Denise Leith grew up in Sydney and has worked in a factory, as a waitress, a receptionist, a counsellor for child abuse prevention and in stockbroking—she was the first woman trained as an 'operator' on the Sydney Stock Exchange floor. She has a PhD in international relations, which she teaches part time at Macquarie University in Sydney.

Denise served on the management committee of International PEN's Sydney Centre for six years, where she and her colleagues received the Human Rights and Equal Opportunity Community Award for work with writers held in Australian detention centres.

She writes book reviews and articles on politics and travel for newspapers, journals, serials and online media. She is the author of *The Politics of Power: Freeport in Suharto's Indonesia*, and *Bearing Witness*, a look at the world of war, disease and famine through the eyes and voices of the world's top war correspondents and photojournalists.

What Remains

Denise Leith

ALLEN&UNWIN
SYDNEY•MELBOURNE•AUCKLAND•LONDON

Published by Allen & Unwin in 2012

Allen & Unwin
Sydney, Melbourne, Auckland, London

83 Alexander Street
Crows Nest NSW 2065
Australia

Phone: (612) 8425 0100
Fax: (612) 9906 2218
Email: info@allenandunwin.com
Web: www.allenandunwin.com

Cataloguing-in-Publication details are available from the National Library of Australia
www.trove.nla.gov.au

ISBN 978 1 74237 692 9

Set in 12.5/17 pt Tibere by Bookhouse, Sydney
Printed and bound in Australia by Griffin Press

10 9 8 7 6 5 4 3 2 1

For my parents,
JOY AND JACK HELSON,
with love

Chapter 1

I SMELL THE SWEET SCENT OF GINGER FLOWERS AND IT BEGINS.
I am the vulture circling, but I'm not as bad as Pete. He stalks.
I insist there is a difference. I pick my way through the bodies
rotting in the afternoon heat: white bones jutting; maggots
erupting through bloated, black skin. Treading on something
soft I look down to see a small hand under my boot: body parts;
tiny body parts; children's body parts. As I move through the
human debris a thick cloud of flies disturbed from their work
rise to crawl their putrid business across my skin. The scarf I
have tied around my nose and mouth can't keep out the sickly
sweet smell of death.

Words forming into sentences: unspoken expressions of
horror disrespectful in the presence of this thing; this obscenity.
Our silence separates us as Pete moves where the lens takes him
and I, rudderless, drift in the opposite direction. The church of
Nyarubuye, this testimony to what man can do, is pulling me

down so deep into its darkness that nothing will ever be the same again.

Wandering deeper into the circle of buildings I hear what I cannot possibly be hearing: a moan. As I enter the church I'm initially blinded by its darkness and stumble, scraping my arm down a raw brick wall, and as the blood begins to ooze the flies descend. Before sight there is always smell: the metallic odour of blood, and the sharp, protein-ripe tang of rape. The bodies of two women and a little girl are lying at my feet, their legs spread wide, blood crusted on their open throats, dried semen spilling out from between their thighs to stain dull, dark skin. As I lean down to close the little girl's legs the flies rise up again and this time they find their way in—up my nose, into my ears, across my eyes—and I am blinded by the soft horror of them and I scream, a deep primeval noise that comes from the recesses of my being, from all the lives and times I have ever lived, and from all that I will ever live, as if the very act can stop the nightmare and it does.

From: Bullwinkle91965@yahoo.com
Date: Monday 28 March 2005 8:24 AM
To: Rocky91956@yahoo.com
Subject:

Dear Rocky,
I had the Rwandan dream again last night. Have you ever wondered why these dreams are always so much more rich in texture, more vibrant in colour, more real than memory? Sometimes it feels to me as if they are being played out in my head like a movie in slow motion or from a faulty projector. Other times they come in disconnected flashcards with dark, troubling

edges. More than the pictures, though, it's the stench of that afternoon that stays with me. I smell Rwanda before I dream Rwanda. Is it the same for you, my friend?

I'm back in London for the funeral. *Funeral*—what a strange word that is. If you say it too many times it sounds all wrong. You'll be there, of course, and Bella and John, but I wonder how many others we know will be coming?

I'm going to keep writing to you. I hope you don't mind.

Your loving Bullwinkle

Chapter 2

London
March 2005

IT'S NEVER BEEN A SOFT LANDING—AN EASY SLIDE—THIS constant shifting from one world to the other. Perched on the side of a vacant baggage carousel I watch the jostling for position across the floor as a little girl begins to cry at her father's feet. Shuffling through the passports and landing documents as he waits for their luggage to appear, he pretends he hasn't noticed her tugging at his trouser leg. The woman next to him sighs before bending down to pick up their daughter. Kissing the child's head as she strokes her fine blonde ponytail the exhausted mother makes loud shushing noises for the husband's benefit, but still he will not hear. It has been a long flight from Australia.

On the train in from Heathrow the very important suited man sitting next to me is having a conversation with his mobile, explaining to it why he needs to fire the woman he's been having an affair with. Sitting opposite is a young girl in a tight black skirt that's riding up with the rhythm of the train. Next to her is a woman applying make-up: contorting her face with strange little moues as she paints and smudges and draws. I look around the carriage to see if anyone else is watching, but everyone is either reading, or staring vacant-eyed into the space in front of them. Why am I the only one concerned with this blurring of the private and public taking place in front of us? Pete would say that I'd been hiding away too long again and he'd be right, for each time I return home it is becoming harder to adjust: to paint my face, or put on clothes that are overtly sexual—too short; too tight; too low; too black. Each time it becomes harder to advertise that I might be single; available; desirable.

'She looked better before she began with the make-up,' offers the man claiming the seat next to me vacated by the suit. Ah, I think, another dysfunctional soul does exist on this train after all. 'You've just flown in, right?' he says, motioning towards my suitcase and the laptop propped between my feet.

'Right,' I say, looking down to see my sandalled feet and the chipped red nail polish on my toes. I am out of place on this early-morning commuter train. Crushed and baggy cargo pants, and a shirt with its sleeves rolled up to reveal arms tanned from five months of the Australian summer. I am a strange brown nut in the middle of all this busy London grey. When I look back up again I see my reflection in the train window and notice for the first time that my hair has grown lighter, streaked blonde by the sun. Reaching up I pull it back into a ponytail, securing it with the elastic I have around my wrist.

'Anywhere interesting?'

'Not really.'

'Just got back from South Africa a couple of days ago myself. Covered the rugby test. I'm a sportswriter, you know. American . . .' He hesitates. 'New York, actually.' Ah, I understand completely. New York is not quite American. No Midwestern redneck here. Educated. Sophisticated. Worldly. With that settled he offers up his name, along with a handshake that carries with it a whiff of stale cigarette smoke and freshly applied cologne. I return his smile and notice that he's a handsome man, probably in his late twenties. His hair is still wet from the shower. '. . . married an English girl and we have a son. That's why I'm still here . . .'

As he talks I realise that I've already forgotten his name, and wonder if you can technically forget something that you didn't register in the first place.

'. . . separated a while back. I'd go home to the States at the drop of a hat except for my boy. He plays "ruggers", you know.' The word does not slip easily off his tongue as if he is trying its Englishness on for size.

'Really.' I just can't dredge up any interest in what he is telling me.

'Yes, he's very, very good.'

I nod. Smile again.

'Could play for England, you know. Of course—' he's leaning in towards me now, bringing with him again the cigarettes and cologne '—I wish it was real football, but he's half English, right?' His body stiffens then and he backs away when he realises the possibility of his error. 'You're not English are you?'

'No, I'm a crossbreed like your son.' I watch him to measure the impact of my words. I see him wince and I regret them immediately. Why did I have to say that? Why did I have to hurt this stranger needlessly? It's not technically true, anyway. I might like to think I'm part Australian, but I'm English by birth and by passport. What I really wanted to say to this man is that things could be much worse . . . much, much worse. His son's still alive, isn't he? He has a future ahead of him, doesn't he? Oh, yes, things could be much worse.

'No, I could tell you weren't English.' We lapse into silence then as each of us retreats back into our own little world. I imagine he's thinking about sons, and real football, and crossbreeds, while I'm trying not to think about anything much at all, especially why I'm back in London.

As the train rocks its way towards the centre of the city I stare out the window again, losing myself in the suburban morning flying past. A young woman is hanging clothes on a line, her breath frosty in the grey of the chilly early morning. Another is sweeping the concrete steps outside her back door with a straw broom as a dog barks at her, soundless, from a patch of mud below. Dirty, brown-grey vignettes flash past until my attention is caught by a shiny red bug of a car pulling out of an old timber garage. A young mother is standing close by with a baby balanced on her hip, her hand raised to wave goodbye, and all I can think of is Thoreau's lives of quiet desperation . . . my life of quiet desperation.

It wasn't always like this.

'I don't want to lose him so I'm stuck here.' The sportswriter's words are dragging me back into the train again.

'That must be hard.' I offer a half-hearted smile to try to make amends for my rudeness, but this only encourages him to tell me about the destruction of his marriage and how much he hates everything about England: the food, the climate, the people. He hasn't actually said it yet, but I suspect his former wife and her proprietary rights over their son are top of that list. I look around the carriage to see how our travelling companions are reacting to his opinion of them and their country, but in true British style they are pretending not to hear.

I have grown too hard over the years and I know it is not an attractive trait and so as the train pulls into Embankment and I begin to gather my things to change lines I turn to him to wish him luck with all his troubles. It is not enough, I know, but it is the best I can do this morning. Yet it seems as if it is more than enough because he beams back at me and shakes my hand once again, only this time he holds it for too long. Once out on the platform I look back to see that he is watching me and we both smile, embarrassed at being caught out. As I manoeuvre my suitcase through the crowd I consider that perhaps he and I are kindred spirits after all, both part of the world's great mass of unattached: the less happy, the hurt, the anxious.

It was not always like this. I used to be someone different.

I spend the morning unpacking and cleaning out the musty corners of the flat I rent for a pittance in Clapham Common—I'm hardly ever there and don't cause my landlord any trouble, he says, so he gives me the place cheap. By the afternoon a misty rain has begun to fall and a new freshness is moving through the air. I take the tube to Bond Street and walk to Berkeley Square, where I find my favourite bench and sit under my umbrella watching the strangers passing by. This watching, I fear, has become my addiction—an unbroken line from my earliest memory to this day—and like all addictions it has exacted a heavy price. I wonder, will it be the measure of my life?

To avoid going back to the empty flat I drop into Ratko's shop in Clapham Common High Street. 'Ah, Kate, we been worried 'bout you. We very glad you still alive. We heard. It was a very, very bad think they did,' says Ratko by way of welcome as he heaves his ever-increasing bulk out of the seat he rests in by the front door.

'How's Mila, Ratko?' I say, changing the subject. I absently pick up an avocado from the display beside him and test its ripeness with my thumb.

'She very difficult. Very difficult.' The familiar ritual of complaints has begun and I smile at the comfort of it. 'She all time is wanting return to old country. What for, I ask you?' Ratko spreads his hands and shrugs his shoulders, as if the absurdity of his mother's longing is obvious. 'Is nothing for her there. Dead. You know. Please you tell her, Kate. She listen to you.' Mila doesn't listen to me, and who can blame her when it is I who was the cause of her misfortune? But there is no point in telling Ratko this for the scene must be played out. 'I do everythink for her. Everythink.'

Suddenly the monologue of complaints falls abruptly short of its predetermined ending and I turn to see Mila emerging from the back of the shop. 'Kate, Kate, Kate,' she says, rushing over to crush me to her black-clad bosom before releasing me to squash my face between her hands.

'My English, she is good now?' Mila says proudly, releasing my face to look pointedly over at her son. 'I am taking English lessons,' she says, leaning in to whisper loudly, 'He think it big waste of money 'cause I old woman who die soon, but bahhh.' Mila waves her hand in the air. 'I speak better than him. What you think, Kate?'

Before I can answer in the affirmative Mila is asking if I've been home. She means Sarajevo, the universal home in Mila's universe, and I reply in the negative, as I have done for years.

'No mind. No mind. Come, come,' Mila says, taking my hand and leading me to the small, overheated flat out the back of the shop to ply me with strong, sweet tea and an array of cream biscuits pilfered from Ratko's shelves. Mila wants to talk about the war in Sarajevo and the time before the war that I don't know about: the time when she was young and pretty and wore flowers in her hair; when Ratko was a baby and she and her husband danced together in the town square. Sometimes, when she's filling me with her tea and biscuits and sweet, sweet memories, I believe she has forgotten my part in her drama, so that instead of being the architect of Mila's misfortune I have become the bridge between what Mila wants and what she can no longer have. And so I sit with her, as I always do, and I listen to her stories and I smile, trying to balance out the scales of my misdeeds against this old woman's loneliness.

Later, back in my flat, I take my cup of tea and sit down at my desk in front of the laptop. As I wait for it to boot up I consider phoning my parents to let them know that I am back in England, but they would only want to take the train up to London to see me and I can't quite face what it is that I would have to tell them.

Opening a new document I watch the cursor pulse on the screen and then type: *Can you ever understand who you were in the moments before your life changed? Is it possible to know what was lost and what was gained in that moment? Who existed before and what remains?* I stop, my fingers balanced over the keyboard as I search for the sentence that will begin the story that was us. But how do you begin a story when you cannot be sure where the beginning is? Was it that day in Larry's office in London when I saw you for the first time? Was it in Riyadh? Perhaps it was Sarajevo? Did it begin in New York, or was that where it ended?

'Why do you always have to make things so complicated?' I can hear you saying over my shoulder. 'Just pick a point, Price, any point, and then go forward or back.'

'It would be that simple for you, wouldn't it?' I say, smiling into the memory of you.

A hard dirt floor in Africa as he cradles me; Bosnia, his hands rough, hurting my shoulders as he pushes me away; New York and a poster of a white ibis and an old Indian chief above a soft, warm bed. Ghosts of times and lovers long gone drift through my head until the weight of all the years we wasted and all the things that were left unsaid settle heavy against my heart.

And so I am going to go back. I will unpack the suitcase, fold back the layers and rummage around in the past so that I might find the truth of how it all happened; so that I might feel more and care less. So I might understand what remains.

Chapter 3

Riyadh
January 1991

SIXTY YEARS BEFORE, RIYADH HAD BEEN A WALLED CITY, PART of the ancient Bedouin trade route in the middle of the wind-blown Arabian Peninsula. By the time the world's press arrived in 1991 for Operation Desert Storm, a hot and dusty souk still crowded around the original wadi that had spawned Riyadh, but little else of that ancient desert settlement still existed. With the discovery of oil the city had become the economic and political heart of Saudi Arabia and the personal fiefdom of the Saudi royal family and its six thousand princes. When I arrived it was a confronting mix of ultra-modern and medieval: invisible women in black abayas trailing the scent of Dior, and Dolce & Gabbana, with heavy gold jewellery dangling from their black-gloved wrists as they stood in line at the local McDonald's wearing impossibly high heels.

Riyadh had been my home for the last two months—specifically the richly appointed Regency Room of the Hyatt, where the US and Saudi flags and a banner reading JOINT FORCES formed the backdrop for the twice daily US military briefings. The consensus among the press corps stationed there was that General Stormin' Norman Schwarzkopf's performances during the briefings were pure entertainment, and as a result were always well attended. When someone lobbed a provocative question—like, 'Was that a baby-milk factory we hit, General?'—we all held our breath, watching the heat creep up his neck. Off to one side his aides shifted uncomfortably, concentrating intently on a spot somewhere near their feet. The old hands from Vietnam especially loved it, swearing Schwarzkopf's briefings were more amusing than Saigon's long-missed Five O'Clock Follies.

My paper, a popular broadsheet in the UK, had dispatched two of its most experienced journalists and one photographer to cover the war. I had been sent because the senior editor of our foreign desk, Larry, told me he wanted to get me out of his hair. My instructions were to cover the military briefings, while trying to find human interest stories on the streets of Riyadh; the other three, would, in Larry's words, 'do the heavy lifting'. Larry's parting advice to me had been, 'Don't do anything too stupid, like getting yourself killed, because I don't want the death of some stupid, green-arsed kid on my conscience.' My senior editor might not have had high expectations of me, but I did. I was going to be the best war reporter in the business. I was going to land the scoops that made my fellow colleagues green with envy and I was going to write copy that changed the world. Unfortunately, I wasn't going to achieve that covering the military briefings or human interest stories on the streets of Riyadh. A war of unprecedented military fire power was about to be unleashed on the Arabian Peninsula and I was stuck in downtown Riyadh. I had to get out.

In the weeks of the bombing campaign that led up to the ground war I had made fruitless requests to go out on US military sorties, or to interview the flight crews returning from their missions, but I was so far down the rungs of who counted in the international press corps that I might as well have been invisible. I also spent hours hanging out in the bar of the hotel just to listen to the other reporters' gossip and try to glean the information and experience that only time on the road could give. I was shameless.

I had a drink in the bar one evening with a veteran journalist from the Vietnam War—I would have a drink with anyone who offered *and* who'd covered a war before. When I tried to impress upon him my worldliness by complaining about how the military was treating the press, he just threw back his head and laughed.

'Look, honey,' he said, swivelling around on his stool to face me, 'the military's happy 'cause it gets to tell its *Top Gun* version of the war that we know is worth fuck-all, and the public's happy 'cause they think they're seeing a real live war movie.'

'But what they're seeing,' I countered, leaning forward and nearly falling off my stool into the bargain, 'isn't real war.'

'Yeah? Really? What do you know about real war? How long you been covering it anyway?' When I failed to answer he muttered something unintelligible and turned back to his drink. 'Let me tell you somethin'. The folks back home don't want to know the real story 'cause it don't sit well with dinner. So the editors don't like to upset 'em, and the advertisers don't like to upset 'em, and who the fuck are we to upset 'em? Right? Video games they know—they're like mother's milk for the kids nowadays. But real dead bodies? No way.'

'You made a real difference in Vietnam,' I said, still believing that if journalists worked hard enough they could put a stop to war, just like they had in Vietnam.

'Oh fuck. What planet you been living on? Man, they're teaching some crap these days in them fancy colleges.' Shaking his head, he ground his cigarette out in the ashtray on the bar in front of him and signalled to the barman for another drink. 'Want somethin' heavier than that soft drink ya got there?'

'No, thank you.'

'Oh sweet Jesus! Think I'm wasting my time here. Look, honey, let me tell you so as you know. We didn't make one bit of difference in 'Nam. Not a shit-kicking, goddamn fucking bit of difference. It was our boys coming home in them there body bags that made all the difference. Do ya really believe anyone cared 'bout the dead dinks? Hey? Do ya? Go ahead, honey, show all the dead rag heads ya want here, but I'm telling you it ain't gonna change a goddamn thing till they start bringing our boys back in them bags. And that ain't gonna happen on no CNN, least not these days.' Did I want to take my soft drink with me up to his room? he asked. I politely refused, and slunk off to the room I was sharing with a woman from one of the Spanish TV channels. I was never going to be like that man. How could he keep doing the job if he didn't think he might make a difference? His cynicism appalled me, but my naivety had also embarrassed me. I needed to toughen up—fast.

Out of over a thousand journalists stationed in Riyadh, only about one hundred and fifty of us at any given time were allowed to see any action through the US military's media 'pencil pool' system. When a journalist finally got into one of these pools and was able to get to the soldiers, they had to submit copy to military censors. The rest of us, stuck in Riyadh or Dhahran, would rewrite this into our own copy. I fretted endlessly. This was not how I had envisaged my first war. Where were the scoops and glory I had dreamed of? Where were the stories to change the world? Larry, on the other hand, would have been satisfied with *a story, any story.*

When I'd first started working at the paper Larry was already one of the top two foreign editors in London. He was respected—even worshipped—by everyone on the floor. Although he was a perfectionist with a habit of publicly summoning people into his office to chew them out, and although he had an intimidatingly gruff manner, Larry was the most brilliant boss in the world. He knew when to push you—I never saw him bawl out anyone who hadn't deserved it—and he knew when to praise you; he'd go soft when you were a little fragile and encourage you when you'd done well.

'Where's the copy?' he yelled at me down the phone from London. 'What the fuck have you been doing for the last week? I've not had anything from you for five days! What've you been doing, Kate?'

'I've been busy.'

'Yeah, well you haven't been busy writing copy. Go talk to one of those women who cover themselves up in those black thingos.'

'I've tried, Larry, but they don't want to talk to me.'

'Try harder,' he said.

'Yes, sir.'

'What's this "yes, sir" shit?'

'Don't know, sir.'

'Christ, Kate, have you gone native on me and been hanging out with soldiers? Is that why you haven't sent me any copy?'

'No, sir.'

'Mmmm,' he said, before hanging up on me.

After making a complete nuisance of myself I got to spend a couple of days with the soldiers of the 6th Marine Corps. Part of my prepackaged holiday info-tour of the desert included the dubious honour of riding in an M1 Abrams tank. Although I was supposed to be buoyed by the knowledge that the Abrams could protect me from nuclear, biological and chemical warfare, I became a little too fixated on how it was going to protect me from incineration. Larry, however, was happy enough with my human interest story on the men who manned the tanks and didn't complain about me hanging out with soldiers anymore.

It would have been impossible for anyone outside Riyadh to understand just how much I envied the few journalists reporting from the Al Rasheed Hotel in Baghdad in the frontline of US fire power. Locked up in splendid isolation in Riyadh, and glued to the briefing sessions like perpetual reruns of a bad movie, by late February I was starting to look and act deeply traumatised. As the rumours began to swirl around the press corps that the ground war was about to begin I became truly desperate. I had to make my name reporting this war or there might never be another chance.

During one particularly boring afternoon briefing session I heard someone from the back of the room comment that we were all dying a 'slow death by briefing'. If I had been sitting further to the front of the briefing room that day and not heard him, or if I had been late or left early or simply ignored the comment, then my life would have been completely different.

I'd first seen Peter McDermott about four years before in our London offices just after I'd joined the paper. At the time he had been photographing conflict for around ten years and had a reputation in the industry. From my lowly corner I'd watched as he offered each photograph to Larry, who would deftly flick

17

the ash from his cigarette before slipping the glasses that lived on top of his head down onto the bridge of his nose. When he'd finished examining the photographs, he'd reverse the procedure before turning to McDermott.

I remember exactly what McDermott was wearing that day, because it never much changed. He had on an old pair of Lee jeans and a navy blue sweater—when he'd walked past my desk earlier I'd noticed that the stitching was beginning to unravel on one of the cuffs—and a scarf was wound loosely around his neck. His mousy brown hair kept flopping over his forehead in a way that obviously annoyed him because he kept dragging his hand through it. When I turned to look at him leaning up against the back wall of the briefing room in Riyadh he looked exactly the same except his hair was now cropped short. He still had the scarf and the jeans, and his sweater, though different, was still navy blue. He had one camera around his neck and another slung over his shoulder. I watched as he said something to the man next to him then turned to the woman beside him. Leaning down, he whispered into her ear and she laughed, smiling up at him as she reached out to caress his arm.

'You know them?' asked the guy sitting to my left.

'I don't actually know them, but I know the tall guy in the middle's Peter McDermott.'

'Yeah, well the other guy's John Rubin. He's also a hotshot photographer. American I think.'

Rubin didn't look like any hotshot photojournalist I'd ever imagined. He was dressed in neatly pressed tan corduroy pants and a caramel-coloured shirt and vest with his light brown hair meticulously parted to one side. No matter how many times I watched John work in the years to come I would never shake the impression that he had been born in the wrong century; he seemed more like a nineteenth-century gentleman farmer than a hotshot war photographer.

'The blonde woman with them is the anchor from CBS and McDermott's latest squeeze,' he continued. 'I hear McDermott and Rubin are getting out of Riyadh tomorrow.'

'Where're they going?'

'Don't know. Ask them yourself. Lucky bastards. I'm going crazy here, but my paper wants me to stay put.'

'You sure they're leaving?'

'What I heard.'

Staring at McDermott, a germ of an idea began to form. This was potentially the biggest opportunity of my life. I could either sit in Riyadh trying to drum up human interest pieces for Larry while the biggest story in the world was unfolding around me—or I could try to convince McDermott and this guy Rubin to take me with them.

Chapter 4

LATER THAT NIGHT I FOUND MCDERMOTT DRINKING IN THE
bar with the woman from CBS, John Rubin and a man I'd never
seen. I was so afraid of approaching him that my hands were
shaking and my heart hammering in my chest. McDermott was
already well respected in the business, even famous in some
circles, and I was nothing, but I figured there was no easy way
to do it. What was the worst that could happen? I asked myself.
I could make a fool of myself, but I'd done that before and was
sure to do it again. They could reject me and I'd be embarrassed,
but who would know or care but me? It wasn't as if it was going
to make front page news tomorrow: *McDermott rejects stupid,
green-arsed kid from London broadsheet!* I bought a bottle of
wine from the bar and five glasses and took a deep breath before
making my way through the crowd to their table.

'It protects me, man,' the guy I didn't know was saying.
'Every time I hold that camera up in front of my face it fucking

protects me from what's happening out there. It's a filter, man. It separates me.'

John Rubin was shaking his head; he obviously didn't agree. Neither did McDermott. 'I don't see that,' he said, pushing his chair to balance precariously on its back two legs. 'I don't see that at all. When I'm looking down that lens and all I can see is what's at the end of it, then that's my world. Nothing else exists. It brings you closer. Definitely. There's no protection in the lens. No way.'

'No way,' echoed Rubin.

'Hi,' I said, clearing my throat, 'I'm Kate Price.' I leaned over and placed the bottle and glasses on the table and offered each of them my hand to shake. It felt stupid and awkward. 'Sorry to interrupt, but I was wondering if I could join you?' When they all just sat there looking at me without responding I wanted to crawl into a hole.

'Sure,' McDermott said finally, breaking the painful silence. With that they all began to shuffle around to make room for me at the table, while John Rubin reached behind him to get a spare chair from the next table.

They stared at me expectantly, clearly wondering what I wanted. I could feel my face going red with embarrassment. I looked at McDermott, who had plonked the legs of his chair back down on the ground and now had his arm draped along the back of Ms CBS's chair. 'I hear you and Mr Rubin are leaving Riyadh tomorrow.' He didn't say anything. I swallowed and continued, 'I'd like to come with you.' McDermott looked over at Rubin, but his face remained expressionless. The third man was busy studying his glass, while Ms CBS just seemed bored. I waited. Perhaps if I'd had a week to try to ease myself into their circle, charm them with my personality while impressing them with my intelligence, I wouldn't have been making such a fool of myself, but I didn't have a week or even a few hours. All I had was now. 'Look, I'm sorry—'

'How long have you been covering conflict?' McDermott asked, studying me with a frown on his face. A fair enough question considering his life might depend on his travelling companions. I stared back at him, all the while wishing I had a better answer. I'd never been so close to the man before, and although I knew he was in his mid-thirties I could see that his brow was already furrowed and the corners of his grey eyes framed by tiny squinting creases—probably the result of peering through a lens for too long. I thought about lying and saying that it was my second war, but that might lead to questions about the nonexistent first one. 'This is my first.' It sounded so pathetic that I offered the name of my paper, which should have made me feel better, but didn't.

I watched the corners of his eyes crinkling as he began to smile and realised that he'd already known the answer. 'Right, and so now you want to come with us?'

'That was my plan.'

Removing his arm from Ms CBS's chair he leaned back, arms folded. 'Oh, so you have a plan, do you?'

'Well, only so far as going with you, wherever that might be.'

'What did you say your name was?'

'Kate Price.'

The frown lines on his forehead deepened. 'Sorry, Kate Price, but we can't afford to take someone who can't look after themselves.'

'I can look after myself.'

'Can't take the responsibility of something happening to you.'

'I'm not your responsibility.' I heard Rubin laugh, but I didn't take my eyes off McDermott.

'Whose are you then?'

'Nobody's.'

'You're going to be someone's responsibility if they take you with them.'

'But not yours.' Everyone except Ms CBS seemed to find this amusing and I felt some of the tension in the air disperse. 'And, frankly, I find it offensive that you think I ever would be.' I couldn't believe I'd said that. What a smart arse.

'Do you just? Well, that's tough.'

Somehow McDermott made me feel like a naughty school kid in front of the principal. His scrutiny was making me nervous. I bit my bottom lip and looked over to Ms CBS, who must have decided that I was no rival and therefore she could afford me a smile. I noticed she was dressed similarly to me, but where I looked utilitarian—which was what my mother called my working clothes—she just looked sexy. Her jeans were stylish and tight-fitting; mine were soft and old and somewhat baggy. The top buttons of her shirt were open to display an admirable cleavage; my cleavage was disappointing. Her thick hair, with its carefully applied blonde highlights, was swept high onto the top of her head, while my idea of styling was pulling my straight brown hair into a ponytail when I stepped out of the shower in the morning. Ms CBS had tiny pearl drop earrings hanging from neat little ears, a gold bracelet on one elegant wrist and a slash of pale lipstick, whereas my face was bare and my ears and wrists unadorned. I was starting to wish I'd at least made some sort of effort.

When I looked back at McDermott he was smiling again. He'd been watching me summing up his girlfriend and had probably guessed that I'd found myself wanting. The guy was a mind reader. *Bastard*. He was having a good time at my expense. I needed to get out of there as soon as I could with some pride intact, but I had no idea how.

He picked up his drink, but before it reached his mouth he paused. 'It's no picnic out there.'

I tried so very, very hard not to smile, but my heart was racing and I could feel the unwanted smile trying to burst through. *Oh, sweet Jesus, Peter McDermott was going to take me with him!*

'What do you think, John? Want to take this baby with us?' He glanced over at John.

'Hell, no skin off my nose,' came the reply. My grin could no longer be suppressed and I turned its full force on John, who winked at me. 'Everyone has to start somewhere, right?'

'I don't know why I'm saying this, but okay, you're on—though if you're any trouble, I swear we'll drop you in the middle of the fucking desert.' With that McDermott tipped his glass to finish off the last of his beer. 'And before you say another word think about this: you can't go home if it gets a little uncomfortable, or you miss your mummy, or you get scared because someone's taking pot shots at your head.'

'I know that, there's no need to be patronising.'

There I went, being the smart arse again. If I could have pulled my words back I would have, but John saved the day by laughing again. 'Atta girl. Give him hell.'

'Listen, one thing you should know right now is that you don't know anything . . . what was your name again?'

'Kate Price.'

'The only thing you got right, Kate Price, is that you're not John's or my responsibility. Agreed?'

'Agreed.'

I only realised I was still standing when McDermott, who I now noticed was a good six inches taller than me, rose to say his goodnights to everyone, with Ms CBS following suit.

'Wait. What time should I meet you in the morning?'

'Five o'clock. Out front. Oh, and by the way,' McDermott added, as if it was an afterthought, 'you need to get yourself some fatigues otherwise we'll leave without you.'

'But where'll I get fatigues?' I blurted out childishly. It was now nearly midnight.

'You're so clever, you should be able to work it out.' As they walked away I heard him asking Ms CBS why she hadn't told him taking me was a bad idea.

She shrugged. No skin off her nose either. 'If you think a pretty face is worth risking your life over, that's your business, Peter.'

'Welcome to the circus,' said John, as he too drained his drink and he and the other fellow stood to leave. 'You might want to take that bottle back to the bar and see if you can get a refund,' he added, motioning to the untouched bottle of wine on the table. 'It'll be good having you along, Kate. See you bright and early in the morning.'

After knocking on a couple of doors that housed some of the female members of the US media contingent, I scored a pair of fatigues in exchange for the only spare pair of jeans I had. The next morning I joined McDermott and Rubin in the lobby to find I was the only one wearing fatigues.

Chapter 5

AS LUCK WOULD HAVE IT—OR NOT, DEPENDING ON YOUR POINT of view—the ground war had started in the early hours of that morning, and with the media pool system breaking down it quickly became a free-for-all as journalists headed out for the Iraqi–Kuwaiti border. Although the military had orders to arrest and confiscate the credentials of stray journalists, the soldiers were more interested in fighting than checking our whereabouts.

Occasionally we passed random piles of garbage, or arid little farms from which it was impossible to imagine a living might be eked out. Rarely seeing another car, the only movement in that great expanse of sand was the odd plastic bag tumbling across its surface, or the occasional scrawny goat or wild camel wandering aimlessly in the distance. Framing the horizon were the fires from Saddam's burning oil wells—orange and gold flames licking the sky as dirty, black plumes of smoke billowed up to block out the sun before drifting back down to cover everything in a thick, oily film that you could taste in your mouth and scrape off your skin. On that first day a sandstorm hit—not the infamous sandstorms we would later see in Baghdad in 2003 that turned the world orange, but bad enough that we drifted off the road a couple of times and had to retrace our tracks before they disappeared.

For those first two hours John and Pete spoke little, causing me to fear that they were regretting bringing me along. Because I was terrified that any comment I might make would mark me as naive or, worse, stupid—thus justifying their regrets—I too said little.

'I spoke to Helen last night,' John said, breaking a particularly long silence. He looked across at McDermott.

'Yeah? How is she?'

'She's agreed to marry me.' John was beaming.

'You're kidding! That's wonderful news. I had no idea you were going to ask her. You didn't say a bloody thing! How long you been keeping this to yourself?' McDermott kept taking his eyes off the road as he shot questions at his friend.

'I'd been thinking about it for a while and . . . you know . . . after I went back to my room last night I got to thinking . . . well, another war, no idea when it'd be over, or when I'd get the chance to talk to her again, so I rang and asked her last night and she said yes.'

'Stupid if she didn't. Seriously, it's the best news I've heard in a long time.'

I had been watching McDermott in the rear-vision mirror when he looked up and caught my eye. 'John and Helen were childhood sweethearts,' he explained for my benefit. 'Never dated anyone else. That's right isn't it, John?'

'That's right. It's only ever been Helen for me.'

'Congratulations,' I said, leaning forward to touch him lightly on the shoulder. I had already decided that marriage was not for me. I couldn't see how it was possible in the profession and was curious to know what his Helen thought of his job and all the time they would spend apart.

John twisted around in his seat to face me, looking so happy. 'We've been together since junior high. She's going to organise everything and as soon as I get back we'll tie the knot in her folks' backyard.' He turned to McDermott. 'And if Pete here agrees, he'll be my best man.'

'I'd be honoured, mate. Honoured.'

As McDermott encouraged John to talk about Helen and the wedding I finally began to relax. I was about to work with two of the best photojournalists in the industry, an opportunity most young journalists would have given their right arm for. I was smiling out the window, thrilled with my amazing good fortune, when I remembered that Larry still thought I was in Riyadh searching out human interest stories. I knew he was going to be furious with me for leaving, but my plan was to get a story that was so big that he couldn't possibly fire me.

We spent that first night inside the Saudi border with the 7th Division, talking to GIs who, after waiting around for months bored out of their brains in the desert, were all hyped up because they were finally going to get the chance to 'kick some Ay-rab ass'.

The following morning, as we were leaving, we noticed a GI running after our car. When Pete stopped I wound down my window. I remembered him from the day before. He came from Wichita and had told me that all he'd ever wanted to do was fight for his country. The soldier pushed a photo under my nose. 'Ma'am, this is my wife Cheryl and our new baby.'

'They're lovely,' I said, taking the photo of a young woman nursing a newborn.

'Ma'am, I haven't heard from Cheryl in over a month now and we're probably gonna see some action tomorrow and I was hoping . . . I was wondering, ma'am, if you wouldn't mind contacting Cheryl for me and . . . could you tell her that I love her and that I'll be home real soon?' I could see the pain and anxiety in his eyes.

'We'll give it our best shot,' Pete said, before I could answer.

The soldier switched his attention to Pete and handed him a piece of paper through the window. 'I've written Cheryl's number here and that's her name.'

'What's *your* name, soldier?' Pete asked, taking the piece of paper and putting it in the top pocket of his vest.

'Pete. Corporal Peter Wainwright.'

'Won't forget that name,' Pete said.

'You'll do it, won't you? Tell her I love her and our little daughter, and I'll see them real soon.'

'We'll do our best,' Pete repeated.

The soldier smiled for the first time as he backed away. 'Thanks,' he said, as I wound the window up and Pete stepped on the accelerator.

While taking instructions from Pete on how to set up the suitcase-sized satellite phone I shared the back seat with, I couldn't help wondering out loud if it was really such a good idea to use the phone when both militaries were monitoring signals.

'We told him we'd try,' Pete said, 'and that's what we're going to do.'

John turned to smile at me, trying to lessen the rebuke. 'We'll be fine. Just see what you can do.'

I tried to get through for at least an hour but all I got was static until finally Pete told me to give it a miss, that he'd try again when we stopped for the night.

We spent the second day driving aimlessly around southern Iraq with nothing to show for it but photographs of blackened tanks and burning oil fields and interviews with guys who professed to be shepherds. Everyone professed to be a shepherd. Apart from the random Bedouin who might possibly have really been a shepherd and not realised a war was in progress, the only other people we met were Ma'san, the southern Iraqi swamp Arabs who would soon heed George Bush's call to rise up against Saddam Hussein, only to be slaughtered in their thousands by the dictator and their wetlands turned into a wasteland of mudflats.

Crossing back into Saudi Arabia we camped with the 6th Marine Corps that night before heading back into Iraq the following morning. As would happen too often in war, it was the wrong decision. Within hours of us leaving the marines were attacked by the Iraqi regular army in what turned out to be the largest tank battle in US Marine Corps history. By the end of that day, oblivious to the great battle taking place little more than a hundred kilometres away—in fact, oblivious to anything that was not happening in front of our eyes—I began to fear that my first war would be over before I saw any action, or filed a story that would save my job.

When John noticed how frustrated I was becoming he told me to be patient. 'All good things come to those who wait,' he said.

Watching my reaction in the rear-vision mirror, Pete added, 'A good part of this job is the looking for the story, Kate. You have to get used to that. A lot of the time nothing much happens.'

'Why don't we go into Kuwait?' I asked, gripping the backs of both their seats to pull myself forward. 'They've got to be fighting there, haven't they?'

'Every man who has ever owned a Polaroid will be in Kuwait at the moment,' said John. 'Pete and I are freelancers and if we want to sell our work we have to be one step ahead of the staff photographers and get something they don't.'

I relaxed back on the seat, remembering that I also needed something nobody else had if I wanted to keep my job and if anyone was going to find it for me it was these two guys.

By dusk we were bunking down on the kitchen floor in a deserted roadside café near the Iraqi–Kuwaiti border that looked as if it had been beamed down into the desert as part of some intergalactic joke. What use it had, and who its patrons might have been, was one of life's great mysteries, although the back of the café could quite possibly have been the repository for the world's supply of broken tyres and empty petrol drums. Out front a couple of struggling date palms clung tenaciously to life as an assortment of rubbish whirled around the yard in little sand eddies. Inside the café everything that had not been nailed, screwed or stuck down had been carried off.

Before we turned in Pete finally got through to the soldier's wife and then began fiddling with the short-wave radio until he picked up the news that Saddam had just ordered his troops out of Kuwait. I could see that John and Pete were pleased with the news.

'So,' I asked, not wanting to sound too stupid. 'That's good for us?'

'Have you seen any other journalist in the last couple of days?' John asked.

'Not really.' I still couldn't understand their excitement.

'It looks like nearly everyone headed to Kuwait and we just might be the only Western journalists still in southern Iraq.'

It was decided that we should grab a couple of hours' sleep before heading south in the early hours of the morning.

Unable to sleep, I was staring into the dark when I heard Pete roll over to face me. Whispering softly so he didn't wake the snoring John he asked, 'What're you doing here, Kate Price?'

'What do you mean?' I said, turning towards him, although I could see nothing in the tiny windowless space.

'Why are you here? Why Iraq? Why war? Why now?'

I wasn't entirely sure he would be interested in my answer because it was so bog-standard boring. For as long as I could remember I'd been fascinated by other people's lives and the worlds they inhabited that seemed so different from my own. Strictly governed by my mother's good manners and her interminable rules, there were no moments of high drama in my home: no whispered secrets, heated arguments, funny parents, rude jokes or broken rules. 'Where there are rules, Katherine, there is order,' my mother would warn her only child. And where there was order, I am sure, she hoped there was safety. All things considered, it was probably the perfect upbringing for a nice young lady, except I didn't want to be a nice young lady. I longed to bring things crashing down. I wanted excitement and I wanted drama.

When I was five we moved from Somerset to Sydney for my father's job and it was there, with the light and dust and the heat of Australia's endless summers, with the flies and bugs and cloudless blue skies so bright and so deep that I imagined I might disappear into them, that I finally felt I belonged. But on my fifteenth birthday—the summer of my first kiss—we moved back to England, and while my mother embraced the return to her ordered country and her ordered life, I floundered. Catapulted unprepared into a grey, friendless adolescence in a house that was chilly ten months of the year and oozed damp and old wood smoke, I was lost until at the age of twenty-one I was offered a cadetship in journalism. It was my free pass to the world and I grabbed it with both hands. Five years from cadet to hack, and then what was generally considered a bizarre decision by everyone but the girl who longed to bring things crashing down, and possibly the mother who knew her too well: war.

Instead of telling McDermott any of this I ventured that I had been looking for something more challenging than covering corrupt politicians, which only made him laugh. 'You've not really come very far, Price. Corrupt politicians and corrupt policies is what war is all about.'

'So why did you start covering war?'

'I thought it would be fun,' he answered. I knew immediately that was what I should have said and made a mental note to try to be less serious and more amusing in future.

'And is it?'

'Most of the time it has enough of its own shameful little thrill to keep me coming back. Look, you need to know that war is fucked and that all of us who cover it are probably fucked, so you need to ask yourself, Kate Price, if you're fucked enough to do this job.'

I laughed.

'No,' he said, 'I'm serious.'

I smiled into the dark. I was serious too. There I was, lying on the floor of a clapped-out café in a godforsaken part of Iraq with a war that I couldn't find raging all around me and for the first time in my life I was deliriously, wondrously happy. This was excitement. This was drama. I had finally made it.

A few hours later we were up and packing in a chilly predawn before heading south toward Kuwait for our first and only real story of that war.

Chapter 6

FOUR IN THE MORNING ON 27 FEBRUARY 1991 ON THE JAHRA-UMM Qasr Highway heading into Kuwait. Catnapping in the back of the jeep I became vaguely aware of John and Pete talking. 'I've no idea what it is. Kate?' Pete reached over into the back seat to shake me. 'You awake? You might want to see this.'

The smoky quarter moon had long gone, but the dawn had not yet lit the night sky. Up ahead in the distance was a strange, flickering orange glow. As we drew closer the light dispersed into hundreds of small fires until it became a crazy man's breakfast of burning, melted, black, bombed-out cars, trucks, buses and military vehicles spread out across the desert as far as we could see. Some of the vehicles still had their headlights on and, more eerily, their radios were still playing.

'What is it?' I asked.

'Don't know,' Pete answered as he cut the engine, turning to grab his cameras from the seat next to me. 'Don't know.'

Through the smoke I could see household items: clothes and children's books, their pages being turned by invisible fingers. A wedding dress, its tulle torn and blackened, was rolling softly across the oily black sand. Trucks and tanks, gigantic pieces of shrapnel—a post-modern sculpture—lay melted and sunk into the earth as smoke curled up through the air currents to hang low and heavy over a scene that was beyond even Salvador Dali's darkest imaginings. Littered among the metal were gruesome pieces of charred meat, burned so badly that the outer extremities had disintegrated. The stench of burning flesh and petrol fumes mingled with the sweet scent of the expensive perfumes the fleeing Iraqi troops had looted from the department stores of Kuwait City. A horrifying little memory was born for me in those moments. Crawling into the recesses of my mind it searched out a corner where it would rest until sometime in the future a whiff of something vaguely unpleasant would call it forth again. Charred human flesh, petrol and Calvin Klein's 'Eternity' locked forever in an obscene lover's embrace.

Something else was happening inside me in those first moments that would also never be lost to me. My sense of smell became razor sharp. It was as quick and as random as that. To this day I can smell what others cannot. I know road kill is ahead before it can be seen; I can smell the sour heat of fear from fifty paces and I can catch the scent of a woman's perfume before she enters the room. I can smell danger. Sometimes I believe I can even smell what others are thinking.

Coming back through the smoke Pete grabbed rolls of film from the back of the car before noticing that I hadn't moved. I could never have imagined anything could be that bad and had absolutely no idea what to do or where even to begin. 'This is war, my beauty,' he said, turning away from me again as he stuffed the film into the pockets of his vest. 'You'd better get used to it if it's what turns you on.' When I still didn't move he shrugged. 'Your choice,' he said, moving off.

'Stick with me, Kate,' said John.

'Fucking napalm,' came Pete's disconnected voice through the smoke. 'Hey, John, come and have a look at this—the bastards have used fucking napalm.'

Stepping up onto the running board of a truck I became transfixed by the face staring back at me. I could smell the fresh blood on his skin, sticky and metallic sweet, seeping out of the cavities of his eyes and mouth. A bright red droplet hung suspended, drying on his ear. I watched the pretty red jewel dangle. Brown eyes, short-cropped black hair, dirty white T-shirt, lips pulled back in a grimace to reveal perfect white teeth. I couldn't see the injury that killed him, but I did notice that his watch was on the right hand. This man was left-handed. Unable to compute the enormity of a thing the brain latches onto small, more readily digestible pieces of information, like a watch being worn on the right wrist.

Another thing I learnt that morning on the road from Basra. When adrenaline kicks in, and your body is in fight-or-flight mode, then cognitive memory takes a back seat. Flashcards of memory, often surprisingly insignificant, are laid down to be retrieved at a later date so that every time you retrieve the flashcards you must recreate again the missing pieces. Memory is not a perfect video. It is not to be trusted.

You think a lot about the first time you will see a dead body and it becomes, in a macabre sense, a challenge. Will you cut and run or will you stay the course? But it's never going to be the way you imagine. That morning I found myself wondering about the man and the life that was lost—which I could not possibly know—about the way he died—which I did not know—and about those he left behind. Did he have children, a wife, a sweetheart waiting for him at home? How long would it take for those who loved him to accept that he was never coming back? How long until they began picking up the pieces of their lives without him? How long would his photo remain on the mantelpiece, in the frame beside the bed, folded and faded in the wallet? Those who were connected to this man through the invisible bonds of love and friendship had no idea that they had just become prisoners of time, condemned to remain wondering, but never knowing. The horror of never knowing; of living with the possibility that one day your loved one might return when in truth they never would.

I could hear someone calling my name from a great distance. I could feel hands on my shoulders. I could see this happening from a great height. I was in the scene and at the same time I was the observer floating above it. A man was standing in front of me but I had no idea who he was. I could see his mouth moving slowly, opening and closing in precise movements as if carefully enunciating each word. Concentrating on the man's mouth I tried to understand what he was saying to me until gradually I was back with him.

'Are you all right, Kate? Kate?'

'Yes.'

'Are you sure?'

'Yes.'

'Okay.' Letting go of my shoulders Pete put his arm around me and began to steer me away from the corpse in the truck. 'You'll get used to it, or you'll find a way to deal with it, or you'll get out. Okay?'

'Okay.'

'Come on,' he said. 'Stick close to me. I don't want to lose you in this.' Weeks later I would remember how offended I had been when he had said that I might become someone else's problem, but within days his words had proved true. I was completely out of my depth.

The three of us walked on, Pete and John shooting in the breaking light as I talked nonsense into my little tape recorder. Little vignettes of smells, sounds, pictures, feelings. Later, in Kuwait, when I turned the tape recorder on to write the article, I would find it blank. I had forgotten to press the record button.

Unable to see an end to the carnage, we eventually decided to return to the car and at some point on our journey forward we began clocking the kilometres of destruction—twenty, forty, sixty. The next day we would learn that the 'Highway of Death'—which was what it would be called by the press—was littered with cluster bombs. Pete, John and I never talked about how we had moved through it unscathed, because there was no way to explain it. Sometimes these things just happened.

When we arrived in Kuwait later that day I contacted Larry, who yelled down the phone at me, 'Where the fuck have you been?'

'I—'

'Don't give me any excuses.'

'I wasn't, I—'

'You're supposed to be in Riyadh covering the human angle, not in Kuwait fucking City.'

'I—'

'What the hell are you doing in Kuwait?'

'Larry, I—'

'I should fire you on the spot.'

'Larry, listen, I've got a story you might want.'

'Yeah. Well, I better want it. What story?'

'A massacre . . . by the Americans.'

'I'm listening.'

'We were the first there.'

'We? Who's we?'

'John Rubin, Pete McDermott and me.'

'You've been travelling with Rubin and McDermott? Anyone else?'

'No.'

'No other journos?'

'None.'

'What the fuck were you doing with Rubin and McDermott?'

'Well, I—'

'Forget it. Have you got copy?'

'Yes, I—'

'How many words?'

'Fifteen hundred.'

'Cut it to six hundred. Can you get it to me within twenty minutes?'

'Yes.'

'Any photographs?'

'McDermott said I can have whatever I want.'

'Any good photographs?'

'Jesus, Larry, you had to be there. Everything's a good photograph.'

'Okay, send the copy and get Pete to contact me.' He hung up. Larry hadn't fired me and I had my scoop but unfortunately the story of the Highway of Death got lost on page six, eclipsed by the euphoria of easy victory in the war against Saddam. While the paper printed one of Pete's photographs, few of the mainstream media outlets were willing to pick up Pete or John's work, claiming it was too graphic for their readers.

I spent the next two weeks in Kuwait City covering the liberation and the return of the first Kuwaiti princes from their homes in Paris, London, Rome and New York, before flying back to the UK with Pete.

As soon as we boarded the plane and the seat belt sign switched off he reclined his seat, pulled out a book and fell asleep, waking only when we were landing. Before we parted he turned to me. 'According to Howard Zinn the outcome of war is always unpredictable and uncertain, and the means always certain and horrible. If you can't find a good reason to risk your life covering something that doesn't make any sense, Kate Price, then I suggest you forget about it.' He was looking at me hard, trying to read my response to his words. When he smiled I smiled back. 'You did okay, Kate. See you round.'

As the automatic doors closed behind him I felt the cold of the London morning swirl around my feet. I was turning to go down the ramp to the tube station when a black Mercedes pulled up, and as I watched, a woman leaned across to unlock the door for him.

Two weeks later I finished my first in-depth investigative piece on what really happened on the Highway of Death that night. After we had heard that Saddam ordered his troops out of Kuwait the withdrawal began immediately. Around midnight, just as we were bunking down in the café in the desert, American fighter planes attacked the retreating Iraqi convoys. Dropping their first bombs on the leading and rear vehicles to block any means of escape, the planes then began bombing and strafing the resultant traffic jam. Aboard the USS *Ranger*, plane after plane returned to reload with whatever ordnance they could find on the carrier's decks to the strains of Rossini's 'March of the Swiss Soldiers'—better known as *The Lone Ranger* theme song—blasting from loudspeakers. During the attack there were so many planes in the air that US air traffic controllers feared there might be a mid-air collision and were forced to divide what they called 'the killing box' into halves. There were no known survivors from the sixty kilometre stretch of road we had been on. Around four hundred and fifty people survived the carnage on a second road that night that stretched a mere sixteen kilometres.

Before the sun had risen on that frosty winter morning of 27 February, Colin Powell, National Security Advisor to President George Bush, had his driver take him to the White House. There he placed before his commander-in-chief the satellite photos of the carnage along the Highway of Death. The war was turning into a massacre, he told Bush. It was un-American, he said, even unchivalrous to continue. George Bush ordered a ceasefire to come into effect the following day.

My investigative piece made it into the weekend magazine, while one of Pete's photos made the front page. Late that night, before the paper hit the streets, Larry called me into his office. I could see the magazine on his desk. When he began patting his thinning grey hair I became nervous, for it was always a sure sign that Larry was going to stray into personal territory.

He turned the magazine around so I could see it. 'You did a good job here, Kate.'

I let out the breath I hadn't realised I'd been holding and smiled at him. 'Thanks, Larry.'

'Don't ever go disappearing on me like that again though.'

'No, Larry.'

'Scared the bejesus out of me.'

'Sorry.'

'Okay,' he said, waving me out, 'what are you doing hanging around here? Don't you have a bed to go home to?'

I did, but who could sleep? I lay awake that night with a copy of the magazine on the pillow beside me, bursting with pride at the thought that my parents would see it the following day. Life just didn't get any sweeter.

Chapter 7

AFTER IRAQ I TRIED TO SETTLE BACK DOWN TO LIFE IN London and my usual political reporting, but I was finding it hard. I missed the excitement I'd found in Iraq. Late one night in early May, a couple of months after I had returned from Kuwait, Larry and I were leaving the building together. As the lift doors opened on the floor below and we shuffled to the back to let more people in I saw him reach inside his jacket for his cigarettes. The building and the company had a no-smoking policy but Larry ignored it. The rest of us who shared the floor with him, from the cleaners up to senior management, turned a blind eye, but lighting up in the lift was definitely not going to go down well.

'You know they'll kill you one day,' I said quietly.

'Probably.' He sighed and put the packet back. 'You been following the news coming out of Jabaliya this afternoon, Kate?' There had been reports of clashes between Hamas and Fatah supporters in the Gaza Strip with riots breaking out in Jabaliya, the biggest Palestinian refugee camp there.

'I have.'

'Be interested in going there to take a look at this military wing of Hamas? See if it's something we should know more about?' As we walked out of the lift Larry waved to the night security guards before pulling the cigarette packet out again.

'Isn't Loewenstern covering Gaza?' I asked.

'Loewenstern's busy with the talks in Cairo. I want to put someone in on the ground until he gets back. I have a feeling the place might explode. You interested?'

'Of course.'

The rain was driving hard against the glass entrance of the building and as we manoeuvred our way through the revolving doors I pulled my umbrella out of my tote bag. With Larry already puffing away at his cigarette we moved off to the side to find shelter under the awning of the café next door.

'Could turn out to be an interesting story for you, Kate. Think you could get on a flight first thing in the morning?'

'Not a problem.' My heart was beating faster. This was the opportunity I had been waiting for.

'Good. Try to contact Loewenstern, but if you can't get hold of him then talk to Brooks. She covered the Territories for us a couple of years back so she can fill you in on whatever you need to know before you go.' Larry stepped out into the rain, his arm already out hailing a taxi.

Coming out of a press conference in Jerusalem two days later I ran into John Rubin. It was the first time I'd seen him since Kuwait. 'Hey, Kate, how you going?' he said, smiling.

'Fantastic. I'm fantastic. And you?'

'Couldn't be better.'

'How was the wedding?'

'Wonderful. Hey, if you've got some time now we could grab dinner and I'll show you the photos.'

John took me to Darna on Horkonos Street, 'the best Moroccan restaurant in the whole world,' he enthused as we entered a vaulted passageway before passing by tiled dining rooms stuffed with cushions to a table in the garden. Gorging ourselves on cous cous and a rich lamb tagine, we shared a bottle of wine and talked happily about our days together in Iraq and Kuwait and what we had done since. When the mint tea arrived John produced a large manila envelope of photos.

Helen was a pretty blonde who'd worn a simple white knee-length dress and daisies in her hair. Among all the family photos there were a few of Pete. He looked strangely different, wearing a suit and tie. In each photo there seemed to be an attractive dark-haired woman in a slinky green dress by his side.

'Has Pete got a new girlfriend?'

'Huh?' John pulled his gaze from a picture of his new wife and leaned over to look at the photo I was holding. 'No, that's Cynthia. She's Helen's best friend. I think she and Pete might have hooked up while he was in town for the wedding.'

'So they're not together?'

'Not that I know of.'

We looked at more photos until, trying not to sound too interested, I casually asked him what the Pete McDermott story was.

I'd already taken the time to research McDermott after Iraq because I found myself thinking about him often, but when I couldn't find much I asked Larry. 'McDermott?' he'd said, looking up over the reading glasses perched on the end of his nose. 'I don't know. Hard to say. Keeps to himself mostly. Got a reputation as a bit of a scratchy character, though can't say I've ever seen it.' He squinted into the cigarette haze shrouding his desk, as if seeking a memory, but came back blank. 'That's about it, I suppose. Why don't you ask him yourself?' he said, returning to marking up the article he'd been working on when I'd knocked on his door.

'Pete's story?' John said. 'Let's see. Grew up in Wellingborough in northern England; lives in London; never been married— although I seem to remember a couple of bad years cohabiting with a neurotic children's book publisher. Mmm, really bad time.' He shook his head. 'Got his fingers burned there, so he's been a free agent ever since. That's about it, apart from the fact that he's the best darn photographer going around these days. Why you asking, Kate? Not interested, are you?' He was smiling at me.

'God, no,' I said holding up my hands as if to fend off the charge. 'Just curious.'

A couple of days after John and I had dinner in Jerusalem news came through that the Israeli Defense Forces had found a weapons cache in a house in Jabaliya which allegedly belonged to a Hamas operative. A number of the press contingent in Jerusalem headed off to Gaza to investigate, but while we were there the Israelis began shelling the man's house and the Hamas fighters fired back, leaving a few of us trapped in the middle.

As another British journalist and I were cowering in the entrance of a Palestinian home waiting for a break in the fighting, McDermott and another photographer came running in. I'd seen them both at the top of the square when the shelling had begun about fifteen minutes before.

'See that shop over there?' Pete shouted at me above the noise of the gunfire. His hand gripped my shoulder to turn me in the right direction until I was looking at a small kebab shop with its shutters still open.

'The kebab shop?' I called back.

'That's the one. That's where we're heading. I was there earlier and there's a way out of the square through the back of the shop. When I say run I want you to run for your life, okay?'

I nodded.

'If you hear incoming hit the ground and crawl to the shop as fast as you can. Neither side is trying to kill us so the only way we'll get shot is if we catch a stray bullet, so keep it low. Got it?'

'Got it,' I shouted back.

As we waited in the doorway, each of us pressed up against the wall, a round hit the side of the building not a foot from my head. I hit the ground as shards of plaster and brick flew into the entrance. Out in the square I could see little spits of dust rising up where the bullets were landing and began to wonder if McDermott had been right when he'd said that they weren't trying to kill us. With my heart racing and my breath coming in shallow little gasps I stood up again, trying to press myself further into the wall. Beside me Pete was taking photos of the inside of the house. When I turned to look I noticed for the first time the terrified family hiding behind a large brocade lounge. A man and a teenage boy were trying to protect a woman. A baby was screaming in her arms, as the frightened eyes of a small child stared out from under the woman's abaya. When a tank shell landed near the building it shook and the woman started to cry. I tried to disappear into the wall again, wondering how these people lived with this constant terror.

'Run!' McDermott shouted after the shell had landed, pushing me out before him. The four of us tore across the central square into the kebab shop and followed McDermott out the other side to the alley behind. 'Where's your car?' he asked.

'Back up at the top of the square.'

'My car's down the hill.' He was still yelling above the noise. 'I was just talking to the Israeli captain and he said they wanted to destroy the house, scare the hell out of the Hamas guys, and then get the hell out of here. The house is just about gone so I think they'll be moving out soon. Do you want to wait to go back for your car or come with us now?'

'I don't know. I think I'll wait, thanks.'

'You'll be okay?' he asked, his hand on my shoulder.

'Think so. Yeah, sure.'

'Where're you staying?'

I told him the name of the hotel and he said he'd call me to maybe arrange dinner that night.

After McDermott and the other two had left, I walked about two hundred metres down the street until I found a coffee shop open, where I sat and talked with the local Palestinians until I'd stopped shaking and the sound of the fighting had died down.

That evening, I spoke to Larry and filed my story then joined McDermott and the others in a little pizza shop in Jerusalem's Old City.

'How'd you go?' Jaap, a Dutch photographer from *De Telegraaf*, was asking Pete when I arrived.

'*Stern*'s taking one of my photos of the family in the house and another of the Israeli tank. I think a European daily has picked up one of the images of the destroyed house.'

'Frankly, I do not know how you guys survive freelancing,' Jaap said. 'Tough business.'

'Well, it gives me a certain amount of freedom that suits me,' McDermott replied.

'It's a freedom I cannot afford. I have a family to feed.'

'Sure, that changes everything.'

As we were making our way back to our various hotels after dinner I caught up with Pete, who was walking ahead. 'Can I ask you something about your photographs?'

'Sure.'

I'd been looking at Pete's published photographs until I thought I could see when the young man who had gone to war because he thought it might be fun had begun to change. Initially his photos had been of soldiers and the explosive mechanics of war, but over time they became focused on its victims. His style had also dramatically changed and that was what I couldn't understand. 'A lot of your images are blurred.'

'Ah, that,' he said, as we walked together up the cobbled street towards the Damascus Gate. 'I made a lot of mistakes at first—too bloody scared to hold the camera still, or to take the time to focus. I used to think of my out-of-focus photographs as fuck-ups, but after a while I sort of came to like the fuck-ups and their vision of war better than a lot of the nicely framed shots. More importantly, the magazines and newspapers liked them too. So, you don't like them, Price?' he said, shifting his backpack to his other shoulder as he smiled down at me.

'I'm not sure, but I do understand what you're saying about how they depict war better.'

'Interesting. Well, let me know when you've decided what you think, okay?' he said, stopping when we reached the Via Dolorosa. McDermott was heading up to the Ecce Homo

Convent, where he was staying, while the rest of us were staying in hotels outside the Old City.

'Anyone want to read this?' he asked, pulling a book out of his backpack. It was Dostoyevsky's *Crime and Punishment*. With no takers Pete laid it on the top of a small stone wall. 'Okay, I'm off to bed.'

'Wait,' called Jaap, picking up the book. 'You're not going to just leave it here, are you?'

'Sure. Why not? I've finished it.'

'Do you always leave books on walls?'

'Not always on walls.'

'I don't understand you,' Jaap said, looking confused. 'Why do you do this?'

'Paulo Coelho says books have three journeys: one in the writing, one in the reading and one in the sharing. If I leave it here someone will find it and maybe they'll read it, or maybe they'll pass it on to someone else who might read it, and then they'll pass it on to someone else, and so on. That way the book will stay alive.' Raising his hand in farewell Pete turned to walk up the Via Dolorosa as the rest of us headed out the Damascus Gate into the noisy Jerusalem traffic.

Over a year would pass until I saw McDermott again.

Chapter 8

Johannesburg

June 1992

I MADE NO SECRET OF MY AMBITION TO LARRY AND I WORKED hard to earn his trust. I wanted to please him, not just because he was my boss and held my future in his hands, but because like so many others in the department I had grown genuinely fond of him. With each assignment Larry threw my way I pushed myself a little bit harder and each time I did my confidence grew. When I began to run into many of the same faces on each assignment—journalists I'd watched on TV or those whose reports I'd been reading in the papers for years—and they started greeting me by name and inviting me to join them in the bar for a drink at the end of the day, I knew I'd made it. Larry, however, was not so easily convinced.

In June 1992 he sent me off to Johannesburg to cover for our South African bureau chief when he went on holidays. It was a time of escalating township violence, with Buthelezi's Zulu Inkatha Freedom Party and Mandela's ANC fighting it out for the black African vote in what would be the country's first democratic elections. I had two days with the bureau chief before he flew out, leaving me in the capable hands of Bheka, whom he referred to cheerfully as 'my Mr-Fix-It Man, Bheka.'

It was a particularly bad day in the township of Boipatong that first day on the job. Inkatha Freedom Fighters had killed forty-six ANC supporters three days before and I was there interviewing people from both parties when the South Africa security forces made their belated appearance. I decided to retreat to a safer distance to see what they were going to do. Crouching in the dry grass on the periphery of the town they then proceeded to fire randomly into the streets. With not much having changed by late afternoon and a long drive back to Johannesburg, Bheka and I headed off. As we were leaving I saw three photographers lying in the dirt by the side of a house shooting photographs as the bullets flew over their heads. I was sure one of them was McDermott.

The following morning word came through that trouble was brewing in Soweto, the largest township on the outskirts of Johannesburg. By the time Bheka and I got there a crowd had already gathered, singing and dancing as they waved weapons in the air. I looked around to see if the constabulary had arrived but they were conspicuous by their absence. 'If we heard that something was going down in Soweto this morning,' I said to Bheka, 'then surely the South African police and security forces would have too, so why aren't they here?'

'We would not expect them here,' was his sombre reply. In the days I'd spent with Bheka I'd never seen him smile or respond to a joke. When I asked him about his family and his political sympathies he remained steadfastly tight-lipped. I couldn't help but wonder whether it was something specifically about me that he disliked or if it was just his nature. 'It is not in their interest to stop this,' he added.

I knew what he meant—the ruling National Party and its secret security forces were doing everything in their power to foment trouble between Inkatha and the ANC in order to split the black vote—but something in his voice made me ask him, 'Do you know what's going to happen here, Bheka?'

Before he could answer a skirmish broke out in the middle of the throng, and as the crowd parted a young man came running past us, his hands raised to protect his head from the blows that were raining down on him. He had only gone about ten metres when he collapsed to the ground, curling himself up into a ball. But there was no sympathy for him and I watched as he was roughly picked up again by those around him. 'What's going on, Bheka?' He either didn't hear me over the noise or was not going to answer.

From close by us a man appeared carrying a tyre and a can of petrol and with a sense of sick foreboding I finally knew what I was about to see. Necklacing was a form of rough justice the ANC meted out to informers and those suspected of collaborating with the apartheid regime.

I can't just stand here and watch this man being killed in front of me. I have to do something. Oh God. I have to do something.

Blood poured from his head as eager hands held his sagging body up. The tyre was placed around his neck and then pulled down to restrain his arms. His eyes were wide with terror but he didn't make a sound. The man with the jerry can emptied it over the victim's head and lit a match, and with a *whoosh* he burst into flames.

Oh God, my brain shrieked in horror.

The crowd moved back in silence but as the burning man began to scream they let out a wild cheer. I scanned the faces around me, looking for someone to stop the killing. A young woman with a baby strapped to her back was looking directly at me. She smiled when I caught her eye and pumped her clenched fist into the air. I looked back to the blazing thing that had once been a man. His screaming was lessening as he ran in blind circles before falling to the ground.

I was so terrified I couldn't move and I had done nothing. I could sense the bloodlust of the mob around me; anyone who tried to intervene would surely be killed too. I remembered reading somewhere that it could take up to twenty minutes for a necklacing victim to die. I prayed not. If God had any mercy he would not let that happen.

With flames and smoke still pouring from the man's body the crowd moved in to kick and beat him again. I noticed that the photographers were also moving in to take their photos, though a few, Pete McDermott among them, had turned their backs and were walking away.

Bheka and I had become separated in the melee, so I found my way back to the car and sat waiting for him to turn up. When he did we drove back to the office in silence where I collapsed at the desk. I wanted to forget what I'd seen, but the gruesome scene played over and over again in my head. Hours later, as the room grew dark, I finally roused myself. 'Oh God,' I said out loud, running my hands through my hair when I remembered that I should have sent the story to Larry. He'd probably already seen the photos on the wire and was not going to be happy with me. I looked at my watch. I had two hours to get the story in before tomorrow's deadline, but first I needed to let Larry know that it was coming so he could save the column space.

With that done, I sat down to write the story only to realise that I had no idea who the victim was and who had killed him. I called out to see if Bheka was still around. When he appeared almost straight away, silhouetted in the doorway, I wondered if he'd been sitting quietly in the outer office all the time I'd been slumped at the desk.

'Do you know the name of the man who was killed?' I asked.

'No,' he said.

'Come on,' I said, getting up and grabbing my bag. 'I need to go to the hotel.' We would go to one of the favourite drinking holes for the international press; someone there would be able to give me all the details I'd failed to get.

As we drove through the streets that night they felt different. I'd been warned often enough that Jo'burg was not a town for lingering, but I could see people standing around on street corners talking. I considered writing my story for Larry about how the necklacing had affected those on the streets, but dismissed the idea immediately. He'd never go for it. The story was not about how it had affected others, but about the man whose name I didn't have, who was killed, by people unknown to me. If no other news eventuated, I could do the effect of the necklacing on the townspeople as a follow-up story the next day.

The noise level in the bar was so bad that I wanted to turn back, but I knew I couldn't, so I continued to push my way in.

'Hey,' someone called from behind, grabbing me by the arm. I turned to see McDermott.

'How are you?' he asked.

'Good.'

'Want to join us for a drink?'

I remembered that he'd been at the necklacing, and although I had no idea who 'us' was, I suspected that if anyone could give me the information I needed, or tell me where I could get it, it was going to be him. As he pushed his way back through the crowd I followed him to a table where two women and a man sat deep in conversation. They all knew the name of the victim and that he was an alleged collaborator with the South African security forces killed by the ANC. The police didn't have a suspect, they said, so no one had been arrested yet. As I was writing all this down I suddenly stopped, realising that this information was probably already on the wire. I wasn't thinking straight. I felt like an idiot. When I looked up, embarrassed, I saw McDermott watching me.

'First necklacing, right?'

'Right.'

'It's okay. It happens to all of us.'

I should have been back at the office filing the story, or even dropping into the police station in Soweto to see how their inquiries were going, but I found I didn't want to leave the comfort of the bar or the hundreds of people around me for the cold, dark office where the memories would assail me again.

The other three at the table, who all worked for the same television station, decided to leave together, but as they did the woman who had been sitting next to McDermott told him pointedly that she'd be in her room if he needed her. He just smiled and wished them all a good night.

'I saw you walking away from the necklacing this afternoon,' I said to him after they'd gone. 'Didn't you want to take any photos?'

'Nope.' He drained the last of his beer before pushing the glass away.

'Why?'

'You ever met Kevin Carter?'

'No.'

He tilted his chair back to lean up against the wall. 'Kevin's a local photographer who covers the violence in the townships. He was the first to photograph necklacing, but then he noticed that he never heard about a necklacing happening except when the media was there. He began to suspect that necklacing was staged for the media, and that if none of us photographed it then it wouldn't happen.'

'That's terrible. So he stopped photographing necklacing?'

'That's right.'

We sat watching me turn my glass of wine around and around on the circle of moisture it had left on the table. 'So,' I said finally, looking up at him, 'you don't take photos of necklacing either because you believe you're causing a killing? Is that it?'

'No, I don't take photos because I don't know whether I am or I'm not.'

'Couldn't your photos stop the act in the future?'

'How?' He banged his seat back down on the floor. 'Did you see any police there today trying to stop it? The police knew what was going to go down—they've got spies everywhere. And I bet your office got a call to go to Soweto this morning, didn't they?' We both knew what the answer to that was. 'Look, Mandela has condemned necklacing more times than I can count but it still happens. If Mandela can't stop his people, and the security forces don't want to stop them, then my photos won't either.'

'But you went there today.'

'I went because I didn't know what was going to go down, but once I realised I left.'

'Okay,' I said, finishing off my drink. 'I've got to get my story out to Larry or he's going to fire me.'

'Do you want the name of the killer?'

'Are you kidding? You know who did it?'

'Nku Cekiso. He's the victim's brother.'

'Jesus, McDermott, are you sure?'

'He's a member of the ANC. His brother was an informer and it was a matter of honour. If he hadn't killed him he would probably have been killed himself, maybe even his family too. As it is, they've already burned down the parents' shack in Soweto.'

'How do you know these people?'

'That's not the point. They know me and they trust me.'

'If you know the name of the killer, why don't you tell the police?'

He looked up at me, a frown over hard grey eyes. 'Don't you think they already know who did it? Go talk to Colonel Hansi Van NieKerk—he's in charge of law and order in Soweto. Ask him why he doesn't arrest Nku. If he's had a few drinks and he's in a good mood he'll tell you that the police and the security forces like the images of the ANC necklacing to go out to the world. Helps discredit the Messiah Mandela and his party. Hansi also might admit that Nku's brother really was his informant and that he didn't bother saving him. If he's in a bad mood, 'cause he lost an informant, he'll just tell you to "fock off".'

'Are you absolutely sure of all that?'

'As sure as I am sitting here.'

'Did you refuse to take the photos because it would look bad for the ANC?'

'No, and don't you ever say that sort of thing to me again. I told you why I didn't take photos.' He was angry with me. 'I don't play politics, Kate. Ever. And here's a free tip for you: it's not our job to play politics, policeman or God.'

I slumped back in my chair. 'I'm sorry.'

'It's okay,' he said, softening. 'It was a legitimate question.'

'Maybe, but I'm sorry anyway. You know, every time I think I'm getting a handle on this job—or the politics of a place—I realise that I know nothing and I'm back to square one again.'

'Don't be so hard on yourself,' he said, pushing his chair back and standing to go. 'It takes time to understand and to build up contacts. You shouldn't expect to do it in five days. I've been back to the townships a couple of a dozen times and I know nothing compared to Kevin and the other South African shooters who're on the ground there every day. It's all degrees of how little we know: degrees of nothingness. But when you do get to know people and they trust you, they'll start opening up—but that takes time. Relax. It'll happen.'

'I should've interviewed the family,' I said, checking the time again on my watch as I too got up to leave.

'I don't think that'd be such a good idea. They're suffering enough. Not everything's our business.'

'Yes, of course. I wasn't thinking. Do you mind if I write that the killer could possibly be a family member and that the victim was allegedly an informant for this colonel in Soweto?'

'The decision's yours.'

'What about photos . . . oh, sorry, I forgot.'

'Take care, Kate. See you around.' He walked off then, looking so very tired.

Thanks to McDermott, it was going to be great copy and Larry might just forgive my tardiness. The whole thing showed me, though, that I had to get a better grip on myself. I had to toughen up.

Chapter 9

Sarajevo
August 1992

FOR JOURNALISTS EACH WAR HAS ITS OWN CHARACTER AND ITS own defining qualities. Some are 'better' than others, some you love and some you hate. For an earlier generation Vietnam was their war; their life-defining experience; their everything. The grunts and the dinks; the napalm and the drugs; Nixon and Kissinger; Saigon and the bar girls; the music and the heat and the whole goddamn stinking, sweating jungle mess of it. Nothing came close to Vietnam. For a later generation it was Central America: El Salvador and Nicaragua; Reagan and the Sandinistas; right-wing death squads and Jesuit priests; dictators and villagers; land reform, communists, democracy, decay. And for the new recruits of the nineties it was the Balkans: quiet villages, lush fields and meandering rivers; freezing snow-dirty winters; snipers, militias, ethnic cleansing, concentration camps; Karadzic, Mladic, Milosevic and NATO; suburban death among the pretty streets of civilised Europe.

Perhaps our attachment to a particular war can be measured by its longevity, so that erstwhile strangers become trusted friends and the place—the war zone—becomes more real than home. Or maybe the attachment comes from something entirely different: from something that has been lost there. Whatever the reason, a particular war signals our coming of age. And horror of all horrors, when it is over, we miss it. Everyone says there'll always be another war, but it'll never be the same war and it will never be your war ever again. The Balkans became my war.

With Larry's blessing, and filled with high hopes of brilliant reportage, I hopped on a plane in late '92 and made my way to the beautiful harbour city of Split, which with its bustling markets, huge private yachts and sparkling blue waters had been a popular European summer vacation spot before the war. After fronting up to the offices of the United Nations to get my official journalist's accreditation, I took a taxi to the airport to hitch a ride on a UN cargo flight into Sarajevo. It was as easy as that. Unlike Riyadh there were no military 'pencil pools' in the wars that reconfigured the former Yugoslavia; no one made me sign a piece of paper to control my behaviour; no one told me who I could and could not speak with, and no one looked over my shoulder to tell me what I could and couldn't write. Perhaps that's why so many journalists died there.

After the communist dictator Tito's death, the Republic of Yugoslavia began to fall apart. Aware that he wouldn't be able to hold all of the former communist state, the ultra-nationalist Serbian leader Slobodan Milosevic pursued his vision of a Greater Serbia and turned his attention to holding Croatia and Bosnia-Herzegovina. The day before Bosnia was to declare its independence, Milosevic's Bosnian Serb forces, together with his Yugoslav National Army, attacked the Bosnian capital of Sarajevo. Under Milosevic's racist vision, ethnic cleansing had once again crawled out from under the slagheap of European history.

On that morning of 6 April 1992, the switchboard operator at the main hospital in Sarajevo was surprised to receive a call from the professor of plastic surgery, who requested that an ambulance be dispatched to collect him from his home. His street, he stated calmly, was coming under sniper attack. Shot in the neck while climbing into the ambulance, the learned professor would become one of the Bosnian war's first victims. At about the same time, machine-gun fire burst from the Holiday Inn and the surrounding apartments in downtown Sarajevo, ripping through a crowd of peace demonstrators gathering outside the parliament building. An ambulance sent to rescue the injured was fired on. Milosevic's Serbs had begun the war in Bosnia the way they intended to finish it: by ignoring every tenet of the Geneva Conventions. They would not be the only ones.

On that first day of the war many of Sarajevo's urbane citizens were blissfully unaware of what was coming down on their heads. When they did hear the rumours, most of them predicted that the fighting would be short-lived, but within days it had become increasingly dangerous to move from one section of the city to another, or even one street to another. Areas quickly became identified as either Serbian or Bosnian, and suburban streets became no-go areas as the frontlines in the racist war began to firm.

Within a month Sarajevo had been surrounded, all roads in and out of the capital blocked, and the airport closed by the Serb guns in the hills overlooking the city, until a reluctant Milosevic was forced to yield to international pressure and the airport was opened again to UN relief flights.

With all its obvious attractions Sarajevo quickly became the world's most popular travel destination for the war tourists and their cheerleaders, the media.

As I sat in the cab of the UN supply truck on that first drive into Sarajevo I couldn't help thinking that this was my first 'real' war. In Riyadh, Iraq and Kuwait it had felt as if I'd been skirting around the edges of war, and although I'd ducked bullets in Gaza, the violence in the Occupied Territories and the South African townships hadn't felt like real war—unless, of course, you actually lived there.

Heading into Sarajevo, I could see the evidence of war all around me. When we passed a bombed-out, pock-marked house with the salutation *Welcome to Sarajevo* scrawled across a wall in large black letters I asked the driver what that meant.

'I think you'll discover it's an "up yours" to the rest of us, who they think have abandoned them.'

'But we have, haven't we?'

He didn't reply.

When we turned onto the six-lane thoroughfare that linked the centre of the city with the outlying residential areas I looked up to the surrounding hills where I knew Milosevic's snipers were sitting watching us and felt my first thrill of fear: I was driving down Sniper Alley, which would soon be declared the most dangerous stretch of road on earth. While that initial drive into Sarajevo had given the war junkie in me my first hit, Sarajevo was the next: it tasted of fear.

By the time I arrived this once vibrant metropolis had been under siege for four months and had already pulled in on itself, dividing along ethnic lines that rapidly began reconfiguring into physical boundaries. And while little shocked the residents of Sarajevo, in the end much angered them, and the thing that angered them most was the sniper who made going about their daily business a life-threatening ordeal. Collecting water, food or firewood for warmth was unbelievably dangerous. Allowing your child to leave the house to play was a monumental risk, and going to hospital in an ambulance made you a prime target. As the cemeteries of Sarajevo became favoured shooting galleries for the Serbs in the surrounding mountains, burying your dead only increased your chances tenfold of being in the next coffin.

At some point all this became normal for the Sarajevans, but it was a strange sort of normality. During the day I would see people moving through the streets as best they could until they came to a certain street corner where they would stop—often in groups—loitering, lingering behind a wall, biding their time, watching and waiting, picking their moment and then they'd run. Around fifteen seconds of safety, maybe twenty seconds if you were lucky—fifteen to twenty seconds between the sniper's first and second shot. With luck you made the distance, if not, if you tripped . . . well, things became a little tricky.

For the sophisticated citizens of Sarajevo such behaviour was an insult to their urbanity. It was, however, just what the great general wanted. Milosevic didn't necessarily need his snipers to kill every citizen in Sarajevo; he wanted them to destroy the fabric of that society. The city had to be taught a lesson. Like a puffed-up schoolyard bully, Milosevic wanted to punish them for daring to defy him. And punish them he did.

My Serbian grocer in London had given me the name and address of his mother, and assured me I would be made most welcome. So after being dropped off in the centre of town I hitched another ride out to the picturesque suburb of Jarcedoli, but by the time I was standing at Mila Deronjic's front door I knew that it was too far from the centre of town to be of any use to me. I decided to at least say hello to Ratko's mother before heading back down into town.

But my knocks weren't answered, and I was about to leave when I heard a faint shuffling sound from the back of the house. Peering in through the swirling amber glass panels of the front door I could just make out a black shape ambling slowly up the hallway, until the door was opened and an elderly woman peered out uncertainly. When I told her my name and mentioned her son, her broad face split into a welcoming smile and she opened the door wide, grabbing my hand to pull me inside and then locking it just as quickly behind me. Ratko's mother lifted my two hands in hers and kissed them on both sides before squashing my face between her old, callused fingers. When she released me she smiled up at me as if I was the Christmas present she had always dreamed of—none of which, I realised, boded well for a quick getaway.

As I was ushered in I deciphered enough of her broken English to learn that Mila had not seen Ratko for over five years. She missed her only child so much that each mention of the beloved's name brought forth a fresh flood of tears. Good manners demanded that her son's dearest friend—there seemed to be some confusion between 'dearest friend' and 'customer in local corner store'—was supposed to stay for a while. After three cups of heavily sweetened tea I felt as if my brain had been rewired, which perhaps explained why I was incapable of telling Mila that the friend sent by her loving son was only an acquaintance and was not really intending to stay.

Before long I was ensconced in Ratko's old bedroom and over the following days was introduced with a certain pride to the old men of the street and, having gained some measure of celebrity status, was invited to play chess, where I soon learnt to refuse their offers of cigarettes and local alcohol without giving offence. More idle hours were spent with Mila's women friends, who plied me with tea and cakes and, disconcertingly, with kisses and hugs. After two days of this I understood that I had come to symbolise all their missing children, of whom there seemed to be a great many.

Although a Serb, Mila hated everything about the war and prayed daily and loudly that NATO would bomb the Serb positions in the hills, kill that madman Milosevic, and end her city's suffering. More than anything Mila wanted her life back. The sporadic electricity, an unreliable water service, and the necessity of dodging snipers' bullets and heavy artillery just to buy food and collect firewood was testing her independence until she was no longer bothering to shelter in her basement when the shelling began. Nor did she venture out for provisions, relying instead on the goodwill of her Croat and Muslim neighbours. But as time passed, and the city became increasingly polarised along ethnic and religious lines, I feared it might prove more difficult for a Serb in Sarajevo to rely on the goodwill of others. Without heating, and having to brave snipers to collect firewood, the coming winter might well prove impossible for Mila.

My time in Jarcedoli gave me a few human interest stories, but I quickly exhausted that genre with Larry, who reminded me I had been sent to cover a war, not tea parties. Desperate to move into town, but unwilling to abandon Mila, I decided I needed a plan for both of us that would include a route out of the city for her and a place in the Holiday Inn for me.

Chapter 10

AT THE UNITED NATIONS HEADQUARTERS I FOUND LITTLE enthusiasm for my plan for the world's largest humanitarian organisation to fly Mila out to Split. It was not within their mandate to evacuate the city of Sarajevo I was told, as if I was a rather slow child. My attempts to persuade the overworked and stressed staffer that this plan did not include the whole of the city, but one old and exceedingly vulnerable lady, produced the retort that there were a lot of old and exceedingly vulnerable ladies in Sarajevo. Why didn't I take a look out the window on my way out?

The next stop, which also happened to be my last stop, was the Holiday Inn, where the world's journalists were gathering, setting up their incestuous little community, their own peculiar beehive. The queen bee—the war—moved and all the worker bees followed. In Saigon it had been the Caravelle Hotel with its rooftop bar and its magnificent alcohol- and drug-soaked view of the war. In Beirut it had been the elegance of the Commodore Hotel on the splendid Corniche, looking out over the Israeli gunships floating in the Mediterranean, and in Iraq it had been the Al Rasheed in Baghdad, in the line of US fire power. In Sarajevo it was the Holiday Inn, an ugly two-toned yellow and brown building resplendent with everything the war tourist could possibly desire: a prime position on the most dangerous street on earth, a gaggle of hyped-up media junkies and its very own sniper with a clear view of the entrance.

Walking into the cavernous interior of the foyer the first thing I heard was, 'Well, well, well, what do we have here but Kate Price.' I turned and looked into the smiling face of Pete McDermott. My first uncensored thought was, *God, he's sexy*, closely followed by, *Not for you*, but I smiled anyway for I couldn't think of anyone I wanted to see more. If anyone could sort out my problem it was McDermott. For a few seconds we stood facing each other, neither of us quite sure of what the greeting should be until he leaned in and kissed me on the cheek. 'Come on,' he said, 'this deserves a drink. When did you arrive?'

'Nearly a week ago.'

'Where the hell have you been for a week?' he asked, frowning, as we walked to the bar.

'I need some help.'

'Ah, yes, don't we all?'

'No, I mean I need some serious help.'

'Like I said, don't we all? What do you want to drink, Kate? We have whisky, whisky and this local stuff that'll put hairs on your chest.'

'Be serious.'

'I am being serious. You should see the number of Bosnian women with—'

'Okay, I'm leaving if you're not going to be serious.'

'Alright, you tell me about your serious and I'll tell you about my serious. Even better, how about you show me—'

'Are you drunk?'

'No, but I probably should be.' When he saw I wasn't amused his smile vanished. 'It's a war, Kate, you need to lighten up.' He pulled the chair out for me. 'John'll be here in a minute so before he arrives there's something I probably should tell you. Actually, you shouldn't be too surprised if John isn't exactly glad to see you.'

I looked at him, wondering what he was talking about. I'd run into John a couple of times since our dinner in Jerusalem and everything had seemed fine to me. 'What've I done?'

'It's nothing you've done . . . well, it *is* actually something you've done.'

'What?'

'Okay, I may as well tell you now that we—John and me, that is—we had a little wager on whether you'd turn up here or not.'

'A wager? On me? And who won?'

'Me.'

'So why won't John be glad to see me?'

'It's not really that he won't be glad to see you, it's just that he won't be glad to have to buy my drinks for as long as this siege lasts.'

'Do you think it will last that long?' I was saying, just as John appeared.

'How'd you be, Kate?' He leaned down and kissed me on the cheek. 'Ah, McDermott, wanting to keep her all to yourself were you, hiding her away in this back corner? You need to watch him, Kate. He's not to be trusted.' John was smiling as he pulled out a chair and sat down.

'And you're my friend?' Pete said good-humouredly.

'I am.' John was still beaming. He certainly didn't look like he was worried about losing the bet.

Pete must have noticed it too because he looked at John and shook his head. 'Okay, what gives?'

'Guess.' It seemed impossible, but John's smile had grown even wider.

'Can't guess.'

'I'm a dad,' he said, tears welling up in his eyes. 'I'm a dad! Exactly four hours ago I officially became a dad!'

'Bloody hell! Congratulations, mate!' Pete jumped up to hug him. 'Boy or girl?' he asked, breaking away.

'A little girl. Amanda. Six pounds five ounces and mother and daughter doing well. I think I'm going to cry,' John said, as the tears began to fall.

'Cry all you want. It's fantastic,' Pete said, putting his arm around John's shoulders again. 'This calls for a drink,' he declared, having already forgotten that John was supposed to be buying.

'That's so wonderful, John. Congratulations to both of you,' I said, standing to give him a hug too as Pete walked to the bar.

As word spread people kept coming up to congratulate John and drinks started to accumulate on the table, but I noticed that John sat on the one drink and Pete hardly touched his. I realised then that although I'd seen both of them with drinks often neither of them really drank much. I'd definitely never seen either of them even slightly intoxicated.

'So,' said John when the excitement around us had died down. 'Did Pete here tell you we had a bet on whether you'd turn up or not?'

'Why didn't you think I'd come?'

'Oh, I'd thought you'd come, alright, I was just hoping you wouldn't.' I frowned, wondering why he would say that. 'Don't get me wrong,' he continued. 'I like the girl I got to know in Iraq, but this job has a way of changing people and I wouldn't want you to change. You're too nice.'

Was the job changing me? I didn't think so, at least, I hoped not.

Pete interrupted my thoughts. 'Apparently Kate has a problem and it's a serious problem, hence we are in the serious end of the bar.'

After I told them about Mila, Pete raked his hand through his hair. 'Impossible', he said. 'All the roads are blocked and there aren't any domestic flights in or out of the city. No one's evacuating. As far as the Bosnians are concerned they don't want any of their citizens to leave because that'd hand a victory to Milosevic. It just ain't going to happen. How does this woman think she'll get to London anyway?'

'Well . . . she doesn't. I mean, I haven't actually talked with her about it.'

'Oh, this is priceless,' he said, throwing back his head and laughing. 'You've been covering war for what? Five minutes? And you're trying to ship this old lady out to London without her consent? Giving war reporting the flick and into the business of kidnapping are we now? Remember what I told you back in Jo'burg? Don't play God, it can get a wee bit messy. Best leave all that stuff to the NGOs.'

'What makes this woman so special?' John asked.

'She's not special. She's just sort of become my responsibility. Look, if you won't help me I understand, but I've got to find someone who can.'

'We didn't say we wouldn't help,' said John, 'but I'm trying to get out of here to see my daughter so I'm not sure what I can do.'

'And I was simply pointing out the moral minefield you seem pretty eager to step into.'

'Pete's right, Kate, it's risky business. Have you really thought it through?'

'No, I haven't, because I've got absolutely no idea how to get her out. All I know is that I have to because I don't think she'll survive. It doesn't feel like I've got a choice. I can't leave her behind in her house all alone.'

John and Pete discussed the rumours circulating about a secret tunnel running under the airport and out past the Serbian lines, but neither of them knew anyone who'd actually seen the tunnel or could even verify its existence. It was agreed that they'd make inquiries and we'd meet in the foyer the following morning.

Like everyone else I had to leave the hotel by the back entrance to avoid being shot. In time the hotel's bored inhabitants, usually members of the world's press corps, would play Russian roulette by poking their heads out a window to taunt the sniper.

Chapter 11

WHEN THE TUNNEL TURNED OUT TO BE A NO-GO I STAYED IN the Holiday Inn the following night and tried to talk Pete, or anyone else sitting around the bar, into helping me devise a plan of escape for Mila. Late in the evening a Bosnian officer blearily informed me that he could help. The only catch was, if I was reading his signals correctly—and there was a slight language problem made worse by an excessive level of alcohol consumption on his part—I had to sleep with him.

During a break in negotiations when the soldier went to the bathroom, Pete, who had been monitoring proceedings from across the bar, came over to ask how much a bed at the Holiday Inn was really worth to me. It was a reasonable question, to which the answer was obviously either quite a lot, or not very much, depending on what value I placed on my body.

'Is he asking for a down payment first, Price, or does he want to try before he buys? Just a hint: I wouldn't sell myself too cheaply if I were you. I'm sure you could raise the price if

you showed him that cute little butterfly tattoo on your arse.'
I froze, along with all those within earshot.

'I don't have a butterfly tattoo on my arse, McDermott.'
Even to my ears the denial sounded too loud and too lame.
'Tell them, McDermott!' I demanded, looking into his laughing
grey eyes, but he wouldn't respond. 'Bastard!' I said under my
breath, which only made him laugh out loud.

As the soldier swayed back to the bar Pete offered, 'Cuts
a dashing figure, don't you think?' and then announced that
he was off to bed. 'I don't think I care to see the end of these
negotiations.'

I didn't really have any intention of trading my body to get
Mila out of Sarajevo and me down to the Holiday Inn, so the
only solution was to get her on one of the UN supply planes
that returned virtually empty to Split every other day. After
three days of driving the UN staff crazy I convinced one tired
and battered ear that Mila, who had mysteriously become my
mother's sister and in possession of a British passport, should
be allowed to leave on a UN aircraft.

That evening in Jarcedoli I raised the possibility with Mila,
but it was never going to be an easy conversation for a plethora
of reasons, not least of which was that she had never considered
the idea of leaving Sarajevo. After I explained my fears for her
safety, she became distressed at the quick disintegration of her
life. I sat with my arm around her for hours as she cried. She
had not planned to die in London, a place she had never seen
nor cared to see, she sobbed. She wanted to die in the house
she had come to after her marriage, the one in which Ratko
had been born, and the one her beloved husband—God rest

his soul—had died in. To try to lessen her pain I then made a promise that would shame me for years: she would only have to leave until the war ended and then she could return.

In the quiet hours of that morning I lay in Ratko's childhood bed racked with fear and guilt, for in my planning I had overlooked an important factor: while I had cleverly devised a plan to get her *out* of Sarajevo, I had not devised a plan to get her *into* Sarajevo. Mila was incapable of the ducking and weaving necessary to dodge snipers while traversing the city. In trying to save her, I might end up getting her killed. Staring into the dark, I marvelled at how quickly events had reached a point that any rational person would describe as out of control. Pete was right: playing God was not all it was cracked up to be. If the good Lord—who I didn't happen to believe in—helped me just this one time, I promised Him, in the future I would do as Pete had suggested and leave playing God to the NGOs.

Our saviour came the following morning in the form of an ambulance driver Pete had befriended who agreed that if it was quiet that evening he would take us downtown in his ambulance.

Of course, we still faced the problem that, despite the Geneva Conventions, ambulances had become moving targets favoured by the Yugoslav army, which had a useful supply of infrared night-vision equipment. The only positive was that infrared proficiency was limited to a single shot, so if a vehicle was able to move fast enough it was difficult to take it out—as long as the driver or a tyre didn't receive a direct hit. The odds were in our favour, I told myself.

That evening, the ambulance driver eschewed the meandering back streets for the main road into town, which we covered in record time. Just before we reached the centre he turned off his headlights and pressed his foot down on the accelerator. We roared down Sniper Alley, taking the turn-off that led to the back entrance of the Holiday Inn at forty-five degrees, and in doing so succeeded in defying all the general laws of physics. Mila, who had been crying when we entered the ambulance, completed the journey in shocked silence and had to be carried into the hotel by a waiting Pete with the help of the driver. After Mila fell asleep in the room I would share with her until she left I went looking for Pete. When I couldn't find him in the bar I went to his room.

'How's Mila?' he asked, taking the book that he had been reading off a chair so I could sit down.

'Asleep.'

'Good. I suppose congratulations are in order, Price. By getting Mila out you will have single-handedly thwarted a cabal of Bosnian politicians, the UN, a number of world leaders—including the British prime minister and the US president—Slobodan Milosevic and the whole Serbian army in the hills. How does it feel?"

'I haven't got her out yet.'

'You will.'

'The truth is it doesn't feel so good.'

'Why? You did what you set out to do—which, I might add, is more than the rest of us are doing. You've probably saved her life.'

'That's just it. I don't know if I am saving her life. In the end I really did it so I could get a room in this hotel.'

'I know that.'

'That's not so very noble.'

'I'll let you in on a secret: I've been around long enough and have seen enough to know that in the end everything we do is for ourselves. I know it's not a popular idea and people like to delude themselves that they're doing whatever they're doing for a higher good—for humanity, truth, justice, love or some such shit. And I'm not denying that some people have higher ideals and live by them. But when you strip all your ideals and all your good deeds down to the lowest common denominator, it's all about us. What we do is about who we want to be, or who we are, or what we want. To put it less charitably, it's about how we want the world to see us and how we want to see ourselves. In any event it's about us—good deeds, bad deeds and anything in between. Those who genuinely do care and know this don't bother wrapping themselves in comforting illusions of goodness. You did it for an old lady because you were worried about her, and you did it so you could get down to the Holiday Inn, and you did it to ease your conscience. If you hadn't been worried about her, you wouldn't have done it. Isn't that good enough?'

'I doubt whether that's good enough to clear my conscience.'

'Well, at least you're not deluding yourself. I'm impressed, Price, and I'm not impressed so easily these days. You're not deluding yourself over your motives and despite all the obstacles that were in your way you did what you set out to do, which, as I said, is better than most of us.'

'You told me not to play God, remember?'

'That's right. So don't do it again.' He laughed then, and in the end he had me laughing too.

After I left Pete's room I went upstairs to the Reuters office to patch through a call to Ratko. The man had been telling me for years that his dearest wish was for his mother to live with him in London and now he was going to get it. I hoped he hadn't been lying. When I told him that all things being equal she would be in Split sometime within the next few days he exploded with joy. 'I knew you save her, Kate. I knew you do it! God bless you! God bless you! She be happy in London.'

'I'm not so sure about that, Ratko. You banked on my good nature to get your mother out, didn't you?'

'Kate, Kate, you mistaken me. I never do like that. I only try help find you a nice home to stay in Sarajevo with my mother, as God is my witness. If you nice and do this for my mother then I am happy too.'

'Promise me you'll be waiting in Split to meet her.'

'Of course, of course, she my mother.'

Two days later Mila left Sarajevo on a UN flight to Split, where her son was indeed waiting for her. As I had suspected, no one was interested in examining my aunt's British passport.

With John back in the US, Pete and I began to check each evening what the other was intending to do the following day and if it suited we'd join up. I soon discovered that Pete was not only fun to travel with, but he could find his way around a town he had never seen; identify an incoming round by its sound; get an introduction to the general or captain who could get us the pass; and had the uncanny knack of being in the right place at the right time. By watching him I began to learn how to look after myself and how to get the best out of a story. And when the fear came, as it inevitably did, he taught me how to step outside myself and observe it moving through my body so I wouldn't panic. Whenever John was back in Sarajevo the three of us would travel together, although John was spending as much time as he could back home with his wife and their new baby.

Covering the Balkans became my permanent gig at the paper and so I spent the next few years moving between London, when

I needed a break, and living in the Holiday Inn in Sarajevo. By late 1993 Pete had moved his base from London to New York after taking a contract with an American magazine, but the friendship continued to flourish. If we were both out of the country we would talk on the phone about what we thought the next big story might be, and when we were both in Sarajevo we usually worked together or with John. If Pete's magazine didn't want his photographs he'd give me first refusal and I'd offer them to Larry with my stories, which pleased Larry no end. If Larry didn't want them then Pete would sell them through his agency. It was a good partnership that worked well for me and the paper. Pete and I were also building a relationship that came to mean a lot to me, but I wasn't fooling myself either. I was attracted to the man, but so were a lot of other women. Pete enjoyed women's company too much to be anyone's long-term partner. I had to remind myself often that working with Pete was the luckiest break I ever got and I was not about to blow that by sleeping with the guy.

Chapter 12

Sarajevo
February 1994

AFTER A SHORT BREAK IN LONDON I'D BEEN BACK IN BOSNIA for a little over a week and had just come in after spending a few days with a group of Serbian militia. I should have been up in my room boiling water to wash while the hotel had its precious two hours of electricity for the day, but instead I was curled up on a lounge in the foyer of the Holiday Inn. From my vantage point near the reception desk I was staring up into the void that was the interior of the hotel when I saw Pete, who I'd been expecting back in Sarajevo sometime that week. As he left his room on the third floor I watched him begin to make his way downstairs. Within minutes he was wafting past, smelling tantalisingly clean and fresh. 'Wake up, Price,' he said, as I smiled up at him and he bent down to kiss me on the cheek before disappearing again. 'Be back soon.'

'Okay.' I hadn't seen him for about six weeks and was thinking how very happy I was that he was back when my attention was caught by a vision of Annie Lennox floating down the central stairs of the Holiday Inn. I knew it couldn't be Annie Lennox because the last time I heard she didn't go to war. I blinked to clear the apparition, but it just wouldn't go away and was now heading in my direction with a somewhat familiar smile on its face. Returning the vision's smile—how could one not when one was so honoured?—I wondered who it was I was smiling at.

'Kate, beautiful woman,' Bella purred in a voice so soft and sexy that even I was in danger of falling in love with her. 'How extraordinarily wonderful to see you again. It's been ages.'

I'd been introduced to Bella by Larry on my first day as a cadet at the paper. While you could say that Bella had taken the raw recruit under her wing, it was probably more correct to say that she had adopted me as a cause. Intent on teaching me the ropes of journalism during the day, this woman with a reputation as a hardcore photojournalist was on a mission to introduce me to all the bars, clubs, restaurants, eligible men and bad habits of London that she knew—which were not inconsiderable. Bella was ten years older than me, but when partying I could never keep up with her and I'd never met anyone who could.

When I saw her that day in the Holiday Inn, she had traded in her familiar chestnut curls for bleached blonde spikes. With green eyes, a sensuously wide mouth and enviable curves, my friend exuded sex. Pure film noir, sculptured and mysterious, from no particular part of the world, although she claimed to have been born in Alabama. According to Bella, her southern belle mama, Celia, had been less than sober when her daughter was born. To punish her philandering husband, who was on his own bender at the time and could not be found for three days, she named their firstborn Belladonna. By the time Belladonna's father had sobered up and found his way to the maternity ward the deed was done, the birth certificate signed, and his daughter was officially named after a toxic plant.

I knew Bella well enough to know that she didn't think herself beautiful, which made me wonder what it was she saw when she looked in the mirror. She was, however, aware of the effect she had on men. 'Oh, it's a chemical thing,' she used to say, as if it was of no importance. I asked her once what she thought made someone beautiful and she had replied, 'When their heart makes me love them. Everything else is fluff.'

After a brief and disastrous marriage to a South African, Bella had introduced me to her new lover, whose name was Sam. Sam looked like a man but was not. In typical Bella fashion she announced that she had given up men forever for the simpler, less complicated delights of lesbian love, making me promise to cut off her hands and gouge out her eyes if she ever touched a man's penis again. Three months later she confessed she had reverted. 'Why settle for a substitute when you can have the real thing?' Indeed. When reminded that I was now obliged to cut off her hands and gouge out her eyes Bella threw her head back and laughed. Had she really said that? Bella's problem, as she saw it, was that she loved the unbearable torments of love.

'God, Bella, you'll be killed with hair like that!'

In mock horror she drew back from our embrace. 'Oh Lordy, do you think I should demand my money back?'

'No, you look brilliant as usual, but you do stand out—and in a war zone.'

Pete had returned but just as I was about to introduce them he leaned over and, putting his arm around her waist, pulled her close and planted a kiss on her cheek.

'It's been a while, hasn't it, Pete?' she said, leaning back to smile seductively up at him. 'How've you been?'

'Got to congratulate you, Bell,' he said as he released her. 'I seem to remember you always loved drama and I think I can now safely say there are two things on earth visible from outer space: the Great Wall of China and your hair. Let me get you a drink to celebrate your arrival. Still a dry martini?'

'Of course.'

'We only have whisky.'

'Of course.'

'I can ask them if they've got an olive to put in it if you want?'

'I see it's still the same charming Pete I've always loved and adored.'

Their body language and their intimate smiles made me wonder what it was they were both remembering about loving and adoring. Had Bella been another McDermott conquest, or had he been a Bella conquest? Probably it had been a meeting of equals. I was surprised to feel a twinge of jealousy. 'So,' I said, shrugging off the feeling as we moved into the bar looking for a table, 'what's brought you to downtown Sarajevo?' After leaving the paper two years before, Bella had been freelancing for magazines and NGOs, mostly in Africa.

'Thought I'd come here to chill out and forget about things back at home, see what this pissy little war's all about.'

'This is no pissy little war,' I replied, a little miffed that 'my war' didn't impress her.

'So I've been told: not much electricity, unreliable hot water, your very own sniper and—' looking around the room '—all the usual suspects. Things must be serious.'

'I thought you were doing NGO work?'

'I was. I came to escape a broken heart.'

'Not such a great place to get over a broken heart,' said Pete, having overhead her remark as he returned to the table with our drinks.

'That's what my shrink said when I told him I wouldn't be subsidising his wife's plastic surgery anymore. But, hey, listen, you tell me a better place to forget your troubles.'

Later that evening Bella confided to me that she had fallen desperately in love with a handsome young Spaniard, but the affair had been a disaster. In the nine years I had known Bella she had not been in any relationship that had not been a disaster.

As the evening lengthened and a crowd gathered, Pete disappeared into the dark recesses behind the bar with a woman in possession of an unnatural mass of red curls cascading down a delicately curved back.

'Does that worry you?' Bella asked, looking over at them.

'Why should it worry me?'

'Sorry,' she said, frowning, 'my mistake. I must have misread the signals. I thought there was something happening between you two.'

'Pete's a player, Bella, and I'm not interested in players.'

Within minutes a well-known French journalist claimed the seat next to Bella. Sporting a dodgy tan and overly long grey hair, and looking as if he thought he was the next big thing, Andre proceeded to engage Bella in as earnest a conversation as could be had with one eye on the room. Andre was never really with you, always with the possibility elsewhere. With a well-earned reputation as an ego tripper who unashamedly dropped names and places, Andre liked to tell you how honoured he was by the list of those who hated him, which effectively was just another form of name-dropping. His charms, as far as I had been able to discern, were invisible to the naked eye, but the unruly liberal masses seemed to adore him—albeit somewhat slightly less than he adored himself.

It surprised me that Andre was even in Sarajevo for it was not his scene to turn up to a war that was actually happening, his preference being to arrive once the danger had passed and make his name by proclaiming how badly the rest of us had covered it. Perhaps Andre was a little confused and had meant to go to St Moritz or Santorini, and had taken a wrong turn at a bar in Paris and ended up in Sarajevo? I considered pointing his error out to him, and perhaps suggesting that quite possibly there was a war going on outside, but after some consideration I thought better of it.

Perhaps Andre knows something the rest of us don't—like the war has ended. Maybe I should check to see if our resident sniper has packed up and gone home? Maybe I should warn Bella that Andre has unattractive little tufts of grey hair growing out of his ears? Maybe I should go to bed.

Chapter 13

BELLA, WHO HAD ARRANGED TO TRAVEL WITH US THE FOLLOWING day to Banja Luka, looked slightly the worse for wear in the morning, although I was not sure if that was due to lack of sleep, over-imbibing the night before or waking up next to Andre. It turned out to be the latter.

'Well, what was it like?' You could ask about a one-night stand, but you never pried into a serious relationship.

Without lifting her head from the backpack she was rummaging in, Bella replied that his technique was perfect.

'That bad, hey?' I hadn't been particularly interested, but now she had my attention. I watched her look up and stare into the middle distance.

'You remember those ice skaters at the Winter Olympics in Sarajevo? You know, the big hulking guy who threw the tiny girl over his shoulder, and round his waist, and then back up through his legs before he started all over again? What were their names?'

'Torvill and Dean, and I don't remember him as being particularly hulking.'

'Whatever. It sort of felt like we had our own Olympics happening in the room last night.' She disappeared back into the backpack and re-emerged. 'I never thought I'd be praying for the missionary position . . . no pun intended.'

No one wanted to drive so it was left to me as Pete settled down to sleep on the back seat, leaving little room for our handsome young driver and fixer, Haran, who also wanted to sleep on the back seat—and, I might add, on the job. Bella, who was in the front with me, wanted to sleep too and pushed her backpack up against the window to rest her head. I suspected everyone but me had had something, or someone, to do the previous night. For some reason I just couldn't find a man I was attracted to, apart from Pete—and that was a no-go zone. Most days being alone didn't worry me, because I didn't want to deal with distractions of the heart when I needed to put all my energies into the job, but on the rare occasion, I felt lonely.

Late February in Bosnia and the winter grass was beginning to poke its head through the snow turning into dirty brown slush by the side of the road. Heading towards Banja Luka we passed fields with pleasant little farms: cows grazing, birds singing, the sun sparkling on islands of melting ice. Just one tranquil rural scene after another. Beautiful. Except in every picture-postcard village were the raw scars of war. The mosques had all been destroyed, the houses riddled with bullet holes and every now and then the skeletal shape of a burnt-out farmhouse could be seen in the chilly winter landscape.

Continually huffing and sighing and changing the position of her backpack to get more comfortable, Bella finally gave up and, after checking that the two beauties in the back seat were asleep she asked, 'Do you remember when what's her name . . . Lordy, you know her name . . .'

'Perhaps if you gave me a few more clues.'

'You know,' as if I really did know, 'the one who interviews people in bed and is married to Bob Geldof and has all those kids with those ridiculous names. Come on, what's her name?'

'Look, I can't remember her name, but it doesn't matter because I know who you mean.'

'Okay, well, she said that on the first night with one lover he did six things to her that were illegal in England.'

'Everything that's fun's illegal in England.'

'Do you think she was talking about Geldolf?'

'I have no idea.'

'I've been thinking about it anyway and they must have—'

'Spare me the gory details, will you? I've been celibate far too long.'

'Are you sure?'

'About what? That I've been celibate, or that I want you to spare me the gory details? It's an affirmative to both, by the way.'

'Why would you choose to be celibate? I assume it's a choice . . .'

'Thanks for the vote of confidence. The answer is when you can't find anyone you want to bed.'

'Mmm . . .' It was probably not a choice Bella understood.

A few kilometres up the road she asked, 'If this was the last day of your life, who would you spend it with?' I groaned inwardly, remembering my friend's low boredom threshold.

'I don't know. What a question. My parents?'

'Boring.'

'You didn't say the answer had to be interesting. Okay, let me think. Gore Vidal? Fascinating man, shame he's so old and so very gay.'

'Okay, what book would you read?'

'That's easy. The Bible. I thought I should read it once but never got past the begot part, and I suppose that the last day of my life might be as good a time as any to try to get a better handle on what might be ahead of me. I'd also be hedging my bets in case there really was something after.'

'What do you think love is?'

This time I did groan. 'Aw, Bella, I don't know. What do *you* think it is?'

'Caring about someone when you really don't want to.' She let out a sigh then, probably thinking about the young Spanish lover.

'Did you get that from one of those "Love Is" cards from the seventies?'

'No, it's true. What about you?'

'I don't know. I guess for me it has to do with being completely vulnerable. Trusting someone so much that—Oh, shit!'

I'd just driven around a corner and about fifty metres up ahead was a Serbian roadblock. From where we were it looked as if militiamen were quite possibly rolling hand grenades across the road. I prayed I was hallucinating.

Sometimes you could forget, but you never should. Rule number one in a war zone: don't ever forget where you are. Days of calm and sleepy rural landscapes could lull you into forgetting that you were in a country where insanity had become the currency. Up ahead was a gutted house. A tank was slowly turning its sights on us, militiamen and soldiers turning their guns on us. Yelling. I needed to stay calm. *Do you want me to slow down? Stop? Turn back? Get out of the car? Stay inside? Just tell me what you want me to do and I'll do it! Just tell me. I don't want to make a mistake here.* A warning shot was fired over the car, waking Pete and Haran. All things considered the warning shot was a good sign—at least they weren't shooting *at* us.

'Slow down, Kate,' Pete said, leaning forward to place a warning hand on my shoulder.

'What the hell do you think I'm doing?' I hissed back at him, my foot already on the brake. Safest not to do anything too fast. Reaching across Bella I opened the glove box and handed her a piece of white cloth to hang out the window. At the same time Pete wound down his window and held up his camera.

'Let's all be calm now.'

'Lordy, Pete, what do you think we're going to do, throw a temper tantrum?' said Bella sarcastically through the smile she had plastered on her face for the benefit of our friends up ahead.

'Okay, okay. Let's just get through this calmly.'

'Shut up, Pete,' I said.

Forty-four-gallon drums of petrol were lined up on each side of the road. A couple of fires were burning in old drums where militiamen with the stock standard red bandanna wrapped around their filthy hair were standing warming their hands through the stock standard fingerless gloves. I could have laughed, they looked so bloody stupid, like extras in a second-rate Hollywood film, but I knew from experience that militiamen were more dangerous than any soldier I had ever met. These guys had schooled themselves for war on violent video games and Bruce Willis and Sylvester Stallone movies. They had not a skerrick of discipline and there were rarely any consequences to their actions. Any one of them could have blown us away without a second thought.

I counted quickly: two soldiers atop the APC and three behind sandbags on the left with their guns pointed at us. Another soldier was on the ground manning a machine gun that was also pointed in our direction. Three militiamen were on a tank to the right, the Yugoslavian flag hanging limply in the still of the early morning. Its sights were trained on us. I could see at least five more militiamen coming out of the doorway of a house by the roadblock, smoking and watching us. There were also the militiamen hanging around the fires. At least fifteen men and we had their undivided attention. Lying across the road were anti-tank mines attached to thick string—and, of course, the hand grenades.

We had come to a stop about twenty metres from them.

One of the militiamen in the doorway flicked his cigarette into the snow, heaved his rifle up over his shoulder and motioned for the others to follow him. It was a bad sign. The militia were in charge at this roadblock, not the soldiers. When the fellow was about ten metres away he began shouting and waving his gun around.

'He's saying we have to get out of the car,' said Haran. No prizes for that translation.

Adrenaline had kicked in, my heart was racing and the blood was pounding through my head. Leaving the motor running, and our doors wide open, we all got out and stood with our hands in the air. Pete and Bella had their cameras held high, trying to tell them that we were harmless journalists, but that could have been the wrong message. It could have made us the moose with the target painted on his forehead on the first day of hunting season. A lot of the militias didn't like the press by that time in the war and we were becoming targets for all those who never knew, or conveniently forgot, the part of the Geneva Conventions that classified journalists as non-combatants. Each night these killers watched CNN and the BBC looking for themselves, cheering as their atrocities were reported by sober-faced journalists. And each day they scoured the newspapers searching for their names and faces. They'd never had so much power. And yet, while most of these hoons were not averse to a bit of cheesy celebrity status, they were beginning to grow unhappy with some of the things we were saying and writing about them so that each time a reporter wrote a critical piece it upped the ante for the rest of us on the ground.

Pushing us up against the sides of the car they began to frisk us. As the fellow rubbed his hands down my body he lingered over my breasts. I could cope with that. But when he moved them back up and his finger probed between my legs I spun around and whacked him. Stupid me! Stupid, stupid me! He whacked me straight back with a force that cracked my neck and whipped my head back and to the side so that my face crashed into the door. With stars exploding in front of me I sank into the mud, aware that he was raising his leg to kick. There was nothing I could do.

With everyone shouting and moving, it was not the ideal time to pass out. In the dark recesses of my slow-turning brain I knew it was my fault that no one was staying particularly calm. Bella and Pete were both yelling, and people were yelling back at them in a jumble of words that I could not understand.

Trying to focus, I looked up to see the militiaman, his face thick and ugly with rage, holding a gun to Pete's head. Was I blanking out or coming to? Everything seemed to be happening in slow motion with little pieces missing. Even through the ringing in my ears, though, I realised that a quiet had descended. Everyone was now perfectly still. No one wanted to miss what was going to happen next. With the gun at his head Pete was not moving. All it would take for this charged-up guy with the filthy bandanna to pull the trigger was one more stupid move.

Fighting the blackness again I tried to find something to do, or say, to defuse the situation.

I could hear someone shouting from far away. *Have I blanked out again? Oh God, where's Pete?* Lifting my head I saw the militiaman had dropped the gun, but as he began to walk away he turned and spat in Pete's face. From the foggy distance of ground level I watched my friend, praying he would not react. Standing perfectly still, Pete ignored the spittle running down past his eye until the fellow turned his back again and was walking away. Only then did he wipe it off.

The voice from far away must have been telling us we were free to drive on because I could sense that the atmosphere was changing again. Pete and Haran helped me up out of the slush to deposit me in the back seat with Bella, who handed me a packet of tissues to blow the mud and blood out of my nose. Tilting my head back on the headrest I pinched my throbbing nose to stop the bleeding. As they pulled the anti-tank mines off the road, Pete, who was now in the driver's seat, moved off slowly. No one spoke until about five kilometres up the road when he stopped the car and got out.

'Get me the medical kit from under your seat please, Bell.' Pulling the cotton wool out of its plastic bag he replaced it with snow from the side of the road and handed me the makeshift ice pack. 'Here, put this on your eye. You've got a real shiner. In fact the whole side of your face is going to turn black. How does it feel? No,' he said, holding up his hand, 'don't tell me—I can see. Do you think your nose is broken?'

'No, I don't think so, but it's hard to breathe with all the blood.'

'I think we should get her back to Sarajevo so someone can look at her,' suggested Bella.

'Not through that roadblock again!' I said, heart thumping with renewed panic. 'I don't want to go back through the roadblock again!'

'Don't worry, we won't. Does it hurt anywhere else?' Pete asked, feeling around my head and shoulders.

'My neck cracked when he hit me. It hurts when I turn my head.'

'Here, lie down on your back on the seat. Bell, can you hold Kate's feet?' Gently he held my head in his hands, probing, lifting, moving it from side to side and up and down and then lightly rotating it. I winced in pain. 'Okay, I'm going to give it a little stretch. It won't hurt.'

'No!'

'Come on, Kate, it needs to be done while it's still warm.'

'Oh God, Pete, I hope you know what you're doing.'

'Trust me.'

'Haven't I heard that before?'

'Not from me you haven't, my sweet. Okay, just relax. I want you to trust me.' Leaning down he whispered in my ear, 'I want you to be completely vulnerable.'

I looked up into his smiling, upside-down face and groaned. When I looked to my left I saw Bella registering the significance of his words. He just laughed. The bastard hadn't been asleep after all. Cupping one hand under my chin, and the other on the top of my head, he started to rotate my neck gently before giving a quick pull that caused it to crack again and an involuntary cry to escape.

'Did it hurt? Did it crack?' he asked as he moved my head around again.

'No. Yes.'

'You'll be okay apart from a black eye, a swollen nose, a stiff neck and a whopper of a headache. Here, take some of these.' Reaching into the medical kit he handed me a couple of painkillers. 'You completely sure you want to go on? You could be concussed, you know. Did you black out at all?'

'Maybe. I think so. I don't know.'

'Okay, tell me if you feel like throwing up or if you feel like you're getting worse, otherwise we'll go back to Sarajevo via Jajce to avoid your friends.'

After Pete and Haran helped me to sit up I heard Bella ask Pete, 'Are you sure we shouldn't go straight back?'

'Bell, believe me, Kate's welfare is my main concern here.'

'I can see that,' she said, hesitating. 'You really won't hurt her, will you?'

'That's not my intention.'

'Okay,' she said. A moment later she climbed in beside me. After driving for about twenty minutes in silence Bella offered, 'I remembered her name.'

'Whose name?' Pete asked.

'Paula Yates. It was Paula Yates who was married to Geldof. It came to me just as you decided to backhand that guy with the bandanna, Kate. Lordy, of all the things to think of in that moment, can you believe it? I didn't bother mentioning it at the time 'cause I didn't think anyone would be interested.' Turning to me bundled up in the corner she said, 'You sure you don't want me to tell you what this guy did to Paula? It'll take your mind off the pain.'

'Not really, Bella.'

'I'd like to know what he did to Paula,' said Pete from the front. 'You have my undivided attention as always, Bell.'

Shivering and fighting off nausea I decided that I could not feel any worse. Besides, listening to Bella's fantasies about Paula Yates and her lover had to be better than drowning in my own fantasies about what could have happened back at the roadblock. Two of the things Bella said I'd never heard of, which made me wonder where this guy had learnt them, and where Bella had learnt them, and if Pete had learnt them, and why I hadn't even heard of them, let alone learnt them.

Chapter 14

A WEEK LATER BELLA FOUND ME IN MY ROOM IN THE HOLIDAY Inn washing out my underwear. Moving aside a T-shirt I had drying on the chair, she sat down and told me that she had decided to give up her career to live in Italy with her young Spanish lover.

Hopping onto the bed and inching myself back until I was leaning up against the wall, I smiled. 'I thought you said to me—when was it?' I looked up at the ceiling as if it held the answer. 'Ah, yes, less than a week ago if I remember correctly—that this guy was very bad for you and that he'd broken your heart.'

'You know me,' she said, beaming, 'always dramatic. I was wrong and now I think he is very fine for me.' I laughed. 'I know, I know,' she said, raising her hands to fend off any further comment from me, 'but let's be realistic here. I'm in my mid-thirties—'

'Excuse me?'

'Okay, late thirties, and time is running out if I want to have children.'

'Children? This is new isn't it?' I asked, stunned.

'I'm not saying I *do* want babies,' she said. 'But if I change my mind then I need to make some decisions soon.'

I understood why she needed to give up the job if she wanted to give this relationship a chance. The only two serious relationships I'd had since starting to cover conflicts had floundered. Chris had bailed about six months into my overseas assignments, telling me I was married to the job, which wasn't very original, but probably true. I'd met Simon the year before I was stationed in Sarajevo, and at the time I really thought we had a chance to build something, but every time Larry would offer me a new story I'd be off. Understandably, Simon would want to know how long I'd be away and I could never tell him, and when I returned I couldn't settle. He used to say that I was shutting him out and I was, because I never wanted to talk to him about what I'd seen or done. With each assignment it just got worse. I was finding it harder to fit back into the life we had together because I just couldn't see the importance of us sitting down to dinner at seven-thirty sharp each night, or what a disaster it was if our local shop ran out of his favourite breakfast cereal. It was completely impossible to care about which laundry detergent was best for his white business shirts or the environment. I didn't care what we watched on TV or what movie we went to see just as long as it didn't require me to think. Not too many people could put up with that for too long and neither could Simon. He left when I took the permanent position covering the Balkans. Since then I'd had a three-week fling with a guy in the office and two unfulfilling one-night stands with people whose names I didn't want to remember.

'Okay,' I conceded, 'but why Italy?'

'Pedro's a very fine artist and he feels that's where he will be able to work best. So now I have a Pete, just like you, only mine's called Pedro.'

'Don't change the subject.'

'Don't *you* change the subject.'

'I don't have a Pete, Bella. I'm probably the only woman in the whole universe who hasn't had a Pete.'

'That could be somewhat of an exaggeration, Kate.'

'If you must know, he's never made a move on me. He's not interested.'

'Lordy, have mercy on us all, the end is well nigh near. McDermott not interested! Are you blind? A word of advice: if you *are* really interested in him you should let him know.'

'I'm not.' Bella might have been one of my dearest friends, but she was not the first person I'd go to for advice on love. She was also not to be trusted with matters of the heart. If I told Bella how I felt about Pete she would have made a beeline for his room the minute she'd left mine, and I wasn't about to let that happen.

'Listen, I've been with the two of you for the last week and even blind Freddy could see the signs.'

I considered this for a few seconds then dismissed it. There was absolutely nothing in his behaviour towards me to indicate he wanted more than friendship.

'Bella, it doesn't matter what I *feel*, what is important is that we keep working together. He's the best in the business and I think that working with him lifts my own work to a whole new level. If we had sex it'd ruin that. Romantic relationships don't last long in this business. You know that. Go on, you tell me just one that you can think of that lasted more than two years.'

She shrugged.

'Don't you see there's just too much to lose if we became an item for a short time?'

'It all sounds very logical.'

'I know it sounds very logical—it *is* very logical. Believe me, I've given this a lot of thought, because even I can see that McDermott's easy on the eye. But it's not just logical, Bella, it's the right decision. I understand now that Simon was attracted to me because of the job, which probably looked exciting from a distance, but once the novelty wore off he found he really wanted the Miss Domestic White Goods he'd professed to hate in the first place.'

'Simon was nice.'

'Simon couldn't hack it. Besides, my mother didn't like him.'

'You introduced Simon to Attila the Hun?'

'I was actually living with him, remember? It was a bit hard not to mention him now and then, and she's not Attila the Hun. She's just overprotective and wants the best for me.'

'Okay, okay, but all that about Simon misses the point. Pete knows you in the job so he wouldn't be trying to change you.'

'No, but when he got tired of me—as he would—he'd move on to the next fake redhead in some dark corner of a bar and where would that leave me and my work? Come on, Bella, imagine what that would be like for me.'

Three months later an email arrived from Bella.

From: Bella Jordan
Date: Tuesday 19 April 1994 6:05 PM
To: Kate Price
Subject: Missing you

Allora, my dear friend,
In the hills of northern Tuscany, in a small villa with terrace
overlooking a magical little dell complete with rivulet, I can hear
the shrill squeal of children's voices piercing the soft Tuscan
afternoon. In fact, it is going straight through my head and it no
longer seems to be as enchanting as it once was. The noise is
shooting across the valley as the *enfants terribles* that belong to
Christopher, the landed lord of the chestnut mill—where I am now
living ALONE—are happily engaged in tribal warfare.

Yes, Kate, I have indeed split with Pedro. I know that this mere
sentence is just not enough to satisfy. WHAT HAPPENED? you
ask. Lordy, what indeed happened to this very, very young man
and me? The cold nights in the Garfagnana are pretty damn hard
and well, let's say it would bring out the bottle in most of us. This,
combined with a recreational use of hash, was not exactly what I
had imagined. In short, I found it impossible to live with. Still, one
has to be philosophical, the sex was pretty good. Naturally, I would
have liked to tell you it was a dream come true but alas, *era non
essere*.

So I'm out of here in a week, having just accepted a contract
with yet another NGO.

Give my love to your darling Pedro (I know, I know, you don't
have a darling Pedro).

Write soon.

Ciao, bella,

Bella

**Pete was in South Africa and I was sitting on my bed in Sarajevo
trying to pack for a short holiday in Venice when Bella's email**

arrived. When Pete and I spoke on the phone later that night I told him about Bella's latest bust-up and our conversation wandered into uncharted territory for us.

'Love's a dangerous addiction and in the end it burns you up and spits you out just like any other addiction,' I said, wondering how we'd got so quickly from Bella's lost love to my pathetic ruminations.

'Such a cynic at such a young age.'

'No, you think about it, Pete. At first the heat builds until it blinds you and all you can see is the perfection in the other instead of the reality that's standing in front of you. Bella's a perfect example. She couldn't see all those things wrong in Pedro, because she didn't want to. My God, she was even thinking about having children with him.'

'Bella? Children? I don't think so.'

'Well she definitely mentioned thinking about them. I think it's lucky she discovered Pedro's problems not too far down the track, because before she knew what was happening she'd have been promising to love him until death they did part.'

'Not Bella.'

'Yes Bella. I'm telling you, she was besotted. Anyway, what is that "till death us do part" thing? Is it an admission of love, a form of self-flagellation or the first lie in a marriage? You might call me a cynic, but it seems to me that making a promise you can't possibly know you'll keep is not the best way to begin a life together.'

'Are you speaking from experience?'

'Could be . . . well, no, not exactly.'

'I don't know, there's a beauty to love I wouldn't dismiss completely. Sure you might be blinded to the other's faults, but sometimes you get to see perfection in the other and they in you, if only for a short time. Who wouldn't be seduced by that? Who wouldn't want more of that? I think it's something worth taking a chance over.'

When we hung up I lay down on the bed thinking about what Pete had said. Sometimes I really couldn't understand the guy. The man who made a profession of serial girlfriends was telling me that he believed in the beauty of love and in taking a chance for love. What was that all about? I thought again about Bella's claim that even blind Freddy could see that Pete was attracted to me. While her comments had thrown me at the time it hadn't taken long for me to see them as Bella's overactive romantic imagination. Anyway, I was off to Venice for a very nice time with a very nice Italian man. Celibacy was about to fly out the window.

Chapter 15

Rwanda
April 1994

FOR ME RWANDA STARTED WITH SARAJEVO, BECAUSE THAT WAS the time when it might not have happened, when there were other possibilities, other futures. If I had stayed with my Italian lover in Venice longer; if I hadn't gone to the Reuters office that afternoon; if Pete hadn't been able to get a call through to me; if Larry had already sent someone; if Larry had said no; if I had said no. 'Sorry, Larry. Big mistake. I don't really want to go.' There were so many ways Rwanda might not have happened and at unexpected moments I still find myself examining those 'what ifs' and what my life might have been like without Rwanda, but it is all pointless because there is only what was, and what was was Rwanda. No need—indeed, no possibility of rushing to tell the story about the church in Nyarubuye, in the province of Kibungo, in the country of Rwanda, on the continent of Africa, in that place of men. The story will unfold in its own time.

At first most of us in the press followed the lead of our politicians and called it a tribal civil war, but those of us who were there and saw what was happening changed the story. Problem was, the politicians much preferred the tribal war story they had been peddling. When old people and babies and pregnant women are being slaughtered, when someone is attempting to obliterate a whole nation, then in anyone's book that is not civil war. That is genocide, pure and simple. When the press finally understood this and began to use the G word they were admonished by their editors, unappreciated by their readers, denied by their politicians.

Rwanda continues to haunt me for so many reasons, not least of which is the failure of all my fine words to change a thing. Not one life was spared because of what I wrote. I helped no one. Rwanda showed me my limits. It is that failure, along with the images I carry with me from Rwanda, and the pain I caused Pete, that haunt me today. Everything changed after Rwanda.

Filing copy at the Reuters office in Sarajevo after my week in Venice, I was given a message that Pete was trying to contact me. He would ring again at six pm local time, I was told. When the call came through he said I had to come to Rwanda with him.

'Why Rwanda and why now?'

'My God, Kate, where the hell have you been? Haven't you heard?'

Actually, I thought, I had been having a very nice little holiday with an exceptionally nice Italian aid worker. Part of the deal was that we would tune the world out: no newspapers, no TV, no radio, no phones, no friends. The parameters of our days were defined by a large, soft bed, and an old bath in a tiny room with a sloping ceiling and a view of the Ponte dei Dai. On the canal outside was a family trattoria with its heady scent of garlic and basil that drifted in through the window of our apartment, and where for seven euros we could eat a huge bowl of pasta rich with anchovies, olives, capers and garlic. A short stroll away was the little grocery store with the golden glass windows and the old, rough-hewn rafters that were slung so low that my lover had to bend his head to enter, where we refilled our empty wine bottle every afternoon for one euro. Further afield, when we bothered to venture out, was the warm delicatessen that made the best olive bread in the whole world. In the evenings after dinner we would walk to Piazza San Marco where the bands played 'Nessun Dorma' just for us while we drank our *digestivos* at a table that for a short time was ours.

'At the beginning of April the Rwandan president's plane was shot down over the capital and he was killed, along with the head of the military and the president of Burundi,' Pete was saying. I knew that, but decided to shut up and let him finish. 'Looks like the downing of the plane was a signal for genocide, although everyone's calling it tribal slaughter. Haven't you seen the photos coming out yet?' Without waiting for a reply he added, 'What planet have you been on?'

Planet Venice.

'Anyway, listen, I'm in South Africa still but I'm planning to fly out to Uganda tomorrow to try to organise a ride into Kigali for us with the Canadian air force, which seems to be the only way to fly in there now. The alternative is overland through Kenya and Burundi of course, but that'll take too long. Anyway, I'll sort out the best option while I'm in Uganda. How quickly can you get there?'

'I don't know, Pete. Larry wants me here in Bosnia and I've just been on holidays.'

'Fuck holidays.' There was a long silence down the phone and when he spoke again his voice was calmer, more measured, as if he was choosing his words carefully. 'This is going to be a big story, Kate. Perhaps the story of the decade if not of the second half of the century. I've spoken to a couple of the guys who've come out of there and this is genocide on a scale you can't imagine. I think you should come.' He paused again and I waited. 'You see things I don't see and you see things differently to the way I do. I want you there with me, Kate. I want us to do this together. It's important to me.'

After those words I would have done anything for the man, gone anywhere with him. If he'd asked me to jump into Mephisto's private hell with him I would've been there. Little did we know that was exactly what he *was* asking me to do. In all fairness to Pete, though, when I think back on it now, he couldn't have understood just how bad it would be. You cannot imagine genocide. You simply cannot.

While Rwanda started for me at that moment in Sarajevo, for the rest of the world it started with the civil war in Somalia when in early October 1993 eighteen American Rangers' bodies were dragged through the streets of Mogadishu. In response President William Jefferson Clinton vowed there would be no more entangling engagements in Africa on his watch and instructed his representative in the UN Security Council, Madeleine Albright, to block any resolutions that would entail sending United Nations troops into Rwanda. For good measure she presented a resolution that effectively reduced the UN mission that was already there from over two thousand men to four hundred. But the US should not carry all the blame, for this resolution suited all permanent members on the council, as well as the pen-pushers behind their desks in that famous building towering over the muddy East River. Rwanda was not a mess any of them believed the UN should venture into. With the debacle of Somalia; Milosevic in the Balkans demanding their attention; and the organisation's scant resources, the UN already had too much on its plate. It also couldn't afford another humiliation like Somalia. Best to stay out of the small African country with its vicious 'tribal war'. The Rwandan delegation, which represented the architects of the genocide, by some freak of fate, or some evil alignment of stars, or some huge gigantic karmic payback, held a non-permanent seat on the Security Council and was well pleased by the council's decisions. Unlike those in the West, few Africans deluded themselves about our commitment to human rights. And so the genocidaires of Rwanda gambled that Western politicians would have no stomach for genocide in far-off Rwanda and they were right.

To get away with atrocity one has to bond the killers together through complicity: everyone must either be a killer—directly, or by implication—or else they must be a victim. That way, when the slaughter happens not only are you killing the victims, but you are either implicating or killing all witnesses. The Hutu Power government had worked prodigiously hard for many years to breed hatred into the Hutus. There was absolutely nothing spontaneous about the hundred days of killing that followed. Anyone who saw it knew that what they were witnessing was not tribal warfare, but a very deliberate and well orchestrated political action called genocide that had been unleashed for political and economic expediency.

I had a hard time convincing Larry to send me to Rwanda.

'James is covering the lead-up to the elections in South Africa and he'll get up to Rwanda soon,' he explained.

'No, Larry—no! He'll be too late. You need someone there right now. Get Bob to cover for me here in Sarajevo. He covered while I was in Venice and he hasn't left yet so please, Larry . . . I really want this assignment. You can leave James in South Africa.'

He sighed. 'There'll be a few noses out of joint over this, you know.'

'I've got broad shoulders.'

'I'm not sure I have.'

'You're a Titan. I owe you big time. Love you, Larry.'

In the end it took Pete and me over a week to get into Rwanda. After strapping ourselves into the mesh seats of the plane, we took off, a gnawing fear in the pit of my stomach. Turning to look out the window, I watched the magnificent Great Lakes region of Africa creeping by below. It was always the same. Going into a war zone was nearly harder than being there. There was always too much free time on planes, or waiting around to catch a plane, too much time doing nothing but imagining what could happen to you. Once you were there, you were usually too busy working or looking for food or shelter or a story or just sitting around bored out of your brain to be frightened . . . at least most of the time. I reminded myself again that things were never as bad as I imagined while trying to forget that they could be much worse. It was the certainty of the uncertainty that always threw me off-centre. I looked down again, trying to concentrate on the clusters of tiny brown huts all laced together by slow ribbons of red dirt. When I looked across at Pete he had his head in a book but I knew he wasn't reading because he hadn't turned a page for at least twenty minutes. We all fought our demons.

Our fixer, who would be our driver and translator, was secured within five minutes of touchdown courtesy of a French journalist who was leaving on the same plane we had flown in on. Pale and sweating profusely with swollen and bloodshot eyes, he warned us that if we valued our sanity we should turn around and get the hell out of there.

'Trust me,' he said. 'I have just travelled from Burundi through this and I have seen things no one should see. If you are not already insane you soon will be. True. It is fucked. Get back on this plane. *Ils sont fous, ils sont tous fous.*' With that he picked up his bag and walked across the runway towards the waiting aircraft. 'I am not kidding you, man,' he called over his shoulder. 'I am saying this for what is your own good. Just get back on the fucking plane and get out of here.'

In those moments on the tarmac, with the aviation fumes and the heat rising off the tar nearly choking me, the guy's words rang in my ears. I wanted to do exactly what he said. The plane's engines were still running, ready for take-off as soon as all its cargo was unloaded. It wasn't too late to tell Pete that we should get back on the plane. But I was scared he'd think less of me. *That's stupid*, I berated myself. *Rule number two in a war zone: follow your own instincts no matter what the hell anyone else is doing.*

'Are they killing journalists?' Pete called out to him.

'They are killing everyone.'

'So they're killing journalists?'

The Frenchman shook his head. '*Non, non*, you do not understand. It is not that they kill you—though they might—it is what you will see. It is not of this world.'

'We'll take our chances. Thanks, mate,' Pete said.

'*Mon dieu, vous êtes fous aussi!*'

Pete and I stood in the heat of the fumes watching him walk up the steps and disappear inside.

'What did he say?' asked Pete.

'He said we were mad. Perhaps we *should* leave?'

'Do you want to leave?'

I looked at him only to see determination in his eyes. Pete was not going to leave no matter what I decided. 'No,' I said.

'You sure?'

'Not really.'

'Not really's not good enough. Do you want to go or do you want to stay?'

'Stay.'

'Okay, I think we might try to get someone to ride shotgun for us.' We picked up our bags and headed for the shade inside the terminal. Neither Pete nor I had ever wanted someone working with us who was carrying a gun—in a war zone it could make you look like a combatant. But this time I agreed we should.

The fixer is sometimes the key to how good your story will be, and, more importantly, to whether you come out alive or in a box. Not only do they act as your interpreter and can double as your driver in a strange land, but you have to rely on them to know the terrain: where safety lies and where danger is. A good fixer—often a local journalist—will hopefully supply you with leads for your stories and get you access to people and places that as a foreigner you cannot source on your own.

Patrice was waiting out front of the terminal, just as the Frenchman had said he would be. 'You will know him,' he had told us, 'because he is the only one wearing a white linen shirt.

He said he'd hang around to see who got off the plane. Looks like he is yours. He is a good man.'

Before we left the airport Pete calculated that Patrice was the most expensive fixer we had ever employed, which could have indicated how good he was, or how bad the situation was. Without too much trouble Patrice found his friend Gisenyi, a man with a gun and quite literally our muscle. While Patrice was shorter than me, with a soft and kindly face, Gisenyi must have been over six foot tall, looked like he did hard manual labour and had an ugly jagged scar down one side of his face. He was, we were soon to discover, a man of very few words.

Pete and I stood in the searing heat outside the terminal building with Gisenyi while we waited for Patrice to bring the car around and looked out over the capital towards the city centre. No one needed a financial transaction to tell them how bad it was. You could smell it. We would soon see it.

Apart from the few well-kept bungalows in downtown Kigali near the Hotel des Mille Collines, much of the capital was a sprawling, tin-roofed shantytown that spilled out across gently rolling hills. When we arrived the killing had been raging for over three weeks, and in the face of the advancing Rwandan Patriotic Front, the Tutsi force from outside Rwanda that would eventually end the genocide, the Hutu Power government had fled to the small town of Gitarama in the south of the country.

With government troops openly drunk at their posts it was immediately clear that the streets had been taken over by the rampaging gangs of militia wielding screwdrivers, clubs, machetes and any other weapon they could get their hands on. Not surprisingly food was scarce and nearly all services had failed, with only intermittent electricity and water. Along the sides of the roads bodies were piling up and rotting. In many of the homes we passed we could see the torsos or feet of the long deceased poking out of the doorway. Everywhere wild dogs and rats as big as cats were openly feeding on the corpses. The stench was overwhelming.

I had seen war before and I'd thought the Highway of Death was bad, but nothing compared to this. As my stomach turned and the hysteria rose in my body I fought it down. The Frenchman was right. I didn't want to be here, but the plane was gone and it was too late to turn back. I wondered how Pete was feeling, but he was in front of me and I couldn't see his face. I looked over at Patrice. He was sweating, his hands gripping the wheel as if they were cemented on, while he constantly looked from side to side, watching all that was going on around us as the car moved through the streets. What were Patrice and Gisenyi feeling as they drove us through their capital, I wondered? Evidence of the depths of depravity their fellow Rwandans were capable of was everywhere. Were they ashamed . . . horrified? Were they as terrified as I was?

Patrice had told us we could witness the aftermath of a massacre if we so chose. We so chose. At the numerous roadblocks we had to traverse just to get through the city we noticed that many of the killers lounging around in the grass beside the piles of putrefying bodies were kids. Whenever we approached a roadblock Gisenyi insisted that we wind up the windows, lock all the doors and push our passports up against the glass. When these kids picked up their bloodied weapons and sauntered over to inspect the car's occupants, they were not only looking for Tutsis to kill, but also for Belgians, their former colonial masters. With no rule of law throughout the country, Patrice explained, there was no telling what they might decide to do at any given moment. Maybe being white would be enough to link us to the colonialists.

After leaving the capital we headed east, moving toward the border with Tanzania. Around lunchtime we turned south towards Kibungo Province and Nyarubuye. For a couple of hours we travelled along tarred roads lined with weeds and rubbish, passing thousands of bodies, luminous green-black under the weight of flies, while in the deep, fathomless blue of the African sky vultures circled. Through the open windows of the car the waft of decay drifted in, sliding down our throats as the dust settled thick and greasy on our skin. Village after village along the way bore testament to the weeks of destruction. Painted concrete houses and adobe mud cottages of the Hutu—many resembling a simple child's drawing with brightly painted front doors and two framed front windows—sat perfectly intact alongside the shells of their former Tutsi neighbours' homes. Already branches of bright orange and magenta bougainvillea had begun to twist their way in through broken glass and grasses had sprung up around empty doorways or pushed their way through cracked paths. The rivers, the main source of drinking water for much of the country, were awash with bodies. Bloated and bleached of colour, the corpses bobbed downstream like macabre blow-up dolls, tangling up in the reeds by the river's banks or piling high around the shallows and under bridges before being sucked free again by the water's current to continue on their journey to Burundi and Tanzania. In the distance the fields were already beginning to sour with the weeds of neglect. Africa was reclaiming its own. Rwanda was returning to the wild.

Mostly we travelled in silence, with Pete occasionally asking Patrice to stop so he could get out and take photos. As the hours passed I began to sink deeper into myself, trying but unable to shut out the horror of what was outside the car. The words of the Frenchman, telling us that no one should see what he had seen, kept coming back to me. Rwanda was too much for the mind to take in. How could human beings sink to such levels of hatred and depravity? I knew something in me was dying, but at the time I had no idea what it was.

As we travelled over a ridge my attention was caught by a movement in the valley below before it disappeared, but as we wound our way down it came into view again. It was a pack of vultures squabbling over the remains of a woman's body. A log on the road ahead became a man; a small bundle of rags by a post on the side of the road was a baby with its head smashed in.

'Good God,' I said to no one in particular. 'What has happened here?' No one answered.

Around yet another hill we were confronted by a macabre picnic scene: a mother and her children sitting in the tall grass under the shade of a eucalypt tree surrounded by wildflowers, weeds and the bodies of the dead. The youngest child was sucking at her mother's shrunken breast, while the others watched us with hollow, disinterested eyes. What point was there in walking on when death would come just as easily there as it would around the next corner, over the hill or a hundred miles up the road?

I would learn later, when I had left Rwanda, that the thing that disturbed the Hutu killers the most was not the sheer number of people they were slaughtering, or that the people they were killing were their neighbours and friends, or even that they were killing helpless babies and old people. What disturbed them the most was that the Tutsi were going to their deaths in silence. After generations of pent-up Hutu anger and rage at their 'haughty' neighbours, the Tutsi were still denying their killers the satisfaction they sought.

After asking Patrice to stop the car so he could get out to take photos of the woman and her children, Pete turned to me in the back seat and asked if I wanted to interview her, but I shook my head. I watched as he walked over to the woman, holding up his camera to show that he was a photographer and seeking permission to take her photograph, but she didn't acknowledge him at all other than to follow him with her eyes. What did it matter to her if this man took a photo? And so Pete worked quickly to cause her the least discomfort, but I could see that the family's plight was causing him pain and that he too was in a bad way. He was pale, his eyes looked tired and he had lost the spring in his step.

When he got back into the car and asked Patrice if we might be able to help this family I remembered his advice to me not to play God. He, more than most, knew that as a professional he shouldn't interfere, but as a human being it was sometimes hard not to. Of all the people you passed in places like Rwanda, who did you choose to help and, in choosing, who did you choose not to help, and what would be the consequences of your decision? Most times you chose not to help anyone, which was no choice at all, or it was a bad choice. In the end, no matter what choice you made, it always stuck uncomfortably in your gut.

'They are Tutsi,' Patrice replied quietly. 'If we take them with us they will be killed at the next roadblock. You cannot save them.'

After leaving the main road near Rusumo we travelled down a dirt road before pulling up in front of the church compound at Nyarubuye. Above our heads a white marble statue of Christ was raising his arms in welcome, while on the ground below was the rotting corpse of a man disintegrating into the stone steps as his bodily fluids dried up.

When we got out of the car the first thing I noticed was the smell. I started gagging and pulled the scarf I had tied around my neck up to cover my nose and mouth but it made little difference. As we were walking in I noticed Patrice and Gisenyi had not got out of the car so I pulled the scarf down again and asked if they were coming in. 'No,' said Patrice. 'We will wait here for you.' They had seen it all before. Pulling the scarf back up I followed Pete in.

Africa is a noisy continent. There are always people around and something is always happening, but on that day, when Pete and I walked into the church compound, it was ghostly quiet, as if we had walked into a place that had separated itself from the world as we knew it. There were no birds singing, no squeals of children playing and no dogs barking off in the distance, although two dogs who were feeding on a body scurried off as we entered. Patrice had warned us to be careful of the dogs, but it was not the dogs I was worried about that day—it was my own sanity. We stood, unable to speak, as we tried to take in what was before us.

The initial attack began on 12 April, six days after the Rwandan president's plane was shot down. Thousands of Tutsis had fled to Nyarubuye for the safety they thought their God and His good disciples would offer, only to discover too late that the churches of Rwanda had become the preferred killing fields for the Hutu Interahamwe—'those who attack together'. When the terrified Tutsi inside the compound successfully repelled the first wave of attackers with rocks, reinforcements were brought in and they were eventually overpowered. After overseeing the collection of valuables the local mayor,

Sylvestre Gacumbitsi, gave the order for the slaughter to begin. No one was to be spared. Mercy, one of the killers was later to say, was not part of the deal. But butchering can be a tiring business and when the killers discovered at the end of the day that they hadn't disposed of everyone they camped outside the church compound for the night. As they relaxed back and drank their *urwagwa*, banana beer, the moans and whimpers for help drifted over the walls. In the morning, refreshed, the Interahamwe returned to finish off the job.

In the confusion, a few people survived by hiding under those who were already dead. For days, even weeks, these people lived among the dead, hardly daring to breathe as packs of hungry dogs fought over the bodies that concealed them. At night, when their thirst and hunger could no longer be ignored, they ventured out for rainwater or wild fruit, only to crawl back to their hiding places before the dawn. So traumatic was what they had witnessed that many of them believed that every Tutsi in Rwanda had died and that they were the only ones left. The world as they knew it had ended.

In front of us the bodies were piled up everywhere, decomposing in the sun, lying in stagnant pools of water, the skin around exposed bones slowly returning to the earth. Many had limbs missing: hacked off by machetes, or torn off in ragged pieces by scavenging dogs. The evidence of rape was everywhere: in the exposed genitals and the grotesquely twisted legs of the women and young girls; in the terror frozen on their faces and in the semen dried between their legs. The stench. Oh God, the stench. With every breath it filled my lungs. It would stay with me forever. As we stood looking at the abomination I realised that for the first time in my life my emotions had closed down. I was numb. I couldn't take it all in.

Pete wandered off to shoot everything—click, click, click-click, click, click-click—and so I began to pick my way around the edges, hugging the walls. The flies were everywhere. I brushed them away, but they kept coming back. When I stepped on something soft and the ground moved beneath my foot I looked down to see a small child's fingers sticking out from under my boot and I jumped backwards, my heart pounding in my chest. I shaded my eyes against the glare of the afternoon sun and looked for Pete, but he was gone. I turned and made my way into the church.

At first I couldn't see anything and I stumbled, nearly falling on the bodies at my feet, so I stood still as my eyes adjusted to the gloom. I could hear a dull background hum, not sure what it was until I realised that it was the sound of the flies: big black and green blowflies. Thousands of them. Everywhere. The floor, the pews and the dais were covered in bodies. They were piled up on top of one another, falling over each other and clustered in such a way that it was easy to see who had been killed near the door as they tried to escape, and who had continued praying as the killers came running in. The bodies told their own stories.

At my feet was a little girl; her legs were torn wide and the flies were feasting. When I leaned down to close her legs the flies rose up and one got caught under my scarf. Frantically I pulled at the material to let it out, but it seemed stuck, buzzing and crawling around my cheek. Unable to breathe I clawed at the scarf with both hands to get it off my face and screamed.

'Kate!' Pete called from outside. When he came running in and saw me pulling at my face he grabbed me, wrapping his arms around me and pulling me towards him until I stopped my frenetic scratching and collapsed into him weeping.

I have no idea how long we stood with Pete holding me as I wept, but at some stage Patrice arrived to remind us of the dangers of travelling at night, pointing through the broken glass of the church window to the pink glow on the horizon.

Chapter 16

AFTER DRIVING A COUPLE OF KILOMETRES I ASKED PATRICE
to pull over and jumped out to bend over double in the long
grass by the side of the road as the bitter fluid spilled out of
my mouth. When I climbed back in the car I was rummaging
around in my backpack for water and toothpaste when Pete
handed over his bottle. They had been discussing our options,
he said, and none of them particularly wanted to stay in the town
of Kibungo, but it wasn't safe for us to drive all the way back
to Kigali in the dark either. What did I think about sleeping in
the car, or looking for somewhere to camp out?

With Pete watching me from the front seat I looked over at
Patrice, who remained perfectly still in the driver's seat, eyes
focused ahead, while Gisenyi, cramped up in the back section
of the jeep, was also silent. I was going to make a decision that
might mean the difference between life and death for everyone
in that car when I had no idea how to protect myself. I was not

particularly happy about taking our chances sleeping by the side of the road, or in the open in the car, but I understood their concerns. The decision was made to try to find an abandoned house to bunk down in for the night, and as the day faded behind us we headed off, putting as much distance between us and the church at Nyarubuye as we could.

About twenty-five kilometres up the road we were caught in a sudden torrential downpour that thundered over the roof of the car, sending thick sheets of water cascading down its sides. When Patrice turned the headlights on the two funnels of light were sucked up into the rain and we had to stop until the storm passed. Just as we were about to move off Gisenyi pointed to a rutted track by the side of the road that was half hidden by a banana grove. With no idea what awaited us at the end of that track, including the possibility of Interahamwe, Patrice backed the car up and we turned in. Our headlights, pale in the fading light, bounced past eucalypts and over crops of sorghum until we entered a clearing of beaten earth in front of a small mud hut. Rising up behind it were rich green terraces, and scattered among them were tiny adobe houses shrouded in the last mists of rain that were sweeping across the valley.

The hut had a rusty iron roof and a metal door newly painted an impossibly vibrant aqua with a water barrel standing beside it. Inside were two small dark rooms with beaten earth floors, one of which seemed to be a tiny living area with a storeroom off to the side. The other was a communal bedroom. The place had been ransacked. Terracotta jugs lay in shards on the floor; a broken plastic chair lay on its side and the sorghum for breakfast porridge was scattered around the room. On one of the walls was a crooked portrait of Jesus on the cross and a framed quote from the Bible. Even at that early stage of the genocide it was clear that many of the Lord's good disciples were complicit in the killing. I wondered how the owners of this home, if they were still alive, would view their church when it was all over. The second tiny room had an old bed made out of packing crates propped up on mud bricks. With no reason for the killers to return, and the owners obviously fled, it seemed as good a place as any to spend the night.

Patrice moved the car behind the house, parking it next to the abandoned cow enclosure. Grabbing my backpack out of the back I rummaged around in its depths for a half-eaten block of dark chocolate that I knew was there and the last of a packet of dry biscuits, but when I offered them around for dinner no one seemed particularly interested, including me. Patrice and Gisenyi said they preferred to sleep in the car so Pete and I ventured into the house to stand together, staring at the sagging wooden pallet bed.

'You win,' he said, throwing his backpack into the tiny space between the bed and the wall. I tossed my backpack onto the pallet only to watch it slide down into the bed's sunken middle. Pete wandered off to have a look around in the last half hour of light and I wandered out into the courtyard, where I found a large rock by the house's banana grove. Sitting on the rock with my back pressed up against a banana tree I watched the outline of the hills above the house, silhouetted black against the disappearing light. The rock, I realised, must have been placed in that precise spot for the view it offered, and I couldn't help wondering if it was a favourite sitting spot for the man of the house, or if his wife used it at the end of her working day.

'Mamba in there,' Patrice said, pointing to the banana grove behind me as he came from around the back of the house. I stood up and began searching for another place to sit.

During the drive down to Nyarubuye Patrice had explained that when he was eight years old both his parents had died and his best friend, Innocent, had invited him to live with his family. If he was very quiet and did not cause any trouble, Innocent was sure his parents would not even notice Patrice among their brood of eight. After a week Innocent's father had summoned Patrice to him and explained that despite what his son might think he was neither deaf, blind nor stupid, but if Patrice could find a place to sleep in the house then he was most welcome to live with them. Innocent was Tutsi and Patrice was Hutu. It had never mattered to the family and when the boys had grown Patrice had married one of Innocent's younger sisters. He had failed to elaborate on where she was now, and I had been too afraid of what the answer might be to ask.

'Patrice,' I said as he was about to go back to the car, 'can I ask you what you are going to do when this is all over? Will you be able to live here after this?'

'I will not live here. No. I will go to my wife and children. They are in Burundi with my uncle and we will live there. Here it is very bad . . . very bad.' Patrice then told me that he had five children. His family had been lucky, he said, explaining that because the genocide had begun in the capital and the north of the country there had been a small window of opportunity for Tutsi from the south to flee. The resourceful Patrice had been able to secure his wife and children's passage by signing over his house and tiny plot of land to his neighbour, who happened to be the local Hutu mayor.

After Patrice left I found a log to sit on and listened to the sound of frogs drifting up from the valley below as I watched the buttery full moon rise over the roof of the hut. 'What are You thinking looking down on this place?' I asked the God I did not believe in, just as Pete came out of the banana crop. I moved over on the log, patting the spot beside me for him to sit, but he preferred to stand.

'We're such an arrogant species, aren't we?' he said, leaning up against the wall near the front door. 'What with our men on the moon, our science, our computers and our weapons of mass destruction we think we're pretty clever, don't we? But for all our cleverness you only have to look at what we do to each other to know that we aren't really very evolved at all.'

'Why would any rational human being willingly screw with their minds by coming to a place like this?' I said.

He groaned and raked his fingers through his hair. 'We're here. Not much we can do about it now.'

'Right,' I said, but it wasn't right and I wasn't right. I was still numb. It definitely wasn't right.

'Did I ever tell you about the time Sam and me came across a wheelbarrow filled with lemons and a sign that said, *Please take*?' Pete had started telling me little anecdotes about his wayward youth with his friend Sam after we'd been working together for a while, and I'd come to understand that they were his way of returning to a happier, simpler time so that he could distance himself from whatever was happening around us.

'No.'

'So we did.'

'You did what?'

'We took the wheelbarrow.'

'And the lemons?'

'Them too.'

Usually his stories were amusing, but that night the humour fell dead between us. A short time later he placed his hands on my shoulders, squeezing them as if we were an old married couple who'd just been watching our favourite show on television. He was turning in, he said.

Alone in the clearing the honey scent of ginger flowers came drifting in on the air currents again to curl around my skin, but within half an hour I was scratching midge bites on my arms and neck and decided it was time for bed. When I walked in Pete was on the floor reading, a small portable torch lying beside him to illuminate the page.

'What're you reading?'

'*An Imaginary Life*.'

'Who's that by?'

'David Malouf."

'Ah, the Australian author. Is it good?'

'It's good.'

I lay down on the pallet only to roll into its centre, where I lay staring up at a gecko on the ceiling who was staring back at me. I heard Pete turn a few more pages before stuffing the book back into his backpack and switching the torch off. 'Goodnight,' he said.

'Night.'

With sleep still not coming I grabbed the side of the bed to pull myself up to its ridge where I could look down at him. He was lying on his back with his hands cupped behind his head watching the gecko.

'Are they nocturnal?'

'No idea.'

'Do you believe in God?'

'Not today.'

'I want to believe in God.'

'Not today, Kate.' He sounded so very tired.

'Yes, today of all days I want to believe in God.'

He turned his head to look up at me. 'You've got to be joking. Tell me you're joking.' I could hear weariness and anger in his voice. 'What sort of fucking God do you want to believe in that would allow this to happen?'

'I don't know, but if there is a God He might be able to explain it all to me.'

'Christ, Kate, *there is no God*. God has left the building. It's official. Rwanda has proved it. *There is no God. There is no reason*. We exist and we get through it in the best way we can and that's all there is. That's all there fucking is.'

'Don't be angry with me.'

'I'm not angry with *you.*'

'How do you think this happened? How can one human being do this to another?'

'Greed, hatred, fear, anger, you name it.'

'It's like someone opened up Pandora's box and let all the evils of the world out to descend on this country.' We lay in silence for a while until I asked him if he knew what had remained in Pandora's box.

'No, why don't you tell me.'

'Hope. Hope is what remained. Pandora was so terrified by all the evil she had let loose that she slammed the lid down and trapped hope in the box.' I reached out my hand to him and he took it. 'Can I lie down there with you?' Releasing my hand, he moved over to make room for me.

'Sometimes something happens,' he said gently, all anger gone now as he stretched his arm out for me to rest my head on, 'that reminds me how much I don't know, and that's the only thing that gives me any shred of hope. Do you understand?'

'Maybe.'

'Well, if what I don't know is so much greater than what I do know—and it obviously is—then there might be a reason for everything that I can't see and that idea's comforting. That is the only hope I can find. Do you follow?'

'Sort of.'

'I don't think there is a God, Kate, and I don't think we're meant to have all the answers. I guess that's the short version.' He brushed a strand of my hair from his face. 'I can't believe you're really serious about wanting to believe in God,' his voice soft and gentle now.

'The way I figure it there's nothing to lose by believing. If He doesn't exist then what's the harm, and if He does exist . . . well, the payoff's not so bad is it?' Despite my words, though, I didn't believe and he knew I didn't, but I was drifting off by then to dream of a man brushing my hair from my face and of fingers tracing down my cheek and a soft mouth on mine and I turned to him. I wanted the comfort of him and his closeness, but more than anything I wanted him. Later, much later, when my body rose to meet his the vision of a little girl in a church with bruised legs spread wide like mine, and a man moving over her, replaced the vision of the man I loved and I froze, pushing him away.

He wanted to talk about what had happened, but I couldn't and eventually he gave up trying and turned away from me to face the wall. When his breathing fell into the rhythm of sleep I went out into the yard to stand naked by the water barrel where I tried to scrub my skin of that day and the memory of what we had done.

Chapter 17

AS THE FIRST LIGHT OF DAY BEGAN TO FILL THE ROOM I
saw that the gecko had hardly moved. When a rooster crowed
outside the window and Pete began to stir I grabbed my backpack
from under the bed and escaped outside. Patrice and Gisenyi were
stretching and rubbing the sleep out of their eyes by the side of
the car. I spoke with Patrice about the route back to Kigali for a
couple of minutes before throwing my bag into the back of the
car and making my way up into the terraces behind the house.

'You need to be careful, Miss,' he called after me. 'The killers
are everywhere.'

'I'm not going far.'

Below me the sun was beginning to spread its warmth out
over a valley dotted with mud-brick cottages and crisscrossed by
a maze of dusty walking tracks and terraced gardens. A deep red
scar scored the side of a far-off hill where the soil and trees had
slipped down into the ravine below. Shading my eyes, I followed

the road we would take back to Kigali until it disappeared over a hill. From a distance all looked well with this world: a gentle rural scene, quiet and welcoming.

Pete emerged from the house and I watched him walk around to the back to talk to Patrice, who pointed up the hill to where I was sitting. I was ashamed of my behaviour the night before and how unfair it had been to Pete, but I had no idea what to say to him to make it better. I also had no idea how we were going to move past what had happened. We had been friends and colleagues and it had worked well, but now I had no idea what we were. I needed a couple of days to myself to take measure of what had happened, but I had to see him in a few minutes. There was no escape.

When it looked as if everyone was ready to go I made my way down to the yard and climbed into the back seat, avoiding his eyes, but as we reversed out he turned to pass his backpack over and looked at me.

'Are you okay, Kate?'

'Fine,' I said, turning to stare out the window, not willing to meet his eyes.

As we drew closer to the capital we would sometimes pass small groups of people moving slowly on the road, their possessions piled high on their heads. As Pete moved through them taking photographs I walked with Patrice, trying to understand where they had come from and where they thought they were heading. As the parents spoke with the *mzungu* their children stood wide-eyed, grasping at the folds of their mother's dress or peering out from behind their father's pants leg. No one really wanted to talk much and I had to remind myself that these people were Hutus, and quite possibly killers, or the families of killers, or the supporters of killers, or simply innocent Hutus caught up in the violence. It was impossible to know. One thing I did understand, though, was that they were all trying to flee the country.

During one stop Pete and I were about to climb back into the car when I noticed Patrice walk over to an old man who was sitting in the drainage ditch by the side of the road. After talking with him for a couple of minutes, Patrice returned to explain that this man came from his village and in the mayhem he had been separated from his family. Could we take him with us? Patrice asked. Pete and I agreed immediately, although the rejection of the mother and her children the day before sat heavy on my mind. Returning to the old man Patrice explained that we could take him to Kigali, but he looked away from Patrice and over to us with rheumy eyes yellow with fever and shook his head. No, he did not want to go to Kigali. He was old and he had seen enough. It did not matter if he died.

As Patrice started the engine I asked whether he knew if the old man was Hutu or Tutsi.

'He is Hutu, of course. Do you think, Miss, that Tutsis be on this road?' For the first time I heard anger in his voice. It had been a stupid question. 'The people you are seeing moving are Hutus, Miss. All Hutus. The Tutsis are all dead. These Hutus are moving because they are frightened now because the RPF is coming and the radio is telling them that the soldiers will eat them. I do not know if these people are killers. That old grandfather, I do not know if he is a killer, but many people are killers: children, mothers, old people. They are all killers. I have seen these things with my own eyes.'

Not too far up the road we passed a group of Interahamwe heading south. When they saw us they began chanting and blowing their whistles, waving their bloody machetes above their heads or dragging them along the road to send off sparks where flint and rock connected. Some were dressed in skirts of tree bark with banana leaves around their necks, their faces painted white with chalk. One man had goat horns on his head and another had a red, black and green cape thrown over his shoulders, but most just wore the clothes of the poor. From within the car I could see their eyes red-rimmed with madness from their killing work and the banana beer they were passing between them and my heart began to pound, the sweat of fear seeping out from under my skin. They had been killing for weeks and I knew that at any time they could turn on us, surrounding the car before they dragged us out and chopped at our limbs with their clubs and machetes. As we drove past they whooped and jumped in the air, banging the side of the car. With Patrice changing down a gear the car lurched forward and we left them behind on our way down into Kigali.

When we arrived at the small pensione Patrice had found for us I went straight to my room, but Pete followed me there and tried to talk again about what had happened the night before. I begged off, telling him that I was tired and needed to be alone. I could see how much I was hurting him, but I felt completely incapable of dealing with it.

It was as if I had arrived in Rwanda to find myself in a parallel universe. I tried to ground myself by thinking about when I returned home to London and how I'd do all the ordinary, everyday things just like everyone else did. I'd shop and cook and clean the flat and I'd read books. I'd catch the tube, maybe even see my parents and have coffee with friends. But when it came to imagining our conversations it felt as if my head would explode with the impossible effort of it. What the hell would I ever talk to them about again? Rwanda had destroyed the vision of a normal world forever and everything I said and did would be tainted by the memory of what I had seen. Even the thought of going back to the Holiday Inn and Sarajevo seemed too much like normal compared with Rwanda.

So many confusing emotions flooding my body: terror, disgust, fear, anger, dread, pity, sorrow, horror and shame . . . shame at what humans were capable of. Most of all, though, there was disbelief. I simply couldn't understand what I had seen. It was too much for my frayed emotions to process, so that all that night I tossed and turned, lost in my first nightmares of Nyarubuye, confused by dreams of sex and rape and love.

In the morning I was woken by a knock at the door, but when I tried to lift my arm to get up I found it wouldn't move. I tried the other one. Both arms were thick and useless on the mattress. When I discovered that my legs wouldn't move either a cold fear began prickling under my skin. What was happening to me?

Another knock and a silence and then Pete called out, 'Kate, are you there? Are you alright?'

'Yes, I'm okay.'

'Are you coming?'

'No, go without me.'

'Are you sure you're alright?'

'Yes, just go without me.' I listened to him standing at the door for a while, imagining his soft breathing, his mind wondering what best to do. But then he turned and walked away and I remained trapped for hours on the old mattress with its prickly, thin blue sheets, watching the shadows shrink back across the room as the day grew old. Where had he gone? What was he doing? It wasn't safe out there and I worried about him.

Just when I was beginning to think I would have to wet the bed my wayward limbs grew a spongy heaviness, and I found

I could lift one arm and then the other until I was able to push myself to a sitting position on the side of the bed. Exhausted with the effort I rested a few minutes before gathering my strength again and, holding onto the wall, I made my way down the hall to the toilet.

'What the hell are you doing here? Are you insane?' I hissed at the pitiful stranger staring back at me from the rusty old mirror. 'You've made a bloody mess of everything. Everything. What will you do now?'

Back in the room I dragged a chair over to the window and stared out over the red and white Marlboro sign that hung outside. Across the hills I could see the shanty settlements of Kigali with their collapsing tin and wood structures and dusty red pathways glowing softly warm as the sun sank lower. There were makeshift roadblocks along the backstreets and bodies lying in random piles along the pathways. On the street below my window a group of men with machetes passed by. Sometimes I heard the far-off pop of gunfire, but mostly the air was still in the city that afternoon. When the sky turned orange, then pink and then purple as the sun disappeared I looked up to see a high trail of vapour from a plane passing overhead and found myself wanting more than anything to be on that plane: to be anywhere but Rwanda.

By the time it was dark and Pete hadn't returned I began to torment myself with visions of him lying bloodied by the side of the road. To stop myself thinking about the horror of it I tried to work up a story for Larry, but found I didn't have the words to describe Nyarubuye. As I sat with the blank pad on my knee visions of Pete and the night before kept catching me unawares, but I pushed them away, unable to think about what had happened and what it might mean for us. Eventually I gave in to the languid heat drifting in through the open window and crawled back into bed. When his knock woke me again the room was in darkness.

'Kate, are you alright?' Relief flooded through me, but still I would have preferred not to see him. After I let him in I retreated to the safety of the middle of the bed. He looked terrible.

'Last night was wrong,' I said, unable even to name it.

He remained standing in the doorway, frowning at me. 'I know. What happened, Kate? Something happened.'

How could I say to him that I couldn't bear the thought of him or anyone touching me, or tell him that I had seen him as one of those monsters? 'I just want to be friends, Pete, so we can keep working together. That sort of thing complicates everything, and I don't want things complicated at the moment.'

'That sort of thing?' he repeated. 'Just friends? Is that all it was, and is that all I am to you? I thought there was something more.'

I had no idea what the night before had been and could no longer say what he meant to me. If only I could just make it all go away so we could get our old lives back again. Had Pete been looking for comfort last night too, or had it really meant something more to him? I had absolutely no idea.

He tried again. 'I'm worried about you, Kate, and I came to see if you're okay. I was also hoping that you might be able to help me understand what happened.' When I didn't respond he asked, 'Jesus, Kate, what is it you want from me exactly?'

'I don't know at the moment. Yes, I do. I want us to still be friends.'

'We are still friends—at least I thought we were.'

'Only friends. I want us to be *only* friends.'

He raked his hand through his hair and shook his head. 'Look, it doesn't have to be wrong. The timing was wrong, granted. And something happened that I don't understand, although I suspect it had to do with Nyarubuye—at least I hope it had to do with Nyarubuye and it wasn't me—but *we* don't have to be wrong.'

Pete had come to the room wanting an explanation and he deserved one, but I had none to give him. I really didn't know what I wanted, other than for everything to go back the way it used to be before Rwanda. I desperately wished he'd go away and give me some time so *I* could try to understand what had happened and what it all meant and where we could go from there, but he seemed to want answers immediately and I just didn't have them.

As I looked at him I saw the expression on his face change. It was as if a light had gone on. His brow unfurled and he almost smiled, except his eyes had gone cold. 'It's a game to you, isn't it? Some people like the game. They get off on the pain. It's always been a game for you, hasn't it?'

'No! *No!* That's not it at all. It's not a game.'

He shrugged. 'You won't tell me what happened to you last night and why you went cold on me so what else am I supposed to think? Nice one, Kate.'

'It's not like that, honestly. Please, can't we just be friends?'

'I thought we had been and I don't know why you keep saying that unless you don't think we are anymore.' He turned and left then, closing the door behind him.

It was all very well for him to demand to know what I wanted, but I had no idea what *he* wanted. Even if he had wanted some sort of relationship—and he definitely hadn't said that—I knew Pete well enough to know that there'd inevitably come a time when he'd grow tired of me, or the relationship would sour for some reason, and he'd be off on some new assignment and there'd be some other woman waiting for him in the corner of a bar somewhere. The only way I could have a relationship that lasted with him was a friendship. The tears welled up when I thought of his anger and the way he'd left. 'I knew it,' I said to the room. 'I knew this would happen.'

I sank back onto the bed and cried over the mess I'd made of everything and the horror that was Rwanda, but by midnight I'd pulled myself into some semblance of order. Castigating myself for my self-pity, I reminded myself that I was supposed to be a professional journalist in Rwanda reporting on a diabolical genocide. I knew that what I was feeling was nothing, *absolutely nothing* compared to what those around me were going through. The innocents who had already died in Rwanda, and those who were going to die if we couldn't stop the slaughter, deserved nothing less from me than my very best, and I was certain that the only hope we had of forcing the politicians in the UN to do something to stop the genocide was by turning the tide of public opinion on Rwanda. To play my part in that I had to write and I had to write powerfully.

By morning I had what I thought was a potent story about Nyarubuye ready to send off to Larry.

When I emerged from my room Pete said a clipped 'good morning' and we set off south to Butare, the second largest town in the country. After spending the night in the dilapidated Hotel Ibis, which was full of suspicious characters, we headed north the following day to try to join up with Paul Kagame and his RPF troops. In all, Pete and I spent another five days in Rwanda, working together as polite strangers who spoke only when they had to.

I had given Larry six articles while in Rwanda, but I was only happy with the first one. There were no Tutsis to interview, while the Hutus I spoke with were either killers and wary of me, or too afraid to say anything against the killers. After that first powerful article on Nyarubuye I was finding it hard to write in any meaningful way about continual slaughter on such a relentless scale. Larry must have felt it too because for the first time he rejected one of my stories, explaining that he couldn't put his finger on the problem but something was missing. He was right, of course—something *was* missing.

When Pete and I parted in Uganda for him to fly back to South Africa, and me to head back to London and then on to the Balkans again, he could barely look at me. I was heartbroken. I had lost him.

Chapter 18

Zaire .
(Democratic Republic of the Congo)
July 1994

HEAVY WITH THE LOSS OF PETE AND THE BITTER TASTE OF failure from my coverage of Rwanda, three months later I flew alone into the refugee camps of Goma in Zaire, home to the hundreds of thousands of Rwandans who had fled the genocide and Kagame's triumphant forces. But again I was left feeling inadequate, unable to express the enormity of what I was witnessing. I wanted to write that Goma was 'indescribable' and what was happening was 'inexplicable', but history was moving before me and I was there for only one reason: to describe and to explain. Over the next two weeks I drew deep on what I came to see as my store of second-rate words and stale phrases, until at some point I began sending copy to Larry in London awash with adjectives. 'The fucking, insane, pathetic, ugly, bastard, killer Hutu bushman still had fresh blood on his large, ham-fisted, filthy killer's hands.' It felt good, but it also felt very, very bad.

Initially I pretended Larry and I were playing a game where I'd send him valid choices and he'd edit me down.

'But if you had to pick one adjective, Kate, what would it be?'

'Fucking.'

'Besides fucking.'

'Bastard.'

'Other than bastard.'

'Pathetic.'

'Okay, I see the problem here. We'll use "alleged" killers.'

'Alleged killers!'

Throughout the conversation I could picture Larry, sleeves rolled up to his elbows, pants hanging baggy on his wiry frame, pacing up and down in the corridor outside his office, puffing away on the cancer sticks that were eating away at his vocal cords. When Larry's patience with me finally wore thin he reminded me that there was no need to bang our readers over the head because they were able to fill in the blanks for themselves. I exploded.

'Just how're they supposed to do that when they're not even allowed to see this? You can't *imagine* what it's like here, Larry.'

'Trust them. They can.'

'No, you didn't hear me. I said *you* can't imagine what it's like here and *you're* seeing the photos, for Christ's sake! The very photos you won't print in the paper because they might upset someone! How is anyone supposed to imagine it when no one lets them see the truth of it and I can't even come close to describing it?'

There was a long silence on the other end of the phone, but I no longer cared if I was pissing him off. I was furious. What did he know, sitting in his nice, safe, air-conditioned office in London with his dinner waiting on the table? I asked him late one night on the phone from Goma, conveniently ignoring the fact that Larry was a bachelor and there wasn't ever any dinner waiting for him when he got home. Luckily for my employment record and our friendship Larry pretended he hadn't heard. There was a lot of pretending going on in those days: the West pretended they did all they could for the Tutsi; the aid agencies in Goma pretended they didn't know the truth of what was happening in the camps and who was running them; and I pretended I was a totally sane person making completely rational decisions covering the horrific aftermath of a diabolical genocide.

Soon Larry began writing long, serious missives suggesting that I get out for a while, and I began writing long, serious missives suggesting that he get a life—which was basically what he was telling me to do, only somewhat more politely.

Twenty-four hours a day, under UN direction, the huge cargo planes came lumbering down the runway in Goma, depositing the trademark white Land Cruisers, medical supplies, food, more and more staff, and, of course, the tents and the bulldozers and the lime. In short, everything that was needed to set up the biggest relief operation in human history, while disposing of the greatest number of bodies safely in the shortest possible time.

Sometimes, when I needed to get out of the camp, I'd sit on one of the surrounding hills looking down over Goma's vast tent city and just watch from a distance the hundreds of thousands of people sitting around in the black volcanic dirt, as tens of thousands more streamed in every day. 'The apocalypse is well nigh upon us,' Bella said as she sat next to me one day, for she was also in Goma doing PR for the aid agency she worked for. I found no reason to contradict her. Below us the large, clean tents closest to the feeding stations gradually gave way to smaller tents, and then to makeshift shelters erected from an old blanket strung between a couple of bushes. On the periphery nothing more than a rag tied between sticks marked the shelter for a whole family. All during the day and long into the night the thick smoke from the cooking fires mixed with the acrid smoke from the Nyiragongo volcano, which in some biblical feat of mystical synchronicity had erupted to shoot flames and spew ash and sulfur over the whole stinking mess. Goma was my vision of hell. A listless, sunbaked place where the stench of smoke, human waste and decay pulled at my stomach until my body no longer registered hunger.

At night, in the tent I shared with Bella, I would toss and turn in my sleep, fighting the nightmare of Nyarubuye and my sadness over Pete, until she would put her hand out to comfort me, telling me softly that everything would be alright. But it felt as if some vital life-giving part of me had been torn away and I despaired that everything would ever be alright again. I missed him so much and thought about contacting him every day, but I wasn't sure whether he would want to hear from me and so I waited, hoping that he would make the first move. When I'd first arrived Bella had asked where he was and when I'd told her that I didn't know she'd not mentioned him again, but we talked about Nyarubuye often. 'I cannot understand what was in the hearts of the men who did that,' I told her, 'and I'm not sure I ever want to know, because I think that to look into their hearts would endanger my own soul.'

One morning Bella and I joined a flow of refugees moving towards a new feeding station, and as we walked I noticed the line up ahead snaking around what appeared to be a bundle of rags. It turned out to be a small child, barely old enough to walk, sitting on the ground pulling at the lifeless arm of a woman in a bright orange and red dress. Squatting down, I closed the woman's eyes while Bella picked up the child and we went off in search of a passing UN vehicle to take her to the orphans' tent. A life gone, another changed irrevocably. It was that simple, and it happened a thousand times a day in Goma. I no longer knew how to write that with the gravity it deserved.

With cholera and dysentery raging in the camps people were dying in the tens of thousands. Bodies were either tossed directly into the mass graves, or stacked by the side of the road to be scooped up by the tractors on their daily rounds. Everyone was talking about this being God's punishment for the Rwandans' unnatural acts. I even heard one of the godless aid workers saying it. No one had ever seen anything quite like Goma before.

'The essence of inhumanity is indifference,' Bella had said as we sat together late one afternoon on the hill again, watching the line of bedraggled human traffic gathering outside one of the feeding stations. 'There's a lot of people down there who don't deserve to be abandoned.'

Bella was a lot like Pete. They both accepted the world as it was, which allowed them to see the value in humanity, while I, according to Pete, always looked for perfection, which only served to magnify its imperfection. He was probably right. I looked back to the mass of humanity below. Bella was right when she said that a lot of the people in Goma didn't deserve to be abandoned; she was also wrong. Victims are not always innocent.

As I stood on the side of one of the death pits, swatting flies in the rising dust as Bella took photographs for her agency, she confirmed the rumour I had been hearing since I had arrived that the killers of Rwanda, the Hutu Interahamwe, the militias and the former Rwandan military, were taking control of the camps. What we were watching streaming into Goma, and what the world responded to with its money and its aid, were rarely the victims of the genocide, but often the killers and their families who had fled the RPF. This had not always been the case. Initially the camps had sprung up with the first Tutsis fleeing the slaughter, but as the Tutsi-dominated RPF moved in to take control of the country, the Hutu killers had in turn fled to the camps. As a result, many of the initial wave of Tutsi refugees had been forced to leave, trekking further north into the Congo.

'No one's doing anything to stop it, right, because everyone's frightened of them,' she was saying. 'The UN is hopeless. In the last couple of days the Interahamwe have even started threatening the aid workers and the UN have done nothing. Listen, I can't speak out because I'm under contract with the agency, but you can. Lordy,' she said, dusting the black dirt off her jeans, 'give me a good old-fashioned war any day. At least I can work out who's the fucking good guy and who's the fucking bad guy, but here . . . I just can't tell the difference anymore.' Like Pete, Bella usually coped with anything that was thrown at her, but on that day she looked worn out. 'I'm getting out of here as soon as the contract's finished and I think you should too.'

What became increasingly hard to stomach, and what would stay with me, was the fact that while the media's accounts of murder and genocide from Rwanda had done nothing to help the victims, our reports of famine and cholera in Goma had moved the world to save the perpetrators. We journalists are not supposed to be judge and jury; we're expected to report the facts as accurately as humanly possible. But few things are ever that black or white. If I failed to report that the camps were increasingly run by the killers would I be negligent in my responsibility? But if I did report that, would I be responsible for the withdrawal of aid and, by association, the deaths of maybe thousands of innocent Hutus? Who would want that responsibility? If covering Rwanda had done my head and heart in, it felt like Goma was finishing it off. Who was innocent? Who was the victim? I didn't know how to draw that line, or how I fitted into that equation anymore.

'Oh, man, this is so fucking complicated,' said Bella, as if reading my thoughts. 'Come on, I want to introduce you to someone. He's handsome, educated, well-spoken and polite. You'll hate the very air he breathes.'

As we walked back past the place where we had seen the little girl that morning there was a new pile of bodies, the corner of an orange and red dress sticking out from the bottom. Crisscrossing the chaotic maze, we finally arrived at a cluster of derelict shelters. I was surprised to see in the middle of them a new white tent. 'This is Silas's little kingdom,' Bella was saying. 'The contented lord presiding over all that he surveys.'

'How did he get the tent?'

'I have no idea, but he takes most of what's handed out to the refugees around here and gives it to his loyal henchmen, or else sells it back to anyone who can buy it. He's supposed to be one of the leaders of the genocide.'

A tall, handsome Hutu man had been sitting outside the tent and stood to greet us. 'Welcome, my friends.' No starving refugee there; no fear, no trauma. Purring seductively that perhaps he and Bella had met before, it took him a few seconds to remember that indeed he had met the white beauty before and she had definitely not liked him. Shrugging his shoulders, he turned his attention to me and acquiesced to the pleasure—my pleasure, that is—of an interview.

'It is your lucky day, Miss Price, for you are my sister, no? We are all brothers and sisters here.'

Silas was a businessman and police chief back in his village so how could he have hurt anyone? Indeed, Silas saved many lives. Ask anybody, he said, smiling through his perfect white teeth. 'They will tell you that I am their saviour.' I spent the rest of that afternoon and most of the following day with this tall, self-proclaimed Messiah. He introduced me to people who all attested to his saviour-like qualities until I began to think that if Silas was half the man he was made out to be, he should get busy breaking bread and feeding the masses so we could all go home.

Because we were supposed to be quasi-friends, and because I was supposed to trust him, and he trusted me, I raised the rumour with Silas that many of the killers from Rwanda were in the camps. This was true, he said, shaking his head in dismay. As luck would have it, Silas could quite possibly introduce me to one of these poor souls.

Gabriel shared a rag shelter with three other men who didn't seem all that keen on meeting with Silas, or me, and got up to slink away as we approached. Silas performed the introductions with a flourish. Gabriel, he explained, had been a big man in his village and a well-respected elder in his community. He had a house, a family, and a good piece of land that his fine, strong sons cultivated with him. They were good boys. Indeed, Gabriel had been blessed by the Lord, but something had gone terribly wrong in him. Gabriel, with his bones jutting out from under thin, papery skin, didn't look like a big man to me.

'Did you kill people in Rwanda, Gabriel?' I asked. No point beating around the bush. My compassion had hit rock bottom.

'Yes,' he replied, examining the creamy hard skin on the soles of his feet.

'How many people did you kill?'

'Many.'

'Children?'

'Yes.'

And so we went on with our question-and-answer session as if Gabriel, the archangel, was an automaton, devoid of emotion except for his eyes, which darted furtively about like those of a caged animal looking for escape. His head, always half-turned, hung as if distancing himself from the things that were coming out of his mouth. Finally I asked the most important question of all, the one I had not been able to find an answer to: 'Why?'

'The devil made me do it,' Gabriel answered. 'The devil took me.'

'How do you know the devil took you?'

'To think about it, even me, I am not like this. If I can say I feel him change me in my body and making me do those things. He was very powerful in my head. Satan, he is very powerful, he can make you do things you do not want to do. So I would say he must have been in me.'

'Is he in your body now?'

'No,' he whispered, beginning to pick at a scab on his elbow.

'How do you know he's no longer in your body?'

'I can say I do not want to do those things now.'

'What did it feel like when he was in your body?' He didn't answer.

Shit, why was I even asking the question? 'Gabriel?'

'I cannot see what I am doing. I shake. Madness is in my head, I think. You cannot understand. Me, it is like I am blind and must do those things I not want to do. I can say it was madness. Yes, it was madness.'

'Why did Satan leave you?' When, I wondered, would the absurdity of my questions end? I had told Bella that I didn't want to look into the hearts of the killers for I feared for my own soul, but there I was, asking the questions, discovering that I couldn't stop.

'I do not know why, but I can say I will never forget what I did. Never. Satan, he was everywhere in my country.' When I asked why he thought Satan chose him and his country he looked directly at me for the first time, confusion in his eyes, his face hollow and drawn as if he too had been grappling with this question, but he had no answer and so, in the end, neither did I.

But I found I had one more question to ask Gabriel. With my heart pounding and my hands slippery with perspiration I was not sure I was ready for what the answer might be but I asked anyway. 'Were you in the church of Nyarubuye?' I held my breath.

'No.'

Years later, when I returned to Rwanda for the Gacaca trials that would supposedly hold the killers to account in their villages, I would realise how extraordinary my interview with Gabriel had been. By that time few were ready to admit to the enormity of their crimes, with the official response from the Hutu government in exile being denial. What the world witnessed was not genocide, but spontaneous intertribal warfare caused by the invasion of the RPF, they claimed implausibly.

After talking with Silas and Gabriel I spent time with people who were not so enamoured of Silas, for already Hutus were trying to offload the responsibility of killing onto the shoulders of those more guilty than them.

'Welcome, my sister,' Silas said again when I returned to his tent for the last time. I suggested to him that he had encouraged people to shelter in a local schoolyard so that they could be killed, and that he had actually been one of the leaders of the rape and slaughter, but he just laughed, flicking away my allegations with a wave of his long, elegant fingers, his beatific smile remaining confidently in place.

'They are mad, my sister. You must understand that because of what has happened many people are mad. You should not trust what they tell you, Miss Price. You should be very careful.' His eyes were hard now. 'Very careful.'

In his 'saviour-likeness' Silas forgave them their confusion for they knew not what they did. To reinforce his saintly qualities, he assured me he would continue to pray for their souls, as should I, but when I stood to leave his long fingers closed tightly around my wrist. 'You ask too many questions, sister. It is not good for you, no? Your United Nations did nothing. No? Your country, Miss Price, they did nothing. No? They are also guilty, yes?'

I tried to pull my arm away, repelled by his feline touch and the horror of his words and beautiful smile.

'What did you do, Miss Price?' He laughed as he released his grip on my wrist and I stumbled out of his tent. 'What did you do?' he called after me.

Chapter 19

London

August 1994

THE STORY OF SILAS AND GABRIEL WAS A SCOOP AND LARRY loved it, but he had been growing increasingly worried about me and was insisting that I return to London to take some time off. Bella was also encouraging me to leave. As she waited with me on the runway in Goma until the UN plane finished loading and I could board she made me promise to see a shrink about my nightmares when I got back to London.

'I know it's not any of my business,' she added, as I was picking up my backpack to board the plane, 'but why don't you contact Pete?'

'I can't do that, Bella. I have to wait for him to contact me.'

'Lordy, don't be so proud.'

'I'm not being proud. I don't know if he wants to talk to me ever again so I have to leave it up to him.'

'Look, I don't know what happened between you, but I can't imagine it could be as bad as you think. If you want, I could contact—'

'No, Bella,' I said, grabbing her arm. 'Promise me you won't say anything to Pete. You must absolutely promise.'

.

A few days after arriving home I caught the tube into the city to have lunch with Larry, who'd booked his favourite table at the local corner pub. I hadn't seen him for about six months and noticed immediately that he'd lost weight and looked even more dishevelled than usual. Larry had never been exactly stylish, but at least his clothes had always been freshly laundered and pressed. As he walked ahead of me, leading me to the table, I noticed that the collar of his shirt was threadbare and the marks of the previous day's wear still lingered around its edges. When I asked him if he was alright he told me he was fine, but he pushed his plate away, having hardly touched the food, to light another cigarette.

With no counselling for trauma offered by the company in those days, Larry had taken it upon himself to look after everyone on the foreign desk so his opening gambit was, 'How are things *really* going for you, Kate?' I suspected he'd been planning to talk to me about my emotional wellbeing, but all I wanted to talk about was evil.

'Do you think evil really exists, Larry?'

He looked ashen. The question probably wasn't easing his concern for me.

'Do you think it's a metaphysical force that has needs, wants and desires, and can direct human behaviour like Gabriel claimed, or is it a human construct like Pete says?'

'Pete says that?'

'Yeah, he says that if you make someone evil then you take away their responsibility for their actions: go to church and say ten Hail Marys and all will be forgiven. It's like Gabriel. He really doesn't like to think he's responsible for what he did so he'd rather blame a force he can't control.'

'I asked a priest once whether he'd ever seen evil,' Larry said thoughtfully, lighting up again. 'He told me that life was like one of those crazy Bruegel paintings they made into jigsaw puzzles, and hidden somewhere within its depths was a tiny piece of puzzle that we could call evil and if we found it we'd recognise it.'

'Was that it?'

'That was it.'

'No other explanation?'

'No other explanation.'

'Jesus, I hope his parishioners could follow his clues to enlightenment better than I can.'

'I must say, he also left me none the wiser.'

I finished the last of my mashed potato and pushed my plate away also. 'I didn't use to believe in evil, Larry, but now I'm not so sure. I think I saw it in Nyarubuye.'

'Do you really think this is what you should be dwelling on now?' he asked.

What else should I be dwelling on, or even what else *could* I be dwelling on after Rwanda? I wondered.

'Apart from the week in Venice before you went to Rwanda, and a few short trips back to that house of yours in Australia, you haven't had a proper holiday since you joined the paper and you've certainly been through a lot with the last few assignments, Kate. So why don't you take it easy for a bit? Stay at home and read some books and go see some movies and hang out with friends.'

Was Larry serious? This was the man who'd probably never taken a break in his whole working life. I distinctly remember this had caused some consternation in the human resources department and within the union, but Larry had somehow been able to placate the powers that be and everyone had conveniently forgotten the matter. Was he really telling me he didn't think I was up to the job? Larry might have known I'd lost it in Goma, but he didn't know about Nyarubuye—unless Bella had told him. *No, she wouldn't go behind my back*, I told myself, but then wondered if she might if she was really worried about me—and I knew she was. I began to sweat. I couldn't afford Larry to think I wasn't able to do my job, and I certainly didn't want to sit around at home doing nothing except thinking about Rwanda and the mess I'd made with Pete. I knew how to cover the Balkans and I wanted to go back. Not only was it the best way to forget Rwanda but Pete was back there and I longed to see him.

'I don't actually want to take time off.'

'I think you should.'

'I want to go back to Bosnia, Larry.'

I watched him pat his hair and wondered what was coming next. Whatever it was it looked like he wasn't happy about saying it. 'I'm sorry, Kate, but I'm pulling rank on you. You have to take a break. As of now you're on four weeks' holiday. Go and enjoy yourself.'

'And after four weeks, what then, Larry?' I said, leaning forward, anxious to know, scared that he was really grounding me permanently. 'Will you let me go back to Bosnia?'

'Relax, Kate. Just take a break.'

'That's not an answer, Larry.'

'It's the best answer I can give you at the moment.'

What was I going to do for four weeks in London? I considered the possibility of flying out to Australia, but I wanted to stay put in case Larry changed his mind and sent me back to Bosnia. That night I ate an omelette on my lap while watching the news, before falling asleep on the lounge. I was desolate.

I tried to settle, I really did. I read books until I thought I might just turn into a library. I gave my flat a spring-clean. I shopped and cooked for myself, and I had lunch with friends and attended dinner parties. I went to the movies, like Larry had suggested. I thought about going to see my parents, but instead I read some more books. Relaxing was not one of my strong suits. When it finally dawned on me that, although Larry was my boss on the foreign desk, he couldn't stop me writing, I did a spec article for the paper's Sunday magazine on the new phenomenon I'd been hearing about called speed dating. When I handed copy to Larry to look over before I submitted it to the magazine I watched him go red in the face. Larry, my wonderful, hardcore senior editor of the foreign desk of one of the nation's most popular broadsheets could take death and destruction on a daily basis, but he couldn't cope with a story about dating. I had to smile.

By October I was back working, but Larry still hadn't given me any indication of when I might be able to return to Bosnia. I was going spare. Bella, who was also back in London now, kept banging on at me to see a shrink, while dear John rang every week to see how I was going. Not a word from Pete. I also noticed that his name was conspicuously absent in my conversations with Bella and John and became alarmed that he might have told them he didn't want anything to do with me ever again. My stomach was in knots every time I thought about him, until I decided that if something didn't give soon I was going to end up with an ulcer. I thought of telling Larry this alarming piece of self-diagnosis as a way of persuading him to send me back to Bosnia, but decided against it. He'd probably think I was turning into a hypochondriac and worry about me even more, or join Bella in telling me to see a shrink.

In the middle of January Larry called me into his office and dropped the bombshell that he wouldn't be sending me back to the Balkans. I was to cover Europe, using London as my base. I sat on the other side of his desk taking in this news. Initially I was stunned, then I felt betrayed and finally I was so furious that it took me some time to be able to collect my thoughts to respond to him in any coherent way without being fired.

'Look, I haven't been to Bosnia since April and it was supposed to be my gig, so I just need to be perfectly clear about what you're saying to me here. Are you telling me you think that I can't cover war anymore and that you'll never send me back to the Balkans? Because if that's what you're saying, you can have my resignation right now.'

'No, Kate,' he said, holding up his hand as a spasm of coughing racked his body, 'that's not what I'm saying.' After regaining his breath he sat up straight again and continued. 'I think you'd agree that Goma following Rwanda was a tough call for anyone, so before I let you go back to Bosnia for a long stint I need to be perfectly sure that you're able to handle it, otherwise you could get yourself killed and I'm not willing to take that risk.'

Despite my anger I knew Larry was right. The Nyarubuye nightmare had been visiting me more often and had recently been joined by a nightmare about a six-lane Sniper Alley highway I was trapped on for eternity. To placate Bella I'd finally visited a shrink, but after I'd talked to the woman for over an hour about

my life she told me that she was going to need therapy herself .
after listening to me. I lied to Bella and told her the woman
had helped. But nothing helped and the nightmares continued.

In February Larry sent me on assignment to cover the newly
set up UN tribunal on human rights violations in the Balkans.
I followed that story with the withdrawal of British troops from
the streets of Belfast and then the extradition of an alleged Nazi
war criminal to Italy. I actually found the stories interesting
and worked hard on them to please Larry, but life in suburban
London was not what I wanted and covering the transfer of a war
criminal in a police van was not what you would call exciting.
I missed my work in Bosnia and my friends there, but most of
all I missed Pete: our easy friendship, the conversations, the
way he made me laugh, the way he looked at me, the thrill I
sometimes got when I saw him come into view unexpectedly.
I just plain missed him and I thought about him constantly,
rerunning the scene in the hotel room back in Kigali where I
would explain what had happened and he would laugh and say
he understood and we would be friends again.

One evening in July I was lying on my lounge feasting on a
packet of corn chips in lieu of dinner while watching a swaggering
Ratko Mladic, the Serbian military commander responsible
for the siege of Sarajevo, on BBC World News. The man was
striding into the so-called UN 'safe haven' of Srebrenica as if
he owned the fucking air everyone breathed. With his sleeves
rolled up he was laughing and sharing a drink with one of the
Dutch UN commanders of the 'safe haven' while his troops
handed out lollies to the children.

'Don't take them,' I called out, throwing a corn chip at the TV. 'They're poison.' Ha, I thought, any fool would know that another round of ethnic cleansing was about to begin. 'Damn it,' I said to the newsreader as my phone began to ring, 'I need to be there.'

'You watching Mladic?'

My heart was racing as I swung my legs around to sit up straight on the lounge, as if Larry could see me in my dishevelled state. *Please, God, let him tell me I can go!*

'Sure am,' I said as casually as I could, although I was so excited it was hard to breathe.

'Think you're ready to go back?'

'Absolutely.' *Remain cool.*

'Okay, let's do it.'

We were about to hang up when I called back down the phone, 'Wait! Larry, are you still there?'

'I'm here.'

'Thank you.'

'You'll be fine?'

'Oh, Larry, I'm going to be one hundred per cent perfectly fine.'

'That's my girl.'

Jumping off the lounge I picked the corn chip up off the floor and threw it and the half-finished packet in the bin before going to the bedroom to pack my bag. I was going back to my real life: to the war I could understand and knew how to cover and to the one I knew he was covering. I was going back to Pete.

Chapter 20

Bosnia

July 1995

MUCH TO THE CHAGRIN OF THE UN SECURITY COUNCIL, IN April 1993 the Canadian head of the UN Protection Forces in Bosnia had told the traumatised citizens of Srebrenica that they were under UN protection. That singular, unauthorised and, as far as the Security Council was concerned, decidedly unwelcome act forced that august body to officially declare the town of Srebrenica a safe haven for Bosnian Muslims. The following month it extended the safe haven concept to include five other Bosnian towns and cities: Zepa, Gorazde, Tuzla, Bihac and Sarajevo. The problem was they weren't safe and they weren't havens.

As soon as the pictures of Mladic were screened around the word he made an audacious move that smacked of complete disregard for the UN. His forces attacked the nearby UN observation posts and took thirty Dutch peacekeepers hostage. The Dutch commander called in a NATO air strike against

Mladic, but he submitted the request on the wrong form and until the paperwork was sorted out nothing was possible. When the clerical error was finally corrected the following day NATO planes attacked Mladic's positions. He responded by threatening to kill his Dutch hostages. No further air strikes were called in.

While I was in the air flying to Split, the good citizens of Srebrenica were being forced to walk past the Dutch peacekeepers and, under Mladic's careful gaze, were herded onto trucks and buses that were to take them to Tuzla, one of the 'safe havens' over fifty kilometres away. During this strange procession young boys and men of military age were pulled out, as were women of a certain pleasing appearance. The UN mandate for its Dutch peacekeepers was to do nothing. Within twenty-four hours around seven thousand Muslim men were dead. Desperate to save the lives of their soldiers still being held by Mladic, the Dutch handed over a further five thousand Bosnians who'd been sheltering in their compound. Someone must have thought it was a fair exchange.

By the time I landed in Sarajevo, Srebrenica was being shelled and nearly twenty-three thousand refugees were arriving in Sarajevo and Tuzla by bus, truck or on foot, bringing with them reports of a massacre.

When I walked into the Holiday Inn one of the first people I saw was John Rubin.

'John,' I called out.

'So glad to see you again,' he said as we embraced. 'How are you now? Back for good?'

'I'm fine,' I said, ignoring the 'back for good' question that I had no answer to. I smiled at him like the Cheshire cat. It felt so damn good to see him again and to be back.

'You heard what's happening in Srebrenica?'

'That, my dear friend, is why I'm here.'

'Good, Kate, you want to come with us then because we're heading out to Srebrenica as soon as Pete's back.'

My heart was doing somersaults. We'd not seen each other for over a year and now I knew that not only was he in Sarajevo, but I was going to be seeing him very soon. Under the excitement, though, was the fear that he might not be pleased to see me or hear that I was travelling with them. It would be so embarrassing for all of us, but especially dear, innocent John. I prayed Pete would at least give me the chance to explain.

As John and I were standing at the bottom of the stairs I saw him. His hair was a little longer than usual and I liked it, but everything else was the same. I watched him come down the stairs to the main floor, clearly looking around for someone and then he saw us. I smiled and immediately his face froze. *God, what if he won't even speak to me?* But he masked the reaction quickly and smiled back. My heart sang.

'How are you going, Kate?' he said when he reached us, although he didn't offer his usual greeting of a kiss on the cheek, or a hug like I'd got from John. But at least he was smiling and talking to me. That had to be a start.

'I'm fine, Pete. Fine.' I kept smiling at him, seemingly unable to change the expression on my face. 'How are you?'

'Couldn't be better.'

'Kate's back to cover Srebrenica,' John announced, 'and I've told her that she's most welcome to travel with us if she wants.'

'Is that okay with you, Pete?'

'Sure,' he said, smiling again, although I wasn't quite sure he was pleased by the prospect. Despite all the easy words and my excitement over seeing the two of them again, I could feel tension in the air. John could feel it too and was watching us closely.

'So we're ready to go now,' Pete said, looking down at my bag. 'I'm assuming you don't want to take that with you. Do you have a room yet you could put it in?'

'No, I need to check in.'

'No time,' he said. 'John, why don't you get Haran? Kate, you can put your stuff in my room until we get back.'

I followed him to his room.

'Just put what you don't need now on the bed,' he said, unlocking the door and standing aside for me to enter.

I saw two books on the bedside table and tried to read the titles but they were upside down. After I'd emptied some stuff out of my bag I repacked what I needed in my backpack and turned to him.

'Ready?' he asked.

'Yep.' If I didn't talk to him now, I wasn't going to get another chance once we were in the car with John and Haran. 'I'd like to explain what happened in Rwanda,' I said. I'd practised my explanation for months.

'No need.'

'But I thought you might want to know.'

'No, Kate, I don't want to know.'

This was it then: a cold silence between us.

At the bottom of the stairs I could see John was waiting for us. I was beginning to think that perhaps I shouldn't go with them if it was going to be awkward when Pete put his hand out to stop me descending. 'It's good to see you again, Kate.'

'Is it really?'

'Why wouldn't it be?'

'You two right?' John called up.

'Haran ready?' Pete called back, and he began to descend.

Within hours we had arrived in the deserted town of Srebrenica to watch as Mladic's soldiers went about trying to dispose of the bodies before the dogs did. The Serbian soldiers I questioned told me unequivocally that there had not been a massacre in Srebrenica—yet all the while we could hear shots ringing out as their comrades scoured the surrounding hills for any stray souls who had slipped through their grasp. There were also no rapes, the soldiers told me in disgust, spitting on the ground as they gave their denials. Definitely no rapes of filthy Muslim women.

After leaving Srebrenica we headed for Tuzla, passing thousands of bedraggled refugees along the way. Women, children and old people, a dejected wave of human misery swept forward on foot, in the back of trucks and in wheelbarrows, as the very old and the very young sat precariously on top of the few possessions the family could take. This is my enduring vision of the Bosnian conflict: hapless caravans of bitter loss and confusion.

To deal with the influx of refugees from Srebrenica the UN set up a makeshift tent city on an airfield in Tuzla, but with the punishing summer heat and no toilets, journalists were being warned of an approaching cholera epidemic. Throughout the day Pete, John and I watched as wave after wave of frightened and disoriented refugees staggered in off the road and collapsed onto the dry grass as aid workers moved among them treating dehydration and exhaustion. Every time I stopped to question a refugee, others crowded in wanting to tell me their story. A toothless old man with a pinched and sunken mouth told me through tears that they had taken his three sons. As a little boy hid in the folds of his mother's coat, she, wrapped in a headscarf and woollen coat despite the heat, thrust tattered pictures of her husband and sons at me with shaking hands, begging me to find them. So many voices and so many stories that I couldn't keep up with the words as they poured out and Haran translated. My hand ached so badly that my writing was all but illegible. Still they kept coming and they kept talking, and Haran kept translating and I kept writing, and Pete and John kept taking pictures. What else could we do?

From the confusion it was hard to understand exactly what had happened in Srebrenica, but the survivors were already calling it a massacre. By the following day, young men who had been lucky enough to escape made their way overland from Srebrenica and began to straggle in. They were greeted with hugs, and tears, and inconsolable wails as they brought news of the fate of missing loved ones. A youth no more than thirteen described, dry-eyed and in graphic detail, how he watched columns of men standing silently as the rat-a-tat-tat of the machine guns moved down the line, propelling them forward in grotesque puppet shapes into the graves they had just dug for themselves. I knew the valley the boy described. It was a place of simple beauty, peppered with wildflowers in springtime; a swift river flowed through cool glades overhung by shady trees. There were so many such tranquil valleys in rural Bosnia—so many beautiful places in which to kill.

There were not so many pretty young girls coming into the camps, I noticed, and my mind flew back to the sight of the little girl in the church in Nyarubuye. I shivered. Now was not the time to freeze up. I had to let Rwanda go or else it would destroy me.

After hearing that a Serb-controlled television station was predicting an attack on nearby Zepa, another of the UN's safe havens, we jumped back in the car and headed south again. The closer we came to Zepa the greater the destruction and the greater the number of refugees trailing along the side of the road. Events fuelled rumour and rumour fuelled events until it was impossible to understand whether the refugees were fleeing because of fighting, or because of rumours of fighting.

Having stopped yet again at a makeshift roadblock, this time beside the blackened skeleton of a house that still had acrid smoke rising from its belly, I was interviewing some of the refugees when I smelt it: the suffocating odour of sweat and human leakage—the stench of fear. Knowing exactly what that smell meant I turned and began to walk towards where I thought it was coming from.

There is a sixth sense that you come to rely on if you have been in war enough times. It both keeps you safe and it leads you into danger. When the rational left side of the brain has done all its logical thinking and still can't give you an answer then the intuitive right side takes over and it is never wrong. It is the one to be trusted. Trust the right side. I knew exactly what I was walking into as much as I knew I would regret it. But how could I not? It was my job. It was what I was there for. The fear drew me. Maybe it was something I could prevent. Maybe this time I wouldn't be so helpless. Maybe this time I hadn't arrived too late.

Not wanting to call attention to myself, I walked casually over to tell Pete and John what I suspected, and we began to wander idly across to the other side of the road together. Rounding the corner of a house we found two cattle trucks packed with live human cargo. As Pete and John lifted their cameras to shoot, a soldier who had been smoking by the side of the house came to attention. Pushing himself off the wall he adjusted his rifle over his shoulder and walked toward us, shouting at us to stop. I continued towards the trucks, leaving Pete and John to deal with the man.

'Hey, Kate,' called John softly, 'come back.'

I ignored him.

'Kate?'

'They're going to kill them,' I said to the air in front of me.

'And what precisely do you think you're going to do about it?' said Pete, materialising behind me.

I realised then that I had no plan. 'There must be something we can do.'

'What are you doing?' called the soldier in perfect English.

'There *is* something we can do, Kate—we can leave,' Pete said softly. He now had his hand on my elbow and was steering me back to John and the soldier. I twisted out of his grip. I still had no idea what I was going to do, or even what I would be able to do. All I knew was that I had to do something to stop this massacre.

'Where are you taking them?' I asked the heavily tattooed soldier who stepped in front of me to block my way.

'To safety.'

'Bullshit. Let me go with you so I can see where this safety is.'

'What is this "bullshit"?' he threw back at me, turning and motioning for his men to get back into the trucks.

'What's your name, rank and serial number?' I demanded, like an actor in a B-grade movie. 'I'm going to report you.' When this, understandably, had no effect I turned to the others. 'All of you,' I said with a great sweep of my arm that took in the trees on the hill behind them, and the two destroyed houses, and the fences and barns. 'I'll report *all* of you.' Somewhere in my brain I knew I should back off but I couldn't stop myself.

I followed the tattooed soldier as he made his way to the cabin of the lead truck. 'You can't do this—it's a violation of the Geneva Conventions. You've heard of them, you moron, haven't you?'

He stopped and turned then, his face swollen with hate. 'What is this "moron"? You are talking about you, I think, lady. We are taking them to Tuzla, to *your* United Nations.' He spat the words out as if 'United Nations' were the dirtiest words in the world. He climbed into the cab and slammed the door in my face.

Overcome by a blinding rage I banged on the window, demanding that he take me with him, show me where this safety was. Even in my unhinged state I could sense that the soldiers were growing agitated, but the blood pounding through my brain made me oblivious to warning signals, flashing or otherwise. *No more Nyarubuyes*, I said to myself. I was not going to let another massacre happen. Never!

I turned then to appeal to the Muslim men I could see tightly packed in the trucks, but they just stared at me, unmoved and unmoving. In that moment I felt a profound sense of helplessness and an overwhelming sadness and I wanted to cry. I understood why they were going so calmly to their fate. These men had lost all hope.

'We're going now,' Pete said loudly, to no one in particular, as he caught my arm in a steely grip, before leading me towards the car, where I could see John and Haran waiting anxiously.

'We're going now,' I mimicked him. '*We're going now. Thanks for the lovely cup of tea. Have a nice day. Hope you have a good life!*'

'Shut up, will you?' he hissed. 'At least until we're out of earshot.'

'Are you completely mad?'

'No, but I think you are.' His hands were gripping my shoulders tightly so I couldn't move as he pushed me into the car.

As we drove past the soldiers manning the checkpoint on the side of the road one grinned at me and raised his arm to pump his closed fist in the air. 'Yeah, and fuck you too!' I shouted at him before turning the full force of my fury on Pete. 'They're going to kill them!' I yelled, pointing back at the trucks we were leaving behind. 'We could have stopped those men being killed back there, but you did nothing. Nothing! What's wrong with you, McDermott? Lost your balls?' I could see him in the front seat, body rigid, but he didn't respond.

'We couldn't stop anything, Kate,' John said quietly from the seat next to me.

'Bullshit. *Bullshit!*' I turned to look out my window, but I couldn't see anything but what was in my mind's eye: the lost faces of those men cramped in the trucks.

After we had driven in silence for a while John attempted to make things right by telling me that he'd been able to shoot photographs while I had been distracting the soldiers who were guarding the men—as if there had been some kind of rationale behind my behaviour. 'We need to get to Zepa as soon as possible,' he added, 'so I can get the pictures out.'

As the adrenaline began to seep from my body the enormity of what I had done began to dawn. I had put us all in danger with my behaviour. I began to shake and then sob uncontrollably. John moved over to put his arm around me.

'I know, Kate,' he said as I cried into his shoulder. 'I know.'

That night, in the room we were all forced to share in Zepa, I made my apologies.

'I've got a wife and two little kids now,' John said. 'I can't take those sorts of risks.'

'I know. I'm sorry.'

'If it makes you feel any better, the photos have been picked up and tomorrow everyone will see what was happening there.'

But we all knew that tomorrow would be too late for those men.

'You need to get out, Kate,' Pete said. He was sitting at the room's small table, cleaning his cameras. It was the first thing he'd said to me since I'd abused him in the car. 'You need to do something different. Get a reality check before you get yourself and everyone else killed.'

'Oh?' I said spitefully. 'You mean a reality check like shopping at Sainsbury's? That's more real than Bosnia is it?'

'You're on edge and that's dangerous. A reality check at Sainsbury's would be just the ticket.' He looked up at me then. '*You* might think dying in some godforsaken country in some goddamned awful war that has nothing to do with you is a good way to go out, but it's not on my must-do list.'

He was right of course. I shouldn't have come back until I'd got some sort of grip on Rwanda and how it had affected me.

We all worked together the following day with the refugees pouring into Zepa and I left that evening to head back to Sarajevo. Before I did, though, I pulled Pete aside.

'I don't know how to apologise to you enough . . . again. I know I stuffed up and I need to sort myself out. Rwanda and then Goma really did me in and I'm so sorry—so, so sorry for the danger I put you all in yesterday. It was inexcusable.' I also wanted to tell him that I was sorry I had lost his friendship, but it didn't look like he was in any mood to hear anything like that from me.

'Go home, Kate. Look after yourself, have a rest and think about where you really want to be.' He turned and walked off.

Chapter 21

London

March 1996

LARRY HAD BEEN MORE THAN HAPPY WITH MY STORIES FROM Srebrenica and Tuzla, especially after one had been shortlisted for a British Press Award. I hadn't told him about what had happened with Pete and John. I knew he'd be worried about me—and this time he might ground me permanently. I came back to London clearer in my head: I knew I could do the job, but I really needed to sort my shit out. So this time I instigated the break and Larry agreed happily, assigning me stories closer to home. On the whole they were interesting enough and again I threw myself into them. And while Bella and I hung out together whenever she was back in London, and John and I would talk from time to time, I heard nothing from Pete. His loss was a huge black hole in the pit of my stomach that I tried to fill with work, waiting for the time when both Larry and I agreed I could go back.

At the beginning of March I was invited to be part of a dinner and panel discussion organised by the London School of Economics. I was on the verge of declining when the organiser mentioned who else was on the panel. When I took my seat next to Pete McDermott at the dignitaries' table in the function room at one of London's better hotels, his attention was focused on a woman to his left—one of the event organisers, I later learnt.

'Hello,' he said finally, registering my presence.

He looked so bloody good in a suit that for a moment I couldn't speak.

'Don't let me interrupt anything,' I said at last, indicating the woman he'd just been talking to, who was now talking with the man on her other side.

'You weren't interrupting anything—she's not my type.'

'Oh, I don't know,' I replied, smiling. 'She has a pulse, doesn't she?'

He threw his head back and laughed. 'Sounds like you're back to your old endearing self, Price. It's good to see.' He looked like he really meant it and I beamed back at him. 'That said,' he continued, 'you look a little bit different tonight from how I remember you.'

'I do?'

'Well, the make-up and the hair, not to mention the little black dress and the Cruella de Vil heels . . . and what's that scent? Chanel? Very nice, Kate, very nice indeed.'

I'd bought the dress and shoes especially for him, deliberately not thinking about what my intentions might be, or where I hoped the evening might end, but already I was regretting it, beginning to feel embarrassed that my efforts were so obvious. 'Sometimes you bore me, McDermott.'

'Crap.'

'No, you're really boring sometimes.' But I couldn't help smiling, even as I was trying not to read too much into his comments; trying not to hope for too much other than not stuffing up with him this time. 'Anyway, McDermott,' I said, 'you don't actually have a type.'

'Really?'

'Well, I've seen you with blondes, brunettes and redheads . . .' I began ticking them off on my painted fingernails. 'Tall women, short women, slim and voluptuous women.'

He laughed. 'Watch that imagination of yours, Kate. Just because you see me talking to a woman doesn't mean I'm bedding her.'

'If I may have your attention, please,' an affable Michael Parkinsonesque type was saying from the stage. We both turned to face him, but I could feel the tension in the air; Pete and I were not finished yet. I found it impossible to wipe the smile off my face, wondering exactly when in the last year I had switched from thinking McDermott was not good relationship material to wanting to seduce him. After introducing himself as the master of ceremonies for the evening, Mr Parkinsoneque invited us onto the stage where I became acutely aware of my too-tight dress and too-high heels. Trying to ensure that I didn't trip over or turn my rear end to the audience, I resorted to what probably looked, and certainly felt, like an awkward crab walk across the stage.

'Nice,' whispered McDermott as he moved past me to his seat.

When we were seated, the MC began. 'Thank you and welcome to the London School of Economics annual Shepworth Dinner. As you're all aware, tonight's discussion is titled "The United Nations' Relevance in Today's World", and I'm absolutely positive that we are in for a particularly lively discussion this evening. So without further delay, let me introduce our panel of distinguished guests.'

Professor Hyphenated-Surname was then called upon to give us a short history of the United Nations, which sounded a lot like a History 101 lecture. His rambling soliloquy finally came to an end with the claim that the United Nations was not irrelevant by virtue of the fact that it had a lot of good work to do. Mmm, not too much heavy thinking going on there.

The next guest talked about something entirely irrelevant—though perhaps if I'd actually listened instead of fantasising about the sexy man in the suit sitting opposite me on the stage I might have seen the connection between French beef subsidies and the UN's relevance.

When it was Pete's turn to speak he stated bluntly that the UN had three choices: it could either continue to be the whipping boy of the only remaining superpower, reform drastically, or dissolve. He discussed the UN's appalling string of failures, ending with, 'It's a utopian absurdity to think that one undemocratic institution, weighed down by bureaucracy and global inertia, and representing the wishes and whims of a hundred and ninety-odd democrats, dictators and despots can be a panacea for the world's problems.'

I looked over at Pete to see him smiling at me, for this was an argument we had often had—only this time he had stolen my argument, which meant I had no alternative but to take his. Smiling back sweetly, as if I was enjoying myself—which for the first time in a long time I was—I began, 'We should ask the previous panellist what his solution is, should nothing materialise to replace the UN? And what would happen if the UN dissolved and the space was not filled?'

'May I remind our audience that in politics a void is always filled?' he retorted.

'Filled with what, though, Mr McDermott? Isn't that the question you can't answer and isn't that the danger?' These happened to be the exact words he had often said to me. I went on to argue reasonably convincingly—I thought—about the importance of the UN, ending with the statement that I agreed with much of what the first two panellists had said (which was a bit rich considering I didn't actually know what number two had said).

'Come on, Kate,' Pete said as we were leaving the stage, 'let's get out of here.'

'I'm with you, but we can't just walk out.'

'We could tell them we have a war to go to,' he said, mischief in his eyes.

'Don't be ridiculous.'

When we reached our table, though, he did just that, announcing to our dining companions that he was dreadfully sorry, but Ms Price and he had a war they had to attend. As he took my hand all I had time to do was grab my handbag and tug at the hem of my dress as I murmured, 'So sorry.'

We had almost reached the hotel's bar when the woman who had been sitting next to Pete at the table came chasing after us.

'Mr McDermott! Peter!' she called. When we saw who it was Pete whispered, 'You go on to the bar. I'll sort this out and be there in a couple of minutes.' My first thought was that he was probably going to quickly organise a date, but I quashed the ugly notion; I knew that on this night, I had his undivided attention.

Down in the bar I settled into an exquisitely large lounge to watch the passing parade outside the window. There was definitely the possibility of mending bridges tonight, maybe even more . . . Kicking off my shoes, I was about to tuck my feet up under me when I remembered just how short the little black dress was. It definitely had to go. So too did the shoes—although, I thought with a smile, they had done the trick. When the waiter arrived I ordered a bottle of wine and two glasses.

'Kate!' When I looked up I saw my old boyfriend Simon beaming down at me. Without waiting for an invitation, he plonked himself down on the lounge beside me. From the smell of him and the bloodshot eyes I knew immediately that he'd been drinking and I moved a little away. But Simon swayed towards me, intent on planting a sloppy kiss on my lips.

'Simon, what are you doing?' I said, recoiling from him in horror.

'I saw on the notice board in the foyer that you were on a panel here tonight, but they wouldn't let me go in. So I thought I'd come to the bar and wait and see if you'd turn up—and hey presto, you're already here waiting for me. Don't you look smashing?' He leaned back to get a better view, half slipping off the end of the lounge in the process.

'Simon, this is not really a good time.'

'Hello,' said Pete, standing over us, smiling as he loosened his tie.

'Pete,' I said, standing. 'This is Simon Davies, an old friend of mine. Simon, this is Peter McDermott.'

'More than just an old friend, hey?' Simon said, leering, as he got to his feet unsteadily. *Oh hell, how was I going to get rid of him?*

'Good to meet you, Simon,' Pete said, holding out his hand.

Simon turned to shake Pete's hand, nearly falling into him. 'Likewise,' he said, after finally connecting with the hand being offered. Something must have registered in Simon's alcohol-soaked brain because he made an effort to straighten himself up before declaring that he should leave, muttering something about a party in a room on the sixth floor. 'Well, good to see you again, Katie, you looking smashing. She looks smashing, doesn't she?' he said, wobbling around to face Pete again.

'Smashing.'

'Still trotting off to the bang-bang are you, Katie Pricey?'

'I thought you were leaving, Simon.'

'Right. Yes. Okay, best be off.' After taking one of my hands, on which he succeeded this time in planting a sloppy kiss, he turned and saluted Pete, then stumbled off to the lifts.

When he'd left, Pete settled into the lounge opposite me. Pulling his tie out from under his collar he folded it and put it in his jacket pocket then reached over to pour the wine. 'Good friend of yours, is he?'

I could lie—but then again, I could tell the truth. 'I used to live with Simon, but he couldn't stand my job, among other things, and we parted.' I was interrupted by the ringing of my mobile. I hesitated, looking at Pete.

'Go on,' he said, tasting the wine, 'answer it.'

It was Larry. The Israelis had attacked southern Lebanon in retaliation for Hezbollah launching rockets into Israel. Did I want to cover it?

It took me all of three seconds to make the decision. I knew I was ready this time. The nightmares were far less frequent and I felt more in control, less emotional. This was my chance to start again and prove to Larry he could rely on me. 'You bet,' I said.

'Good. There's a flight to Tel Aviv tonight at ten-thirty—can you be on it?'

The realisation of the choice in front of me fully registered for the first time. *Pete or the job? Pete or the job?* Larry was waiting. *Pete or the job?* I looked at my watch and did a quick calculation. 'Sure, I can make it.'

'That was Larry,' I said to Pete as I put the phone away. 'Israel's launched an offensive into southern Lebanon and he wanted to know if I could go.'

'And you said?'

'Yes.'

'And he wants you to go . . . ?'

'Now. Ten-thirty tonight out of Heathrow.'

He looked at his watch. 'Well, that's that.' Taking a mouthful of wine he stood and took out his wallet. 'We'd better get you a cab,' he said, leaving a few notes on the table.

I grabbed my bag and followed him out to the foyer of the hotel.

Shit, shit, shit. I want to go, but I want to stay. Maybe I could ring Larry back and tell him I'll get a flight first thing in the morning? Would he accept that?

The doorman was motioning and one of the waiting cabs was moving forward.

Oh God, I've been throwing out hints for the last couple of months that I want back in and now Larry's offering me a potentially huge story. I can't disappoint him.

The cab had pulled up and Pete was opening the door for me. I met his eye. Was he reading my mind again? I climbed into the back of the cab.

It'll be okay. I'll ring Pete from Israel first chance I get and we'll talk. We're friends again. Everything will be alright.

As I leaned out from the back seat of the cab to say goodbye, Pete bent down and rested his forehead against mine.

'Stay.'

The word came out so softly that I couldn't be sure I'd even heard it. But before I could react he was pushing the cab door shut, and banging on the roof to signal the driver to move off.

It will be okay. It will definitely be okay.

If I didn't hurry I was going to miss the bloody plane.

Chapter 22

Chechnya
October 1998

BEFORE THE WAR BEGAN IN 1994, THE ARMS BAZAAR IN central Grozny did a roaring trade. Just a short stroll from the fruit and vegetable markets you could, if you were so inclined, haggle over the price of a rocket launcher or a machine gun. If you had a spare American dollar you could procure for yourself one or two hand grenades. If it was a Russian Kalashnikov you desired, you could probably get one from a young Russian conscript in exchange for food or a bottle of vodka. Life was tough in the new Russia, and vodka was still the dulling lubricant of choice. With every male over twelve years old seemingly armed to the teeth, what followed in the fight for independence in the former Soviet republic of Chechnya was a conflict of unspeakable cruelty.

According to the Russians, Chechnya was fundamental to the Russian state. According to the Chechens, it was a state in and of itself. In his vexation, the Russian drunkard Yeltsin became intent on destroying everything that was Chechen under the infamously twisted logic of 'we had to destroy the village to save it'. In turn, the Chechen fighters were intent on obtaining their independence, or, failing that, their martyrdom. The problem was, and remains to this day: Chechnya has oil. It literally oozes up out of the ground. Black crude.

By all accounts Grozny was already in a state of pitiless disrepair before the war, but by the time I got there in 1998 it was nearly uninhabitable and immediately reminded me of all the photos I'd seen of Dresden after the fire bombing in World War II, which, in turn, reminded me of scenes from a Mad Max movie only worse. Much of the capital was a wasteland. Street after street of apartment blocks were destroyed with the buildings' carcasses backlit by black plumes of smoke twisting up in the freezing air. Metal streetlights had been bent double under the force of the Russian bombardment, while the ghosts of what must have once been beautiful trees lay broken in the filthy winter slush.

After Israel Larry began to give me more assignments in conflict zones again until I was back in the old routine, although London rather than Bosnia had become my base. I had called Pete from southern Lebanon and we started talking again. Gradually we began to run into each other, and while there were no more hints of romance, we fell back into our old working relationship, although I was painfully aware that we never quite recovered that easy teasing way we'd momentarily recaptured that night in London. Still, I was more than happy to be working with him again. And so we dealt with what had almost happened in London the same way we had dealt with our near miss in Rwanda: by not ever mentioning it again.

The first night in Grozny we camped out in what used to be a hotel in the centre of town and met up with Bella, who had taken up conflict photography again and whose hair was now a luxuriantly thick curly chestnut that hung down her back in a plait like a medieval bell-pull. Exhausted from travelling for the previous week with a group of Chechen rebels over the snow-covered Caucasus, she had arrived with only one camera, having lost her second one when they had been forced to break camp in a hurry after coming under Russian fire.

Our fixer in Chechnya was Umar. He was a walking, talking moustachioed cigarette packet with a thinning patch of hair he contrived to make the best of by way of a scraggy ponytail and woefully thin comb-over. Having spent a number of years in England before being deported for crimes unknown, Umar had formed a rather jaundiced view of all Westerners as both extraordinarily wealthy and extraordinarily keen to part with their hard-earned cash. During negotiations Umar made some simple calculations, and presented Pete and me with a bill for his services and the use of his car that would have put his six kids through Oxford. Eventually we agreed to pay for only three kids' college educations and three exceedingly generous dowries.

Prigorodnoye, the village Umar took us to on the second day, had been razed, its orchards destroyed, and all its inhabitants had fled. All, that is, except those who were no longer able to leave, their frozen bodies having leaked a brilliant red out into the freshly fallen snow. Confusingly, the Russian bombardment of the village had continued intermittently all that day, which led Pete and me to the conclusion that the Russian conscripts had been instructed to bomb something, everything, anything, anywhere, all the time. Prigorodnoye was not a good place and the longer we stayed the higher my fear barometer rose until the mercury was about to burst out through the top of my head. Umar, Bella and I had told Pete—who wanted more photos—that we needed to get out so we could begin the thirty-kilometre journey back to Grozny before nightfall. Traversing icy roads and Russian roadblocks was dangerous enough in daylight, but at night it was suicidal. In the early afternoon, and with the light fading quickly, the three of us sat in the car waiting impatiently for Pete to finish.

Tossing up whether I valued my lungs over hypothermia, and deciding that my lungs won the day, I was winding the window down to let the toxic mass from Umar's cigarettes escape when my eye was caught by a movement in the car's side mirror. It looked like a greatcoat with legs was running into one of the few houses across the square that remained standing. So fleeting was the image that I could not even be sure I had seen it until I saw Pete come into view, running after the greatcoat. Swinging the car door open I jumped out, calling back to Umar to keep the motor running in case we needed to get out of town in a hurry. As I ran off in Pete's direction I heard Bella take off after me. Umar, who played by his own rules, totally ignored my instructions and took off after her. When I entered the house Pete was standing in the middle of what had once been somebody's lounge room. 'Did you see a boy run in here?' he asked, as if he too could not quite believe the vision.

'I didn't see anything,' replied Bella from behind me.

'I think I did,' I said. 'At least I saw what looked like a coat with legs run in here.'

Bella was looking from Pete to me. 'What's going on?'

'This room's all that's left of the place but there's no one here,' Pete said, ignoring Bella's question.

'He could have run out the back,' I offered.

'Not possible. The house behind has collapsed onto the back of this one and there's no way into this room or out except through the door we just came in.'

'Can one of you please tell me what's going on?' Bella asked again as Umar arrived, gasping for breath.

From deep within the building a muffled cough was heard and all of us stood perfectly still, listening for the sound again so we could locate its source. When it came we all moved to the staircase, under which we discovered a trapdoor. As Pete opened it the smell of urine and faeces and stale air made us all reel back.

'Is anyone down there?' Pete called, then turned to Umar. 'Umar, ask if anyone is down there.'

When no reply came I told Umar to go back to the car and fetch the torch out of my backpack. When he returned we all crowded around Pete as he shone the torch down into the void. Someone moved and there was another muffled cough. Switching the torch off Pete asked Umar to explain to whoever was down there that we were not going to hurt them, but Umar's words were greeted by silence. 'Tell them again,' Pete said, 'and this time tell them we are British and American journalists, not Russian soldiers, and that we would like to talk with them.'

A whispered conversation could be heard from the darkness below, and then more coughing, until finally there were footsteps, and the top of a ladder appeared against the edge of the trapdoor. As Bella and I watched Pete and Umar descend into the void, a paraffin lamp spluttered into life to cast long shadows up the damp cellar walls. Squatting down to get a better view, I counted at least eight children of varying ages, including a baby resting on the knee of an old babushka sitting at a table. Beside her, one arm wrapped protectively around the back of her chair, stood the greatcoat. The children were huddled together on mattresses, their tiny frames covered in blankets.

After Pete and Umar had talked with the woman, they motioned for us to come down. Even as we did, the ladder shook with the force of a shell landing overhead, causing lumps of masonry to break away from the ceiling.

There had to be at least fifteen children, although the dark recesses of the cellar could have hidden more. Everyone was filthy, seemingly all angular bones and dark, hollow eyes. The light from the lamp cut deep grooves in the angles of the old woman's face, framed by a scarf tied tightly under her chin. She looked exhausted.

There were a total of eighteen children in the cellar, she told us, ranging in age from the six-month-old baby on her lap to her fourteen-year-old granddaughter. The boy in the greatcoat was her twelve-year-old grandson. As my eyes grew more accustomed to the gloom I noticed that all the children had shaved heads and were wearing oversized clothing, which made it almost impossible to tell their age or sex. Except for her two grandchildren, she explained, all the children were orphans, with their parents and families either missing or dead following the destruction of the village.

'Okay,' said Pete to Umar. 'Tell her they all have to leave because this house is probably going to come down around their heads soon.'

After some conversation between Umar, the boy and his grandmother, Umar informed us that the babushka refused to leave because some of the children were too sick, or too young to walk. We could take some of them in the car with us, Pete told her, but we could not fit them all in. Eight children, he said, holding up his fingers to emphasise the number. We could take eight children now, and we would try to come back for the others in the morning. Another shell exploded overhead, causing more masonry to dislodge and dust to drift down through the cracks in the wooden floorboards. No one moved. We were all holding our breath, waiting to see if the next shell was going to bury us alive in the house.

Umar, the boy and his grandmother began another discussion until Pete interjected again, telling Umar that the woman needed to choose who was to go with us—and the decision, he said, needed to be made immediately, as it would be dark within half an hour. 'Does she understand the urgency?' he said, exasperated at the slowness of their deliberations.

'Yes, yes, she understands,' replied Umar, 'but you must understand this is difficult for her. She wants to know where you will take the children and who will look after them.'

'Tell her we'll take them to one of the aid agencies in Grozny so they can be cared for, and we'll come back to get her and the others in the morning.'

Umar stared at Pete, knowing as well as we did that there were no services in Grozny to care for orphaned children. I knew Pete's first priority was to save their lives by getting them out of the house. We would worry about where to take them later. After hesitating, Umar turned to translate Pete's words to the old woman.

Bella, who had wandered off into the recesses of the cellar, reappeared carrying a small child lost in the folds of a dirty blanket. 'This kid's really sick and the others are not much better, including the old woman's grandson with the cough. Sounds like pneumonia to me.' Unwrapping the blanket, she showed me the sores on the child's tiny blue feet.

Indicating the child in Bella's arms, together with those who were most ill, the old woman then selected the smallest children and, finally, her two grandchildren, but the boy refused to leave. Nodding in agreement, Umar translated the boy's claim that as the oldest male it had become his responsibility to look after this family in the cellar.

'Tell him,' said Pete more urgently, 'he has to make up his mind. We've got to leave here before dark. Come on!'

Another blast overhead and Bella and I began collecting some of the smaller children to take out to the car. The boy, his grandmother and Umar, who by this time appeared intimately involved in the family's deliberations, began another round of discussions. I wasn't entirely sure whose side Umar was taking, but it looked suspiciously like the boy's. He probably agreed that this male child had become the de facto head of the household. Finally, losing patience, Pete cut across their deliberations to tell Umar that he would stay with the grandmother and the other children if the boy went to take care of his sister and the smaller children.

'What the hell do you think you're doing?' I asked him furiously. 'Do you want to die here too?' He told Umar that the boy needed to decide immediately, or the car would go without him and his sister. With the urging of his grandmother, the boy's thin frame visibly deflated and he agreed to go.

'You don't have to do this, Pete, please.'

Ignoring me, he began to help Bella with the children.

'If you stay I stay,' I said in desperation, hoping that would make him see reason, but the only response I got from him was that I was a 'fucking idiot', which was exactly what I was thinking.

'Are you really sure you want to do this, Kate?' asked Bella.

'Okay, there'll be room for four more kids if Kate and I both stay, so who else is going? And the decision needs to be made *now*!'

'I don't think I have much choice,' I told Bella. There was no backing out after Pete's announcement. No opportunity to ask if I could possibly have a few more minutes to reconsider my options. Another lesson in war reporting: think before you speak.

Wrapping the blanket tightly around the boy's sister I helped her to her feet, while taking the baby from the old woman, who was now sitting dazed and unmoving. Passing the smaller children up the ladder until we were all gathered outside the house, I put my arm around the girl, who leaned into me, and we began to move towards the car. When we got there I passed a baby to Bella in the back seat and then I turned to see Pete reach out to help the girl into the car, but she recoiled in horror from his touch. His eyes met mine above her head and he backed away, pretending to busy himself on the other side of the car. Her androgynous haircut had come too late. My heart went out to this poor child. Visions of the little girl in Nyarubuye, never far from the surface, flashed in my mind, but as I had learnt to do, I pushed them away.

'There's room for you in the car, Kate,' Pete said. 'You could go.'

'No, let's get another child.'

After we'd handed the child into the car Umar tapped his head in a gesture that had so far punctuated all his conversations, and could roughly be translated as 'trust me, I know what I'm doing', before promising to return for us first thing in the morning. Revving the motor as if the starting flag was just about to fall at the Indianapolis 500, he roared off, spraying snow and slush up our legs. Watching him go I offered a prayer that three college educations and three dowries were enough to ensure Umar's return, while wondering if, all things considered, we should have offered Oxford for all.

'This is another fine mess you've got us into, Bullwinkle,' said Pete, smiling as he draped his arm around my shoulder.

'Mmm, I don't seem to remember it like that.'

Not particularly happy with spending the night in the cellar, I thought we might try to find a different place to shelter. Telling Pete that I'd meet him back at the house in five minutes, I was just heading off, intending to explore a side street off the central square, when a rush of noise filled the air. *Too late*, my mind screamed. *Too late.* A suffocating wave of hot air filled my lungs as a loud roar lifted me up off my feet and sent me flying through the air until there was nothing but silence and blackness.

I had no idea how long I'd passed out for, but as soon as I was conscious again I got to my knees and began crawling as quickly as I could through the smoke and dust until my head hit a brick wall. There I curled up in a ball, waiting for the next mortar. Silence. Silence.

Where is Pete? Oh, sweet Jesus, where is Pete? I called his name, but I couldn't hear my own voice, or even be sure I had made any sound. I called again. Silence. 'No, no, no, no!' I screamed. '*Not this. No, no, no, not this!*'

As the smoke and dust began to settle and my vision began to return, I saw him lying motionless in the middle of the square. '*Pete!*' Unable to stand I propelled myself forward on all fours through the muck, but it wasn't fast enough and so I tried to stand. When I fell down I tried again until, dizzy with the ringing in my ears, I made it to where he lay. He wasn't moving.

'*Nooooooooooooooo! Noooooooooooooooo!*' I screamed, falling to my knees beside him, but as I reached out he began to stir and then tried to sit up. 'Pete!' I gasped. 'Are you okay?' But he couldn't hear me. We had to get out of the square and find cover in case another round came in. 'Come on, Pete, help me here.' Slinging his arm around my shoulder, I pulled him up to his feet.

'My cameras,' he was saying, searching blindly on the ground at our feet for them.

'They're in the cellar. Remember? You left them on the table while we loaded the kids into the car. Come on, Pete, we've got to get out of here.' As the snow was beginning to fall I pulled his arm tighter around my shoulder and, with him leaning heavily on me, we hobbled back to the house.

Down in the cellar, I used the tiny medical kit I always carried to clean up his face as best I could. He had a few minor cuts, but one gash over his eye looked particularly bad and would need stitching.

'Go on, stitch it then,' he said when I told him.

'Maybe we should wait?' I suggested.

'What?' He still couldn't hear properly, although his hearing was slowly returning. I repeated my words again, speaking closer to his ear.

'It won't bloody stop bleeding unless you do it, Price.'

'It's going to hurt.'

'What?'

'Nothing.'

Pulling out the needle and thread and some painkillers, I handed him two tablets and then lit a match to sterilise the needle.

'I don't have anything to wash my hands with, and I guess we don't have time for those tablets to work,' I warned him.

'Whatever you're saying, just fucking do it quickly.'

'Okay, but you need to know I failed sewing class.'

'You what?'

'I failed sewing class in school,' I yelled.

'Jesus, Price, why can't you be like every other woman? Didn't you ever want kids and a family and all that shit?'

'Shut up, McDermott.'

'What?'

I pressed the flesh together and pushed the needle through. He winced as sweat broke out on his brow. I pushed it out the other side and tied it off.

'Christ, Price, your hands are shaking more than mine. Stop shaking and stop bloody crying, will you?'

'If you don't like the service, do it yourself.' He flinched again as I pushed the needle in a second time. After three stitches I wrapped a bandage around his head then stuck a piece of wadding over the eye to try to catch the blood, before grabbing his beanie out of his backpack and pulling it down over his head to try to hold the wadding in place. I sat back then, feeling his face, checking to see if anything else needed to be done.

'For Christ's sake, Price, what are you crying for?'

'I thought you were dead.' I didn't add that I could not imagine my world without him in it.

'But I'm not, so stop crying and help me get these kids settled down for the night.'

We distributed the little food and water we had taken from the car and then helped the babushka push all the filthy mattresses together before sharing the remaining blankets around for communal warmth. Once the lamp was extinguished it was pitch dark in the cellar and there was nothing to do but try to sleep until Umar arrived in the morning.

I was squashed on a mattress between Pete and a young girl, trying not to think about the overwhelming smell of piss and shit, or what the damp was that was seeping up through the mattress around my hip. Without a blanket to share, I pulled the young girl in closer before reaching over to pull Pete's arm around me.

The explosions had moved off some distance from the town, but with the cold, and the old lady's snoring and mutterings, and the children's coughing, and the smell of the urine, not to mention the fact that it was probably only four in the afternoon, I found it impossible to sleep. And so with nothing better to do I took the opportunity to mentally torture myself. How much could I take before I cracked? Would I quit before I died, or die before I quit?

When I had begun in the industry I was like most young people and believed myself invincible—dying was never a reality. By the time I was lying in that cellar in Grozny I had seen enough to know that it could happen to me at any moment of any day. There were so many variables I could never control, and no one's behaviour in war was predictable, including my own. Most of us who cover conflict are usually superstitious in one way or another, and would sometimes talk about the statistics of surviving in the job. Some, including Pete, argued that for every war you survive your chances of surviving the next increase, because each time you become better at reading the danger signs. But in my mind the converse argument held just as much sway, if not more. The more time you spent in dangerous places the more chance you would become a statistic. How many times could you play Russian roulette and survive? Every time you played your chances were theoretically the same, but if you spun that cylinder enough times, surely one day it would stop at the chamber that held the bullet? The more you go to war the better your chances of surviving; the more you go to war the greater your chances of dying. In the end the arguments cancelled each other out and it all came down to being in the wrong place at the wrong time, and that always came down to one simple decision: do I walk to the left, or do I walk to the right? Following my miserable train of thought, I began combing back through the day in Prigorodnoye looking for the mistake. It didn't take a genius to guess where the wrong turn was—apart from the decision to come to Chechnya in the first place.

I didn't want to be buried alive in that cellar and considered the possibility of making it through the night upstairs, but survival was just as uncertain up there, perhaps even more so. In the absence of any better guarantees of living, I made my usual pact with God: *Just let me get through this one and You know the deal.*

Taking my stiff arm out from around the sleeping girl I rolled over to face Pete. Staring into the darkness where I imagined his face to be, I asked him what he thought bravery was.

'What?'

'What do you think bravery is?' I repeated, leaning over to speak into his ear, my lips brushing against his cheek by mistake in the dark.

'What?'

I reached out then to find his face with my hands and spoke directly into his ear.

'What do you think bravery is?'

'Christ, Price, where did that come from?'

'I don't know; thinking about our chances of dying here.'

'Great.' He was quiet for a while before he answered. 'I guess I've always thought there has to be an element of fear for it to be bravery. You can't be brave if you don't feel fear.'

'Were you fearful when you decided to stay this afternoon?'

'What?'

I leaned in, wanting to brush his cheek again with my lips, but refraining. 'Were you fearful when you decided to stay this afternoon?'

'No, I wasn't, so there was no bravery there. But I have to tell you, the fact that I wasn't fearful makes me fearful. Feeling fear when someone is lobbing mortars at you is a normal, rational human response. What about you?'

'Definitely no bravery here either. The babushka is brave, don't you think?'

'She is, and so was the boy and so were you when you decided to stay.'

'I don't know about that. I don't feel brave, but the boy was definitely. He really was scared, wasn't he, although he tried not to show it. Are you afraid of dying?'

'Price, what are you trying to do, scare the bejesus out of me? Of course I'm afraid of dying.'

We lay in silence for a few minutes, listening to the sound of shells exploding way off in the distance. I was shocked by the discovery that I was happy. Pete was alive, he was lying close, holding me, and we were talking like we used to for the first time in years.

'I think we're going to make it, Price,' he said.

'Mmm, me too.'

'What did you say?'

Again I leaned in and spoke in his ear. 'Me too.'

Satisfied, I turned back to cradle the child, who had begun to cough, and noticed that my other hip was now wet as well. I must have drifted off when an artillery barrage nearby shook the building.

'I like you a lot, McDermott,' I whispered into the dark and felt him shift behind me.

'I like you a lot too, Price.'

'Shit—you bastard! You could hear perfectly well all along!'

'Shh . . . you'll wake the children. Have I ever told you, Price, about the time Sam and I burned down the local bus shelter after we'd written something rude about the constable's daughter on it and couldn't work out how to get rid of it?'

'Yeah, you told me that one, McDermott, but tell me again.'

When Umar returned the following morning he carried a note from Bella to say she had gone back across the mountains with her Chechen friends and that she hoped we were still alive. It had two postscripts.

> *PS My friends have told me that the Chechens are stockpiling weapons under that fleabag hotel you're staying in. Just thought you might like to know if you're still alive.*
> *PPS If you're not (still alive, that is), can I have your cameras please, Pete?*
> *Much love,*
> *Bella*

There was also a second rescue car, driven by freelance Dutch photographer Luc Vos. I'd heard of Vos—he had a reputation as a good and fearless photographer—and I'd seen him working a few times over the years, but we'd never met. After we shook hands he took photos of the babushka and me carrying the kids to the car before moving off with Pete to take a look at what was left of the village. Realising his car was not really needed to carry any of us back to Grozny, he decided instead to head off to the Argun Gorge, about thirty kilometres away, where heavy fighting had been reported between the Chechens and the Russian army.

On the way back to Grozny the babushka said something to Umar that I had heard her repeating to herself in the dark of the cellar. When I asked him what it meant he told me it was a Russian saying that translated roughly as: *Too many tears, not enough sweat.*

'It about the village,' he said. 'She say they mixed too many tears in foundations and not enough sweat and that why it is destroyed.'

When I asked about her grandchildren's parents she told us that the Russians had killed them. Their father—her son—had been shot in front of the family and the boy's mother and two younger sisters had been killed two weeks later when their house was shelled. The boy and his sister were the only survivors. Mohammed was never part of the resistance, she said wearily, but the Russians had arrested him anyway outside the rubble of their home, along with his sister. He'd been held for two weeks and tortured.

The old babushka was relating the bare details of her family's fate in a measured, dispassionate tone, as if it was just another piece of family history, which I guessed in the scheme of their hard lives it was. Umar explained that the Russians liked to torture children because they gave up the village's secrets more readily than the adults. After the Russians were finished with

Mohammed they'd blindfolded him and taken him into the forest, telling him that they were going to execute him. After tying him to a tree in the snow they had left him. His sister had found him two days later close to death.

When I asked about the girl, Umar spoke to the babushka, who replied with just one word. Umar turned his attention back to the road ahead.

'Umar?'

'She was raped.'

'Where did you take the other children?' I asked him.

'My sister, she has farm about fifty kilometres from Grozny. She still have animals and still some food.' He let out an ugly laugh. 'The Russians, they have not found it yet. The children yesterday are at my home, and my wife and I will take them all to my sister tonight.'

Held up at innumerable roadblocks and forced to take detours, our progress back to Grozny was infuriatingly slow, especially when two Russian soldiers wanted to know why two foreign journalists were transporting Chechen citizens around the countryside.

'If we'd run into trouble back there, and they'd asked me to pay a ransom for you, I want you to know I would have, Price,' said Pete, leaning over from the front seat in an attempt to charm the little girl sitting on my lap with his most brilliant smile.

'What would you pay for me, my hero? What do you judge my worth to be?'

'About a thousand pounds would do it, give or take a couple of quid. I don't know,' he said, turning around again to look me up and down. 'Maybe thirteen hundred, tops. You're a bit skinny for the likes of the punters around here.'

'That's all I'm worth? I'm deeply offended.'

'You shouldn't be. A thousand pounds could buy a lot of vodka.'

'I seriously don't know why all the girls love you, McDermott. Your charm eludes me.'

'Do all the girls love me?' he said, smiling again at the little girl on my lap. She clearly did not love him. 'Well, possibly not all of them,' he sighed.

Chapter 23

WHEN WE GOT BACK TO THE HALF-DESTROYED AMMUNITION DUMP masquerading as our hotel, it was too late to look for somewhere safer to stay that night. We'd have to test our luck one more time.

I was sorting out the children and Pete was standing by Umar's door making arrangements for the following day when I heard a voice call out, 'Pete McDermott! Well, well, well, who would have thought?'

I looked up at Pete to see him peering across the bonnet of the car, his face initially registering confusion, which was quickly replaced by a smile. I turned to see Ms CBS from Riyadh standing with her hands on her hips in the hotel's entrance. Where the hell had she come from?

'Hello,' he called out, waving as he made his way around the front of the car to her. I knew immediately from the way he greeted her that he couldn't remember her name. 'How are you going?' I heard him say. He still couldn't find her name and I smiled to myself, before deciding to put him out of his misery.

'Hi, I'm Kate Price,' I said, walking up to join them, holding my hand out to shake hers. 'We met years ago in Riyadh and then Kuwait, but I'm sorry, I can't remember your name.'

'Of course, Kate,' she said, taking my hand, although I could see in her eyes that she had absolutely no memory of meeting me. 'I'm Catherine Taylor.'

'It's been years, Cathy . . .' he said.

'Catherine.'

'So, Catherine, what've you been doing?'

Neat, I thought, he's got the name now and he's off and running with it—shame about the little error with calling her Cathy. It was obvious to me that Catherine Taylor was still into Pete and that he was already picking up on those vibes. The two immediately fell into a conversation that didn't include me about what they each had been doing since Riyadh.

'Excuse me,' I said, 'I hate to interrupt, but when you're free and want to discuss our plans for tomorrow, Pete, I'll be up in my room.'

'Sure thing. I'll see you soon.'

'Nice to meet you again, Catherine,' I said.

'You too . . .' She'd forgotten my name already.

Back in my room I threw my bag onto the bed and fell onto the mattress after it. I waited an hour and a half but there was no sign of Pete.

McDermott's a player. Don't you ever forget that, Price. He's a player and you can only ever be his friend.

I needed company.

Following the sound of laughter and the aroma of cigarette smoke mixed with voodoo magic and weapons-grade whisky,

I found a party in one of the rooms down the hall. When I appeared at the door, Colin, a freelance journalist with a contract to cover Chechnya for *Newsweek*, told me to come and have a drink because I looked like I could use one.

'I could do with company more,' I said to the room in general.

'Ah, well, if it be company you're after, Sunshine, and 'tis enjoyment you'd be seeking, you're probably in the wrong place,' offered Hamish, the correspondent from the *Scottish Times*. 'May I humbly suggest, me darling, that you exit door left, stage right, and walk about two and a half thousand miles to Paris where you'll be sure to find some company on such a bonny winter's evening. Come on, Kate,' he said, patting the floor beside him, 'take a pew and let me dazzle you with me latest escapades in beautiful downtown Grozny with me mad Russian pals. Sure you'll not be wanting a wee dram?' He proffered a flask.

'Quit with the fake accent, Hamish.'

'Right. So why don't you just sit next to me, Kate, and make my day.'

As I settled in next to Hamish he put his arm around my shoulder and offered me his flask. 'Here, it'll do you good.'

I shrugged his arm off before taking a long swig of a fiery liquid that burned my throat and took my breath away. 'Holy cow! What is that?'

Everyone in the room laughed.

'I've no bloody idea,' Hamish said. 'The Ruskies gave it to me.'

When I was passed a joint I hesitated only a second before taking a long toke. I had never liked marijuana much because it usually made me giggle and feel out of control, and I hated hangovers so I seldom overindulged in alcohol, but on that evening I was on a mission to wipe myself out. Pete and I had nearly died the day before, and the fact that we were still alive and we were friends again surely deserved some sort of celebration. And since Pete was obviously organising his own celebration, there was no option for me but to create my own.

The main topic of conversation was the fact that this was the most vicious war anyone had seen, and the general consensus was that we all needed to leave the capital in general, and that hotel in particular, as soon as possible. A few people mentioned that they'd seen a number of journalists making camp a little way out of Grozny in a former kindergarten, where they had turned the playground into a huge transmission station crammed with portable satellite dishes. There followed a general agreement that everyone would head off to the kindergarten in the morning.

The room must have been Luc Vos's because he had prime position on the only chair. I couldn't help staring at him and he caught my eye a few times until I no longer knew if I was watching him or he was watching me, which may or may not have had something to do with the amount of illegal substance I had inhaled.

A psychologist friend had once told me helpfully that if I met the eyes of a male stranger across a room three times, each time longer than the last, then he would instinctively interpret it as a signal to approach. Apparently it was a deep primal mating urge. The critical issue about real attraction, she stressed, was the time factor. I needed to increase the length of eye contact on each glance. Personally, I'd always found this eye thing a bit deceptive, and was not sure I could be so clear about the signals I was giving and those I was receiving. Sometimes I found myself not at all attracted to someone I was making eye contact with, but was looking at him because I had noticed that he was looking at me. Or conversely, he was looking at me because he'd noticed I was looking at him. But wherever it had started, it definitely was not attraction.

Luc Vos's attention, however, was rarely unwanted. With dark curly hair, olive skin and the deepest blue eyes on the planet, Bella had once described him to me as eye candy. Looking at Luc Vos, she said, was good for the soul.

I suspected I was probably making a fool of myself with Vos and was just considering leaving when he got out of his chair and stepped over me to reach the window, where he peeled back an edge of the gaffer tape and plastic that covered the space where the glass should have been. In any normal town, in any normal country, if that much smoke had billowed out of a hotel window the fire brigade or the drug squad would have been banging down the door within minutes, but on that night in Grozny all that arrived in the room was sub-zero air. Stepping over me on his way back to his chair he dropped a jumper into my lap, motioning for me to put it on. I giggled. Christ, no more dope for me.

'Are you a fucking Eskimo, Vos? Close the fucking window!' complained Colin, turning his jacket collar up around his neck.

'Shit, Luc, always knew you had a perverse streak.' Hamish rose somewhat unsteadily to his feet, which made me want to giggle again. 'Anyway, there seems to be something happening here that I'm not included in.' There were muffled clearings of throats, and the collecting of glasses and bottles as everyone got up to leave. Not particularly sure if I should leave also I stood, but Luc caught my arm. For my part I simply wanted to forget everything and lose myself in whatever the man had to offer—another reaction to the dope.

About twenty minutes later I gradually became aware again of the sub-zero temperature in the room. I also become aware that there was nothing elegant about lying on a bed with a T-shirt up around my neck and no knickers on, next to someone who was in a similar state of disarray and was, in all respects, except for the fact that our bodies had just been rapturously intimate, a complete stranger. To cover myself with the blanket would imply I was intending to stay, which I was not; I never fancied waking up in the morning with my naked limbs entangled with the naked limbs of someone I hardly knew.

As Luc reached for the blanket I pulled my T-shirt back down and got up to gather my clothes. Picking his clothes up from the floor at the same time I tossed them onto the bed without looking in his direction, offering him his dignity and hoping that he was allowing me mine. When I was fully dressed I turned to see that he was not. Having taken the rest of his clothes off, Luc was now under the blankets watching me.

'Hello, Kate Price,' he said with a smile. 'So very nice to meet you again. You could stay, you know, and we could keep each other warm tonight. Perhaps take things a little slower and get to know each other better until the morning.' He was holding back the covers, enticing me into his bed with a reminder of what I'd just enjoyed and what I would be missing.

'I can't.' I mumbled about needing to sleep and other things of no importance until I found myself at the door and could make my inelegant exit.

Hours later, unable to sleep, I lay alone in my bed feeling miserable. The alcohol and drugs had worn off and I had a massive headache building. I wanted nothing more than to forget what little I could remember of the night before.

Later that day most of us moved on to the kindergarten, and although Luc and I shared a room we did so with a couple of dozen others, all bunking down on the floor of an abandoned classroom. Everyone was hungry, dirty, tired and short-tempered. We all smelt, some snored and few slept, while any thoughts of sex were lost in the struggle to survive and report in any meaningful sense on the war whose carnage, for the second time in my career, sometimes left my reportage wanting.

In the afternoons or evenings, when Pete and I returned, I would find Luc, or he would search me out, and we would sit and talk. I discovered that he cared deeply about his job and what he hoped to achieve with his photographs, but he also cared about the destruction of the natural environment. It didn't take me long to realise that this man was so much more than eye candy. While Luc didn't make me laugh, and we didn't tease each other the way Pete and I did, I found myself looking forward to seeing him and our time together.

With the former Ms CBS moving on, and me spending most of my free time with Luc, I noticed that Pete spent a lot of time by himself. Sometimes he'd talk briefly with one or two other journalists, but mostly at the end of the day he'd find a quiet corner where he could read undisturbed. Occasionally, when I might look up unexpectedly, I'd see him watching Luc and me.

One afternoon, about two weeks after we'd moved to the kindergarten, Luc returned from a trip south of Grozny to take me around the side of the classroom and give me a long passionate kiss before telling me that he was leaving. When he'd gone, I found myself missing him. About a week later word came through that he'd been seriously injured after being caught in crossfire between the rebels and the Russian military. I tried to find out the extent of his injuries and if they were life-threatening but the Russians had airlifted him out and because he freelanced I didn't know how to contact him. I eventually heard that he'd been in and out of hospital for months to repair a shattered leg.

A year or so after that I heard that he was working for *National Geographic*, spending his time in some of the most remote places on the planet rather than the most dangerous. Many of those who had worked with him explained his failure to return to the job with the old adage that if you couldn't run, you couldn't do war, but I wondered if Luc was finally where he really needed to be.

When Pete heard the news about Luc he was solicitous, asking me every now and then if I was okay. 'Sure,' I said at last, 'it wasn't as if I was in love with the guy.'

With both Luc and Ms CBS out of the picture, Pete and I fell back into our old ways, but for a long time, and on the oddest of occasions, I'd find myself thinking of Luc.

Some days Pete and I returned to Grozny to spend the day moving through the city with the militiamen who had remained living in the hotel we had abandoned. One afternoon, as we watched them heading out of town and were wondering if we should just pack it in and go home, one of them turned from across the road and called to Pete, 'Hey, big shot photoman, we're going to front. You want come?'

'Her too?' Pete said, hooking his thumb my way.

'Sure. Her too. Of course.' With that we grabbed our bags, paid Umar off and were gone.

Chapter 24

ROLLING OVER STIFFLY ON THE DIRT FLOOR, I WINCED. MY hips and shoulders were bruised from sleeping rough with the militia for nearly two weeks, and the right side of my face had developed an ugly red rash from a hitherto unknown allergy to dust, or straw, or bedbugs, or maybe even the Chechens.

When first light began to filter in through the cracks in the old barn walls, and I heard a rooster crow far off in the village, I climbed out of my sleeping bag and picked my way over the sleeping bodies of the militiamen. Closing the barn door on the musty smell of cow shit, wet wool and old sweat, I stepped out into a crisp, mud-scented morning, moving past the bloody carcass of the cow the militia had slaughtered the night before to stand under an ancient fir tree. Six inches of fresh snow had fallen overnight. I shivered and, pulling my jacket tighter around my neck, buried my hands deep within its pockets. I'd been freezing for so many weeks that it felt as if winter had taken up residence in my bones.

Down in the valley a river, black and swollen by an unseasonable melt high in the Caucasus, rushed towards the sea, while high up in the mountains the first rays of sun were turning the ice on their peaks to fire. The morning was so quiet and still that it seemed the world was holding its breath. When a light came on in a farmhouse below I watched until a twist of smoke curled up from the chimney and pictured someone poking at the embers with a practised hand until a lick of flame caught under the newly laid wood. A couple of minutes later the door opened and a farmer and his dog stepped out into the snow, to be framed by the light fanning out over the frozen ground. But when the door closed it took with it the promise of home and hearth and of a loving warmth. Perhaps, I mused as I leaned my back up against the fir tree, my imagination had run away with me again. Perhaps the door had been closed on the farmer and his wife's own private war of silence: cold backs in a bed that no longer saw love.

With a woollen beanie pulled down low over his forehead, the farmer shuffled along a well-trodden path towards his barn, his dog following close on his heels. Soon chickens were scurrying out through the barn doors, squawking and flapping their useless wings as they scrambled between the legs of the cows, who were skittish from the farmer's prods. Somewhere deep in the valley another rooster crowed; a dog yapped; a tractor spluttered into life and doors began opening and closing. The village was waking up as a fog rolled down over the river to block the farm from view.

Aware that someone had come up behind me I turned to see Pete just as he was reaching out to pull a piece of straw from my hair. He looked exhausted, the lines etched heavy down his face. After throwing the straw on the ground he lifted his gloved hands to his mouth and blew a cloud of warm air into them. 'Here,' he said, taking my beanie out of his pocket. I must have left it in the barn.

'Your scar's not too bad,' I said. I reached out to touch the still-raw jagged line above his eyebrow but pulled my hand back. The time with the militia had taken its toll on both of us. There was no more bantering. No laughter between us. For nearly a fortnight we had moved with them, listening to their tales of death and heroism. Russian helicopters, they told us, dropped the broken bodies of young Russian conscripts into the woods under the cover of dark. The kids were deserters caught trying to escape the war and had been killed by their own commanders—desertion was a term their political masters back in the Kremlin had become somewhat sensitive about. With their bodies so disposed their files would be stamped with the more acceptable MISSING IN ACTION.

A young fellow who carried a kitten with him in his greatcoat and petted and talked to it incessantly had told me quietly as we sat together by a fire one evening that he no longer had the heart to kill the Russian boy-soldiers. I peered at him through the flickering glow, our faces red from the fire's heat and our backs freezing. His erupting adolescent skin and slight frame made me think he was no older than the Russian boy-soldiers he could no longer kill. 'I hear them crying in woods sometimes in night so I shoot them in leg so their mothers come take them home again.'

We both turned to gaze into the flames. What a strange upside-down world it was when shooting someone in the leg could be seen as an act of compassion.

During the day I often found my eyes drawn back to this boy, easily able to imagine him as someone's beloved son, but never as someone's lover. I watched him as he played with his kitten, feeding it before he fed himself; showering love onto the furry little bundle. Even the toughest, the most battle-hardened among the militia, found time to pet the little kitten.

On the previous afternoon the militia had blasted their way into the house of a man they claimed was a Russian sympathiser, executing him along with all his family. Pete and I had no idea beforehand what their intentions were, and it had all happened so quickly that there was nothing either of us could do. After dragging the furniture out of the house, the militia had reconstructed the family's lounge room in the barn where we had slept that night. With the traitor's supply of homemade ninety-per-cent-proof alcohol warming their veins, and one of his cows filling their bellies, the militiamen tried to forget the misery of their lives for a while. From my bed in the corner of the barn I watched a couple of the men leave to return only a short time later dressed in the traitor's wife's dresses, her pink lipstick smeared across their lips. The party had ratcheted up a notch after that and with Pete and the young boy with his kitten positioning themselves between me and the men I had turned away, and prayed for the oblivion of a dreamless sleep.

Trapped in a muddy ditch with our militia friends two days before as shells split the air above our heads and the acrid smell of cordite filled our mouths, the bile of terror had risen up again in my throat and I had made yet another of my pacts with the God I did not believe in. How many pacts with how many gods until my luck ran out? Was the great guru in the sky keeping a tally? I hoped not. Would He one day proclaim from on high, 'Well, my child, look at the list: Sarajevo, Palestine, Rwanda,

Goma. How many times have you broken your word to me? Do you really feel that you deserve another saving?' And I would agree that I was a miserable soul who did not deserve another saving, but if He could just see His way clear this one last time I would change. And in those moments I swear I believed my own lie, but when the terror had passed and I was high with the exhilaration of survival I would forget my promises—until the next time.

As Pete and I stood together I reached into my pocket for one of the eucalyptus leaves I collected whenever I returned to the old house in Sydney, but when I rubbed a brittle fragment between my fingers to release its sweet memory of the garden by the sea all I could smell was the stench of decay under my nails.

The Chechen militiamen, coughing and cussing, were beginning to straggle out of the barn to piss in the snow, warm air rising up from their thin yellow streams. I was tired of the heavy grey of this country, of the militia and the Russians and their stinking war. These men would be moving down through the valley soon and the Russian tanks would come rumbling along the narrow village roads after them, destroying everything in their path. The thoughts of warm days and sunshine in an old house overlooking the blue Pacific constricted my throat and I realised I no longer had the stomach to watch their work.

'I'm going home to Sydney,' I said to Pete. 'I don't know when I'll see you again.'

'It'll happen when it needs to happen.'

Larry loved the story about the babushka and the children in Prigorodnoye. He also loved the one about the young boy-soldier with the kitten and the Russian boy-soldiers, which saw me nominated for my second British Press Award. The Russians were less appreciative of my writing, informing Larry that my journalist's visa for Chechnya had expired and would not be renewed. I didn't care. I never wanted to go back.

Chapter 25

Sydney

January 1999

I WOKE IN THE DARK DISORIENTED AND, AS USUAL, I WAITED. It is the smells I notice first. Always the smells. On that morning it was the sweet, honey scent of orange jasmine floating over a heavier, pungent odour of neglect: mothballs and the dust of years. Tantalising fragments of memory began floating around in my head, filling my heart with the sweetness of summer, but the memory of where I was and what bed I was in remained maddeningly elusive. I continued to lie with my eyes closed. It was a game. Seaweed and sea salt, the sound of surf crashing on rocks, but the clue that placed me in that bed, in the room over the ocean, was the creaking of the tin roof overhead as it expanded with the first warm rays of the morning sun, and my heart swelled with the old joy and I opened my eyes. I was in my parents' bed in the old beach house in Sydney.

When I was a small child and we moved to Australia with my father's job he had rented the old 1920s fibro cottage on the hill above the beach. With its pink bath and matching pink hand basin stained rusty brown by a persistently dripping tap, it was not what my mother had been expecting. She detested the orange and brown checked carpet in the bedrooms and the split cane furniture with faded green covers in the lounge room. The old timber cupboards in the kitchen that held the owner's chipped holiday crockery and dented aluminium pots were also not to her liking. The cracked linoleum on the kitchen floor, the red-brick fireplace that never worked and all the rubbish left in the garage whose door would never close completely were nearly more than she could take. To her unalloyed horror, my father went a step further and purchased the house and all its furniture on the day we returned to England. His punishment for such daring had been my mother's refusal ever to set foot in Australia again and my father, his spirit of defiance broken, acquiesced.

As the house's sole visitor over the years I had not changed a thing, partly because I didn't have the funds to do so, and partly because I liked to imagine my father's delight when he returned to find the place exactly as he remembered it. Mostly, though, I didn't change a thing because I loved it just the way it was. Returning to that house was like returning to my childhood: a gloriously simple time of floppy hats and baggy swimming costumes; of zinc-painted noses and salt-encrusted skin and a freckle-faced girl with hair bleached the colour and texture of straw. My memories of perfect happiness may have been illusory, but I treasured them beyond nearly anything else. When I thought I could no longer bear to look at what was happening around me, when I thought I was losing my mind or had lost my faith in humanity or both, then I would reach into my pocket for the eucalyptus leaf and its delicious medicinal scent would carry me back to this simpler time and place. Pete had his stories of his wayward youth with Sam, I had my house by the sea.

I swam at dawn every morning in the warm ocean currents until within a month the house and the sea and the old friendships of my childhood had worked their magic on me again. With my soul soothed I was once again strong enough to return to work.

Flying into Riyadh, I did a story on an eight-year-old girl married to a sixty-five-year-old man. I wasn't allowed to speak with the girl, but she sent me a message professing her love for her husband. The cleric I interviewed told me there was nothing wrong with these pairings, adding that, 'If girls are raised properly, they are ready for marriage at that age, sometimes even earlier.'

I then travelled to the Punjab in Pakistan to cover the story of women disfigured with acid by their husbands because they didn't want sex or were thought to have been unfaithful.

Back in London I did some articles for the paper's Sunday magazine. There was the battered women's refuge where one woman told me that being hit was not the worst of it—being hit was the release. It was waiting to be hit that was unbearable. I interviewed a victim of sexual abuse who said her sense of self-preservation was so honed that she could smell a sexual predator from twenty paces.

'Did you know evil has a smell?' she said.

'So you think evil exists?' I asked, curious to hear her answer.

'Once, on a train, a man sat behind me. I never saw his face, but I was literally scared stiff. My legs went numb and I could barely breathe. I felt the presence of evil in a way I'd never felt it before. No one will ever convince me that it was imagined; that it was a blip in my sanity. I could smell him the same way I could smell the other men who had abused me. Evil was seeping out of his skin.' She sat silently on her lounge, lost in her memories. 'When you've seen it, felt it, smelt it, and when you've looked into its eyes,' she continued at last, 'then you know without any doubt that evil exists. I'm sorry, lady, but if you're asking me the question then you've never come across evil.'

Then there was the story I sat on for six months. At eighty-six years old, Coral had euthanised her husband of sixty-six years. Bert, she told me with tears streaming down her face, had terminal bone cancer and had been in terrible pain, begging her to help him die and because she loved him so much she had complied. When I asked how she knew what to do she just laughed, 'Oh, my dear, it's everywhere on the web if you know where to look.' Larry and I were concerned that should the authorities discover Coral's identity the ramifications for her would be serious, but Coral insisted that she had only told me the story so it would be published. 'What's the worst they could do to me? Put me in jail at eighty-six years of age? Now that could be interesting!' Her daughter filled my inbox with emails begging me not to publish, but in the end we changed Coral's name and printed the story. Coral was well satisfied.

I thought about the nature of love a lot after Coral's story—which had to be better than thinking about the nature of evil. Love, I decided, wasn't always expressed in ways we necessarily understood to be love, and was not always found where we would expect it to be. In the end it was Pete who would lead me to a story of love in the most unlikely of places.

Chapter 26

KwaZulu-Natal
February 2002

WHEN PETE RANG FROM JOHANNESBURG TO SEE WHAT I WAS doing I told him I was in back in London trying to interest Larry in a really brilliant story on Mugabe and Zimbabwe. His response was less than flattering. I needed to go with him to a hospital in KwaZulu-Natal, where he had been commissioned to shoot for *A Day in the Life of Africa*. When I asked what was so amazing about this hospital he told me: 'AIDS.'

'You really crack me up, McDermott. You're telling me not to go to Zimbabwe because no one cares, but you want me to do a story on AIDS in Africa. That's the deadest story on the planet, if you will excuse the pun.'

'They'll be interested in this one, I promise. How about I come to Zimbabwe with you and let Mugabe's men take potshots at me instead of at your sorry arse, then you come to Tugela Ferry in KwaZulu with me? You won't regret it, I promise you.'

After returning from Australia I'd worked on various stories that Pete wasn't particularly interested in, and then for much of 2001 I had been covering the lead-up to Milosevic's trial in The Hague, while Pete had been working in Macedonia, the Sudan and then in the US, covering 9/11 and its aftermath for his magazine. We hadn't seen each other for twelve months, although we continued to speak often on the phone and were in almost daily email contact. After focusing on Milosevic for months I needed to get out into the real world and I wanted to see Pete again. The Zimbabwe story clearly didn't have legs and my enthusiasm had been waning anyway so I approached Larry with the idea of KwaZulu-Natal. When he told me the paper wasn't interested in the AIDS story I took leave—with his blessing—and flew myself to Johannesburg where I met with Pete and Bella, who had also been commissioned to shoot for the book.

It was the first time I had been back to Africa since Rwanda and Goma, and I hadn't realised until I was on the plane just how the prospect of returning filled me with dread. What had happened between Pete and me had long been buried by both of us, but the images of Nyarubuye could not be buried and the nightmares were never far from the surface. The possibility of triggering them again filled me with horror.

At dinner that evening at a little Austrian restaurant, Pete was in fine form. 'Did I ever tell you about the time Sam and I did a gig at the local hall?' Without waiting for an answer he continued, 'I'd been practising this Pete Townshend move with the guitar where he does a huge great arch with his arm and slams down on the chords and, well, I thought I was doing pretty good, but just as I was about to finish—'

'No, don't tell me you went all the way and smashed your guitar onstage?' laughed Bella. Clearly she had not heard the story before.

'Close. I might have if I'd got the chance, but just before we finished some tosser jumped onstage and kicked the speaker in. Smashing my guitar seemed a little anticlimactic after that and I really couldn't afford it anyway. You know, I didn't think we were that bad—at least Sam could sing in tune by then.'

'I thought you were the lead singer,' I said, knowing full well that he wasn't and why he wasn't, but Pete must have forgotten I knew and had no idea I was setting him up.

'It's not that I didn't want to, I just had a minor impediment. I'm tone deaf. They wouldn't let me near a microphone. Actually, before I discovered how bad I was I used to sing without realising they'd turned my microphone off. In the end they just took it away.'

'No, come on, surely you can sing,' said Bella. 'You can do everything, Peter McDermott.'

'Go on, Pete, let's hear if you can sing,' I said, laughing, as I refilled our glasses.

Grabbing the pepper mill Pete launched into the opening lines of Van Morrison's 'Moon Dance': *'Well, it's a marvellous night—'*

'Stop—enough,' begged Bella. 'You'll have us thrown out.'

'Go on, Van Morrison,' I encouraged, still laughing. 'Sing some more.'

'No,' said Bella emphatically.

'Okay,' I said, 'tell Bella about your very first gig.'

'Ah, well, that would be the fifteenth birthday party. We thought we were pretty hot, but the parents made us set up in the lounge room, because they didn't want the noise to disturb the neighbours. All the kids were outside in the garden secretly getting trashed, while we were playing in the lounge room to the oldies, who couldn't really appreciate our musical talents and sat there staring at us. In the end the father switched the power off and told us that we sounded better without the noise.'

'What's your friend Sam doing now?' Bella asked.

'I've no idea. We lost touch.'

I simply loved being with the man. The three of us had a wonderful night together, and later, back in the hotel room Bella and I were sharing, she and I talked until dawn about all the places we had been together and all the secrets we shared. With Bella flying out to Malawi for her gig and Pete and I flying on to Pietermaritzburg, from where we would make the two-hour drive to the hospital, we parted immediately after breakfast.

After driving an hour west of Pietermaritzburg, through land neatly cultivated by the white settlers and planted with the fir and pine of their distant ancestors, the road began to incline, and the soft verdant greens and ordered forests gave way to a pebbly, dry brown land shimmering under a deep, empty sky. Small abodes in various states of disrepair began to appear, along with the odd dilapidated roadside kiosk with the obligatory old man and mangy dog lolling around outside in the shade. Rounding a high, wide corner on the crest of a hill, we suddenly found ourselves looking down onto a valley bleached dry by the African sun.

Covered in thornbushes and littered with great masses of exposed rock glistening in the late afternoon sun, the valley, which stretched as far as the eye could see, appeared deserted except for the occasional goat sheltering in a dusty spot under a bush. On the drive down we passed small groups of children in neat red uniforms ambling up the hill as the afternoon heat swam liquid on the hot tar under their bare feet. We passed a woman sweeping a dry patch of dirt in front of her home as chickens pecked around her skirt. Further along another woman looked up from lifting washing stiff from the sun off the bushes around her house. A man with a skullcap of crinkly grey hair, bent low with the weight of his years, shuffled along the side of the road pushing two cows before him with a stick. Children resting on a dry stone wall with their school bags thrown in the dirt below them cheered and waved as we sped by. The deeper we travelled into that valley the more the little bush communities began to appear through the low shrub: rondavels, the traditional round mud huts with their thatched roofs, and the ugly besser brick houses topped with rusty tin, belonging to the more affluent of the villagers. At the valley's centre, where the heat hung heaviest, snaked the muddy Tugela River and the township of Tugela Ferry. The Church of Scotland Hospital was sprawled along its far reaches.

After crossing the single-lane bridge that had long ago replaced the old ferry service for which the town had been named, we turned away from the blaze of the sun sinking purple and red behind the hills and made our way up the dusty main street. On either side of us were stalls and temporary kiosks displaying over-bright plastic goods and an assortment of packaged groceries. A woman selling a meagre few vegetables from an old felt blanket sat in the gutter next to a pile of rotting cabbages. Faded signs for Coca-Cola, Surf and OMO adorned the sides of various buildings, while a billboard that held pride of place at the top of the street extolled the virtues of an alcoholic beverage that promised: *True Greatness Comes From Within.*

Turning into the gates of the hospital we waited as a scabby dog rose stiffly from the middle of the road, stretched, then moved off to a spot just beyond our tyres' reach. As we pulled up, Tony Moll, the doctor in charge of the hospital, hurried out to greet Pete, who introduced us. Hastily apologising for not being able to welcome us properly, he instructed our driver, Sembesi, to take us to his house so we could meet his family and settle in before he joined us for dinner.

The following day Pete rose before dawn to start shooting for *A Day in the Life of Africa*, intending to catch the sunrise and early activity along the main road before joining us in the hospital. His only brief, like all the photographers commissioned for the book, was to photograph positive images of the continent. When I asked Pete how he was going to do that in a hospital filled with AIDS patients he just smiled.

Built at the beginning of the 1900s, the Church of Scotland Hospital had grown in a hotch-potch manner to accommodate the increasing demands of the community, with old red-brick buildings giving way to the more fragile prefab constructions. Although the wards were spotlessly clean, when the AIDS epidemic hit Tugela Ferry in the mid-eighties, there were never going to be enough beds or funds to deal with its demands so that patients were soon relegated to thin vinyl mattresses on the floor, or old army-issue iron beds on the covered verandas. On average, two people died each day in the hospital from AIDS and its related illnesses, Tony told me as we moved around the wards.

'Twenty per cent of the patients we have are from here while the rest are from Durban, Pietermaritzburg, Dundee, Greytown, Ladysmith and all the neighbouring towns and cities,' he explained. 'They have walked past their own hospitals to come to us and you have to ask why. What has brought the Church of Scotland Hospital to the fore is the fact that we are doing something positive about AIDS. In many of the other hospitals you have the thinking that says there is nothing you can do for AIDS patients because the person is going to die anyway. When you have that attitude then you have a climate of hopelessness. We try to create a positive atmosphere. We keep patients in the wards if they need help; if they need blood we give them blood, if they need expensive medication we will give it to them. We have come under criticism from our government department, which says we are keeping patients too long, but don't blame us for trying to do our work.

'Our nurses, who really do . . . how should I say it? . . . the dirty work of looking after AIDS patients, they understand that the small help that you give makes a big difference to that individual. So we are doing our very, very best for AIDS patients, and our nurses and the community understand that we are trying our best.'

As colourful mobiles drifted in the faint breeze in the children's ward, mothers sitting on the floor nursing or playing with their children seemed to occupy every available space. I spoke with some of the women but they were shy, not understanding what it was that I wanted from them. Not one of the mothers would say that her child was sick because of the AIDS virus. Most professed not to know what was wrong and then they smiled with their children for Pete's camera.

Because I wouldn't be able to offer any of Pete's photos from that day with my story I also had to take photos, but I was a reluctant shooter. The AIDS patients, either used to photographers, or with no energy to turn away, looked directly down the lens at me. I had never come to terms with taking photos of another's suffering and was uncomfortable with what I had to do, but Tony was keen for me to get some good photographs.

In one of the iron cots we passed was a boy about two years old. His skin no longer fitted over his skinny frame as he lay motionless, staring out through the bars of the cot. Noticing I had stopped Tony returned to explain that the nurses did what they could for the boy, but they were overworked and there seldom was enough time to give the dying orphan the attention and love he deserved. As I leaned down to pick the little fellow up his stick arms fell limp and his head flopped against my shoulder. He weighed about five kilos. Turning to walk with him I caught Pete taking a photograph of us and was furious, angrily telling him that he should have asked permission first. With the boy lying against my shoulder I walked the wards, patting his back and murmuring little endearments impossible for him to understand.

On the covered veranda of the women's ward a woman of indeterminate age lay on a thin, grey blanket on the floor. A clear plastic bottle of water, a tin cup and her history chart were arranged against the green concrete wall beside her. As Pete lifted his camera to shoot and Tony pulled the woman's gown up over her shoulder to cover her naked breast she looked unblinkingly into the lens. Her husband, Tony explained as we began to walk on, used to return home once or twice a year from the mining hostels, and on one of these visits had given his wife AIDS. Now he no longer returned, or sent money to support her and their three children. He was probably dead, as she soon would be. Whenever the woman went into hospital her children were farmed out to various families so that even as she lay dying, she was constantly worried about who would care for her children when she was gone.

In African society, orphaned children used to be absorbed into extended families, but the scope of the epidemic was making this impossible. Unlike any other epidemic, AIDS destroys the strongest in society so that only the old and the very young are left.

When we finished the rounds in the men's ward and it was time to visit the outlying villages I returned the baby to his cot. As I laid him down his body collapsed into the mattress like a rag doll, and without the energy to move himself he lay motionless where I had placed him, staring up at the ceiling. I leaned down to turn him over to face the bars of the cot again, my heart aching for the life he had been given. Before leaving I blew up coloured balloons I had stuffed in my pockets for the children, ashamed at what I now saw as the miserliness of my gift.

We had six patients to visit that day in the villages. They were all part of the hospital's outsourcing program designed to manage the disease. Teaching volunteers how to look after terminally ill patients in their own homes relieved some of the pressure on the hospital and its scant resources. Each carer visited her patients once or twice a week, and should she feel the patient was deteriorating or not managing at home, she would contact the hospital and Tony would visit.

Near the end of the day, as we pulled into the last village, perched on the high side of a hill, we were greeted by a horde of children running behind the car, the older children carrying the very young on their hips. Some had shorts on that were way too big, or oversized T-shirts that fell below their knees, while the youngest were blessedly naked in the scorching heat. The local carer explained that this village had lost nearly all its young adults so that the responsibility for all the children, and any surviving AIDS patients, had fallen to the old woman we could see standing with her arms folded in the shaded doorway of her rondavel.

Opening the back of the car, the nurses began to distribute clothes and toys donated from around the world. Picking up a pair of ice skates from some well-meaning Norwegian, they laughed and tossed them into the back again. Most of the children ran off with their newfound booty, except for one little toddler who, wearing nothing but a pair of red shoes that were far too big for him, stood staring at the pull-along train now resting in his hands. Squatting down to his level I smiled reassuringly and gently took the train to show him how it worked, but the dry earth was covered in stones and rough wiry patches of wilting grass so that every time I pulled the engine it tumbled over. Frustrated, I looked around for a better idea and saw that the ground outside the grandmother's hut had been swept clean of stones. Hoisting the boy up onto my hip I headed up the hill. Sensing that something was up the other children came running to the hut, but every time I pulled the train on this new ground it still tumbled over, until everyone except the train's new owner and me was laughing.

'You've such a way with kids, my beautiful Kate,' said Pete, laughing as he shot photograph after photograph.

Defeated by the train, but determined to win the little man's approval, I decided on a diversionary tactic. Pulling balloons from my pocket I began to blow them up, handing the first balloon—a red one to match his shoes—to the little boy. Blowing up a few more, I offered the packet to Pete for him to help me, but he was busy taking photographs of the children in the dirt outside the hut holding their brightly coloured balloons. Soon the toy train lay forgotten at our feet as Pete, Tony and I all took photographs of the children with their balloons. Noticing Pete's attention had turned, I looked to see what had caught his interest. Two little boys were ambling away. One was about three years old and naked but for an oversized T-shirt. He had his arm wrapped across the shoulders of another naked boy about two years old. They looked like two old men out for a Sunday stroll except for their beautiful, soft coffee-coloured bottoms, and the blue and pink balloons bobbing along behind them.

As our little crowd dispersed we moved off to the rondavel of the AIDS patient Tony was there to visit, and permission was sought for Pete and me to enter. After the glare of the midday sun, and the hot crush of the back seat of the car, the traditional mud home with its thatched roof was blessedly cool. Lying on a bed, covered by a blanket, the patient offered us a shy smile as we took our seats with the others along two benches that had been placed against the wall. When my eyes adjusted to the dark I saw that this home, with its dirt floor and neatly stacked cooking pots and containers of grain, was spotless.

After taking our seats we sat in silence. We sat and we sat. This was Africa time, I kept reminding myself in an attempt to still my impatience. Unlike Westerners, Africans usually found no need to fill empty spaces with chatter. Eventually the carer began a soft, slow conversation with the man. Questions were asked and answers given. Slow, reflective Africa time. When the carer had finished, one of the nurses from the hospital asked more questions of the patient. There was no need to hurry. More questions. More answers. More soft voices. More Africa time. When it seemed that everyone's concerns had been satisfied, Tony rose and crossed the dirt floor to examine the man and the decision was made to admit him to hospital. Tony sat down again and the silence returned. Just as I was surrendering to this slow-moving Africa time and the silence within the cool, dry hut, one of the nurses breathed in deeply and raised her strong and clear voice in a beautiful Zulu hymn. One by one each of the Africans in that room, including the patient, joined in until that cool dark hut with its mud walls and its dirt floor, in that barren valley in Africa, in a country and a continent blighted by the scourge of AIDS, became a place of grace, more reverent, more beautiful, than any place of worship I had ever been.

Tugela Ferry was a love story and it gave back to me what Rwanda had taken away. So overwhelmed was I by the depth of emotion that swept through me, the singing in that hut would become the most profound memory of all my years on the road, while the photos of the two little old men-children would be my most cherished.

As we walked down the hill to the car I watched Pete, just ahead of me. Throughout the day he had gone about his business quietly and with respect for those he was photographing. He never pried or demanded to see the worst there was, like so many other photographers. I would always love this man, I thought. No matter what happened between us in the future, I would always love him. Catching up with him I linked my arm through his and smiled up at him. Smiling back, he squeezed my hand then pulled away. 'I've got to talk to Tony,' he said, and strode off.

Pete's photograph of the two little old men with their pink and blue balloons was used in *A Day in the Life of Africa*.

Chapter 27

London

March 2002

FOR A NUMBER OF YEARS MY PARENTS HAD BEEN ASKING TO meet Pete, for despite my protestations to the contrary they believed, perhaps even hoped, that there was more to our relationship than a friendship between work colleagues. When we left Tugela Ferry, Pete flew back with me to England to see his family before he was due to head back to New York. Under renewed pressure from my parents I took the opportunity on the plane to invite him to have lunch with my family and to my surprise he said yes. It was awful.

When I arrived Mother asked if I had brought something nicer to change into. So I changed into a red velvet dress that used to be hers and wound a fine silver necklace around my ankle before appearing back in the sitting room barefoot. She must have recognised the dress for she went pale when I walked into the room, but she didn't say anything.

I was on my third glass of wine when Pete arrived and watched with alarm as my parents nearly knocked each other over in the race to open the door for him. I reached for the wine bottle again. In a serious charm offensive Pete had arrived with two dozen pink roses for my mother and some outrageously expensive Belgian chocolates, along with a bottle of French wine for my father. I then sat in dumb astonishment as my mother fluttered around Pete—I could only call it fluttering, though I could not remember ever having seen her flutter before. When she announced lunch was served, Pete took her arm to escort her into the dining room where he proceeded to pull out her chair. She fluttered up at him again, perhaps even giggled, but by then I was past being shocked and way past being sober. I did, however, notice we were using the best crystal and silver, together with the setting that was only for very special occasions, such as possible visits from the Queen. I groaned and reached for the bottle again, after which my father moved it to the far end of the table.

During lunch Dad sounded like he was quizzing Pete for a prospective son-in-law position, while Mother fussed around him as if he was the potential father of the long-awaited first grandchild. Offering extra helpings of meat, she inquired about his taste in food, for what I could only assume would be future happy family get-togethers like weddings and christenings. I drank, and when I wasn't drinking I was telling my parents that Pete was not interested in whatever it was they had to offer via way of food or conversation. By the time coffee was served the four of us had retreated into an uncomfortable silence. No one really knew how to behave except Pete, whose behaviour was impeccable. He did not say 'fuck', or goad me into saying 'fuck'; he engaged my parents in polite conversation, seemingly fascinated by their responses, and when he left he did not tell them he had a war to go to. I made my apologies and retreated to my room with a headache as soon as the door closed behind him.

The next day I caught the train up to London nursing a filthy hangover made worse by each hot memory of the previous day. Pete and I had arranged to meet in a coffee shop in Marylebone High Street before he flew back to the States. We were ostensibly going to discuss the latest news on Afghanistan and the rumours we were hearing about the possibility of a US invasion of Iraq. My first priority, though, was to apologise to him for the whole fiasco.

When he arrived he placed a large manila envelope on the table between us. 'What're you reading?' he said, indicating the unread magazine open on the table in front of me. I told him I was learning how to turn my man into a tiger in bed. 'Really? Have you got a man you can turn into a tiger in bed?'

'I'm working on it.'

'Who's the lucky candidate?'

'Well, I don't know that yet.'

'I wonder if you're getting out enough, Kate.'

'Now you're channelling my mother.'

'Speaking of which, your mother is delightful. I can see where you get your charm and beauty from.'

'Are you being facetious, McDermott?'

'Certainly not.' He picked up the menu, declaring he was starving.

'I need to apologise for yesterday.'

'Really, which part?'

'All of it.'

'Accepted. Are you going to apologise to your parents also?'

'I already have.'

'Okay, let's eat.'

After talking about Afghanistan and the possibility of us both going there he asked about my Tugela Ferry story and I had to tell him that, despite his promises, I was already having trouble finding a mainstream publisher so I'd been thinking of offering it to an NGO to use in their in-house magazine. 'With any luck it'll get picked up somewhere and maybe do some good.' As I was talking the waitress arrived with my muesli and his mixed grill with a double helping of mushrooms. I eyed his plate, wishing I had ordered something that at least had an aroma.

'You expect too much, Kate,' he said, as we started to eat. 'You're a great journalist, but it's never enough for you. You're always hankering after some utopian dream that will change the world, but haven't you ever thought that maybe it's not your responsibility and that perhaps it's also a little bit arrogant to think that you know better than anyone else how the world should be?'

'Ouch.'

'I'm not trying to hurt you. I just don't like to see you hurting yourself. The world is the way it is because enough people want it to be that way. Let it go, my sweet, let it go.'

'Jesus, McDermott,' I said, dropping my spoon, appetite gone. 'What brought that on? Are you in a bad mood?'

'No, like I said, I'm saying this because I care about you. I hate watching you beating yourself up over things you can't change. You live on hope, Kate. It's your adrenaline. You keep hoping that everything will change, but that's just plain naive. Don't you think that if enough people cared about AIDS in Africa there'd be more resources channelled into the place, and if they didn't want wars there wouldn't be any?'

'I have to have a reason to hope, McDermott.'

'Hope is a waste of good intentions. I don't need hope. Do you think the nurses in Tugela Ferry live on hope? They do what they can do and then they let it go and that's all any of us can do, otherwise we'd go insane.'

'Then why did you want me to go to Tugela Ferry if you knew nothing would change?'

'I thought you might change.'

I had no idea how to take that.

'I thought it might be good for you . . . after Rwanda.'

I inhaled deeply and then let the breath out slowly. How did he know Rwanda still haunted me? I'd never told him about the nightmares and we'd never talked about what I'd seen that night. 'And besides, I think you're a good enough journalist to write something that people will want to read and should read. Here,' he said, pushing his plate with the last of the mushrooms towards me. 'You've been eyeing them off since they arrived.'

'And take this too,' he said, pushing the manila envelope across the table to me as we stood to leave. 'Get someone to print this with your story, with my compliments.'

'What is it?'

'You'll see.'

When I went to open the envelope he reached out and touched my hand. 'Not now, Kemosabe. Later.' Outside the café, as we were about to part, he asked if I knew what *kemosabe* meant.

'Yes, it's a Native American name—the Lone Ranger's friend.'

'But what does it mean?' he persisted.

'Who cares?'

'I care.'

After he'd left I opened the envelope to pull out a photo of me holding the dying boy in Tugela Ferry. His tiny wizened face was burrowed in against my neck and I was looking over my shoulder straight into the camera. Pete must have taken it milliseconds before I registered my anger at him for taking the photograph, because all you could see was the sadness in my eyes. It was one of the most beautiful images I had ever seen. As the tears began to run down my face I looked for him, but he was already gone. When I got home I found a message on my answering machine.

'Kemosabe means trusted friend.'

I sat on the lounge for hours after I listened to the message, thinking about our years together, unaware that night had fallen until I noticed I was freezing and needed to turn the heating on. *Kemosabe means trusted friend.* I thought about all the years of denial, the ducking and weaving around each other and the misunderstandings. I had, for some time, begun quietly hoping for more between us, but it seemed to me that evening that I had left it far too late.

In the end it was Baghdad that finally undid me, but it was also Baghdad that brought us together, and for that I can only be grateful.

Chapter 28

Baghdad
January 2003

THERE WERE NO SUNBAKERS LATE THAT AFTERNOON UNDER THE dusty date palms; no guests frolicking in the bright green algae of the pool. Rising Sphinx-like out of the dung-coloured Baghdad landscape, the Palestine Hotel had been hit hard by the years of sanctions: its tourists long gone and the once-lush gardens a crackly, wilted brown. I would rather have been at the Sheraton next door, or the Al Rasheed across the river, but the Palestine was cheaper. Safer too . . . perhaps. Who could tell what was safe when bombs began falling out of the sky?

Early in January 2003 the lobby of the hotel was crammed with the junkies checking in for the coming war under the watchful eyes of the suited gentleman casually lingering around the reception area. His twin, the moustachioed Saddam lookalike at the front desk, informed me with a smile that it was his pleasure to offer me a room on the fourteenth floor with a view across the Tigris River to one of Saddam's palaces—business had never been so good. Bursting his welcoming bubble, I informed him that I would much prefer a room on the eighth floor, having figured that the eighth floor was high enough to command a view of the city, and at the same time low enough to be able to get to and from my room when the electricity failed and the lifts no longer worked.

He shrugged. I was a Western female journalist checking into a hotel in a city that was soon to be bombed by the greatest military power the world had ever known, so what was rational? After reconfiguring his bookings amid much sighing and scribbling, he handed me the keys to a room that looked and felt like a red-carpeted shipping container with sliding glass doors. The toilet leaked, tiles were missing from the shower recess, and it smelt like an old ashtray. Dumping my bag on one of the two single beds, I sighed. The other bed would be taken up soon by a stranger as the hotel filled up with press, desperate for a bed anywhere.

I moved out onto the balcony and watched as a speedboat flew up the Tigris, rushes quivering in its wake as the call to prayer rang out from the blue-tiled mosque in Firdos Square below. I was satisfied. The view across the muddy Tigris to the grounds of Saddam's palace and beyond was perfect, for the palace was sure to be one of the first targets in the war. The only thing missing for me was Pete. The last time I'd seen him was in Afghanistan. We'd been travelling with the Northern Alliance, but I'd left when winter had started to set in and he'd stayed on, moving between Pakistan and Afghanistan.

The obligatory first port of call in the morning for all journalists was the Ministry of Information, a ten-storey building just over a kilometre across the river. While I registered for my satellite phone, Mr Kadim, another moustachioed Saddam lookalike, informed me that I could only send emails and make calls from within the ministry building while I was in Baghdad. I solemnly promised to obey the rules. I was also informed that I needed to apply for a renewal of my visa every ten days, and should I violate the rules of my work permit—such as using my phone outside the ministry building—my visa would be revoked. I had no intention of breaking the rules, I told him, masking my insincerity with my most charming smile.

Because Larry hadn't given me anything like a $33 million budget for the war, I could not afford to rent one of the offices inside the building alongside CNN and the BBC, and was instead relegated to a white plastic desk in the ministry yard among the tents, satellite dishes and chaotic comings and goings of those others of the world's press similarly lacking in resources.

During the registration process I was politely asked whom I would like to interview and what I would like to see. It sounded like I was being offered a smorgasbord of choices. As I mentally perused my wish list I was assigned an interpreter (minder) and driver (minder) to make sure I saw only what the regime wanted me to see, and spoke only with those it wanted me to speak with. Finally, I was encouraged to attend the press conferences (propaganda sessions) held by the ministry each day. I was also encouraged to avail myself of the ministry's free sightseeing tours for journalists to all the must-see points of interests around Baghdad, like bombsites, baby-milk factories and underresourced hospitals.

It didn't take long to learn that the best policy was to keep a low profile with the ministry, although not so low that you were never seen at the press conferences or on their travelling magic bus. Every day, lists of journalists who were ordered to leave the country because their visas were not being renewed were posted on a notice board in the ministry. Twice in three weeks my name appeared and twice I paid five hundred US dollars to make it disappear.

It took approximately five minutes for me to realise that my minder, Haifa, was a loyal, fully paid-up, card-carrying member of Saddam's Ba'ath Party, as was my driver, Hassan, an overweight, humourless chain-smoker in a shiny suit. Big-busted with thickly applied lipstick and eyeliner, Haifa teased her faded bottle-orange hair into a tight beehive and squirmed her way into suits that stretched dangerously across the expanse of her ample rear. For a flash of colour, she tied a different nylon 'Dior' scarf around her neck each day. She also carried a vinyl 'Gucci' handbag over her arm just like the Queen. Haifa would not allow me to speak to anyone or go anywhere she personally considered would make Saddam unhappy. Like the Queen, Haifa was not to be trifled with.

After a month in Baghdad our relationship had deteriorated to a nearly unworkable state. Haifa questioned every request I made for an interview, which made me suspect she didn't even seek permission to visit places or people on my ever-diminishing wish list. Repeating the refrain that it was 'not allowed', she would then produce an alternative itinerary that bore little resemblance to the one I had compiled. More worryingly, I feared she was interpreting creatively, for she would often argue with the person I was interviewing before turning to me with an exhausted sigh to say, 'What he means to say, Miss Price, is . . .' I was out of luck. Although none of the foreign press was given an entirely free rein, most had more creative minders who would, with a little encouragement, turn a blind eye to minor indiscretions.

Unlike Haifa and Hassan, who were definitely taking it all far too seriously, the other minders knew which way the political wind would blow after the war and were keen to amass as many American dollars as they could.

My attempts to evade the constraints of the dynamic duo soon became the standing joke of the press corps in the hotel. If I told Haifa that her services were not needed for the day because I would be working in my room, she and Hassan would be waiting in reception for me when I exited the elevator. Their commitment to the job had earned them a certain degree of notoriety among my colleagues, who took every possible opportunity to enthusiastically commend Haifa on the itinerary she had planned for me that day. When I mentioned that there was no need to tell everyone what I was doing and who I was interviewing, she puffed out her bosom and looked thunderously offended. Although it was frowned on, sometimes a journalist might try to steal your fixer if he or she was particularly good, but sadly no one tried to poach Haifa, despite the fact that I would have paid them to take her.

After six weeks I had produced a number of set-piece interviews with very important men who all bore a striking resemblance to Saddam, and who all had grand houses and grand titles. Entertaining me in their *diwaniyah*, they would ply me with cups of sweet spiced tea and sugar treats, telling me of their love for Saddam, of how he would defeat the Americans—and, by the way, was I married? I interviewed Shiites in their cinder-brick homes in Basra who loved Saddam; Sunnis in their mansions in Mansour who loved Saddam; street vendors, mothers and daughters in Baghdad and date growers in Nasiriyah who all loved Saddam. I looked at village life and the clan system. The village and the clan loved Saddam. All of which helps explain why Larry was soon on the phone from London telling me that he was under a lot of pressure. Actually, Larry said, he was coming under 'overwhelming pressure' and was clearly trying to offload some of this 'overwhelming' onto me—as if I didn't already have enough of my own overwhelming.

'What with your bribes every ten days to the ministry'—as if I personally wanted to pay bribes—'and the fact that you need to rent a second hotel room for the duration of the war, and what with everything else . . .' All my colleagues who could afford it were renting a second room in another hotel in the event that the one they were in was blown up, and in the event that they were not in it when it was blown up. I could not think what the 'everything else' that Larry was talking about might be. All I had been doing since I arrived was hanging out with Haifa and Hassan, which was not exactly hitting the high spots of Baghdad. I decided my darling Larry was having a very bad day and the best line of defence was not to speak to him until a question was actually addressed to me.

'Are you there, Kate?'

Finally, a question I could answer. 'Yes.'

'Look, I'm sorry,' he said, with a wheeze and a sigh of exhaustion. 'I'm having a bad day.' *I knew that.* 'I know it's difficult out there, and I really do appreciate what you're doing—you know that—but I'm getting a lot of pressure from upstairs. Iraq is the *hot topic* here.' *Doh! That's a no-brainer, Larry.* 'Word is, the war is about to start any day now, so tell us something we don't already know.' *Tell me something I don't already know, Larry!*

'Okay,' he said, 'what about the peaceniks? Some of them are Brits.'

'I'm not too sure they call themselves peaceniks, Larry. I think they prefer peace activists or human shields. Peaceniks are sort of from the sixties.'

'Whatever. I've got them to keep two and a half thousand words in the Sunday magazine for you, which is huge, so for Christ's sake give me something different.'

'And you're actually suggesting the human shields are something different?'

'Okay, okay, not them—but something.'

'Right. Not a problem.'

I'd already spent a couple of days with the shields because Saddam quite liked them, and because Saddam quite liked them Haifa quite liked them, and because Saddam and Haifa quite liked them I would quite like to write a story about them, right? Wrong. That's a shame, because Hassan was quite fond of them also.

I was not going to do the human shields story because they had been covered by every foreign journalist in Baghdad twice and there was nothing new to say about them. Yet I could not see how I was going to get something of interest for the paper in the next three days with Haifa directing proceedings.

Chapter 29

WHILE RENEWING MY VISA AT THE MINISTRY THE FOLLOWING day, I got caught up in the melee of journalists now trying to get out of the country, because the rumour was that the war was only days away. Before you could leave, though, you had to pay a couple of hundred dollars cash for every day you had spent trying to report from Iraq, and without that receipt you were not allowed out of the country. I think it's called war profiteering.

The longer I spent talking with the journalists trying to get out, the more the hot panic was rising in my chest. I had no intention of leaving, and while I did not actually think the Allies would raze Baghdad, I was concerned that Saddam might consider taking hostages again. A couple of hundred of the world's journalists tied to posts in ministries, oil facilities and electricity grids just might do the trick. Then again, it might not, and we could all be blown to smithereens. I also had seen enough bombing campaigns not to believe in the accuracy of 'strategic' bombing or laser-guided missiles and I was not happy about being caught in a prolonged ground war on the streets of Baghdad either, because I'd seen the amount of weaponry being passed out—it would have made the National Rifle Association proud.

While hundreds of journalists were joining the queue to leave Baghdad, others who had left it late to come into Iraq, like Pete, were stuck in Jordan trying to secure visas to get in. Each day we spoke he sounded more desperate, until even I began to doubt that he would make it in time, and as stupid as it may sound, I just couldn't imagine the war beginning without him.

As I sat at my white plastic desk uploading a story for Larry about the media exodus, a shadow fell across my work and a thrill ran up my spine. Without taking my eyes from the keyboard, I said casually, 'I'd always thought Pete McDermott was God, but when it looked like he wasn't going to make it for the war I was starting to thinking that he'd been lying to me.' I looked up to see him grinning down at me with that crooked smile.

'So I must be God after all, hey, Price?'

'You surely must, McDermott, you surely must. Did I ever tell you how deliciously handsome you are?'

'No, but don't let that stop you now.' Looking around the courtyard, he kicked the leg of my table. 'Nice little office you've got for yourself here, Price. You've obviously got friends in high places.'

'I have a system here that works.'

'Looks like it's closely modelled on all your other systems.'

'Which is?'

'Chaos.'

'Did I ever tell you I love you, McDermott?'

'Not that I recall.'

'I do, you know.'

He just smiled. 'That so?'

'So what took you so long?'

'I couldn't find someone willing to take my money *and* return with a visa. So what's happening?'

'Precious little. Have you registered with our friends here yet?'

'Yep, so let's get out of here. Are you done there?' he said, motioning towards the computer.

'Sure, but I need to find my minder. They given you a minder?'

'No, and they're not likely to.'

So there it was. The ministry was beginning to fall apart and I'd just paid my fourth bribe to renew my visa. As I was packing up the desk a reed-thin, solemn-looking fellow with threadbare clothes came to stand behind Pete. He was sporting the standard bushy moustache and the yellow fingers of a lifetime's nicotine habit. Pete introduced him as Amin, who had been his driver on previous trips to Iraq. I returned the compliment by calling Haifa over to introduce her to Pete, who pulled me aside to tell me I needed to ditch the iron lady.

When I informed Haifa that I would not need her for the rest of the day, she stared daggers at Pete. Gathering my courage, I also mentioned that I might not need her the day after that either. Puffing herself up to her full four feet eleven inches Haifa looked like she was quite possibly going to strangle me. 'This will appear badly on my record of employment,' she said. I was not entirely sure if she was referring to my strangulation, or my dumping of her. I politely refrained from mentioning that there probably would not be any record of employment very soon.

'No one need know,' I offered confidentially and with a smile.

Slowly she began to compute this strange piece of information, as if she could never have imagined it all by herself. Just when it looked as if she was beginning to see the possibilities she discovered a glitch: the matter of payment for services rendered. Stuffing a wad of nearly worthless Iraqi dinars into her hand, I thanked God that she was too loyal to demand American dollars, like all the other Iraqi minders. My official minder then officially informed me that she and Hassan would be waiting for me the day after tomorrow in the lobby of the hotel, and she hoped that I would be feeling better by then. For a very brief second a wave of affection for Haifa passed over me as I watched her turn on her heel and walk away, until I remembered that I would have to face her wrath again the day after tomorrow.

Pete, who had been listening to this exchange, was shaking his head at my cowardice. As he turned to walk with Amin to his car, I grabbed my laptop and ran after him, throwing my spare arm around his neck.

'Jesus, Price, are you trying to strangle me?' he said, laughing.

'I'm free, McDermott,' I whispered in his ear, before pulling away and yelling out loud, 'I'm free.'

A war may have been looming but Baghdad suddenly seemed brighter because he was there.

On our way to the car Amin told me that he had been waiting for weeks for 'Mr Pee' to arrive. Looking from Amin to 'Mr Pee' I smiled in appreciation of the name and the mileage I would be able to crank out of it.

'Don't even think about it, Price,' Pete warned.

Unable to secure a room in the Palestine, Pete booked himself into the Al Rasheed Hotel, and with the aid of a hefty bribe was given a suite on the southern side of the hotel, where he was able to connect to the portable Inmarsat terminal he'd brought so he didn't have to go to the ministry every day to make phone calls and upload his photographs. After unpacking the small satellite dish, we taped his windows—a rather delicate operation because you had to use just the right amount of masking tape to allow the window to shatter, but not so much that it would blow in. We were about to head off to the Palestine to repeat the procedure in my room when I remembered to ask him what book he had brought for this war.

It turned out he had three. He laid them on the bed. 'Alice in Wonderland,' I said picking up Lewis Carroll's children's book. 'That's scary.'

'I've never read it and they tell me it's a classic.'

'Spooky that you'd be reading it anyway, McDermott. So what else?' I picked up the other two books. 'The Lovely Bones by Alice Sebold—read that, it's very good—and Bush at War by Bob Woodward. Timely, but in a couple of weeks you'll know a lot more about Bush at war than Woodward. Bad choice really.'

'Well, thank you for that,' he said, taking the books from me and throwing them back on the bed. 'I'll see what you brought, Ms Clever Arse, when we get to your room.'

Back in the Palestine Hotel I laid my meagre supply of safety equipment on the bed for a final check. I had a flak jacket that Larry insisted I carry but I had never worn, because how could you wear a bulletproof vest when the people you were interviewing didn't have one? I had a chemical suit, also unused. Like most of the other journalists under contract, I had also been sent off to a hostile-environment training course, the physical challenges of which I sometimes failed, leaving me a technical KIA—killed in action. In the end I graduated none the wiser about how I was supposed to work with both the flak jacket and the chemical suit on in the fifty-plus degrees of an Iraqi summer, should the war drag on that long.

Pete had thirty-five thousand US dollars in cash. I had sixteen and a half, which might prove to be a problem once the war started because it was unlikely anyone would bother to restock the automatic teller machines. I also noted, not for the first time, how much more generous the US employers were to their staff. I made a note to talk to Larry about this small problem. I did not own a bulletproof helmet, or any helmet for that matter. I was beginning to wish that I did. Pete wished I did too and made a disparaging remark about my preparedness before taking some ampoules of Atropine and syringes out of his bag to add to my supply. When I protested, telling him that he might need them, he said that he had specifically brought extra for me. He also threw a small package on the bed in a casual manner that belied its importance. It was a ten milligram, self-injectable canister of diazepam to be used in the event that I could not get my chemical suit on in the crucial ten seconds before my lungs were blistering and I was bleeding internally and going to die an excruciating death.

'I don't need that,' I told him, throwing it back at him.

'Probably not, but you should take it anyway.'

We checked and rechecked the cables for my computer and recharger for my phone. I was concerned that I didn't have enough batteries in my stash, and made a note to buy more the following day. I also made a note to buy a torch like Pete's. He had a head torch that left his hands free to do things like put on his chemical suit and flak vest in ten seconds in the dark. I had two crushed packets of cigarettes to bribe my way out of tricky situations, like possible rape, and a medical kit that I had been carrying around for so long that everything was probably out of date.

I remembered how in Bosnia Bella had spread all her possessions out to dry after dropping her backpack in the Drina River. I had noted at the time that she had a whole packet of condoms. I had three condoms. She took lacy Christian Dior underwear to war and I had serviceable cotton. I sighed. I really needed to be more optimistic. I also had a wedding ring on the appropriate finger and a photo of 'my husband'. Not being able to decide who was going to be the lucky fellow, Bella and I had gone through all the actors or famous musicians I fancied only to realise that a photo of Bono or George Clooney might have been a dead giveaway to the discerning killer. We then looked through *Vogue* and *Vanity Fair* for a photo of a male model that I wouldn't be averse to spending at least a few nights with, but they all looked a lot prettier than I did. With thoughts for my own safety overriding vanity—or fantasy—I eventually opted for a photo of my friend Callum, complete with double chin, glasses and comb-over. You just had to believe he was my husband—there could be no other possible reason for carrying around a photo of such a man.

When we had finished the full inventory Pete commented that he didn't think I was taking the coming war seriously enough. 'You need to watch out, Price, your attitude could get you killed.'

'Yeh, well, thanks for the vote of confidence.'

'Just making an observation. So what books did *you* bring?'

'I might not win on quantity, but I think I win on quality.'

'You've only brought one book. You don't think this war's going to last too long then?'

'Doesn't matter 'cause I knew I'd be able to borrow whatever you'd brought.'

'So, end the suspense. What did you bring?'

'The Day Diana Died.'

'You're kidding me.'

'No, honestly, that's what I brought.'

'I don't believe you. Show it to me,' he said, putting out his hand.

When I pulled out the copy of *Tuesdays with Morrie* I feigned surprise. 'Oh no, I've brought the wrong book!'

Pete and I spent the rest of the day looking up old acquaintances, and retired with them en masse to a local *chaikhana* behind the hotel. Relaxing back on the richly embroidered cushions, we indulged in quantities of apple and mint tea together with rosewater sweets, while some of the guys gave the hookah pipe a good workout. Arguing good-naturedly over the distorted strains of the famous Egyptian singer Umm Kulthum spitting out of the overhead speaker in competition with the Saddam speech being rerun on TV, we discovered we could not agree on anything. Did Iraq have weapons of mass destruction? Were the sanctions justified? How soon would the war begin? Would journalists be taken as human shields? How long would the ground war in Baghdad last?

Afternoon tea slid into dinner and we all slid across the road to a kebab house seductively lit by flickering blue neon lights. When it became apparent to the Turkish proprietor that he would have no other customers that evening, he closed the shutters over the door, drew the lace curtains, and produced a number of black market bottles of raki for our enjoyment. We all laughed too loudly, smiled too brightly and drank too much, for we had gathered to witness a war and we all knew it was no laughing matter. As the hours passed amicably enough, and the noise level rose steadily, the proprietor retired to a chair behind his cash register to sleep. It was one of those nights from which not too many coherent memories survive, but I do recall quite vividly looking around at all the faces I knew and wondering how many of us would be there at the end. It also hit me that we all looked too old and too haggard to be doing the job, but that could have been the result of the unkind overhead fluorescent lights, or the quantity of alcohol I had consumed. I also remember feeling overcome with love for each and every one of my friends there on that night. They were my family.

When the first rays of the morning crept in through the curtains from the alleyway outside, and the call of the muezzin cranked out of the mosque in Firdos Square, our host roused himself to take our American dollars and lock the door behind us before he scurried off to pray. Hugging and kissing goodbye, we each swore that the other was the best journalist/photojournalist in the world and the wisest, the best, and the most loyal friend that one could ever find.

Walking back to my hotel with Pete, who had hold of my elbow to steady me, my feelings of love for all my colleagues channelled themselves into a single, intense, overwhelming love for him and an obsessive desire to seduce him. 'Come to bed with me, McDermott,' I slurred.

Waiting for his reply—because the gravity of the offer demanded my close attention—I abruptly stopped walking and forced him to do so also. I looked intently from one Pete to the other. Unable to discern which was the real Pete I decided to concentrate on the space between the two of them.

'Despite the charm of your invitation, Ms Price, I must decline.'

'What's the problem? C'mon, Pete. This is my first attempt at seduction and you're turning me down. A girl could get a complex over this.'

'Surely not your first!'

'Well, the first time I've asked someone outright like I just did you. I did just ask you, didn't I?' For some reason this seemed incredibly funny and had me collapsing onto the front steps of the hotel, laughing.

'You did,' he said, pulling me back up again and propelling me through the front door. 'Don't think of it as a rejection, sweet Kate, think of it as the answer you really want. You'd only regret it.'

'Nah, I wouldn't.' I wanted to appear sober to him, to stress the seriousness of my proposal, and so—as Mother would say—I tried to wipe the silly smirk off my face. *Ooooooh, she would not be happy if she could see me now*, I thought, which made me double over with laughter again, which made it harder to walk despite the supporting arm, which made me seem very drunk, which I was.

'Come on, Kate, you've had too much to drink,' said the man I'd never seen drunk as he steered me into the lift.

I was finding it hard to stand up straight, so I rested my hands on my knees, but that only made the lift spin.

'Oooooh, c'mon, McDermott, I know you want to sleep with me—admit it,' I said, trying to straighten up.

'How many years have I waited for this conversation?' he said quietly to himself.

'What? What?' I asked. 'What'd you say, McDermott?'

'Your timing's brilliant, Kate,' he said, as the lift doors opened. 'Come on, sweetness and light.' Tightening his grip on my arm he led me down the hall to my room. 'Let's get you to bed.'

'Good, that's what I want too.'

Unable to fit the key into the door, I finally handed it over to Pete. The hallway was starting to spin now. As the liquid contents of my stomach began to rise up into my mouth I clasped it shut with my hand and concentrated on not throwing up as Pete helped me to the bed. No sooner had he taken off one of my boots than I pushed him away and rushed into the bathroom.

When I'd stopped vomiting I staggered back to the bed.

'Jeez, McDermott, I hope they don't start this war today 'cause I'm in no state to cover it . . . Larry's gonna kill me. Will ya just lie down with me for a minute, please?'

'How about I tell you a bedtime story instead? Once upon a time,' he began as he sat beside me and began to unlace my other boot, 'there were two friends called Pete and Sam and they wrote a rock opera.'

'Enough.'

'Don't you want to know what it was about?'

'Nope.'

'It was about two lesbian vampires . . .'

'I don' wanna hear 'bout two lesbian vampires.'

'Okay then, now you'll have to wait until it comes out to know what happens.'

'Wake me up if it starts, okay?'

'What, the rock opera?'

'Nah, stupid, the war.'

'Of course, my sweet, of course. I'll be over here in a flash.'

Chapter 30

WHEN I FINALLY WOKE I WAS NAKED UNDER THE SHEETS WITH a foul taste in my mouth and a headache that only increased in intensity as fragments of the morning came spinning back. Swallowing a couple of aspirin, I showered propped up against the cool of the wall tiles. It was past noon and I needed food, and I needed to throw up, but first I needed to see Pete. No, first I needed to throw up.

When I stepped out of the lift I ran into a colleague who looked me over then asked if I'd got the number of the truck that had hit me. Ignoring him, I headed past reception only to be confronted by the ever-vigilant dynamic duo loitering in the foyer. Confused, because I thought she was not supposed to be there, I watched Haifa rise from her chair and move purposefully in my direction. When she drew near I raised my hand.

'Not now, Haifa. I'm walking over to the Al Rasheed and I don't need an escort.' When she opened her mouth to speak I raised my voice louder, 'Not now, okay?

Pete wasn't in his room and I discovered from another journo that he'd gone to see Saddam in one of his palaces, which only made me want to throw up again. *Fuck!*

When I got back to the Palestine, Haifa asked where I wanted to go and I told her to bed. Then I bestowed my sweetest of smiles on her.

'Could you please, just this once, get me a pizza and bring it up to my room, Haifa?'

She looked at me as if I was the strangest creature she had ever had the misfortune to meet and then surprised me by asking what type.

'Any type,' I said, waving her away. 'Any type.'

When I woke I could see the pinkish-grey light of evening through the balcony doors and realised that I was, thankfully, feeling slightly better. Opening the door I nearly trod on the pizza box in the hallway. I bent down, tore off a cold piece of Hawaiian pizza, and stuffed it into my mouth.

Down in reception there was no Haifa or Hassan to be seen, so I hurried across to the Al Rasheed to find Pete in his room going over his photographs from that day.

'Did you see Saddam?' I asked, eaten up with envy.

'Maybe I did, and maybe I didn't.'

'Come on, Pete, don't be such a jerk. I don't have the energy for this today. If you saw him I'm going to kill you right after I slit my wrists. Why didn't you come and get me if you were going to see him?' He looked up at me, raising an eyebrow without saying a word. 'Okay, okay. So did you see him, or didn't you?'

'I spent the day waiting for him, or one of his doubles, to appear in a very baroque waiting room the size of Buckingham Palace. A lot of people came who looked like Saddam, but I couldn't tell if one was him, and no one was about to say. So how are you anyway?' he asked, swivelling around fully in his chair to take a closer look.

'I've been better.'

'You have indeed.'

'I want to apologise . . .' I shook my head, disgusted with myself. 'I always seem to be apologising to you, don't I? Anyway, I want to apologise for this morning. I don't think I've ever drunk so much.'

'No one's ever drunk so much.'

'Yes, well, if it makes you feel any better I *am* suffering. As I was saying, it must have been horrible for you and, um, I wanted to ask you . . . I woke up naked . . .'

He laughed. 'It wasn't me, I promise. You must have undressed yourself.' He swung back around to the computer screen, clearly intent on getting the photographs out. I thought about pulling a chair up next to him to see what he had shot, but decided leaving was the better option. As I opened the door he twisted around in his seat again.

'You know, Price, I've been thinking about something Mark Twain said. In twenty years' time, he said, you wouldn't regret the things you *had* done, only the things you *hadn't* done.' He hesitated, watching me. 'I'd welcome the proposition you made this morning in another time and place.'

'Okay,' I nodded, closing the door so he wouldn't see the effect his words had on me. I leaned back against his door, reminding myself that a war was about to begin and neither of us could afford to be distracted. I didn't want to make any more mistakes with Pete. Next time, we had to get it right.

Chapter 31

WHEN I SAW PETE THE FOLLOWING MORNING, MY STOMACH contracted and I felt my whole body blush with the memory of his invitation. Very nicely, he pretended not to notice, and we headed off with Amin to collect the last of our war provisions from one of his cousin's stores: cartons of bottled water, toilet paper, candles, matches, kerosene lamps, canned food, dried food, paper, pens, soap, batteries and earplugs. We split the booty between our two rooms, agreeing that if one of our hotels was deemed too dangerous we would move in together. I phoned Larry immediately to give him the good news that I wouldn't need to pay for an extra room.

'I don't give a toss whether you have to pay for an extra room or not, Kate. I just want you safe. I was a bit stressed the other day, sorry 'bout that. Be careful, my girl, won't you?'

'Sure thing, Larry.'

'How's the story for the magazine going?'

'Fine, just fine.' I hung up and bit my lip. I still had no idea what I was going to write. If some miracle didn't happen that day, I'd have to ring Larry back and 'fess up so he could get something else to fill the space.

As we were getting in the car again outside the hotel, on our way to do another set-piece interview at the Ministry of Culture, Pete asked Amin how he and his family were preparing for the war.

'You all fixed up?'

'Fixed up?'

'Are you all prepared for the war?'

Amin let out a bitter laugh. 'We always prepared for war, Mr Pee. This Iraq. My children, they tired of living like this. My wife, she tired. We all tired. We want Saddam to go, but Americans must go too when this over.'

The germ of an idea for a story was starting to blossom. I explained to Amin that this was the first time an Iraqi had said anything to me other than protestations of undying love for their great leader. When I described my frustrations with Haifa and Hassan he spat, 'Ba'athists! Everyone too afraid to speak. Friends too afraid to speak. Ba'athist ears everywhere. No one say what they think. Too dangerous to think. You listen, Miss Kate, to what people don't say and then you know what they think, what they saying.' As he started the car Amin asked if I wanted to speak to some people.

'What people?' I said.

'Just people.'

'People who live in Saddam City?' Amin lived in Saddam City, I knew.

'Yes, people who live in Saddam City.'

Haifa did not much like Saddam City. Nor did Hassan. And despite the fact that it was built by him and named after him, Saddam did not much like the place either. Ergo, I had not been to Saddam City. Situated in the north-east of the capital, and home to Shiites from the south, the slum would be renamed Sadr City after the war and would become the first centre of Shia resistance against the Americans. As one of the poorest and probably most unattractive districts in Baghdad, and with few of its inhabitants supporting the dictator, journalists needed a special permit from the government to enter the place, and when they did they had to be accompanied by two minders—one from the local Ba'ath Party and another from the ministry—just to make sure that none of Saddam's loyal citizens said what they really thought to the international press.

Of course I wanted to go to Saddam City. This might be the story I was looking for.

Leaving the breezy boulevards and traffic of modern Iraq behind, we entered a maze of dull brick and concrete houses in various states of disrepair, their windows and doors shuttered tight against a hostile world. The monotony of its suburban streets and alleyways was broken only by the odd date palm or eucalypt, which would offer scant relief in the burning heat of a Baghdad summer. Illiteracy and unemployment were widespread in this quarter, and with many of the criminals Saddam had just released from his jails disappearing within its walls, it was not a place for the faint-hearted. As we moved deeper into its rabbit warren of alleyways and dead ends, the sophisticated Iraqi women of the cafés and department stores in the more affluent districts of Baghdad were replaced by women in black abayas trailing hordes of small children. I noticed that there were fewer photographs of Saddam on the sides of buildings.

Stopping outside a forlorn bicycle-repair shop built of rusting tin, Amin manoeuvred the car so that Pete and I could alight without stepping into the puddle of sewage festering by its entrance. Nearby a goat with a plastic bag stuck on its head moved about blindly, while down the alley a group of boys played war games behind a clapped-out vehicle, running barefoot over the broken footpath as they ducked to evade the enemy's bullets. A breeze blew up the alleyway, carrying with it bits of plastic and paper in little dusty eddies. As the fronds at the top of a palm tree began clicking together in the gathering wind, Amin looked up.

'We have *sîmūm*,' he said, referring to the choking desert storm that would soon turn the world a dull orange and send all living creatures scurrying for shelter.

Picking our way over the contents of a burst black garbage bag, we crossed the alley so Amin could buy a glass of tea from two little girls who'd set up shop on an upturned crate out the back of their house. From behind the wall I heard a baby crying, while a donkey brayed close by. As Amin drank his tea Pete crouched to take photos of the girls, but when he lost his footing and almost fell back into the muck behind him the girls collapsed in giggles. Regaining his balance he laughed too before handing over an extravagant sum for a glass of tea, a gesture that only set the little girls into fits of laughter again. Just as we were about to move on a street vendor appeared around the corner pushing a cart of rags. Pete stood transfixed, changing cameras to frame more images.

When Pete had finished Amin motioned for us to follow him across a plank covering an open sore of a drain. As he pulled open one of a pair of rusting metal doors, he called to his wife, Hanan, to warn her that visitors had arrived and that she must

cover herself. Delaying our entrance for a few minutes, Amin
introduced us to Jawal, his three-year-old son. The boy looked
up fleetingly from his game in the dirt and smiled at his father,
but the man he was playing with, whom Amin had pointedly
not introduced to us, took no notice of the strangers who had
arrived. All his attention was focused on the stones the child
was placing before him. Behind their heads a rotting piece of
hessian covering a tiny window flapped in the breeze, while
over our heads a loose sheet of metal screeched, lifted by the
wind. Hidden in a corner near the gate, I noticed a fountain
heavy with naked cherubs and festooned with hearts and metal
leaves of ivy was disappearing under layers of dirt and the rust
of neglect. The only thing growing in the dustbowl of that little
courtyard was a bunch of faded plastic roses sticking crookedly
out of the side of a broken plastic pot that sat under a huge old
date palm. With the tiny child instructing his silent partner in
the rules of his game, Pete asked permission to take a photo
and Amin agreed, stipulating that it must only be of the boy.

As we took our shoes off in the doorway Amin explained
that his family shared this house with another, pointing to the
curtain in the hallway that divided their spaces. As we entered
directly into the kitchen an old woman in a black headscarf
heaved herself up out of her chair, and after offering a few
words to Amin and a gap-toothed smile to the strangers, she
disappeared behind the curtain. At the end of the table a
little girl was hunched over a colouring-in book. Ruffling her
curly black hair with a few words of Arabic greeting, Pete was
rewarded with a radiant smile that lit up two heavily lashed,
almond-shaped eyes.

'This is Soraya,' Amin said with pride, introducing his
six-year-old daughter. Admiring how much she had grown since

he last saw her, Pete asked if he could take a photo of this dark beauty with the honey-coloured skin. Amin smiled, but then waved his hand in the air dismissively, as if her beauty was of no consequence. 'Yes, yes,' he said, 'take photo.' I watched as Soraya's face came alive for the camera.

Inviting us to sit, Amin explained that Soraya was doing her homework because her brother, Mohammed, would be home from school soon and she would be leaving to take his place in the classroom. There were not enough classrooms and not enough teachers in Saddam City, so the school day was conducted in relays: boys in the mornings, girls in the afternoons.

As he spoke, I realised that a woman in a black abaya was standing in the doorway. Heavily pregnant and carrying a sleeping baby, Hanan smiled at the scene. Acknowledging our presence with a shy nod, she entered the room, bringing with her the clean scent of soap and another, more elusive scent, conjuring up visions of springtime in my mind.

With a soft voice Hanan asked if we would take tea with them, before turning to give instructions to Soraya. Jumping up, her daughter cleared away the dirty tea glasses on the table and began making preparations for these new guests. A kerosene burner that served as a stove sat in a corner on tins of cooking oil, with sacks of grain stacked beneath it. Next to it a small fridge was host to a fly-speckled fan and an equally ancient aluminium saucepan. As Amin tipped water from a jerry can into the jug Soraya was holding, Hanan explained that their water supply was not always reliable.

They were the survivors of the Iran–Iraq War and the Gulf War, and ten years of sanctions, and they were Shiites. They had learnt to live without. The little girl skipped around the kitchen until she found some dried apricots and nuts and then looked up at her mother expectantly. When Hanan nodded she arranged the offerings prettily on a plate and placed it on the table. Hesitating only a second, she pushed it towards Pete. The man and the child smiled at each other again.

Apples. The fragrance Hanan wore was of fresh, crisp, green apples. I could not stop looking at her. As she spoke with her daughter and her husband to coordinate the tea-making, I watched her wide sensuous mouth and her almond eyes, for apart from her hands that was all I could see. For the first time I understood the seduction of the abaya. Surely a man could go crazy with the longing to uncover the exquisite jewel hidden behind the floating layers of black? Next to Hanan I felt ugly and ungainly with my ponytail, my boots and jeans and my shirt with the sleeves rolled up.

Many women in her condition were leaving Baghdad before the war started so I ventured to ask if she too was intending to go. Shaking her head, her hand moved unconsciously across her thickening belly. 'This not possible,' she said. It was not safe for Hanan to travel so late in her pregnancy, Amin offered, and in any event they had nowhere to go. He had a brother and a sister who both lived in Syria, but there was no money to travel there. Hanan's family were all dead except her brother. I wondered why they could not go to the brother's.

As Amin was speaking, eight-year-old Mohammed, their eldest child, burst into the kitchen chattering in rapid-fire Arabic. Having just returned from school he was still full of the excitement of it, but Amin and Hanan spoke to him harshly until he lowered his head, ashamed at his bad manners in front of their guests. They were proud that Soraya was going to school too, Hanan explained as she passed the baby over to her newly arrived son and began gathering up her daughter's colouring book and crayons for her afternoon class.

'Thanks to Mr Pee, who help Amin when he come to Iraq,' she added shyly. There was that smile again.

'Families here do not have money to send their children to school and they play in the streets, or sell things like the little girls we passed selling tea,' offered Amin.

'Girls are especially unlucky,' Hanan broke in as her long fingers deftly wrapped a pink scarf around Soraya's head, then tucked in the stray curls. 'It is very bad,' she continued, lowering her voice. 'The family on other side of curtain no longer can afford send their daughters to school. But we always send Soraya,' she added defiantly. 'My daughter will have education, and this new baby if she girl—' her hand involuntarily caressed the mound under the abaya again, '—she also have education. And, *Insha'Allah*, we one day leave this place.' Hanan then excused herself, explaining that she had to walk Soraya to school.

Reluctant to see Soraya go, I asked her what she wanted to be when she finished school, but Amin was already answering for her. 'Soraya, she will be doctor. She go to great American university and she be famous doctor.'

They might hate the country, I thought, but they still wanted a piece of the dream.

'So you want to be a doctor?' I said, turning back to the child.

'Yes,' she answered in English. 'I make babies better.'

As Hanan and Soraya left, Pete and Amin began discussing the difficulties of keeping his car running under sanctions and petrol rationing, when they were interrupted by Jawal, who ran into the room and jumped up onto his father's lap, swinging his tiny legs to get his father's attention. After failing on the first few attempts he placed his chubby hands on Amin's face and pulled it toward himself. Amin frowned and chastised the boy, but Jawal was satisfied, for now he had the attention he had been seeking and immediately broke into a rat-a-tat-tat of pleading. Amin frowned and shook his head. The boy pouted and started the rat-a-tatting again, smiling magnificently when he had finished. Despite himself Amin smiled too, and sliding down off his father's lap, Jawal scraped his little hand across the plate of leftover apricots and nuts until his fist was full. Closing one hand over the other to keep his treasure safe, he turned and ran back out into the yard to share the food with his silent friend.

We all watched the pair for a minute until Amin drew our attention back to himself by tapping the side of his head. The man outside with Jawal was Hanan's older brother, he explained. Akba had been conscripted into the army by Saddam in 1990, but he had not returned when the war ended. 'Many not return,' Amin said, shaking his head with the weight of Shiite loss. Three years later, Akba had been spotted working on a farm not too far from the village where Hanan's family had lived. The man who owned the farm explained that he had found Akba wandering alone in the desert unable to speak, with no memory of who he was or where he had come from. The farmer had taken him in and given him work. By this time Hanan's parents had died, so Akba had been brought to Hanan and Amin in Baghdad. No one really knew what had happened to him, but the farmer thought he might be a survivor of the Highway of Death.

'Akba, he forgot to bring his mind home,' said Amin, 'but, Insha'Allah, one day he will remember.'

Pete and I stole glances at each other with the memory of the carnage on the Highway of Death.

'He has bad dreams,' added Mohammed, who apparently shared a bed with his uncle.

Photographs of sombre family members wrapped in black and looking distrustfully at the camera dotted the walls. I noticed there were no photos of Saddam. Reading my mind, Amin stated simply that Saddam was not welcome in that part of Baghdad and neither would the Americans be if they stayed.

'They will shame us, coming here to rid us of this butcher as if we are not men. We have long memory of the first Mr Bush. We not trust this new one. They must leave.'

Larry was happy with my story of Amin and his daughter with the toffee-coloured eyes, which handsomely filled the double-page spread in the Sunday magazine. He also took Pete's photos of the man hawking his wares in the alley, and of Soraya sitting at the table with her crayons and paper, smiling prettily.

Chapter 32

THE PEOPLE OF BAGHDAD MADE THEIR PREPARATIONS FOR WAR. As shops began to draw down their metal shutters, those who were able to piled their families into vehicles for the long trip to Damascus or Amman, or to relatives in the country. Those less fortunate stocked their homes with food and jerry cans of water, before hunkering down for the long haul. In the streets below the Palestine Hotel, Iraqi soldiers dug useless ditches, becoming the butt of Iraqi jokes in the few cafés that remained open. As a dull weariness of inevitability settled over the city, the speedboats could no longer be seen racing past the bend in the Tigris, towing waterskiers. *Where are the Americans?* everyone kept asking, wanting it all to be over. *Where are the Americans?*

With the distant sound of thunder rolling across the city at five-thirty on the morning of 20 March, only one and a half hours after George W. Bush's ultimatum to Saddam expired, the cry rang out through the Palestine Hotel that the war had begun. With a sense of relief, everyone grabbed their cameras and phones and crowded onto the balconies to watch.

Each night after that, the American planes whined overhead, invisible to the crackling anti-aircraft gunfire and the tracer bullets of the Iraqi army that arced through the sky. As the bombs landed on their targets, they lit the night in a red and gold fireworks display that reflected prettily in the oily waters of the river. A couple of times missiles passed so close to the hotel that it swayed. When a bomb exploded nearby, the glass in the sliding doors rippled. We had no way of knowing exactly what was being hit in the city for we had no maps of strategic buildings and, even if we had, we could not have reported direct strikes in our stories, which were still being posted from the courtyard of the ministry building. Each morning we dutifully hopped into our cars or into the ministry sightseeing bus and sped off to the latest disaster—lest we forget what the pretty fireworks were really for.

Our electricity and water supply became so unreliable that we all filled our baths with water at every opportunity. Some of the larger agencies provided their crews with generators, which were shared when we needed to file or send photos from somewhere other than the ministry. Room service had fallen by the wayside, and some of the hotel's inhabitants started throwing their rubbish out into the hallways. With few of us using the air-raid shelter in the basement—we were being paid to cover a war, not hide from it—our places were taken by the wives and children of the hotel and ministry employees in the belief that the Americans would not bomb a hotel housing the world's press, which only proved that they had more faith in American weapons technology and our worth than we did.

After receiving countless warnings from London that the Al Rasheed could be a target because of the possibility of underground passages linking it to Saddam's palaces and ministries, Pete moved in with me at the Palestine. Cordoning off the small space into two minuscule areas, we worked ferociously and slept little. Any chance to dwell on his closeness or the invitation he had issued that day before the war started and what might lie ahead for us was subsumed in the rush to keep working and to stay alive.

Although the ministry had insisted we use its building to file stories, as the war continued to rage we became increasingly bold, relying more and more on the satellite dishes hidden on various balconies. In random bursts of energy, ministry personnel would raid rooms, while on one memorable night it succeeded in confiscating thirty phones, seven of which belonged to the Associated Press. To thwart the ministry's raids we set up our own rudimentary, but reasonably effective, early-warning system, aided and abetted by ministry employees who had become more reliant on the US dollars supplied by the journalists than the department's worthless dinars.

The first five days of the war were the hardest for me because I didn't seem to be able to turn myself off. While Pete was able to upload his photos as soon as they were taken and sleep whenever the opportunity presented itself, I had to compose a story and try to meet a deadline. Sometimes I tried to take my cue from him, and when I discovered he was asleep I would lie down on my bed, trying to lock into his rhythm of breathing, but it was no use and I'd lie watching him, wondering what kind of future there might be for us after the war. In the end, though, I'd usually just leave the room so I didn't disturb him. I wasn't eating and I was running on adrenaline, so I knew from experience that at some point I would come crashing down. But not today, I prayed each day, not today.

It felt like my head was crystal clear, my perceptions razor sharp, my thoughts lightning fast. It felt like I was doing my best work, and I had no complaints from Larry, although he always ended each call or email with a question about how I was holding up. Sometimes I worried that I wasn't really feeling enough when I was confronted with dead bodies, but rationalised that at least I wasn't cracking up like I had in Rwanda and Goma.

Pete began nagging me to eat and sleep more, but I no longer felt hunger. One afternoon, while I was on the bed trying to quiet my erratic thoughts, willing myself to sleep, he crept in. At first I couldn't believe what my nose was telling me, but then, after days of only nibbling at food, my appetite returned in full force. Rolling over on the bed I smiled at him. 'Okay, buster, hand it over.'

He produced a barbecued chicken from behind his back and outside on the balcony we pulled the bird apart with our fingers, grease smearing my face and hands and running down my chin as pieces of flesh lodged under my nails. He and Amin had scoured the city for the bird for me, he said, and Hanan had cooked it. In my excitement I talked non-stop as I ate until Pete told me to slow down because I was giving him a headache. Within twenty minutes it all came heaving back up.

'Right, I think we can do better, my sweet,' he said, producing an orange from his backpack, also courtesy of Hanan. Peeling it for me he rationed out the segments one by one to make sure I ate slowly. When I'd finished I leaned over and kissed him on the cheek, tracing my finger across the scar above his eyebrow.

'Remember when you got that?'

'I do.'

'We've been through a lot together, haven't we?'

'We have, but do you think you could stop talking as if one of us is about to die?' he said. He got up and walked back into the room to grab his backpack off his bed. 'I have to find Amin.'

'Thank you,' I called out as he left.

Each afternoon at two o'clock we trotted off to the ministry building to hear the highly imaginative ramblings of the indomitable Mohammed Saeed al-Sahhaf, Iraq's loyal Minister of Information, better known to his international fans in the media pool as Comical Ali, or Baghdad Bob, the Minister of Disinformation.

Although he afforded the West some amusement, al-Sahhaf was, like Haifa and the Queen, not to be trifled with. When CNN disobeyed the ministry's rules and moved its equipment from the press centre, refusing to transmit al-Sahhaf's conferences live, it was kicked out of the country. By and large, we journalists made ourselves known at most conferences and tried to at least give the appearance of obeying the rules.

Despite any and all evidence to the contrary, al-Sahhaf's message was always the same: Iraq is winning the war and the infidels will be vanquished—that is, those who had not already committed suicide by slitting their own throats in shame. Having grown used to years of officious American and British military briefing sessions, I was initially bewildered by his flowery pronouncements, but it didn't take long to decide that he was a joke. One of the *New York Times* correspondents even referred to him as the Iraqi equivalent of Donald Rumsfeld, famous for mixing fact with fiction.

At some stage I started to keep a list of my favourite al-Sahhaf utterances. 'We have them surrounded in their tanks; we have destroyed two tanks, fighter planes, two helicopters and their shovels.' And, 'You think their tanks are in an endless line coming towards us. Wrong. There are only a few of them and they turn around and then return as if to make a long snake.' Later, when the rumour began to spread that the Americans had taken Baghdad airport his response was, 'Now that's just silly! They are nowhere near the airport . . . they are lost in the desert . . . they cannot read a compass . . . they are retarded.' When it became obvious that a battle was being waged at the airport, al-Sahhaf claimed that only four or five American tanks had survived. Following that particular pronouncement another rumour spread around the hotel that with the Iraqi lines of communication destroyed a Republican Guard general had been dispatched to the airport by Saddam to report on the situation. According to the story, he returned with the words, 'Four or five tanks! Are you out of your minds? The whole damn American army is at the airport!'

When the Americans finally did enter Baghdad and al-Sahhaf was asked for a comment he declared, 'I triple guarantee you—' which was clearly much better than just guaranteeing or double guaranteeing '—that there are no American soldiers in Baghdad.' Someone should have told him to look out the window.

I liked it most when he said Donald Rumsfeld needed to be hit on the head. At least al-Sahhaf and I agreed on something.

Still, for all the amusement he provided, who would have thought that our dear Comical Ali would prove to be a sooth-sayer? 'They are trapped in Umm Qasr, they are trapped near Basra, they are trapped near Nasiriyah, they are trapped near

Najaf. They are trapped everywhere.' And that was before the Americans really were trapped.

Standing with the press pack, half listening to al-Sahhaf's lunatic act, I turned to the journalist next to me one afternoon and commented how much more amusing he was than Schwarzkopf had been in 1991. In that instant I realised how far I had descended and it was a sobering moment. It had taken only twelve years for me to sound like one of the cynical journalists I had so despised at the beginning of my career. For the remainder of the briefing I stood silently wondering what that said about me, too frightened to examine where the thought might take me.

Chapter 33

ON 28 MARCH, THE EIGHTH DAY OF THE WAR, PETE AND I were standing against the back wall talking with friends while waiting for al-Sahhaf's arrival when Mr Kadim rushed in all excited, screaming that the conference was cancelled and that we all had to come to the al-Shaab marketplace.

As the bus provided by the regime drew near the scene we began to hear the howls of pain and we fell quiet. Avoiding eye contact, lost in our own worlds, each of us searched deep within for the resources that would steel us against what we knew was to come—but when the bus pulled up and the door opened we tumbled over each other in the rush to get out.

The bigger picture assails you first: two smoking blocks of a wide boulevard; burning cars; smouldering buildings; confusion; rubble, dust, desolation; yelling and weeping. Then, as your brain begins to process what you are seeing, the focus narrows: two shallow craters about two feet deep and six feet long pitting the

273

middle of the square. People were standing around in shock, talking and gesturing as water red with blood tracked around their feet. A large group of men, possibly a hundred, were standing to one side in front of a gutted building, pushing their fists in the air and pounding their chests as they shouted out in an elaborate dance of grief, frustration and anger. *'La ilaha illallah, la ilaha illallah.'* There is no God but God. There is no God but God. It was the only way they knew how to claim back power from an enemy they were, as yet, unable to reach.

Dead bodies wrapped in plastic were already being piled high on the back of a truck. Another was being wrapped in its plastic shroud in front of me. The most severely injured had already been taken to the hospital, I was told. A child with a bandaged head and a man with his arm in a sling were being comforted in the dirt by two women. Another woman close by me was screaming hysterically, pulling at her hair and clothes and beating her breast as she stood helpless in front of an incinerated car that had become a coffin for an Iraqi mother and her three small children. Those around the woman tried to calm her, but their efforts were half-hearted. What right did anyone have to deny her her grief and pain? An old man sat in the gutter behind her crying, his eyes drawn with suffering as ash drifted down to settle like dirty snowflakes on his head and shoulders.

My mind screamed at the sensory overload. I needed to calm down, disconnect my emotions and anchor myself to where I was so I could start working. I used my usual trick: focus in on one thing, anything. On that day it was a foot resting in a scuffed brown sandal. The buckle was broken; there was cracked grey skin rimming the sole of the foot, the toenails were uncut and curling yellow with age.

A man rushed up to me in his white dishdasha, its hem splattered with black water. He was angry, waving his arms, until he calmed a little and spread his hands out before me. 'No military targets. Look. *Look!* We are just people. Why? *Why you do this?* It is abomination. Murderers. Bush and Blair are murderers.'

I looked down at the hands held out to me in—what? Supplication? Pleading? For what? What did he think I could do? There was nothing I could do for him. We stood looking at each other. He asked me again, softly this time, more desperate for the answer, 'Why?' It was the same question I asked myself over and over again; the one I could never find the answer to. Why?

And so we remained facing each other, locked in our shared helplessness, until a sob burst from his chest and he sank to the ground by my feet to crumple into a ball. Instinctively I stretched out my hand to comfort him, but the gesture was pitifully inadequate and remained stillborn. Who was I but a voyeur? How could I offer solace when I was one of 'them': a Westerner? I could do nothing to stop the carnage or to help him, yet I had no idea how to walk away from his pain. And so my hand lingered uselessly above his head, not touching, but not knowing how to withdraw either. Steeling myself, I lifted the hand, as if I was about to adjust my sunglasses, then turned and walked away.

A young man stood staring at the charred remains in the car. He looked composed so I walked up to him. Without Amin to translate I asked in broken Arabic, 'Do you speak English? Did you see what happened?'

I waited, but he didn't react. He was in shock, unable to reply. Another one of the walking wounded that no hospital would count.

I was looking around, wondering where to move next, when a Canadian journalist who'd been on the bus with us walked over. As casual as could be, as if we were discussing the weather, he said, 'These missiles were meant to kill people, not destroy infrastructure. Look.' He pointed to the craters. 'Those holes aren't deep enough.' Bending, he picked up a piece of shrapnel and offered it for my inspection.

Feeling its heaviness, the sharpness of its twisted angles, I turned it over in my fingers and then, not quite knowing what else to do with it, I slipped it into my pocket.

'These bombs are meant to explode horizontally. See? Maximum collateral damage. Look at the buildings. Gutted but not destroyed. Probably HARMS.'

'HARMS?'

'Small, high-speed missiles. Cost about three hundred thousand each. Imagine what that six hundred thousand dollars could have done for the people who live here instead of this present out of the sky.' He looked around again. 'Wait till we go to the hospital, you'll see. They'll have limbs severed and they'll be riddled with puncture wounds. I've seen this before.'

'Where?' I started to write all this down, finally beginning to work.

'In Libya. They used them to bomb Gaddafi's palace in '86 when they killed his kid. Got the wrong piece of collateral then. Wonder if they got the right ones this time?'

I winced at his words, but he had already turned and was walking away.

Two men approached.

'You can speak English?' I asked them.

'Yes.'

'What happened here?'

At around eleven-thirty, they told me, just when the market was most crowded with shoppers, two missiles hit.

'Look around and you will see with your eyes that this, it is where people sleep . . . how do you say it?'

'Residential.'

'A residential, yes. Residential. Restaurants, shops, places for food. Look!' One of the men grabbed my shoulder and pointed. 'Poor. This is poor place. We all poor.'

'Yes, I know,' I replied. These people were Shia, the poorest of the poor in Saddam's Iraq.

'Did you know any of the victims?' I asked.

'Yes, yes,' they said together, drawing me to a blackened hole in a building that they told me used to be a restaurant. 'Go, go.' They pushed me forward, urging me to enter. I should see for myself so that I could see for the rest of the world. Surely if the good, decent people of the world could see this for themselves they would never forget, and they would never let it happen again. That was their reasoning, their belief. That was how much power they thought we journalists had.

White plastic chairs had been propelled into the street with the force of the blast. Inside cement debris covered the floor and bits of raw flesh were stuck to the walls. Blood, mixing with the water from the hoses used to put out the fires, was flowing out in a slow trickle onto the pavement outside. Following its flow with my eyes I looked down to see that I was standing in it. I turned and walked back out.

Malek Hammoud was eighteen. Saliah Nouri was twenty-eight and a father of five and Abu Hassan was forty-five. All were working in the shop preparing lunch for their customers.

'That is what they did every day and this is what is left of them. Look for yourself. See.'

I looked for myself again, wondering if my traitorous brain would be filing it all away for later so I could look at it again and again.

'Um Juana, she just come out of her house over there,' one of the men said, pointing across the street. 'She is dead. She was burned and now the baby in her belly is dead, may Allah have mercy on their souls. That is her husband there. See the man sitting in the dirt?' A young man was sitting in the gutter with his head in his hands, his world torn to shreds.

More names. Sarif Albari and his son; Safe and Marwan Issan, seventeen and twelve years old, and their father. All dead. I wrote them down.

'Who will look after their families now? Will Americans look after them? They not fighters. Not hurt Americans. Not like Saddam.' Finally they asked the question everyone always asks. 'Why?'

We stood looking at each other, my pen poised above the notebook. I wanted to tell them I was sorry this had happened to them and their friends. I wanted to tell them that I didn't support the war. But I said nothing. We looked in different directions then, avoiding each other's eyes, conscious of the distance between us once there was no more business to be done.

As I was looking around, deciding where to go next, I saw him not ten feet from me, crouching perfectly still as he framed a photograph: Luc Vos. But before I could react Pete ran past, grabbing my shirt and pulling me along with him.

'What? What?' I yelled, trying to match my pace to his so I didn't fall.

'Amin and Soraya've been hit.'

'What?'

'I was talking to Jamil, a cousin of Amin's who has a shop here. We need to get to the hospital!'

'What?'

He stopped abruptly and I ran into him. Taking hold of my shoulders he spun me around and pointed. 'Look.' And then I saw it: Amin's car. 'Jamil says they were here this morning. Come on.'

We couldn't find them at first as we walked among the injured on trolleys or deposited in chairs in the corridors of the Al-Numaan Hospital. Loud wailing, hysterical people, too many people, too many hysterical people and the rush of confusion made the job of seeing difficult. A little boy in the corridor with a drainage tube in his abdomen; a man with a plastic bag holding his small intestine; a small body covered in a sheet, and a doctor yelling at someone to get the body off the bed because it was needed for the living. A mother screaming.

The Canadian was right.

Through the confusion I saw Amin standing in the hallway by a bed soaked reddish-brown with blood. His arm and chest were bandaged and he was holding a little dimpled hand that was poking out from under a sheet. She wasn't moving, but there was a saline drip hanging from a nail in the wall behind her, so she wasn't dead. As we approached I saw what the bomb had done. The skin on her tiny face had already peeled off in red strips. Where the burnt skin had lifted a watery blood-stained fluid was weeping. Her bare chest and little arms were a mottled black. As we stood over Amin, Pete put his hand on the other man's shoulder, but neither of us spoke. A doctor moved over on the pretence of adjusting the drip, but what he really wanted to do was take the opportunity to tell these two Western journalists about the horror that had been visited upon his people. He wanted us to tell the world so that when the world understood they would make their governments stop. All I could think was that someone had to tell Hanan and I didn't want it to be me.

That afternoon I sent my first story of the al-Shaab market-place bombing and the possible use of HARMS to Larry in London and told him a longer story was to follow, asking him to save a thousand words for me. It was a huge ask, but I promised him he wouldn't regret it. I worked furiously through the night, writing the story of all those killed in the marketplace, giving their names and the stories of their mothers, brothers, fathers and children. I wrote about Soraya and of Hanan's collapse when Pete told her the news, and of having to rush her to hospital through the bombing so that her premature baby daughter could be delivered in a corridor awash with blood.

As soon as I'd sent the story and Pete's photos I called Larry and told him that if the paper wanted to print the story it also had to print the before and after shots of Soraya. Larry argued that it was not possible. I insisted, telling him that it had to be possible and that it must be possible. Again he told me he could not run the photos of a burnt Soraya and Hanan's grief because our readers could only stand so much clarity. I would not capitulate. He would not capitulate. I was breaking my contract, he reminded me. Yes, that was exactly what I was doing if he wouldn't run both sets of photos with the story, adding that he didn't have any balls.

'Do you need to get out, Kate?' he asked gently, as he did every time we spoke.

'No. Definitely not. No. Just run the photos.'

There was a long sigh at the other end of the phone. I could picture him flicking the ash off the end of his cigarette and shrugging his reading glasses back up on top of his head as he waited for me to give in.

'Okay, so you'd rather the story of what happened to Soraya never reached the world if you can't have the photo of her burnt face?'

'Yes,' I said, full of anger.

There was silence on the other end of the phone.

'Wait.' I thought quickly, trying to think through what it was I wanted the most. 'Okay, no photos.' I hung up.

Larry ran the full story with all the names and both sets of photos. He didn't cut one single word and one of the photos made the front page. I saw it on the internet. I had no idea what that cost Larry with the powers that be in London, but I suspected it cost him a lot. I also had no idea if our readers complained, but at that point I no longer cared and I don't think Larry did either. The man had more balls than anyone I knew.

That night I saw Rumsfeld on CNN telling the world, 'The images on television tend to leave the impression that we're bombing civilians in Baghdad. The coalition forces are not bombing civilians in Baghdad.'

I liked al-Sahhaf's stories better.

Chapter 34

STRANGE MEN BEGAN APPEARING IN THE LOBBY OF THE Palestine Hotel, sitting around in a thick cloud of cigarette smoke drinking tea. Unlike our Iraqi friends from the ministry with their suits, portly bellies and neatly trimmed Saddam moustaches, these men were a scruffy, skinny lot with thin beards and unkempt hair. Most had Palestinian kaffirs wound around their necks as the hallmark of 'the cause'. I guessed they were waiting for the street battle to begin. The staff gave these men a wide berth and I took my cue from them, but Pete had ignored their unfriendliness and was able to take photos of their unsmiling faces. A couple of years later I realised that he probably held a complete set of mug shots of the Syrian and Iranian insurgency leaders, if the CIA or MI6 were interested.

After the ministry building was hit by a missile its employees moved into the foyer of the Palestine Hotel, setting up a desk by reception with a sad, handwritten cardboard sign that read

PRESS CENTRE. It was clear that they had lost heart, no longer interested in where or how we used our phones, but although we were more or less given free rein, and we might have been at the epicentre of a war, there was little for us to report. Snippets of information reached us in the hotel from outside, either from surfing the net when there was electricity, or from speaking on our mobiles with family and colleagues back home who sat glued to their TVs and often knew more about the war than we did.

When rumour reached us that the Americans had taken the airport, we were unable to verify it. We did know, however, that the Americans had been fighting on the outskirts of the city, for in the previous twenty-four hours new sounds were beginning to fill the air: the crackle of machine-gun fire and the thud of artillery shells in the middle distance. I had spent the morning talking to any Iraqi I could find, but the streets were eerily quiet. I found a café owner and his two customers, a man scouring the streets for food for his hungry family and a couple of soldiers sitting behind their sandbags waiting for the Americans to come, but that was all. Pete and I had also visited Amin and Hanan and their new baby, Talia, who looked as if she had inherited the toffee-coloured eyes of her mother. We were also spending as much time as we could with Soraya in the hospital, but she was still drifting in and out of consciousness; the hospital was unable to give her the painkillers she needed, or the medicine required to treat her burns.

We were sitting on the balcony eating a lunch of tinned dolmades and packets of nuts when there was a knock on the door. 'Come in,' I called. I had my back to the door and didn't bother to turn around, but I saw Pete's eyes light up and his face split into the widest of grins.

'You look fucking terrible!' he called, jumping to his feet.

I turned to see John walking into the room, cameras and backpack slung over his shoulder. Pete was right, John did look terrible, as if he hadn't slept or washed for months. After the hugs and back slapping he joined us on the tiny balcony and filled us in on his war so far.

Having covered the invasion embedded with the American troops, John had grown tired of waiting on the outskirts of Baghdad and had simply walked across the frontlines and into the city. He confirmed that the Americans had secured the airport and were bogged down in the suburbs. We were so anxious for information that we plied him with too many questions, too fast. As he answered I watched him closely, thinking that underneath the smiles and bonhomie of our reunion, something was not quite right with our friend.

'I've been around this shit for a long time, right?' We both nodded in agreement. 'But when I stopped and thought about it the other day, I realised that I'd never travelled with our boys when they'd been fighting.' He took a swig of water from the bottle on the ground. 'I can smell it. I can. It's bad. It's going to be real bad. I don't want to go there anymore. I remember seeing a couple of soldiers torturing a fourteen-year-old kid once. He was just a stupid shepherd, right?'

Pete and I looked at each other. Was he talking about Iraq? It didn't sound like it.

'Anybody could see that he was just a shepherd, but they sat each side of him—they couldn't have been much older than he was—and they kept pushing his head from side to side. Ah, man . . . I'm thinking, you know, it didn't look so bad in the scheme of things, a bit of schoolyard-bully stuff, but they were scrambling his brain and they knew exactly what they were doing, right? I went to find this kid the next day in the Jabaliya camp and he was in real bad shape.'

Pete and I looked at each other again, confused. John was talking about the Occupied Territories.

'He died, you know—a couple of days later he died. He was just a shepherd and I never told anyone about that, not even Helen. I can't cover that shit there anymore. They'll never stop until everyone dies and these kids . . . they're just young kids here—our guys. These soldiers are just young kids and they don't even understand what it's really all about. They think it's about 9/11 and revenge. They think they're fighting for all those who died in 9/11.'

'Perhaps you should just rest for a while, mate,' Pete said, but John wasn't finished and didn't seem to hear.

'And that might be why they're fighting, but it sure isn't why Bush and Rumsfeld sent them here. You should see them. They've still got pimples. They should be back home playing basketball and trying to make out with their college sweethearts. They're so young they can't even fucking legally drink back home, but we think they're old enough to go and kill for us.' He stopped for another swig of water. I wanted to say something reassuring, but had no idea what that might be.

'What I've seen makes me think that Iraq is going to be like that for us.' He was back to the Palestinian conflict. 'It's going to destroy us just like it's destroying them.'

He leaned his head back against the glass door, the food untouched at his feet. I reached over and squeezed his arm, but it seemed he still wasn't finished.

'It's hard, you know, when it's your own guys. I saw Iraqis waving white flags being blown away 'cause our guys had been fooled one too many times. I saw it, you know. I saw Iraqis pretending that they were surrendering and then opening fire. So our guys just said fuck 'em and they shot everyone. They weren't going to be fooled again, right? And really, you know, what were they supposed to do? Everyone was scared. A lot of innocent people get killed, but hey, that's war, right? But you know what it's like. Some are worse at it than others. Some like the killing, and you get to know who they are. Everyone knows who they are.'

'Listen, John,' Pete said, getting up and moving to sit next to him, 'how about you just have a rest for a while? Have a sleep on one of the beds here?'

But with the word spreading that John had just arrived from behind American lines people were already knocking on the door, and soon the room was crowded with other journalists wanting to talk to the man who had been the first travelling with the troops to make it through to Baghdad.

I was still sitting on the balcony, watching everyone milling around John in the room, when I saw Luc Vos walk in and my heart skipped a beat. Apart from a glimpse of him at al-Shaab, I hadn't seen him since Grozny. I knew he must have been late coming in because I hadn't seen him working or renewing visas in the ministry and I hadn't seen him at the Palestine. I wondered where he'd come from. As people started to spill out onto the balcony I got to my feet and, leaning against the rail, watched him, trying to understand the confusing emotions that seeing him again after so many years had stirred in me. When I finally took my eyes off him and looked around the room I saw Pete watching me. He walked over to greet Luc.

'Hear a rumour you came in via Kurdistan, Luc. That right?'

'I wasn't even sure until the last minute if I was going to come or not, so when I'd left it too late to get a press pass in Jordan I had to come in through Turkey.'

'How was it up there?'

'Quiet when I left, but gearing up to stake their claim in the new Iraq. If you'll excuse me, Pete . . .' Luc said, as he turned and walked out to where I was on the balcony. 'How've you been, Kate?'

'Good. Okay,' I said, reaching behind to pull at my ponytail and then blushing when I realised I was worrying about how I might look to him. I had no idea what to say after all the years, so I said the lamely obvious.

'It's been a long time.'

'It has.'

It unsettled me seeing Luc again. Feeling awkward, I quickly excused myself, explaining that I needed to go downstairs to reception to see if I could get a room for John, otherwise Pete, John and I would all be sharing the two beds in my room.

As I moved through the room to the door people kept stopping me, wanting to say how good it was to see John again, but I had also noticed that conversation was already beginning to taper off as some began to register that something was not quite right with their friend. I'd seen it all before. We all had antennae for this sort of thing in our business, but no one really knew how to deal with it, and certainly no one ever talked about it. I knew that whatever had to be done to help John was going to be up to me and Pete.

With the ground war in Baghdad about to begin, and no one knowing how long it would last or how dangerous it might be, quite a few of the media companies were pulling their staff out, and so it was easy to secure a room for John. When I told Pete what I'd done he informed me that he'd move out and bunk in with John.

'You don't have to do that, you know.'

'Someone should be with John, plus I think it'd be good for you to have some space right now.'

'I don't need space. It's not necessary.'

'Oh, I think it is.'

I couldn't ask him if that decision was made out of his concern for John or because of Luc's return, but I knew he'd been watching us.

When John finally fell into a fitful sleep later that afternoon, Pete returned to my room to collect his gear. Neither of us knew whether we should put a call through to Helen or to his agency to let them know that John might have problems, so we decided to wait a few days to see if he improved before contacting anyone. In the end John took the decision out of our hands and left for home through the north of the country three days after he had arrived.

That first evening John had appeared the city had been quiet—too quiet—but the next morning, alone in my room, I woke to the sound of grenades, mortars and machine-gun fire close by. When I went out onto the balcony I saw American tanks across the Tigris.

We all worked hard during the next weeks covering the fighting, the taking of the capital and, finally, its looting. Three weeks after the Americans arrived, Pete came to my room to tell me that he was leaving, heading off to see what was happening in Basra and Fallujah. At first I didn't realise that I wasn't invited, but when he told me that Amin would be remaining in Baghdad as my driver and interpreter because Hanan hadn't wanted him to leave her and the children alone, I understood.

'Have I done something wrong, Pete?'

'No, of course not.' He was purposely not looking at me as he leaned on the balcony railing to stare out over the city.

'I'm sorry, but I don't understand. You don't want me with you, that's what you're saying, isn't it?'

'I think you and Luc have some unfinished business and you should perhaps give yourself time to sort that out.'

'That's crap,' I said, furious with him. 'Bullshit.' Either he was making up excuses because he no longer wanted to work with me, or he didn't want to be with me. I wanted to scream at him, 'Whatever happened to another time and place?' but my pride wouldn't let me. By the next day he was gone.

Chapter 35

Late 2004

AFTER PETE LEFT BAGHDAD WE HAD KEPT IN CONTACT—ALTHOUGH working in Iraq in those days was not conducive to easy communication—but as time passed, and each of us had returned to our respective homes and new assignments, our phone conversations became less frequent, until they had eventually tapered off to the odd phone call once a month or so. I missed him constantly, but after he had left Luc had started coming to my room in the Palestine to talk—much as we had done in the kindergarten in Chechnya—until we eventually became lovers again, only this time we took it far more slowly.

I learnt that he had a mother and one sister whom he was close to and that his father, whom he admired, had died the week we were together in Chechnya. With his father's death and Luc being injured in the space of a few days, his mother had begged him not to return to conflict, and he'd stopped until the war in Iraq had proved too great a temptation. Normally Luc spent his time commuting between Paris, where he had a small bedsit apartment, and Amsterdam, where his mother and sister lived, but after the US had taken Iraq he stayed on in Baghdad to cover the uprising. Whenever I returned to relieve the paper's permanent correspondent stationed there we'd spend our nights together. In the day, though, we'd go our separate ways. For Luc, it meant venturing outside the Green Zone, but for me it meant searching out stories on the streets of Baghdad with Amin.

Back in his room in the Al-Fanar Hotel at night our conversations were always about politics or the mechanics of the job; stories covered or not covered; what had happened that day and the debacle that Iraq had become; who was doing what to whom and where it all might end. We said little about ourselves. Sometimes, when I woke in the early hours of the morning, I'd lie in the dark trying to visualise the face on the pillow beside me: the way Luc's eyes crinkled in the corners when he laughed, the texture of his skin and the curl of his hair. But I was unable to draw the breadth and depth of him without another, more familiar face getting in the way. And so the man whose bed I shared those last nights in Baghdad remained a mystery, and the possibilities of what might have been with him, the imagined him, and the imagined relationship, remained out of reach.

My third last day in the city proved to be another bad day in Baghdad. A suicide car bomb had killed seventeen people near the oil ministry and the police academy. When I arrived bodies still littered the street as warm blood wound its way down the footpath. While the recruits from the police academy were thought to have been the intended victims, most of the people killed on that day had been innocent bystanders. Seven of them were women. When I finished talking to witnesses and gathering as much information as I needed for the article, I sat down on the kerb and rested my head in my hands, wondering how I was going to write one more meaningful article about a suicide bomb in Iraq.

I hadn't seen Pete in months, but both he and Luc had been there that day, and as I watched them work I saw for the first time how much alike they were. Fluid, intense, engrossed in the world through a lens; driven to find that elusive shot that would capture the moment, the one that would capture the war and lodge forever in our collective memory—Iraq's flag raising on Iwo Jima; Iraq's napalmed girl; Iraq's vulture in the Sudan. They had that elusive quality of stillness that I'd rarely seen before: an easy acceptance of who they were and their place in the world. They each fitted perfectly within their skin and because they did they found no reason to rail against the world and all the things they couldn't change. Stillness, I was discovering, was a powerful aphrodisiac. They were good men, I thought, and I smiled to myself until I realised that perhaps the attraction of Luc was that he was a safer, less complicated version of Pete.

I knew Pete had seen me and wondered if he'd come over, already having decided that if he didn't I'd go to him. I watched him work for a little longer then he strolled over to sit beside me on the footpath.

'How's it all going, Kate?'

He was close enough for me to feel the warmth from his arm and I felt my body sway towards his.

'Okay. And you?'

We were both watching what was happening in front of us as the ambulances arrived to take the bodies.

'Good. Good. Seen John?'

'I saw him two days ago. He's around somewhere. He doesn't look good. Have you seen him?'

'Not for a while, but we talk a quite a lot and I've also been talking with Helen . . .' He looked over then and added, 'Don't tell John that, will you? She's worried about him still. I'm not sure there's anything any of us can do, though, until he decides to do it for himself.' He picked up his camera and adjusted the focus before shooting a couple of photographs of a body being lifted into the back of an ambulance.

'It's nice to see you, Pete,' I said, nudging him with my shoulder. 'I've missed you a lot.'

'Missed you too, Price, but shit happens. Life goes on.'

'Yeah, I know.'

We sat in silence for a while, then I asked, 'So when did you arrive in Baghdad?'

'Last night. I've been up in Mosul, but have to fly out tomorrow.'

'Anywhere I should be interested in?'

'Not really. Back to New York. Got to get ready for an exhibition at the ICP.'

The International Centre of Photography was pretty prestigious. I was impressed, even though I knew it wasn't the first time he'd been invited to exhibit there.

'Congratulations, Pete, you deserve it, you really do. Maybe when I leave here I should fly over to see it? You'll have to email me the dates.' I turned my head to smile up at him.

'Sure.' As we both turned back to watch the police clear people away he asked, 'You and Luc good?'

'We're good.'

'That's great to hear. Seen Soraya lately?'

When my article about Soraya and the al-Shaab bombing had been released, a benefactor had materialised, offering to pay for her to go to London for a series of skin grafts and plastic surgery. When I'd excitedly asked Hanan and Amin who this benefactor was they had, to my mind, professed an uncomfortable ignorance. I tried pressing the paper to find out, but Larry said that I should just let it be. In the end I was simply content that my story had done some measure of good. 'I saw her last week. She's looking better all the time—and Talia is just beautiful, of course.'

'She's pretty isn't she?' he said, smiling. 'Anyway, I really should go over and talk to Amin before I leave. Look after yourself, Kate.' He squeezed my shoulder as he got to his feet and walked over to where Amin was waiting for me by his car.

I knew Pete spent a lot of time with Amin and his family whenever he returned to Baghdad because Amin was always full of stories of Pete's visits. I'd always smile when Amin talked about him, but inside I was hurting. I was no longer part of Pete's life and it felt lonely.

The story I filed that day was headed SIXTEEN PEOPLE KILLED IN BAGHDAD BY SUICIDE BOMBER. I didn't even get the number right. The lead was that the presumed target was either the oil ministry or the police academy. I added a few paragraphs about who was thought to have been responsible, and how it might affect the coming elections in Iraq. As horrific as the bombing was, I wondered if any of our readers back in the UK really cared. I suspected, perhaps uncharitably, that most of them would read the headline and then turn over to the sports page. I wrote nothing about the individuals whose lives were lost. It was not a big story in the course of that war—hardly worth mentioning really.

That evening I made my way to the roof of the Al-Fanar Hotel where I was now staying and where I knew everyone would be gathering to discuss what everyone was always discussing: the occupation; how long the Americans would stay; what new group had claimed responsibility for the latest suicide bombing or kidnapping; when the criminally incompetent Rumsfeld would resign; and at what stage were we allowed to officially call what was happening in Iraq a civil war? I also secretly hoped Pete might be there, but he wasn't.

By the massive air-conditioning unit, half hidden by broken terracotta pots and a stack of pavers and rubble, I saw John sitting alone. Our friend had never lost that haunted look he brought with him after being embedded with the Americans over eighteen months before. I said hello to the group drinking, which included Luc, and then picked up one of the spare plastic chairs near the stairwell and climbed over the rubble to join John. We sat in silence for a while, side by side, watching the last of the sun's rays creep up the walls of the Palestine Hotel opposite as the scratchy old tape from the mosque below began calling the faithful to their knees.

'How's the family?' I asked.

'Helen rang last night to say that our marriage is over.'

'Oh no, John. I'm so sorry. So, so sorry.' I leaned over and put my hand on his arm. The pain I saw in his eyes nearly broke my heart. Without having been married, without children, I couldn't even begin to understand what he was going through and had no idea what more to say to him, but 'I'm sorry' didn't seem nearly enough. I looked back over to the others, searching for Pete, but there was still no sign of him. He and John were so close, he would surely know the right thing to say.

'I know it's hard on her, honestly,' he began, 'and I often feel guilty about leaving 'cause when I'm away I sometimes forget about Helen and the kids. Did you know that?' I shook my head. 'It's not that I don't love them, but I don't have to worry about Amanda being sick, right, or Oscar's failing grades or the new neighbour's dog that barks all night. Truth is, Kate, I'm not holding it all together anymore—you know, the family life back in the 'burbs and the stuff I see here. Sometimes it feels like my head's gonna explode, and you know the worst thing of all?' I shook my head again. 'It feels more real here than it does back at home.'

'I know. I know.' And I did know, and sometimes that fact scared me more than I liked to admit.

With the sun now gone and the gathering on the roof breaking up, I saw Luc watching us. He looked worried, and frowned as if to ask if everything was okay. Everyone liked John, and if there'd been a popularity contest he would have won hands down, but they also knew he wasn't coping. I shook my head to let Luc know that things were definitely not okay.

'I don't want our marriage to end. I want to be there for my kids growing up, but what'm I s'posed to do when this is how I pay the mortgage? I used to love this job, Kate, really love it, but I don't know anymore. Helen says it's destroying me and now it's destroyed our marriage.'

Of all the people I knew, John had tried the hardest to make his marriage work. He'd often spend huge chunks of time at home with his family instead of chasing the career. And I'd never seen him cheat on Helen—and that wasn't because of any shortage of opportunities. But it had always surprised me that anyone in this job believed they could have it all: the career *and* the nice faithful loving family waiting at home for them. Those things just never seemed compatible to me.

Luc picked his way over the rubble to tell us that a few of them were going to dinner at a restaurant nearby if we'd like to join them, but John declined and I followed his lead.

'I don't mean to pry, Kate,' John said, as we watched Luc leave, 'but is this thing serious between you and Luc?'

I was a little stunned. Not only had John never asked about my private life before, but it was the question I'd been asking myself a lot lately. Luc had recently begun talking as if there might be a future for us, and he was a lovely man, gentle and kind. I liked him a lot, but was that enough to build a future on? 'The truth is, I don't really know,' I told John.

'A couple of weeks ago Luc asked me about you and Pete.'

I was hurt and a little confused that Luc had not asked me himself. 'What did you tell him?'

'The truth.'

'Which is?' I was starting to feel sick in the stomach at the turn our conversation had taken.

'That you and Pete are in love and would've got together years ago if you both hadn't been so damn pig-headed and keen on your careers.'

'Please tell me you didn't say that.'

'Okay, I didn't. I told him to ask you himself.'

We were silent for a few seconds as I tried to absorb what he'd just said. Did John really think Pete was in love with me?

I shook my head and sunk down into my chair. 'I don't know about Luc and me. I honestly don't know. We've been seeing each other on and off for nearly a year now and he's such a lovely guy, but I can't quite see us lasting . . . I just can't see myself lasting with anyone.' I sighed.

'You sound lonely, Kate.'

'Maybe because I am lonely.' I was shocked by my words. I'd never admitted that to myself before, let alone said it out loud.

'C'mon,' he said, patting me on the knee, 'there must be a thousand men out there who'd want a woman who's married to her job, is only home about five weeks of the year, and doesn't like cooking, shopping, washing, ironing or cleaning.'

'Yeah, I'm a real prize, I know. Thanks for reminding me.' My words sounded bitter even to my ears and I regretted them immediately, but poor John had hit a raw nerve. I knew I'd grown hard over the years. My temper was shorter and I was far less tolerant. More importantly, I knew I wasn't feeling things properly, as if my emotions had been buried so deep that I couldn't reach them anymore. I thought back to earlier that day when I'd gone to the scene of the suicide bombing. I'd looked at the bodies of those innocent women and I had felt nothing for them. That wasn't right. Jesus, I thought, rubbing my forehead, where the hell was I heading? I'd made such a bloody mess of everything.

'I was only joking,' John said, clearly sensing my distress. Sitting forward on his chair he turned and put both his hands on my knees. 'He's lonely too, you know.'

'Who? Luc?' I looked at him in surprise.

'No, Pete. He's lonely.'

'Ha,' I laughed. 'We're all lonely, John. Don't you know that? Goes with the territory. Besides, Pete has so many lovers he makes Mick Jagger look like a monk.'

'I think that might be a bit of an exaggeration,' John said, and smiled. 'Loneliness doesn't have anything to do with how many people you sleep with. In fact, probably the more you sleep with the lonelier you are.'

'Then Pete must be a very lonely man.'

'Perhaps he is. You shouldn't be so hard on him, Kate.'

I searched John's face. Was he serious? Was Pete really lonely? I'd never thought of McDermott as lonely, maybe because I'd never been able to look past all the women in the bars at the end of the day.

'How long have you and Helen been married?' I asked, needing to change the subject.

'Thirteen years—nearly fourteen.'

'That's something worth fighting for. Christ, that's something worth fighting for! I don't really know Helen, but you've talked about her and the kids so much that I feel like I do know her, and from what you've told me I don't think she's the kind who'd ring to tell you the marriage was over unless it was a cry for help. She's probably wanting you to come home and sort things out.'

'Do you think so?'

'Well, obviously I can't know really, but if I was you and I had what you had, I wouldn't be hanging around here talking to me—I'd be on the first plane out of here.' And it was true. If I had what John had I *would've* been on the first plane out of there.

'You're right,' he said, rising, but then he hesitated and stood looking down at me. 'Listen, I'm really sorry I said that about you . . . you know, married to the job. A million guys would want you, Kate, it's just that you always seem so, I don't know . . . self-sufficient?'

'Yeah, I know.' Tears were stinging my eyes.

'Did I say the wrong thing?'

I stood up then and smiled at him, giving John the biggest hug I could. 'No, John, you have never said the wrong thing to me ever. Now why don't you go and ring that beautiful wife of yours and tell her that you love her and that you're coming home because you'll do whatever it takes to keep her. I wasn't joking when I said that if I had what you had I'd be out of here.'

With John gone I was left alone on the rooftop. Leaning on the stack of pavers I watched the lights of Baghdad splutter on in the grids across the city. Was Pete lonely too? Had he and John talked about it, or was it just John's imagination? I'd been feeling Pete's absence so badly the last six months, and seeing him that morning had only made it worse. I also realised that what I said to John was the truth: if I'd had what he did, I wouldn't have been hanging around in Baghdad.

Sometimes you bury a truth so deep below the layers of the years that it can never find the surface again. But sometimes, if you are really digging for it, if you really want to know it, then it might just push its way back up to the surface so that you can finally recognise it. As I stood in the cool of the evening looking out over the rooftops of that ancient city, I knew as surely as I had known anything that if I didn't change my direction then this would *be* the rest of my life. In ten years' time I'd be in the same place doing exactly the same thing and I'd still be lonely.

I tore down the stairs to my room and rang reception to ask if Pete was staying in the hotel, waiting on the line while the woman checked, muttering 'Come on, come on.' When there was a knock at the door, my heart skipped a beat. Perhaps it was Pete? Perhaps John had spoken to him? I slammed the receiver down and rushed over to fling open the door only to see Luc standing there smiling at me holding a cardboard box filled with food from a nearby deli.

'I didn't think you should be alone tonight,' he said.

I burst into tears.

Chapter 36

THAT NIGHT WE SAT ON THE LOUNGE IN MY ROOM AND FOR the first time really talked about ourselves: the things that had brought us the greatest joys and those that had brought the greatest sorrows, where we'd been and what we hoped for in the future. We talked until the early hours of the morning, until I confessed to him that I was never going to be free until I'd given it a go with Pete. In his gentle way Luc told me that he had always known this. Before dawn he left for Basra.

Shortly after I closed the door on Luc and lay down on the bed there was another knock at the door. I looked at my watch on the bedside table. It was four am.

When I opened the door I saw Amin, his face stricken. The jihadists, who were about to officially claim responsibility for the bombing, had arrived at his house in the middle of the night to say that they wanted me to meet them at six that morning. They stressed I was not to bring anything with me other than a notebook, pen and camera, and that I was not to tell anyone about the meeting. My first uncharitable thought was that Amin was somehow involved with these killers, but when I began to collect my things for the meeting he grew agitated and tried to dissuade me from going. He did not know these killers and had no idea where they might be taking me, meaning he would not be able to protect me.

'You should have nothing to do with these people,' he said, looking sick.

'But, Amin, they know where you live. What if I don't go? They might hurt Hanan and the children.'

'You should not go, Kate.'

It's easy in retrospect to argue that my going was a bad decision—that I should have turned right instead of turning left—but if you'd asked any of the journalists in Baghdad at that time if they would have gone, most would have told you yes. It was a breaking story and I was being given the opportunity to get ahead of the pack. I considered the possibility of being taken hostage by these guys, but calculated that this group had just killed seventeen people so they didn't need to kill one more person or take anyone hostage to get attention. In the end, my decision to go came down to what it always came down to: a gut feeling.

There is no confusion now. I can see clearly what I should have done differently. I can pinpoint with absolute precision the time, the place and the reason my life changed forever.

As I was leaving the hotel I saw Pete checking out. Walking over to him, I asked if we could talk in private for a second. When we'd moved away from the reception desk I asked him when he'd be back in New York because I needed to talk with him.

'Can't we talk now?' he asked, looking worried.

'I've got to go somewhere right now. So when will you be home?'

'Tomorrow morning. What's wrong, Kate? Something's wrong.'

'Nothing's wrong. I'd like to talk now, but I really have to go. Honestly. I have to go.' I started to walk away, but he grabbed my arm.

'Tell me what's wrong.'

'Nothing's wrong, I promise. Let's talk when you're back in New York tomorrow, okay?'

'Is it John? Has something happened to John?'

'No, he's going home to Helen. It's not John and for goodness' sake, it's not bad. At least I hope you won't think it's bad.' He let go of my arm and I gave him a smile. 'Maybe I'll see that exhibition of yours after all.'

When I got to the front door I turned and waved. He was just standing watching me, looking confused.

I stood alone on the deserted street corner at the back of the hotel until a battered red car pulled up to the kerb and I was pushed roughly into the back seat. The fellow who jumped in after me patted me down before pulling a hood over my eyes. After a drive of about forty minutes, which for all I knew could have been around the block twenty times, I was hustled out of the car and led stumbling into a room that smelt of old sweat, stale cigarettes and last night's dinner. I could feel my pulse racing, already regretting my decision to come with these men. Rough hands pushed me to the floor before the hood was removed.

In front of me were five men seated on a small raised dais adorned with a threadbare Persian rug. My first reaction was relief. They were all wearing balaclavas, which meant that they were not intending to kill me—you do not need to kill someone who cannot identify you. On the wall behind the men were photos of two martyrs, one of whom looked like the young Palestinian man who'd blown himself up in Israel only a few days earlier. Two flags, an Iraqi flag and an Islamic flag, were propped up against the wall framing the photographs. Between the flags was a sign in Arabic and English which proclaimed these men to be the Warriors of Allah. On either side of me were masked men brandishing AK-47s.

I quickly understood that they had brought me there to lecture me on how the Warriors of Allah were going to defeat the Americans, and that my job was to deliver that message. Refusing to answer my questions, they had me take photos of them with their sign before bundling me back into the car and dumping me unceremoniously around the corner from the Al-Fanar.

That evening Amin and I sat in my room watching the video that had been released on Al Jazeera of the previous day's suicide bomber. I recognised him as the man in the second photograph hanging in the room that morning. I knew the Warriors of Allah were expecting me to impress upon the world, via the front page of one of Britain's largest newspapers, that they were important new players on the Iraqi scene, and that they needed to be taken seriously. Instead I sent copy to Larry with a few sentences saying they were cowardly butchers of innocents who were without honour. For good measure I added that their Allah was a warped and evil fabrication and filled the rest of the article with profiles of each of the suicide bomber's victims. Larry rang and tried to talk me into toning the article down a bit, but I told him I couldn't see the point really. And that was the end of my career. Just like that.

The following morning I woke to Amin pounding on my door again. The Warriors of Allah had been so offended by my blasphemy that they'd decreed I must die. As I was trying to calm Amin, explaining that this was ridiculous, Larry rang on my mobile to tell me that the paper had just received a message from the Warriors of Allah saying the same thing. He was getting me out of Iraq immediately, he said. Someone from the British Embassy would be at the hotel within ten minutes so I needed to be ready to leave. When he hung up the phone rang again.

'Jesus, Bullwinkle, I leave you for three seconds and you go off and paint a target on your fucking forehead. I'm looking at a very fetching photo of you right now on CNN. Who are these Warriors of Allah anyway? I've never heard of them. Oh, and before I forget, was this the nice surprise you wanted to tell me about and what the fuck were you thinking?'

With the death threat being the lead story on Al Jazeera, BBC and CNN that morning, my room was quickly filling with journalists, and as everyone began talking at once the noise level was rising.

'This is crazy, Pete.'

'You getting out, Price?'

'I can't hear you,' I said, putting a finger in one ear and walking to the space beside the window. 'This is crazy. What did you say?'

'You getting out?'

'Looks like it. This is stupid.'

'Yeah, you keep saying that. How're you getting out?'

'The British Embassy, I think.' I was starting to feel numb. The other part of me that was still operating registered that I was probably descending into shock.

'I'll call you in an hour. You okay?'

'Yeah, I think so.' Hanging up on Pete I beckoned Amin over and told him that I needed to see Soraya before I left.

'I'm afraid you're not going anywhere, Ms Price,' said the suit walking into the room. 'And come away from that window.' He grabbed my arm and pulled me into the centre of the room. 'My name's Francis Gorman and I'm from the British Embassy. Who is this man?' He was looking at Amin.

'He's my friend.'

'Right, well I have instructions to get you out of here now. So if you've got everything you need we should go.'

'I have to pack.'

'I'm sorry, but there's no time to pack. The organisation that has made threats against you obviously knows where you are staying. One of my men will bring your things later.'

I looked around the room, which had suddenly turned quiet. Everyone was looking at me as if I was already dead.

'Can we have the room cleared, please—immediately?' said a fellow with a walkie-talkie, herding everyone out. 'I have to ask all of you to clear the room now, *please.*'

Grabbing Amin's hands before he disappeared I promised him that I would be back soon and asked him to say goodbye to Hanan, Soraya, Mohammed and Jawal for me, and to kiss little Talia and tell Soraya that I'd visit her every day when she was in London next. Everything was moving too fast. As they shuffled me out into the corridor men with submachine guns and flak jackets crowded around me, bundling me into a flak jacket and then into the lift and through the back entrance of the hotel into an armoured car with blacked-out windows. Welcome to the Green Zone, I thought, as I climbed in. A man jumped in either side of me and the car was moving before they had even closed the doors. We were waved through the US military checkpoints, and arrived at the airport and waiting plane in what was definitely record time for Iraq. Insurgents with shoulder-fired missiles had come close to downing a DHL cargo plane on its approach into the airport only a few days earlier, and so our take-off was unusually steep. I remember looking down into my lap to register that the only things I had with me were my passport and mobile phone. I had on a T-shirt and a pair of jeans I'd hastily pulled on when Amin had knocked, but no shoes and no watch. I also remembered that I hadn't paid Amin for the previous week's work and his family needed the money. I made a mental note to get the money to him as soon as I could.

As the dun-coloured city with its two ancient rivers disappeared beneath us, I sat in a state of shock. Could it really all be over so quickly? Could it be that easy; that simple; that complete? I had been such an idiot and my judgement had been so haywire that I had actually been suspicious of Amin, the most trustworthy and gentle of all souls, while willingly going off with killers. I'd then written a story that I knew was going to piss them off. What the bloody hell was wrong with me? I should never have gone back to Baghdad. I slumped down in the seat. I'd been tired for too long: exhausted by the effort it took most mornings just to get out of bed and find a story. For the last year I'd been getting on planes that took me to places that didn't even light a flame of interest in me. Somewhere along the way I'd moved from being a character out of a Kafka novel, my nervous system so flayed that every touch was recorded as pain, to an automaton who rarely registered anything unless it cut down to the bone.

Chapter 37

London

BY EARLY EVENING I WAS SITTING IN ONE OF THE PAPER'S
timber-lined boardrooms in London, having been ushered in
the back entrance with two 'chaps', as Larry was calling them,
from 'the company'. 'The company' appeared to be a private
security firm the paper had hired to 'deal with the situation'—
which was what people were calling what was happening to
me when they weren't referring to it as 'Kate's predicament'.
Everyone was talking in inverted commas, no one was handing
out business cards, and it felt like I was the only one who had
no idea what was going on.

The 'chap' doing most of the talking, who was obviously
the man in charge, was a Mr Smith—no prizes for guessing
that was not his real name. It was clear to me that Mr Smith
was relishing my 'predicament' as he leaned back against the
mahogany boardroom desk, hands lightly balanced on its edge,
feet elegantly crossed.

One of the first things I noticed about Mr Smith was his shoes—polished to within an inch of their life. Military. His nails were buffed to a smooth pearly white. Money. Everything about Mr Smith bespoke military and money: lots of military and lots of money. There was nothing even slightly 'chappy' about him. Yet he did not look like a spook or a mercenary, and I should know; I'd seen enough of them in Iraq. Wearing an impeccably tailored suit, a white linen shirt and a navy blue silk tie, Mr Smith looked like the CEO of a Fortune 500 company. Mother would have liked him very much. The security business was paying very handsomely these days, as everyone in Baghdad knew. It was Mr Smith's hands, though, that gave him away: huge, ham fists, gnarled and twisted from too many fights and too many broken bones. Tough hands. Lots of military; lots of money; lots of tough. Just what you needed when someone was trying to kill you.

'We know very little at the moment about this group you've had the misfortune to run up against, Ms Price, and so our best advice is for you to go to ground for a while, preferably out of the country.' He spoke with an accent that I was unable to place. Mr Smith was a man of the world. He also spoke very softly so that I had to lean forward in my chair to hear him. Mr Smith knew how to command attention.

'You mean out of Iraq?'

'No, Ms Price, we mean out of England.'

The room went quiet as I absorbed this information. Then Mr Smith spoke again. 'It's not safe for you to be anywhere you would normally be. I see here,' he said, picking up a file and turning to the second page, 'that your home address in London is listed in the phone book, as is your telephone number.

Someone in your line of work should always have an unlisted number, Ms Price.'

'I'll keep that in mind for the future, Mr Smith.' I looked at Larry and at the other man in the room, who I had not been introduced to, but who sat silently studying me. Turning back to Larry I offered him a wan smile and suggested that this all seemed a little too cloak-and-daggerish for me.

Larry looked uncomfortable. I also noticed he wasn't smoking. Probably Mr Smith had asked him not to while he was in the room. Mr Smith was a man who commanded respect. Mr Smith cleared his throat and shifted his weight, before leaning back and folding his arms across his chest. Larry might be uncomfortable, but Mr Smith was definitely having a very good time.

'Let me remind you that they just killed seventeen people and are saying they want to kill you. Your employer is taking these threats against your life very seriously, Ms Price, and we suggest you do too. So, is there anywhere you'd like to go?'

Anywhere I'd like to go? Was he talking about anywhere I'd like to go for a holiday, or anywhere I'd just like to go generally? There was a difference.

The phone on the boardroom table started ringing. Larry picked it up. 'I told you no calls,' he said angrily. 'No, tell him we don't know anything yet. No, listen, we've got a situation here . . .'

I smiled. I'd never heard Larry talk like that before: never heard him say 'we have a situation here'. It sounded stupid. I put my hand over my mouth, trying not to laugh, but Larry had seen me and frowned. I saw then how sick he looked and I could no longer see the humour in the situation. 'Tell him,' he said, looking directly at me, 'that I'll let him know as soon as we hear anything.' A pause. 'Yes, she's safe. Yes, you can tell him that she is safe and we're looking after her and that I'll let him know of any changes.'

'. . . anywhere that you might feel comfortable staying for a while where people don't know you?'

'What?' Mr Smith had been talking to me, but I hadn't been listening.

'Is there anywhere you could go, Ms Price, where no one knows you?'

'Where no one knows me?' People didn't know me all over the world. 'Actually,' I said absently, a thought beginning to form, 'there's an old cottage about an hour north of Sydney that I lived in as a kid and I go there sometimes, but I don't know anyone in the street anymore and it's mostly holiday homes and weekenders. No one knows me.'

'Give me the address and we'll check it out and get back to you. If it looks okay we should have you on a flight to Sydney within twenty-four hours. Remember, Ms Price, you must not—I repeat, *must not* speak with anyone for a while, and that includes your parents, your friends, your landlord and your pet hamster. Is that clear?'

'My parents,' I said, thinking about them for the first time, 'must be worried sick. Has anyone contacted them to let them know I'm alright?'

'We've taken care of that,' Larry said.

'Pete—what about Pete?'

'He doesn't need to know anything,' interjected Mr Smith. 'I assume you're talking about Peter McDermott. It really is best for everyone, including Mr McDermott, that he's left in the dark.' After consulting his file he looked up again. 'You have a friend, a Mr Luc Vos, who's currently in Basra. Is there a message you would like us to deliver to him?' I realised then I hadn't given Luc a second thought. We'd said our goodbyes, and by now he would have heard everything, including the news that I had been taken out of the country. I told them there was no message.

Within less than twelve hours Mr Smith and his people had apparently gathered a great deal of information about me. They had also, it seemed, taken control of my life. They had confiscated my mobile phone on the plane, explaining that it could be traced, bundled me off to a hotel in the middle of London and told me that I wasn't to contact anyone. They'd also delivered all my belongings from Baghdad shortly after I had arrived in the hotel. A man had then appeared to ask me to make a list of all the things I might need from my flat in Clapham Common. Need for what? had been my first reaction.

'Right, then we'll get you back to the hotel and, all things being equal, on a plane to Australia tomorrow.'

'Wait,' I said, as everyone began to stand, seemingly satisfied with the arrangements. 'Wait. This is going way too fast.' I stopped and drew breath, stalling for time as I tried to collect my thoughts. 'Look,' I said, feeling my way even as I spoke, 'I did something really stupid in Baghdad, and I agree that it's not a good idea for me to go back there right now. I also see that going to Australia for a while might be a good idea, but there's something that I have to do before you book me a one-way ticket to Sydney.'

Mr Smith was not happy. He turned to Larry, completely ignoring me, as if I wasn't even there. 'We know virtually nothing about this organisation, these so-called Warriors of Allah. We don't know their capabilities, what their aims are or where their funding is coming from. Until we know more, we need to keep Ms Price safe. You must understand that we cannot be held responsible if she does not follow the plan. She could be putting herself in grave danger, and if—'

'Mr Smith, I am in the room, you know, and I am capable of making decisions for myself, so if you wouldn't mind, you may address comments about me directly to me.' I turned back to Larry. 'Frankly, I think we're all getting a little carried away here. These Warriors of Allah are probably some tin-pot, fly-by-night group that will disappear into oblivion in no time. I agree that until we find out more about them I should lie low, and I'm more than willing to do that, but as I said there's something I have to do first and I won't be moved on that. After that, I promise I'll go to Sydney until this all blows over.'

Larry was not happy and it made me feel bad that I was causing him more pain.

'Kate, this is a very grave situation. Do you know what you're doing? Are you sure?'

'Please, Larry, don't worry about me. I'm going to be just fine, and yes, I've never been surer of anything in my life. I'll contact you when I get to Sydney. Okay? I promise.'

Larry was looking so frail that I walked around the desk and gave him a hug. It was the first time I had ever touched him and his face flushed a bright crimson.

'I want to thank you, Larry, for all you're doing, I really do. But I promise you I'll be fine.'

Chapter 38

New York

THE TAXI PULLED UP OUTSIDE A BLEAK THREE-STOREY BUILDING that had seen better days. Standing outside the circle of light at the front door I rang the buzzer.

'Yeah?'

'Can I come up?'

'Kate? Is that you?'

'Yes.'

'Jesus. Third floor.'

There was no lift and the only light, which failed to illuminate the entry, came from a naked light bulb suspended from a long chain in the middle of the staircase, sticky and fly-speckled from years of neglect. The handrail hinted of the polished mahogany of grander days, as did the marble stairs worn low through more than a century of footfalls.

It was one o'clock in the morning and nothing stirred behind the heavy doors on each landing. When I got to the third floor Pete was waiting by an open door in a pair of jeans he'd obviously just pulled on in a hurry. Neither of us spoke as he moved aside to let me in.

The apartment was not what I expected, although who could say what I had expected? There was none of his work; no tools of the trade. Nothing. Initially it appeared to be one cavernous room made theatrical by thousands of books lining bookshelves that reached to the ceiling, and one very large bed with the sheets rumpled under an old, hastily pulled up chenille bedspread. Above the bed was a poster of a white ibis and another of a famous American Indian chief whose name escaped me. The apartment didn't look like a home so much as a library housing an oversized bed.

As I moved further into the room I noticed an alcove off to the left with a small kitchenette, an old ripped leather lounge of indeterminate colour and age, and a coffee table piled high with newspapers. On the wall above the lounge was another poster: a simple drawing of a stick-figure child in a field of daisies and doves captioned with the words, *What if they gave a war and nobody came?* It came from the peace movement during the Vietnam War years.

'Are you out of your mind, Kate?' Pete said from behind me. 'What are you doing here? Larry said you were going to a safe house.'

'Yeah, well . . . plans change.' I turned to face him. 'Actually, I am going to a safe house—well, it's not strictly a safe house, just a house far away from everything—but I needed to see you first and then when I got to JFK I realised I didn't even know your address. How stupid is that? We've known each other for how long, and all I knew was that you lived in New York in the Meatpacking District. That's email for you. I wanted to phone you, but the security guys Larry hired said I shouldn't use my phone for a while so I left my old SIM card in the office and got a new one, but it meant that I didn't have your number, and you're not in the phone book so I had to look up John's number—luckily he's in the phone book—which he shouldn't be, by the way, in his profession, and I noticed that you're not . . . in the phone book, that is. Anyway, before I could ring John to find out your address I had to buy one of those phone cards, and I didn't have US dollars so I had to find an ATM, but I didn't have any credit cards because they're getting me new ones, and then I had to use one of those public phones to ring John, and none of them worked. In the end I borrowed a stranger's mobile, and—'

'Kate, Kate, stop it,' he said, taking me by the shoulders. 'How long have we got?'

'A few days . . . maybe a week at the most.'

Chapter 39

ON THAT FIRST MORNING A SHAFT OF LIGHT FOUND ITS WAY through the canyons of New York to rest on the chenille bedspread on the end of the bed. In my happiness I imagined it to be a blessing, a rare and beautiful thing, and so I looked for it each morning after that but it never returned. Because Pete had work to do for the exhibition he left before lunch each day, while I remained behind in the apartment. With his scent and the taste of him lingering long after he was gone, I would lie in the bed thinking about what had happened until hunger drew me out. After pulling up the sheets and plumping up the pillows, I'd make myself a late breakfast, or grab something from the deli on the corner, but with no real desire to leave his apartment I'd quickly return to spend the rest of the day lost in his bookshelves.

Wandering, fingers drawing softly over titles I had seen him reading and many that were new to me, I searched him out, wanting to know more, loving the fact that he kept so many books. I wondered what else I didn't know about him and was eager for the unfolding.

When it rained on that first day, and I lay on the bed waiting for him with the damp and the smell of old books settling musty on my skin, I understood why he didn't keep his photographs there.

In the afternoons, before he returned, I would sit on the old lounge marvelling at what had come to pass, watching as the frozen winter sun fell across the old wooden floorboards and that library–bedroom became a magical, mote-filled place. Hungry for him. Always hungry for him. After all those years it felt as if I would never be able to get enough of the man. At night I lay awake with the warmth of his body wrapped around mine in a giant bed floating in a library, so removed from anything I had ever experienced before.

As we lay on the lounge by the window on the second night and he held my left hand, absently twisting the wedding ring I had taken to wearing many years before, he confessed that he was uncomfortable with personal detail. Gradually, though, especially in the early hours of the morning when we found each other awake, the process of discovery began as we slowly unpacked the secrets we had kept. He had never mastered the intricacies of intimacy he told me—fingers walking up my spine. It was a small frustration, and one he was now determined to overcome—fingers dusting light as feathers across the hollow in my collarbone. He was comfortable with the itinerant life he had chosen. But I knew that, didn't I?—his mouth moving across my skin, his tongue teasing out my nipple. He had given up believing I would ever come to him. He knew loneliness. He began to move inside me. We both had. My hips moving to take him deeper.

On the third day he asked me if I'd brought the red velvet dress and the fine silver chain that I'd worn the day he'd had lunch with my parents, so I ventured out after he'd left and bought sexy red underwear before spending the afternoon with an Egyptian woman who painted my feet and one shoulder with a delicate lacy henna pattern then pummelled and pumped my body, oiling and perfuming it for my lover. My lover. What a strange and wondrous thing it was. I could not stop smiling.

The posters above the bed of the ibis and the Indian were presents from a former girlfriend, he said, who had told him that his totem was the white ibis, and his spirit guide was Geronimo. I registered surprise that he might believe in such things and he laughed, claiming that he didn't, but the posters looked like they had been there for a very long time.

And so over the days I began to make images of him in my mind's eye for the time when I would have to leave him again—unguarded moments of grace: his profile in repose; a hand resting; a bare foot; a naked back. Some of these things were familiar to me, but others were not. At night I listened to his breathing, locking mine into the rhythm of his, and I remembered those nights in Baghdad when he shared my room after the war had begun and I would watch him sleeping, imagining a time like this.

When I thought he was asleep one night I propped myself up on one elbow so I could see him more closely. 'What're you doing?' he said, surprising me. His eyes still closed.

'Making a map of your face.'

'I thought you would have seen enough of my face.'

'I would have thought so too, McDermott, but there you go.'

He smiled, pulling me down so my head rested on his chest and I could no longer see him, but I could breathe in the smell of him to make more memory pictures. Each day I fell deeper into the mystery of the man I had thought I knew so well. When he shaved, towel wrapped around his waist, I leaned against the door of the bathroom and we talked, he looking in the mirror, I making my images.

He cooked us a meal late one night, testing and tasting, reaching for the pepper mill as he talked, and I recorded each moment of it.

'Do you remember when we first met?' he was saying, but I was watching his hands move, hardly taking in the words.

'Mmm?'

'Did you really think I hadn't noticed you back in Riyadh?'

I looked up, smiling into his eyes with the memory. 'Do you really think I hadn't noticed you before then either, McDermott?'

'Me first,' he insisted, pointing at me with the fork he'd been using to separate the pasta.

'Okay.'

He leaned up against the kitchen bench. 'I noticed you the first day you walked into the briefing room in Riyadh, and I saw how hard you worked, and how you drove everyone crazy with your incessant questions. God, you were a pain. I read all your articles, Kate. I watched you and I knew who you were before you schemed your way into coming with me and John.'

'And Ms CBS. Let's not forget Ms CBS,' I said, walking over to put my arms around his waist.

He laughed. 'Is that what you called her?'

'Oh, come on, McDermott, you still can't remember her name and I certainly never could.'

He laughed again, then said, 'Do you really think John and I would've let you come along with us if we hadn't known anything about you?' He wound his arms around my shoulders and pulled me in closer to him. 'I've been a patient man, Kate Price. God knows I've been a patient man.'

'And I bless you for it.' I reached up and ran my finger over the tiny scar from Grozny before drawing my hand down the side of his face. 'I saw you years before that, Peter McDermott. I saw you years before. I've been a patient woman.'

'After Rwanda . . .' he said, becoming serious.

I stiffened. 'Do we have to talk about Rwanda?'

'Let me finish. After Rwanda I decided that I'd never make a move on you again. I wanted you to come to me and . . .'

'But Larry grounded me in London, Pete. I wanted to come back, but he wouldn't let me.'

'Well, I didn't know that, did I? I watched your reporting and all I saw was that you were working in London. You didn't come back to Bosnia and you didn't try to contact me. What was I to think? Anyway, I did pretty well except for that one night in London after the conference. Do you remember? You looked so unbelievably beautiful.'

'Smashing, I think it was,' I said, laughing.

'Smashing, yes,' he said.

There was silence between us then as we remembered how the evening had ended.

'You would have taken the assignment too, Pete, if you'd been in my position. Larry hadn't offered me anything since Srebrenica. I was desperate.'

'No, you're wrong, Kate. I wouldn't have taken it that night. I wouldn't have gone anywhere that night. I hadn't seen you for so long and I'd missed you so bad and then when you turned up looking so beautiful nothing would have made me leave you. Nothing.'

'Were you so sure I'd come to you after all the years and all the misunderstandings and mishaps?'

'Frankly, no. Sometimes I thought you were close, but then you'd always back away. I tried just to enjoy working with you, but sometimes it wasn't easy, Kate, and in the end, when you were with Luc, I didn't want to do it anymore.'

There was none of the shyness of new lovers. Our bodies were comfortable where they touched: his hand on my stomach; my foot across his leg; his head resting on my breasts. He spoke and I watched his mouth; he laughed and I watched his eyes; he moved and I was lost in him. It was a private thing. I drank him in as if I would never get enough. I wanted him—the smell of him, his touch, his mouth—oh mercy, the places his mouth could take me to. I wanted him again before the memory of our sex had even faded.

And so we tested the water, wading in deeper in those first few days. Fragile secrets, seemingly inconsequential stories that had lain hidden between us for years. Stories that said something, but not all. Nervous that it might all come tumbling down, we felt our way cautiously, laying out threads that might, if prepared carefully, weave the fabric of something different between us: something we could build on that might last.

Early one morning, careful not to wake him, I moved my hand over his skin creating an image with my touch. When he stirred and grabbed my hand I froze until his breathing returned to sleep.

While showering one morning, my eyes squeezed shut against the shampoo bubbles, I felt cool air float over my skin and I knew he had entered the room and was watching me. I waited, wondering where the touch would be. When it came his tongue felt cool against my skin until it reached my mouth, warm and soapy.

There is another memory I have from that time. He is humming Van Morrison's 'Tupelo Honey' while making breakfast. He is naked and I am watching him until I realise he is becoming aroused. 'Ah, McDermott, is my mere presence turning you on?' I said, pulling the T-shirt up over my head and stepping out of my knickers. We made love on the old rug between the rows of books. So many ways to make so many memories.

'Have you ever thought what the world would be like,' he said, as afterwards we lay looking up at the bowed shelves towering over us, 'if there was only ever one copy of each book? It would move carefully around the world from hand to hand and then people would appreciate just how precious books are, they'd understand the reverence of words and of stories told. We don't appreciate something we have too much of,' he added. Was he still talking about books, I wondered, or us?

On the fifth day he came back to the apartment early, arms loaded with packages, and disappeared into the bathroom with the warning that I was not to come in until he called. When he ushered me in I saw candles flickering through the steam, and new fluffy white towels hanging over the side of the hand basin. On the cracked black and white chequerboard tiles of the floor sat two champagne glasses and a bottle of bubbling golden liquid, droplets of condensation slipping down its sides. As I slowly undressed for him he sat on the side of the bath watching me, but when I began pinning my hair on top of my head for the bath he stopped me. Putting his hands on my bare hips, he turned me around so my back was to him.

'Do it again,' he said, 'more slowly this time, so I can see how it's done.'

Shaking my hair free I gathered it up and retwisted and pinned it, before unpinning again and passing the tortoiseshell clip back over my shoulder to him. He tried but his fingers were unpractised and his efforts collapsed, so that my hair floated loose around us like fine silk on the steamy surface of the water.

In a hundred different moments I wanted to tell him I loved him, but the words stuck in the back of my throat, impossible to move forward, weighed down by the fear that to speak of love would be to lose it. And so I watched, and in that watching I hoped he would see what I was too afraid to say.

Sitting on the floor the second last night, balancing our dinner plates on our laps, he leaned across to wipe crumbs from my mouth and his fingers lingered. 'Sometimes you only smile with the corners of your mouth, Price. Did you know that?' His fingers moved down then to trace over the intricate henna pattern on my foot resting on the floor in front of him. That night in bed he talked of when I would be gone and how our lives were not conducive to stable long-term relationships and I wondered why we were always afraid of the good things that happened to us. Why, when we finally found something worth keeping, were we already looking past it to the time when it would be gone? I wanted to tell him this. I wanted to say that we should fight for the thing that we had found, but I remained silent, his words having already lingered too long in the air above the bed; the time to respond had passed. Which one of us loved more, I wondered as he fell asleep. There is always the lover and the beloved: the object and the subject. There is always the one who loves more.

Chapter 40

ON OUR LAST FULL DAY TOGETHER WE WOKE TO A CRISP, white New York Sunday morning and I convinced him to venture out with me. Every leaf that crackled under our feet, every passer-by, every bird, every hawker, every madman and every building I saw with fresh eyes that morning—a strange eroticism of observation that made every object a thing of wonder and beauty.

Finding a seat on an uptown bus we watched an old man intent on telling the bus driver a long and complicated story as the line of people behind him twisted and turned and craned their necks in their impatience to see what the hold-up was.

'Yeah, yeah, c'mon, move along,' said the driver, hooking his thumb towards the back of the bus. Eventually, losing all patience with the old man, he leaned in close. 'Listen, buddy, I can do directions, but I don't do stories, so just move it.'

I watched the rejection register on the old man's sad face and my heart ached for his loneliness. As he shuffled past us I wanted to move over and pat the seat next to us and say, 'Come, sit here and tell *me* your story. I can do stories.' But I didn't quite trust the lover's compulsion for kindness and he was gone and the moment had passed.

New York's street vendors on Fifth Avenue, wrapped up under a wintery sky, blew into their gloves, as oblivious to the lovers passing by as they were to the litter swirling around their stomping feet. Out front of Tiffany's, Pete wrapped his arms around me and pulled me in closer to ask if I aspired to own jewellery like that in the window. Laughing, I pulled off my gloves and held up my hands to the cold. 'A fake wedding ring. Probably fake gold.' I wriggled my right hand then so that the coat sleeve fell back to reveal a wooden Buddhist bracelet. 'This bracelet was given to me by a friend when she returned from Dharamsala.' Fingering my earlobes, 'These crystals were my mother's from centuries ago, as was the red dress and the silver chain you seem to be so attached to. So the answer to your question is, no, I don't aspire to own jewellery like that. At this very moment I don't aspire to own anything more than the moments I have left with you.'

'Come on,' he said, grabbing my hand and spinning me around. 'I want to show you something.'

A short cab ride brought us to the Bowery and a door hidden between a reconditioned whitegoods warehouse and a Chinese spice merchant. The men running the warehouse, and an elderly Chinese fellow who sat gently stroking his long thin beard, were lounging around a small metal table where a game of mahjong was in progress. As we climbed out of the taxi conversation at the table ceased, and with Pete's hand on the small of my back urging me forward we passed the men, Pete promising that he would play a game with them the next time he came.

Winding our way through the guard of rusting whitegoods and cardboard cartons of spices and dried mushrooms on upturned wooden crates, we entered a doorway where the warm aroma of exotic spices mixed with the hard metallic odour of wet iron. After closing the grille of the old service elevator we rattled our way to the second floor before coming to a bone-jarring stop. Pulling back the metal grate Pete pushed the door open with a flourish and all the dreams I had been weaving disintegrated before me.

His studio had small utilitarian pieces of equipment. Four dark grey filing cabinets, a desk with a computer, printer, fax machine and mail neatly stacked across its surface. An Agfa loupe half-hidden under an unopened parcel, a projector, a notice board and a door leading to a room carved out of a loft, possibly a darkroom. There was a light table and a blank whiteboard on a wall with little silver magnets standing neatly to attention along its bottom. By one of four windows that ran from ceiling to floor and let in thin winter light from the alleyway below was a small wooden table with a mended broken leg and three old coffee cups, a coffee plunger, a kettle, a spoon and two glass jars with sugar and coffee. An opened packet of tea bags sat precariously on the edge of the table beside an old leather couch atop a worn Persian rug. Small balls of fluff gathered on the floorboards under the couch and in the corners of the room. Expensive photographic books, old newspapers and magazines were stacked neatly on the floor and across the couch. But the unremarkable minutiae of a working life turned into something entirely different when you looked up at the walls. The largest black and white photographs I had ever seen: terrible photographs of people, so beautiful and harrowing that they seduced as they repelled. I had seen many of his photographs before in magazines and newspapers, and I had seen all of the things they recorded with my own eyes, but never had I been so profoundly confronted by photography.

They had a mutual history, this man and his photographs—points of intersection between lives. He had stolen a moment; a fragment; something from them that was now his. Yet who, I wondered, looking at the lost eyes watching me from the walls, was the possessor and who the possessed? These people had moved on, or they were dead. In any event, I doubted any of them would have remembered the photographer, but he would never forget them. He would always be with them; their lives would always define his.

Standing in his studio on that silvery winter's afternoon I felt myself teetering on a precipice as the photographs drew me back into a world where life and death somehow seemed to matter more. Back into the places where you were confronted by the stripped-off depths of humanity and forced to face your own: the war journalist's bittersweet self-flagellation. The apartment back in the Meatpacking District was not Pete; it was simply where he slept and ate. This room, with his work lining the walls, was the soul of him and there was no room for me there.

Moving slowly around the space, not walking, but turning myself three hundred and sixty degrees from a spot in the centre of the room, I looked over to where he was standing, watching me to measure my reaction. I had no idea what to say. Any comment would have been superfluous, irrelevant, banal, misunderstood. In the end I asked one unsatisfying question, but it was the only one that ever really mattered and this time I knew what the answer must be. To the uninitiated it was a small question of seeming innocence: a question of one syllable whose depth and breadth were immeasurable. 'Why?' I asked. 'Why do you do this?' Was there any other question ever? Didn't life come down to just this one question?

He looked puzzled for a second, perhaps disappointed. 'I thought you of all people would know the answer to that.'

'But I want to hear it from you.'

He laughed then, breaking the rod of tension that had been running through his body since we'd entered the studio. Moving his arms wide to embrace the whole of the room he looked at me again. 'This is who I am, Kate. There's no more you need to know about me. This is who I am. This is where it begins and ends for me. But you know that already.'

Of course I knew that. The problem was I had forgotten it and, in that forgetting, I had begun to believe that there might be room for me; a space for us. But there it was: such simple words with such powerful force and such terrible consequences. *This is who I am.* The seduction of being where history is made; the hit of feeling achingly alive rather than suburban dead-boring numb. It excited you, it fuelled you and it burned you up and spat you out like any other addiction. I no longer wanted to be my job. In the previous five days I had been shown the corner of something that might have been possible. I wanted it. I needed more. He did not.

Having no idea how his words and photos had affected me he began shifting a pile of books aside for me to sit on the lounge and then busied himself making me a cup of tea. As the tea grew cold in my hands I watched him move about the studio working, already having forgotten the woman perched on the edge of his world. If I had slipped away then he wouldn't have noticed immediately. It didn't mean he loved me less; it meant he loved his work more. And so I turned back to the walls to create my last images of him.

Such beautiful pictures of such terrible suffering. A little baby in Africa, flat eyes devoid of emotion: no malice, no accusation, no plea. No need. His eyes are like those of a soldier who has just left a terrible battle. Ask the soldier what he has seen at your peril, for he might just tell you the truth and you would not want to hear. The child's head is lying on the shoulder of a woman whose eyes look as if they have registered all the pain of the world. I used to know that woman, who once went to an AIDS hospital in Africa and found beauty there. I believed she was a good woman.

There is another woman. This one is lying on a makeshift bed, possibly in Afghanistan or just as possibly in Iraq, or the Sudan, or Rwanda, or Ethiopia, or any other of a hundred different places. A young boy . . . or perhaps it is a girl . . . rests his or her head on the woman's chest. Her hand rests on the child's shoulder. A private moment between a mother and a child, you might think, but it could just as possibly be a grandmother and a granddaughter, or an elder sister, or aunt, or cousin. It could be whatever you imagined it to be, and what you imagined it to be might not be the truth.

My eyes moved along the walls until I reached the photograph I had been avoiding all along. A man is crouching in a pool of rubble and garbage, bloody water at his feet. His knees are drawn into his chest, folds of his white dishdasha clutched to his breast as its hem sinks into the filth. Smoke is rising from a car smouldering behind him in the al-Shaab marketplace where the bodies of a mother and her three children are trapped. Tears are tracking down his blackened face. You would be forgiven for thinking he was looking directly at the photographer, but he was not. He was definitely not looking at the photographer. I know because I was there. He was looking past the man with the camera into the interminable years of grief spread out before him.

There is another lie in this picture. Over his head a hand is hovering. It is an elegant hand, a woman's hand, floating like a blessed halo in a gesture of grace. The man in the picture is unaware of the hand and the grace it offers as he rocks back and forth like a child in his pain. It is the hand that is the lie—or, rather, it is the woman. The hand and the woman offered no solace. Seconds after the photograph was taken the hand withdrew and the woman adjusted her sunglasses and walked away. She was not always a good woman, I think.

And so on that cold afternoon in New York I returned to the centre of the years that lay behind me, and the days and the months that lay ahead of me, and to the puzzle of how I was to construct a life when its centre was finally gone.

Chapter 41

I WOKE TO THE EERIE WHITE LIGHT OF THE FULL MOON flooding the room. If I'd smoked and I had been living in a 1940s movie I would have lit a cigarette and sat on the windowsill. And as the smoke curled up into the thin morning air I would have watched my lover sleeping. Instead, I lay close to his face bathed in the light from the moon and the fluorescent glare from the streetlights below and I watched him. I could see the morning stubble on his skin, the lines etched deep in his face, the flickering of an eyelid in sleep. It was time to go.

Rain had begun to fall lightly about half an hour earlier until the sound of tyres swishing across the wet road began to filter up through the closed window. If I could have held back that dawn I would have, but already the watery new day was in the room and he would wake soon. I rose and slipped into his shirt and stood at the sink shivering as I thought about making a cup of tea.

'Good morning,' came his voice husky from sleep through

the folds of my hair as his hands reached around under the shirt. 'Come back to bed.'

His tousled sleep smell was nearly more than I could stand but I had a plane to catch.

'I have to go.'

'Right now?' He pulled away.

'This morning.'

When I came out of the shower he was working on his laptop. 'I think it's better to be safe than sorry until they work out who these Warriors of Allah are, so I've set up two Yahoo accounts for us: Rocky91956 and Bullwinkle91965. They should be relatively untraceable.'

'Rocky and Bullwinkle.'

'We could have Kemosabe and Tonto if you don't like Rocky and Bullwinkle.'

'Only if you're the horse.'

'Tonto wasn't a horse, Price. No one was a horse.'

'Right, I knew that.'

'Yeah, sure.' He was smiling as he looked back down and continued to type. 'Let's just stick with Rocky and Bullwinkle, shall we?'

'Good choice, Kemosabe.'

He groaned. 'Price, get with the program. We've moved on from Kemosabe and Tonto. It's now Rocky and Bullwinkle. They're not related.'

'I knew that.'

'Yeah, sure you did.'

How quickly we had fallen back into the old relationship. We had our last breakfast together, discussing John's phone

333

call from the night before and the news that he was moving his family to Connecticut and taking a job on a local newspaper to try to keep his marriage together. It was only when we moved on to Soraya's operations that I remembered I would not be able to keep my promise to Amin and Hanan to see Soraya when she was next in London. I asked Pete to apologise to them for me and to pay Amin's wages for that last week I had been in Baghdad. Soraya's specialist believed her age was in her favour, Pete told me, and there was a very good chance there might not be too much scarring.

'We haven't discussed where you're going,' he said finally, as I stuffed the last of my things in my bag, 'but I think I know.'

'I'm going home, McDermott.'

'I thought so. How long will you stay?'

'As long as I need to. I've got a lot to think about.'

'Us?'

'And other things.'

When the taxi arrived I wouldn't allow him to come down to the street with me, insisting that we say our goodbyes in the room.

'Don't forget me, Price,' he called over the banister as I was making my way down the stairs.

'As if that were possible, Kemosabe,' I said, looking up and smiling at him. 'As if that were possible.'

'I'm Rocky, remember, and you're Bullwinkle.'

'Whatever.'

'You've got the email addresses and your password, haven't you?'

'In my pocket,' I said, patting my jeans.

'Don't make me wait too long.'

I waved over my shoulder without looking back before disappearing through the door.

Chapter 42

Sydney
January 2005

THROUGH THE HAZE OF MOSQUITO NETTING, FRAGILE AND yellowing with age, I could just make out the old angophora silhouetted black against the disappearing night and my heart swelled. I knew exactly where I was. Kicking the sheet off I rolled over onto my side in that airless predawn, drew my finger down the netting until it found the hole that had been there since I was a child, and began chipping away at the flaking paint on the old wicker bedside table with my nail. Throwaway furniture, Mother used to call it, although she had never thrown it away. Perhaps to do so would have meant replacing it with something more permanent, which might have indicated to my father that she was considering staying in Australia—'and that,' she said a hundred times, 'is quite frankly not an option.'

The old red leather travelling clock that had stopped plotting the passage of time in that slow-turning house sat on my parents' bedside table exactly where it had been left the day we had returned to England some twenty-five years before. Just as my mother had never been able to throw away the cane furniture I had never been able to throw away the clock, which in my mind represented a strange sort of honouring of my father and his eventual return.

Sinking back into the bed I laid my hands in the soft hollow between my hipbones and memory flew off to a crushed red velvet dress on a cold winter's night and a bedroom library. So tempting to surrender to the sweet stirrings the memories evoked, but I knew it was dangerous territory. And so with an effort I pulled myself back to the room by the sea, in that old fibro cottage, on that summer's dawn, a world and a lifetime away from New York, and as the rickety old fridge whirred into life I drifted back off to sleep.

At half past six the screeching of the cockatoos roused me. Stretching the last of the sleep out of my body I rolled over in search of the coolness on the other side of the bed, but the sun was already streaming in and the sheets were too warm. I could see Buster, the dog from next door, sitting outside the glass sliding doors that opened onto the back deck and the sea beyond, his tail beating an impatient rhythm as he waited for me to take him down to the beach. Not long after I'd arrived Buster had started visiting, and before too long had started coming to the beach with me every morning under the happy misapprehension that we were best mates. Since there were no other best mates in the offing I was more than happy to accommodate him.

There was only one other swimmer doing laps in the ocean rock pool that day and by silent consent we retreated to opposite sides of the pool. I swam peacefully for about forty minutes until my body began to tire and I climbed out over the side onto the rocks to slip into the ocean. After swimming out past the breakers I turned over onto my back and closed my eyes against the morning glare, letting my body drift with the rise and fall of the swell. Nearly two months since Baghdad and I could still feel the dust and rubble of that ancient city on my skin, still taste it in my mouth.

Back at the house I rinsed the salt off under the garden shower that my father had built of lattice when I was a child. Years later, when I first returned to the house as an adult, I had found its walls so overgrown with jasmine that I could no longer decide whether the jasmine was holding the lattice up or trying to pull it down. After laying my towel over the deck rail to dry I moved inside, walking through the house opening all the doors and windows. When I noticed the little balls of dust drifting around the lounge room floor I said to the house, 'I must sweep you today.' Perhaps I hoped that the words, spoken aloud, would lend some weight to the intent. The forlorn little tinsel Christmas decorations that I'd retrieved from a dusty cardboard box under the house twisted a crinkly dull green and silver in the morning breeze. I made a mental note to take them down, adding it to the ever-increasing list of things I had to do: cut back the wisteria that covered the garage; trim the jasmine around the shower; pull out the asparagus fern that clogged the gutters; string fishing wire along the deck rail to stop the cockatoos devouring its brittle saltiness and arrange for someone to repair the dry rot in the deck. The whole cottage needed repainting. Nothing ever got done.

Since returning to the house I had fallen into a routine dictated by the movement of the sun. Rising at dawn I'd head down to the beach for a swim, have breakfast, shower and check the news on the internet then sit on the deck waiting for my hair to dry and inspiration to strike. When I'd finally accepted that I wasn't going to do any of the chores that needed to be done I'd read, or mostly reread, everything in the house left over from the years we had lived there: *The Old Man and the Sea, Death of a Salesman, The Female Eunuch, The Wind in the Willows.*

Like nomads the old books and I travelled around the garden in search of shade as the heat built throughout the day, but before too long I'd drop whatever I was reading onto my stomach and drift off to the sounds of the day. When it was particularly hot, and the ocean hardly breathed, the cicadas in the eucalypts and the bees in the sweet orange jasmine would drown out the sound of the surf lapping gently on the sand below and I would dream for hours.

My daytime catnaps were contributing to wakeful nights, but that didn't really matter when there was nothing to do. The strands that equated living with achieving were slowly severing as the threads of my former life were cast adrift. As I sank deeper into torpor, sleepwalking through the daylight hours, I was initially surprised and then pleased to discover that I didn't much care any longer.

When they had first told me I needed to go away I had panicked and asked Mr Smith what I was going to do with my life. You could write, he had offered helpfully.

'No, I mean *my life*. What will I do with *my life*?'

Everyone, including Larry, had looked at me blankly before they looked at the floor, and then out the window, until finally we were all looking out the window as if the answer might come flying past. It had crossed my mind that any other journalist in my predicament might have taken the opportunity to write the first draft of a novel, but I was surprised again when I discovered I no longer wanted to write. Life was indeed changing.

Lying in bed at night I would feel the warm air currents drifting in through the window to move across my skin and Pete would be with me again—the scent of him, his touch, a finger tracing across my breast, between my legs—and I would be lost. With no other distractions my body had become the centre of my universe. In the mornings and evenings after my showers I lavished it with lotions, mesmerised by its changing angles and the new, more rounded, more womanly shape. My skin, no longer a sickly London grey, had turned a soft golden brown. Freckles, long forgotten from childhood, began to reappear. My hair, too, had grown and lightened.

In the middle of one drifting day I walked into my parents' bedroom and turned the full-length mirror around so I could study the naked woman standing before it, but my eyes began to play tricks on me and she began to blur and shimmer, no longer a shape but a moving thing. Trying to see myself as a stranger would, as a lover would, I followed the line of my back curving down to my waist, over the rise of my buttocks.

I turned, trying to look over my shoulder. I walked away then strolled back towards myself. But it was no use—no manner of twisting or turning could show me anew. Unpinning my hair I let it swing down around my face until it enveloped me in a shampoo cloud and I was lost again in the memory of an old cracked bathtub and my hair floating across its surface. What did he see then and would he notice the difference now? Which one would please Pete more? And so he was there, as always, in those slow, drifting, watercolour days: his hand lying flat across my thigh, his laugh, his seriousness, a finger circling light as air on my skin until my body was alive with stirrings, seduced by the mere memory of him, and I, fool that I was, tried to remake endings that would not be remade.

'You didn't need to write it,' Pete had said that last night as we lay together before sleep.

Did he think I might not have considered that possibility? I had crossed over into forbidden territory then and had asked him if he loved me.

'Of course,' he had whispered, tightening his arm around my waist to pull me in closer. 'Always.'

The shame. Oh, the shame of it. What else could he have said? How I wished I had been nobler, more sanguine, less desperate in those last hours together, but the words were out, and the memory, each time it returned, brought afresh the old humiliation.

And so the days and weeks passed . . .

Chapter 43

IN LATE JANUARY I RECEIVED A LONG AND UNACCUSTOMEDLY lyrical email from Pete.

From: Rocky91956@yahoo.com
Date: Saturday 21 January 2005 6:44 AM
To: Bullwinkle91965@yahoo.com
Subject: Good morning

Dearest Bullwinkle,
I am writing at the beginning of this new year in the pitch dark up on the edge of the Yorkshire moors—Brontë country—after spending Xmas with my parents and brothers. After bringing in the wood, and coal, and lighting an open fire which casts occasional flickering orange on the electronic light off the computer screen, it is touch-type practice at six-thirty am . . . punctuation, which I can only occasionally locate on the keyboard, is absent or erratic/

the cold is gripping my toes one by one in a tightening vice while my face is hot from the small flames and my brother's snoring (he shares this small room with me) has been interrupted which means tea may need to be made fresh soon . . . well perhaps not . . . he's off again.

I don't think I ever told you about this farmhouse my father bought. It was supposed to be his retirement home but it has never been used as such. Its story, my dear Bullwinkle, has more twists and kinks in it than can be told. One day, though, when we are together again, I will amuse you with some memories

Been thinking about you . . . have attached a photo taken in Afghanistan.

X

In the photo I have a scarf wrapped around my head so that all you can see are my eyes. Standing in front of me is a small, frightened child with wide dark eyes. My hands are resting on his shoulders and I am looking down at him. We had just come in from three weeks covering the fighting in Afghanistan with the Northern Alliance when Pete decided he needed more photographs of the refugees fleeing across the border into Pakistan. It was a miserable place, full of dirt and flies and shit and listless, lost people. Even in winter the odour was unbearable. I remember clearly that all I wanted that afternoon was to get the hell out of there, sink my aching limbs into a steaming hot bath and turn my brain off. The photo pulled me back to Afghanistan and the life I used to have, which was probably Pete's intent, but it also showed me how far I had come by then from the idealistic young journalist who wanted to change the world. For the hundredth time I wondered when the rot had set in. Could it all be blamed on Rwanda?

After checking the news I stood under the shower and watched the water flow over the last scraps of the henna decoration on my feet before swirling down the drain. Would the freckle-faced little girl who had first stood there over thirty years before recognise the woman she had become? I wondered. Would she even like her?

I'd been lonely before, but the way I was feeling after a few months alone in the house was beyond lonely. I spoke on the phone to Pete, Larry, my parents, Bella and sometimes John, and I had exchanged a few words with the young girl at the checkout in the local supermarket and nodded to strangers in the pool, but essentially I had been living without any meaningful human contact. No one had touched me, not even a handshake, for months. I joked with Pete that I was losing my mind, unable to tell him that I thought I might be losing myself.

We'd all been checking the chatter on the internet and as far as we could see no one had been talking about me or my article after the first commotion, while the Warriors of Allah seemed to have disappeared without trace. At the beginning of January Larry informed me that, in Mr Smith's learned opinion, it was safe for me to return to work, but I should not return to Iraq for at least two more years. When I told him that I wasn't quite ready to return to work I could tell he was disappointed and he reluctantly informed me that I would need to use my long-service leave to cover any extra time off. So be it. I really didn't care. But I did care about Larry. The poor man worried about me when I was working and worried about me when I wasn't.

Larry stopped asking me when I might be coming home after that, but my parents continued to ask—not because they wanted me to, but because they didn't want me to. In their minds Australia was as far away from a war zone as you could get. Pete never asked when I was coming back.

'Are you doing any writing?' Larry asked one evening in early February.

'Not too many stories happening in this house, Larry.'

'No, I mean are you doing any writing at all?'

'Not really.'

'Um . . . well, I'm obliged to tell you that next week your long-service leave will run out.'

'Right. Okay. I've got a little money saved that could last me a couple more months if I live frugally, which is not too hard here.'

'Ah, I don't know how to say this, Kate, but . . . do you feel safe?'

'Christ, Larry, what sort of question is that?'

'Just a question. Do you?'

I wasn't completely stupid and Larry wasn't very good at subtlety or subterfuge. I could guess why he was asking that question. One of the symptoms of post-traumatic stress disorder was believing that the world was an unsafe place. I knew I should have told Larry I felt safe in the world, but the world was not a safe place and you didn't need to have PTSD to know that. I considered it a trick question and decided not to respond, so Larry changed tack and asked if I was having any dreams. He'd either been reading up on PTSD, or some shrink now employed by the paper to handle all their possible nutcases had suggested he ask me these questions.

'Larry, what's going on? Have you turned into my psychiatrist?'

'I'm just worried about you.'

'I know, I know, but you don't need to be. I am safe and I'm relaxing and I promise I'll be back at work soon. I just need a little more time.'

'Well, I was thinking that when your long-service leave is gone we could put you on sick leave if that helped with the financial situation.'

'But wouldn't you have to say that I was wacko?'

'We wouldn't put it like that. Post-traumatic stress is a valid reaction to what you've been through. Listen, Kate, take all the time you want, but do you really think it's a good idea being in that house on the other side of the world all by yourself?'

'Larry, people do live in Australia, you know, and things do happen here. I'm not the only one living on the continent or even in my street. Besides, you'll be pleased to know that I've got a friend I'm spending a good deal of time with.'

'That's good to hear. An old friend?'

'No, I think Buster must be only about six years old.'

'Oh . . .'

'Buster's a dog, Larry.'

'A dog?'

'A dog.'

'Kate, don't you think that's—'

'So, Larry, do you want to hear a dream?'

'Yeah, sure, fire away.'

'I call this one my heaven dream.'

'Right.'

'I'm in a white building. All the corridors—and there are only corridors—are lined with shiny white tiles. There are no stairs, only ramps leading upwards, which is a strange thing really when you think about it. How do I know they only go upwards?' I paused, waiting for a comment, but Larry didn't respond. 'Anyway, following the ramp closest to me I reach a place at the top of the building where two elderly men are sitting at old-fashioned school desks busily writing in large ledgers with white quills. These men are definitely not your stereotypical heavenly archangel types with wings and halos, although I consider the quills and the inkwells a fine touch.' I smiled down the phone, waiting for Larry's chuckle, but again there was only silence.

'As I'm standing before one of the men he raises his right hand, and without looking up at me he points to the wall and tells me I have to write three things that God is. Taking a thick black marker from a box at the front of the desk I try to write, but each time I begin I see that someone has already written on the tile before me. While I'm searching for a free tile I never think to cheat by reading what others have proclaimed God to be.' I paused. 'Are you still there, Larry?'

'Sure. Keep going.'

I was getting worried. Perhaps telling him the dream was not such a good idea after all. 'Okay, well, finally I locate a blank tile and I write the words *love* and then *forgiveness* without hesitation, but I can't think of a third. When I return to the desk the fellow lifts his right arm again, only this time he points to the corridor behind him, indicating that I should enter. Just as I'm about to do so, a man comes running out of the corridor, terrified. When I ask him what's wrong he tells me that he's never going back down the corridor again. You're tested on the words you have written about God. I ask what he'd written and he tells me "love". I didn't need to know what else he wrote, "love" is enough. He failed the "love" test and I know I'll fail it too. I'll probably also fail the "forgiveness" test, so I decide I'm not going to chance it.' That was the end of the dream, but Larry hadn't said anything. 'Larry, are you taking notes?'

'No, did you want me to?'

'No, of course not!'

'Take all the time you need, Kate.'

'Did I freak you out, Larry?' Thank God I hadn't told him about the Rwandan dream. Even I knew that was too fucked up to see the light of day.

'Not too much.'

'Bullshit.'

'Okay, a little bit. I'm pretty sure I can get you sick leave,' he said, breaking into a hacking cough that seemed to go on forever.

'Larry, you need to do something about that cough. It's definitely getting worse.'

'Yeah, yeah, I know.'

'Will you stop those bloody cigarettes and see a specialist?'

'What are you now, my wife?'

'Well, if you can be my psychiatrist I can be your wife.'

'Like I said, Kate, take all the time you want and let me know if you have problems with money.'

'Because you'll lend me some?'

'Well, if you need it, I—'

'Thanks, my friend, but I don't need money. Now promise me you'll see a doctor, Larry.'

'Yeah, sure. I'll talk to you again, Kate, in a few days.'

'Larry,' I said, before he hung up, 'do you know what the other descriptor of God should have been?'

'Not really.'

'I've been thinking about this a lot, Larry. Hope. God is love, forgiveness and hope.'

Chapter 44

THE SMELL OF SMOKE AT DAWN BROUGHT WITH IT THE MEMORY of the early-morning cooking fires of Bali. All that was missing was the pungent scent of kreteks and the *pling, plong, pling* of gamelan music wafting out from a *warung* by the side of the road. A liver-pink haze hung heavy that morning across the horizon from the westerly that had come howling down Pittwater the previous afternoon. Whistling through the rigging and swinging the boats around on their moorings, the wind had brought with it the ash and smoke of the fires ringing Sydney.

That morning on the beach the rank odour of three-day-old seaweed, unclaimed by the shrinking tide, lingered in the air, while the screeching of seagulls circling overhead sent my best friend into a barking frenzy. The high tide of the previous afternoon had left a jagged line of bluebottles stranded on the dry sand. Skimming my eye across the pool's surface I checked none were in the water before slipping in. After swimming a few laps I stopped at the far end of the pool to check on Buster, who was busily rolling in the seaweed. My best friend was going to stink. Sinking back under the water I pushed off again.

Normally I paced myself, leaving the hard swimming for the final laps, but that day I felt a need to pull hard from the beginning, to punish myself, working the tension out of my shoulders and back with every stroke. By the time Buster and I arrived back at the house it was eight o'clock and the sun was high and white in a sky of the softest hazy blue. With the Bali theme still playing in my head I put some gamelan music on the CD player before wandering into the bedroom to pull up the sheets and tie the mosquito net back into its knot above the bed. Picking the clothes up off the floor, I carried them to the laundry under the house. It worked for a while—this pretending there was some purpose to my day—but it didn't take long for the constant plinging and plonging of the gamelan music to irritate, or the small diversions to lose their appeal, and it all began to unravel. Before picking up my current book and heading out to the backyard I put that morning's breakfast plate on top of the other dishes in the sink and sat down in front of the computer where I found an email from Pete.

From: Rocky91956@yahoo.com
Date: Friday 4 February 2005 4:12 AM
To: Bullwinkle91965@yahoo.com
Subject:

Dear Bullwinkle,
Thinking of following your lead and spending my days swanning around a pool and working on my tan. I was in Thailand yesterday and I found myself walking around looking at the devastation caused by the tsunami, thinking that this was not as bad as

watching people being hacked to death or bodies torn apart by bullets. Somehow it always seems much worse to me when humans are doing the killing. Still, the horror is beyond imagination. Didn't do my best work. Maybe I need to think about retiring, settling down and getting a mortgage, a house in the country and two dogs, I could do a spot of gardening. Tuesday-night bridge sounds civilised. What do you think?

I have to tell you that Amin blames himself for what happened to you despite what we all tell him.

Should also mention that I got so drunk last night that I was stuck in a corner with myself, listening to my own extreme political views. Miss your incessant bloody questions . . . miss you . . . miss everything about you . . .

x P

I missed him too, but that wasn't what I wrote back. I told him that I wasn't swanning around a pool, and would have liked to write that I wasn't working on my tan either, but that would have been a lie. I had no idea what to say about the mortgage and settling down bit and for a few brief moments I considered he might have been serious, but when I tried to imagine him living a life like that—tried to imagine *us* living a life like that—the little movie of domestic bliss wouldn't crank out. Having decided that I'd been reading too much into his words I ignored the comment completely, together with the one about being drunk. Pete never got drunk. I emailed back with a message for Amin, explaining again that it had been my fault and my fault alone. I remembered very clearly that he had warned me against going with the Warriors of Allah. He must stop blaming himself.

Making a cup of tea, I took it out to the deck to sit staring at the ocean. Too many paths led back to this man who said he loved me in my mother's red dress; too many paths that, no matter which way I played them out, appeared to lead nowhere. Yet, like Bella, visions of babies and happy families had unexpectedly begun to float across my horizon, stirring up the first creeping tendrils of biological panic. In the lonely light of some morning in a distant future I could not see, in some second-rate hotel room in some far-off land, would I wake up alone to discover that the one thing I wanted most in the world had passed me by? Pete's words that you only regret the things you didn't do had begun haunting me. Perhaps my mistake had been trying to imagine an ordinary life for us when ours could never be ordinary.

Grabbing the beach towel off the rail I decided to wander down and have another swim. I had no idea what our life together might look like, but I had begun to realise that we had to at least give it a try. It wasn't until mid-afternoon that I realised it was my fortieth birthday.

That evening I celebrated with a takeaway pizza, which I shared with Buster. As were were sitting on the deck munching away, watching the moon rise over the ocean, the phone rang.

'Hello, precious, happy birthday. I hope we didn't wake you.'

'Hello, Mother. No, I was still up, and thank you.'

'How are you, dear?'

'I'm fine, just fine. And you?'

'Oh, we're fine too. Did you do anything wonderful for your birthday?'

'Well, I went to the beach with the neighbour's dog.'

'Mr Weston has a dog?'

'No, Mother, Mr Weston is dead, remember? This is a new neighbour.'

'Yes, of course. Well, Peter says that things are looking quite good for you, but perhaps you should wait a bit longer before coming back.'

When had she spoken to Pete?

'He said you would come back when you were ready, but I think it's best not to push it, don't you? Hold on, dear, I'll give you over to your father.'

'Hi, sweetheart, did you have a good birthday?'

'Great birthday, Dad, great.'

'How's the old house?'

'Oh, you know, falling down beautifully, awaiting your return.'

'Yes, yes, well, we'll see. Your mother and I have sent you a little present in the mail . . . oh, hold on, dear, your mother wants to speak with you again.'

'Hello, Mother.'

'Now remember, Katherine, don't rush anything. Make sure everything is safe before you come back home. Everyone really has your best interests at heart and I'm sure Peter knows what he's talking about.'

Since when was my mother so buddy-buddy with Pete? Since when was Pete the font of all knowledge? I was surprised to realise I was annoyed. I was forty years old—didn't my parents think I could make decisions for myself?

'Hold on, dear, *there is someone else who wants to talk to you.*'

I could hear Mother talking to someone and the shuffling handover of the phone.

'Happy birthday, Bullwinkle.'

'Pete?'

'Who else calls you Bullwinkle?'

'You're with my parents? This is surreal. What's going on there?'

'I was passing by and dropped in.'

'You were passing by Somerset and you dropped in?'

'No, I was passing by London and your parents and I decided to meet for breakfast.'

I was having trouble absorbing this extraordinary information.

'Larry gave my number to your mother when you had to go to Sydney and she very sweetly calls me every now and then to discuss your welfare.'

I groaned, imagining them together, discussing my welfare.

'We've had a delightful breakfast and I've been greatly entertained hearing about your childhood exploits.'

I groaned again. 'Listen, McDermott, this is not allowed. You are definitely not allowed to buddy up with my mother . . . Oh, this is too surreal even for you. Maybe I'm dreaming.'

'If you are, I would have hoped it would be about something entirely different. I'm happy to accommodate you whenever you want to fill my bed again.'

His words sent a thrill through me, but I wondered what my parents were making of all this. 'McDermott, can my parents hear you?'

'No, I've walked out onto the balcony.'

'I miss you,' I whispered down the phone.

'Same here. So, how did you celebrate the big day?'

'Well, apart from an intimate dinner party with one hundred and twenty of my very best friends and the expectation of a telegram from the Queen organised by Mother, I thought I'd have a quiet one. Where's my present by the way, McDermott?'

'You know where to look, although I'd like to deliver something personally.'

'I wish you could.'

'It's been too long, Kate.'

'I know,' I said. 'So where are you off to now?'

'Baghdad.'

'Not Baghdad, Pete. Don't go back, please. Please.' I'd been hearing that journalists were being targeted by the insurgents to the point where they'd taken to driving around in the backs of cars with Arabic newspapers in front of their faces.

'I've got a couple of things I need to do there. Won't take long. It'll be fine.'

'Please don't go back.'

'I'll see you soon, okay, and we can take up where we left off—yes?'

His words sent another thrill through me. I wanted to see him so badly that I could no longer understand what I was doing in Sydney. I still had no idea what I was going to do about work, or what our relationship would look like, but I no longer cared. Somehow we'd work it out.

'Yes—most definitely, yes.'

'So when're you coming back?' It was the first time he had asked that question.

'I'll meet you in New York when you return from Iraq. How long are you planning to stay?'

'Just a couple of weeks.'

'Okay. Ring me when you're leaving Baghdad and I'll fly out to fill your bed again.'

'Come now, Kate, and I won't go to Iraq.'

Despite Pete's words, I knew him well enough to understand that he still wanted to go to Iraq. We had waited so long that two more weeks would make no difference. 'No, I'll see you in a couple of weeks.'

After hanging up I was excited for the first time in months. I would be with him in only a couple of weeks. I turned on the computer to find Pete's present.

From: Rocky91956@yahoo.com
Date: Saturday, 19 March 2005 10:16 AM
To: Bullwinkle91965@yahoo.com
Subject: Happy Birthday

Happy birthday, Bullwinkle. Missing you like crazy. Happy birthday
from Amin and Hanan too. Soraya is doing well.

   x P

Attached was a photo of Pete with his arm around Amin, who was standing next to Hanan. She was holding baby Talia. Hanan's brother Akba was also in the photo, staring blankly into the lens, while little Jawal sat cross-legged in the dirt, smiling up at the camera. The photo had been taken under the date palm in their courtyard. Mohammed was not in the photo so I assumed he was practising his photographic skills with a little help from Pete. Soraya was sitting on a plastic chair in front of her mother. Although the photo wasn't the best, I could just make out some white scarring on her face. The photo made me cry. I wanted to be with all of them.

In those last weeks the rhythm of my days and the way I moved through them changed. No longer did it feel like I was rudderless, becalmed on a still blue ocean. Now I was only resting one last time before the breath of wind came that would fill my sails and lead me back to him.

Chapter 45

I HAVE ALWAYS BELIEVED THAT YOU SHOULD HAVE A PREMONITION of your own death. You should wake up in the morning and somewhere in the depths of your being you should know: this is the last day I will walk this earth. The moment before you die you should know: this is the last breath I will take. Before you fall in love, or find a dear friend, you should know: this is the day I will meet someone whose memory will touch my heart and change my world forever. I believe the ability to do this is buried deep within each of us, and if we could find it we could imprint on our minds what the world looked like before so we could take the full measure of what remains. I believe with all my heart that we can do this.

Australian seasons don't descend. They slip and slide and leak into one another until one season loses the battle and quietly steals away. Subtle changes: a paler morning light; a new coolness in the air; winter crawling in through the cracks in the windows at night, through the holes in the floor and under the back door. New smells and new sounds. One day the cicadas are gone and there are no more snakes, no more bees making busy in the garden. You put the mosquito coils away for another year, place that extra blanket on the end of the bed and close the doors when the sun leaves the garden at the end of the day. Jeans and sweatshirts replace sarongs and swimming costumes. And then one morning you wake up to find summer has gone and winter has arrived. Not a thick, heavy northern winter of lonely, grey landscapes, of snow, mittens and woolly coats, but a deeper gossamer peace of descending cool and the sweetest solitude.

On that last day the sun, when it finally woke me, was a watery puddle no longer able to pull me out of bed with its prickly heat. For the two previous days it had rained, the puddles on the road filling with mud, the ocean turning a friendless, churning grey and the garden heavy underfoot. By mid-morning the weather had changed again, a light drizzle and a cooling mist had rolled in from the sea, but by lunchtime the heavens had opened and the beach was hidden by a downpour that thundered across the tin roof of the house to wash away the last of the summer dust from the trees. Within half an hour the wind had picked up and was howling around the houses as the storm began to turn back in on itself. Out on the ocean a lone wave jumper skimmed across the tips of the waves, spume flying out behind him under an angry pewter grey sky.

I was sitting in front of the computer with Buster snoring contentedly at my feet in front of the two-bar radiator when my mobile phone rang. Going into the kitchen I picked it up off the bench to hear Larry on the other end.

'Kate?'

'Larry, what's up?'

'Oh, Kate . . .'

You always know. Something in the voice or the way the words are framed tells you, and in the nanoseconds it takes for you to draw breath you have promised your life away to a God you have never believed in if only what you are about to hear will not destroy you. Larry's voice, when it came, was no more than a whisper; the words no more than a gulp, as if I might have been spared the hearing and he the telling.

'The news has just come through on the wire and I wanted to tell you before you saw it on the news. Pete's dead.'

The mind baulks at taking the measure of the thing. The world winds down into silence as words and thoughts fall through you. There is no meaning until the too-full moment begins to vibrate and you see it, the far-off wave of pain, as it builds and builds, rolling towards you until it hits with a roar that fills your ears with thunder and the ground opens up below you. Physical responses, quicker than emotions, literally brought me to my knees. Throwing my hand out, I caught the side of the kitchen bench as I went down. It happened as quick as that and I was outside myself watching the strands of my old life unravel into the beginnings of malfunction, one moment forming the unimaginable shape of the next, and the next, and the one after that. Going nowhere. I didn't cry and I thought about the fact that I wasn't crying even then. Outside myself.

'Kate, did you hear me? Are you okay?'

'How? Where?'

'In Iraq—the double suicide bombing in the marketplace in Sadr City yesterday afternoon. He was taking photos of the aftermath of the first bomb when the second went off.'

'Amin?'

'No word yet, but we're trying to find out.'

'But I just got an email from him this morning.'

'Oh, Kate . . .' He groaned in pain and my heart went out to him.

'I need to go.'

As I hung up, my mobile rang again and I switched it off. Sitting down at the computer, I opened my email and scrolled down the screen to find him.

From: Rocky91956@yahoo.com
Date: Thursday 24 March 2005 4:12 AM
To: Bullwinkle91965@yahoo.com
Subject: A poem for you

Dearest Bullwinkle,
I hope you find this before you go to bed tonight. I found this poem and thought you might like it as much as I did. It reminds me of you . . . of us . . . I am waiting for you to return as I always have and always will.

Wild nights! Wild nights!
Were I with thee,
Wild nights should be
Our luxury!

Futile the winds
To a heart in port,—
Done with the compass,
Done with the chart.

Rowing in Eden!
Ah! the sea!
Might I but moor
To-night in thee!
    x P

His email had an attachment: another photo of Pete and Amin, this time taken in front of Amin's car at the entrance to the alleyway in Sadr City, next to the bicycle-repair shop.

I had seen people die. One second they were in their bodies, full of plans and memories, hates, loves and fears—a movie going on inside them—and then there was nothing. An empty vessel with unseeing eyes. Where did they go? I don't believe . . . I cannot believe there is nothing left. They must have gone somewhere.

Turning away from the turmoil raging inside, I stared out into the storm unable to recognise the demarcation between what was inside me and what was on the other side of the glass. Great gusts of wind were whipping the foam across the surface of the water as black waves came rolling in from the horizon, smashing up against the rocks of Barrenjoey Headland before pounding the shore. The wave jumper had gone. A lone seagull cried outside the kitchen window, flapping furiously into the wind, going nowhere. I could feel it again: the slow twisting pain welling up until I was thick and bloated with its bitterness, unable to swallow, choked by it. I needed to escape before I exploded.

It was a green-grey, unwelcoming sea. Leaves threading through branches and old fishing line smacked down in dirty, brown seaweed bundles by the water's edge. Plastic bags and bottles tangled in the ocean's garbage. As I headed north along the sand the wind lashed me from behind, stinging the backs of my legs and whipping my hair across my face. At the far end of the beach I stripped off my half-sodden clothes and waded in. Tossed back to the shore, dumped and tumbled, lost in the white silence under the water as scratchy seaweed clawed at the soft skin of my face and belly. Swimming as hard as I could out towards the horizon, I pushed myself until I could no longer see the house on the ridge through the rain sweeping in. With eyes stinging and my lungs and throat burning from the mouthfuls of salty brine I had swallowed, I could go no further. Rolling over onto my back I floated and, as the sheets of rain beat down on my face, the wind began to push my body back towards the line of breakers until I was spat out on the shore, rejected, along with all the other debris. A flock of seagulls huddled close to where I lay naked and cold, their bodies turned towards the oncoming rain. Near the shore a sleek black cormorant surfaced with a fish flapping in its beak. Life went on without Pete. I dressed, the sand on my skin gritty under the wet clothes as I headed back to the house.

Throughout the night the storm raged as I tossed around in my little girl's bed under the pink nylon bedspread. Thundering great waves of rain swept in from the sea to batter the bedroom wall, shivering the broken pane of glass, cold air and rain whistling in through its crack. Towards dawn, as I lay on my back staring into the dark, I felt him near me and I turned to see him leaning up against the doorframe, his arms folded across his chest, smiling. I knew he could not leave me. I knew he would come. Smiling back at him, I moved over to make room for him.

When I woke in the thin light of the new morning he was gone, the bed cold where he had lain.

Leaves and hard little gumnuts littered the deck and hurt my bare feet as I took my cup of tea out for the last time. Down on the beach a jagged tideline of seaweed and yellow scum marked the storm's high point. There would be no swimming that last day. There was a message from Larry on my mobile to say he'd booked a ticket for me back to London. The funeral was scheduled for later that week.

Leaving all the doors open to let the house breathe one last time, I stripped the sheets off my parents' bed before positioning the red travelling clock back in its place in the centre of the bedside table. While I was cleaning the kitchen Buster arrived at the back door, wagging his tail in anticipation of our walk. I crouched down to bury my face in his neck by way of an apology, breathing in his musty dog smell as he nuzzled my cheek. Sensing something was wrong, he followed me around for a while until I told him to go home and, for the first time in our friendship, he obeyed.

Before the taxi arrived I walked around to the back of the cottage to collect my eucalyptus leaves, the emotional compasses that would bring me back to this place when I needed it the most. But when I put the leaves into my pocket my fingers found a hard fragment of shrapnel. The memory of Baghdad and a marketplace running with blood caught at my throat, and he was with me again. How many times would this happen until it no longer hurt?

Chapter 46

Yorkshire

FIELDS, ICY WITH THE LAST OF THE MORNING'S FROST, slipped past the train's window. We stopped by a crossing and I watched a farmer open his barn door. The cows, their breath frozen in little puffs, lumbered out into the chilly air and I was back in Chechnya with Pete, on another cold and broken morning, and I saw again his hand reaching up to untangle a piece of straw from my hair.

Making my way out from the station onto the cobbled high street I pulled my jacket tight around my chest and gazed up at the watery spire of a church on top of a rise. *The hills are too close here in England, the sky too low. This country is not generous with its space*, he once told me. When a misty rain began to fall I opened my umbrella and set off in the general direction of the church.

'Is that St Bartholomew's?' I asked a young mother trying to manoeuvre a clear plastic rain cover over a baby in a pushchair. I reached down to help her, but my unpractised hands only seemed to get in the way.

'Ay,' she said, pulling on the hand of the child in pink bunny ears standing next to her. 'I s'pose you're here for that funeral. We didn't see him much around these parts, but me Da knew him. He says he was a famous photographer. Me Da and him were friends, you know? They used to be in a rock band together. If you listened to me Da talking you'd think they was famous. Never shuts up about it, he doesn't.'

'Wait,' I said, touching her arm as she began to move on. 'What's your father's name?'

'Sam. Sam Worthingham.'

'Will he be there today?'

'Nah, he says the guy wouldn't even 'ave remembered him.'

'I worked with him . . . your dad's friend.'

'You one of them photographers then?'

'No, but will you tell your dad that he did remember him? Tell him Pete McDermott did remember him and that he talked about him often.'

'No!' she exclaimed. 'Get away with ya!'

'Will you tell him for me?'

'Yeah, 'course I will. Ta. He'll be right chuffed, he will. Make his day. Who'd have thought? You know, we all thought he was kinda making it all up . . . all that stuff about his friend the famous photographer.'

At the stone wall of the church I stood scanning the crowd for a familiar face. Some in the profession didn't want to acknowledge this sort of thing within our ranks, others were simply away working: the nature of the business. It allowed you to avoid the things that punctuated normal life, like paying the bills, fixing the car, mowing the lawn, going to funerals.

John and Bella were standing under an old yew tree at the side of the church. A pretty woman in a neat, black suit with blonde hair pulled back in a tight ponytail had her arm linked through John's. He looked even worse than he had in Baghdad. Pete's death would have hit him hard. When John introduced me to Helen she unlinked her arm from her husband's and reached out to shake my hand before threading her own quickly back through his arm again. It didn't look as if Connecticut had proved to be the cure John needed.

Bella was standing the other side of John in a figure-hugging tomato-red dress, wearing a large black hat and long black gloves. She looked for all the world as if she had just stepped off a 1950s catwalk in Milan. As we hugged I noticed Larry off to the side talking to a group of journalists. When he saw me he broke away and walked over.

'You okay, Kate?'

'Sure. Yep.'

'Good, good,' he said, squeezing my arm.

'Have you heard about Amin?'

'Yes. He's fine. Not a scratch.'

'Good.'

Larry turned to John. 'I hear you've moved to Connecticut and are working with the guys at the *Hartford Courant*? I used to know one of the editors there . . . what's his name? Anyway, doesn't matter, probably not there any longer. How's it all going?'

'Not too bad really. It got like it was time to stop, and the kids were growing. Amanda's thirteen now and Oscar's eight. Amanda went to her first dance the other night.' He smiled at his wife. 'Should have seen her all dressed up.'

'Dying at forty-eight taking a photo of another damn suicide bombing in Iraq is no way to die. No fucking way to die at all,' said Bella into the silence that followed and I realised she was crying. I put my arm around her. As others who had worked with Pete wandered over to join us under the tree conversation turned, as it always did, to Baghdad. While they talked I pulled my handbag closer under my arm, thinking about the photo of Pete and Amin I had secreted away inside. I considered sharing it with everyone under the yew tree that morning, but it seemed such a morbid thing to do that I decided to keep it hidden, wondering if that was an even more morbid thing to do.

'I don't think I can do this,' Bella said.

'Come on,' I said, taking her arm. 'We can do this together.' We all walked into the huge stone church, following Helen and John halfway down the long aisle before shuffling along a pew together. I looked anywhere but the coffin, unable and unwilling to imagine his broken body lying within.

Pete's father and two of his brothers spoke of his early years, what he had been like as a brother and a son, but there was no one to speak of the man we knew.

Afterwards, people gathered at the bottom of the steps around an elderly couple, quiet, middle-class people broken to the core. I found a spot near them and waited.

'Yes, a tragedy.'

'We will miss Peter, yes.'

'Too young, yes, he was too young.'

'Thank you.'

'Yes, thank you for coming.'

'Please, we would love you to come back to our home afterwards . . . Peter would have wanted you to.'

'Yes, incredible photographer.'

'Yes, terrible accident.'

'Iraq's a mess. Don't know what we're bloody well doing there anyway.'

'Yes, it is, indeed.'

'Hello,' I said, when there was a break in the crowd. 'You don't know me, but I was a friend of Pete's. My name's Kate Price.'

His mother smiled broadly and took both my hands in hers. 'Kate, I am so glad to finally meet you. We've heard so much about you from our Peter, haven't we, David?'

'Yes, we have indeed,' his father said in a voice so familiar that I nearly came completely undone. Taking my hand, he thanked me for coming.

But it was no use, no use at all, for no matter how much I tried I couldn't find any words. Sensing my helplessness his mother began talking, telling me how much Peter thought of me and thanking me for being such a special friend through the years. When people moved in again I mumbled something about being sorry for their loss and slipped away.

John, Helen, Larry and a couple of guys from Pete's magazine and agency went to the wake, but Bella declared that she couldn't face it and went instead to a pub with some others to send him off in their own way.

From the church it was only a short walk to the two-storey bluestone farmhouse with rosebushes lining its gravel driveway. Ivy covered an arched portal over double wooden doors that had been thrown open despite the cold. Accepting fine bone china cups from a neighbour we were ushered in the direction of the conservatory at the back of the house. Standing with Larry, half-listening to Pete's uncle recall his war experiences, I watched as his mother moved around the garden. With a smile she put her arms around a young woman who was crying, and then patted another's hand before giving someone else a hug. All the while she kept smiling. When she walked back into the house I saw her thread her arm through that of the brother who did not speak at the funeral. Drawing him in close to her she whispered something in his ear and they both smiled. What was she saying? That he would not want us to cry? That he'd had a good life? That he died doing what he loved? Would that be enough to get us through this day?

Finding the overheated room with its stilted conversation and offers of cut sandwiches and teacakes too claustrophobic, I wandered out into the hallway. Pushed up against the wall was a spindly card table I hadn't noticed when I had come in. Its surface was covered with Pete's awards and pieces of memorabilia that marked the passage of his life. Above the table was a black and white landscape in a thin black seventies frame that sat uncomfortably alongside the old family portraits and Yorkshire landscapes lining the wall.

'He took that with the first camera we ever bought him,' the voice I loved said from behind me. If I didn't turn around I could imagine it was him talking. 'Couldn't really see the promise then, could you? All things considered he turned out to be not too bad a photographer, don't you think?'

'Not too bad at all.'

'Go upstairs if you want, Kate. Peter's room's first on your right.'

At the top of the stairs I stood on the landing to see his cameras lying on the bed inside the empty room, but as I walked in I sensed I was not alone. Leaning up against the wall, hidden from the door by a cedar tallboy, was Pete's mother, her face drawn in pain as tears streamed down.

'I was the first woman to love him and I will be the last. I loved him before he was born, and I will love him until the day I die. You cannot . . . you cannot know what it's like to be a mother. It is our lot to love them, but by God it is not supposed to be our lot to bury them. It aches, God how it aches.'

Pushing herself off the wall she blew her nose, and wiped her eyes on a crumpled handkerchief. 'Do you know I used to be jealous of you, Kate?' She saw my confusion and smiled to soften her words. 'Of course not, how could you? Oh, my dear,' she said, sitting down on the side of the bed. She swept her hand across the bedspread, as if to smooth out the invisible wrinkles for me to sit next to her. 'I knew he was in love with you. A mother knows these things. You had so much time with him, so much precious time. How I envied you that. We hardly ever saw him once he moved to New York.' Raking her hand through her hair in that old familiar gesture, she added, 'Oh dear, don't take any notice of me. I'm a stupid old woman.'

'I have something for you,' I said, taking the photo from my bag. 'This is the last photo taken of Pete. He sent it to me the day before he died. I'm sure he would want you to have it.'

'Thank you, my dear,' she said, reaching out to take it from me. 'They were great friends, weren't they, he and Amin? What will happen to Soraya now, do you think? I know Pete would want us to continue looking after her so we must see to that; we must see what we can do for the family, too. I didn't want him to go back to Iraq the last time he was here, but I never said anything. One never does. It's their life, but our children always carry a piece of us in them, and if they are hurting, that piece of us is hurting too, and when they die,' she said, the tears pouring down again, 'that piece of us dies with them.

'That was the reason he went back,' she said, changing the subject abruptly. 'But of course you know. He said he was trying to organise her next operation in Baghdad rather than have her travel all the way to London and away from the family each time.'

She looked up from the photo then to see the look of shock on my face. 'Oh, my dear, you didn't know, did you? I *am* sorry. Pete didn't want anyone to know, but I thought he would have told you. I've shocked you, I'm terribly sorry.' She leaned over then and laid her hand on my arm, the way I had seen her do for others grieving in the garden. 'I'm being very selfish. You must miss him very much, my dear.'

I mumbled some words that are lost to me now and somehow found myself in the lane outside the house sitting on the ground under the hedge crying, offering my faithless God one last faithless deal. If only He would let me get through the next weeks and months without breaking into pieces I would do whatever He wanted.

There would be dinners and parties and all of us, the survivors, would mend and move on. And there would come a time when I would no longer be able to pull the pieces of him back into the whole—the way his hands moved, a gesture, a word, his smile, little habits of his that had become invisible with the familiarity of years. In time he would become a vague shade of himself, his name a tormenting emptiness in my heart, and I would begin to remake him in whatever image my memory chose. It was a blasphemy.

From: Bullwinkle91965@yahoo.com
Date: Monday 24 March 2008 9:45 AM
To: Rocky91956@yahoo.com
Subject:

Dear Pete,

It is three years to the day since you died and I am writing this, my last email to you, because I have finished the book about us and there are things that I must tell you.

Did you ever hear the story about the indigenous hunter who was asked to put his hand on the Bible and 'tell the whole truth and nothing but the truth'? He looked at the strange book he had never seen before that clearly possessed great magical powers for truth telling and considered his options. After a time the hunter turned to the judge. 'I don't know if I can tell the truth. I can only tell what I know.' And that is what I have done, Pete. I have only told what I know, but I have felt you often reading over my shoulder and I have heard you say, 'No, Price, that's not how it happened,

371

you've got it all wrong,' and you may well be right, but this is the way I remember it.

I have not been back to Iraq, but everyone tells me things are getting much worse. I hear the only way to report from some places is to travel with the US military inside the houses and across the rooftops to avoid the street snipers. Photographers have been reduced to paparazzi, taking photos from behind newspapers through the windows of moving cars. No one trusts anyone anymore and all the fixers carry guns. You would not like it, my friend. The other night CNN said the best place to buy real estate was in Baghdad. Good old CNN.

Soraya is doing well and only needs to come to London once a year, and whenever she comes I am with her. Things are not going too well for Amin though. After being warned off working with Western journalists he's still unemployed and the family have been forced to live off the trust fund your parents set up for them. He is shamed by it and I am shamed that I am the cause of his troubles. He still misses you, Mr Pee. We all do.

I see your mother and father from time to time when they come to London. To them I am the woman their son loved and they want to be close to me so they might be close to you. For my part, I am content to watch your mother rake her hand through her hair when she is tired, and listen to your father speak of books in that voice I know so well. I wish I could give them more. Your mother told me at the funeral that she was the first woman to love you and she would be the last. I didn't understand it then, but I do now. Her pain has not diminished.

Bella has settled somewhat permanently in Italy with the young lover again, although he is not so young anymore and neither is she for that matter . . . neither are we all. It's hard to believe that our beautiful friend is fifty years old this year and just keeps getting sexier. She calls herself a serial monogamist, but I think you were right when you said Bella is in love with love.

I've never been back to the house by the beach in Sydney.
I couldn't seem to get over the irrational feeling that the house had
betrayed me, for it was there that I spent the last months of your
life when I should have been spending them with you. Mother tried
to talk my father into selling the house last spring because none of
us—which really means me—spends any time there anymore, but
I asked her to wait a bit and she agreed. I think she understands.
I haven't told them yet, but after I give this manuscript to the
publishers I have decided to go back to Australia to live. It feels
like I need to settle and that is the only place that ever felt like
home. I am happiest where the silences are these days. I miss
the old house and the ocean and am thinking of getting a dog.
Don't laugh!

And so I have made a decision not to go to war anymore, but
to concentrate on the stories that have fallen through the cracks—
the ones no one else seems interested in. Larry supported me in
this decision and before he retired organised a section for me
every six weeks in the Sunday magazine. It was one of the last
things he did before the cancer finally claimed all his vocal cords
and his job. We had a huge party for him. Hundreds of people
came from throughout the industry, and we all pretended he was
simply retiring, but it was the saddest thing. Everyone knows
Larry's job was his life and that when the party ended he was
going home to his sickness and an empty house.

The column is going to be called 'Between the Cracks'. I hope
you're not laughing too hard, McDermott, because it was Larry's
idea. You will, however, be pleased to know that the first piece is
going to be on Dr Tony Moll and the Church of Scotland Hospital
in Tugela Ferry and the paper is going to use your photos. I am
content these days to let someone else have their chance at
changing the world and while I know you'd still be out there
fighting the good fight, I was never you, and I never had your
dedication. Now that I no longer feel the need to go where history
is being made I can't help wondering if it is because you and John

and Bella won't be there with me, and Larry won't be back in London saving my sorry arse. He died last spring, Pete.

My parents were so upset when they heard about you, especially Mother—how you charmed her! She seems happier these days, content that I no longer go to war, although I know she wishes I would meet a nice young man. But I did meet one—didn't I, McDermott?—and maybe one nice man is all we get in a lifetime.

I think you were wrong about something. You used to say that you didn't need hope, and that hope was a waste of good intentions. I think the true consequence of the loss of hope is the death of all that is good and worthy within us. If I have no hope, I have no future. I lost that hope somewhere along the way, but I think I'm getting it back again and it feels good. I do not bruise so easily and I can see beauty again in this world. I am moved once again by the simplest of things: the sun rising over the ocean; a bird singing; the memory of a man peeling an orange for me in Baghdad. I think you will also be pleased to know that I no longer make my deals with God, and I am happier for it. He probably is too.

I have a confession. Not long after the funeral I hacked into your Rocky email account—I have to say that 'Bullwinkle' was an obvious choice of password. Joy of all joys I found you had kept all our emails during that time I was in Australia and I've reread them many times. Thank you!

John and Helen and the kids were in London last weekend and I spent the day with them. They seem happy enough in Connecticut and their marriage looks fine. The children are very much like John, especially Amanda, who's now sixteen. She told me over lunch that she wants to be a great photojournalist like her dad, but I fear she is cut from the same pure cloth as our friend and the job will take its toll on her too. Helen took the kids off to see the Houses of Parliament so John and I could have time alone and I have to tell you that he is still not over the loss of you, nor is he completely well. I wonder if he ever will be. Before we parted,

John quoted a line he had memorised from a book and I'm giving it to you because I think it is a good line: *There was a vividness to seasons lived as we lived that summer.* 'That's how we lived it, wasn't it, Kate?' he asked me—his honesty has always been so fine and uncomplicated—and I told him, yes, that was how we lived it and it was, wasn't it, Pete?

I try not to think of all the 'what ifs' anymore. What if I hadn't gone with the Warriors of Allah? What if I hadn't written the article? What if I hadn't left for Australia? What if you'd not gone to Baghdad? If you think about it, Pete, there are a million 'what ifs' to change the fabric of just that one day. Enough 'what ifs' to drive me crazy, and for a while I *was* crazy, lost in the possibility of them, unaware of the days and weeks passing by unnumbered. But the 'what ifs' can also take away New York and the time I wore my mother's red dress for you, the nights in your bed and the way you looked when I caught you making *your* secret pictures of me. I will not give up my memory pictures of you either, but they are fading, Pete, and that distresses me more than anything. You cannot know how many times I wish I had turned in those last seconds before I left you in New York to make one last memory picture, but I didn't. We cannot say every goodbye as if it is our last, can we?

Do I miss you? I ache for you every day, but you are not the wound that never heals as I thought you would be. It hurts less, and for that I can only be grateful.

There is no one in my life at the moment, but if you were to ask me if I am happy I would tell you honestly that I have my measure. Life is good, the sun is shining and I'm not sure we should ever ask for more than that.

All my love,

Kate

Author's note

THIS NOVEL IS WOVEN AROUND HISTORICAL EVENTS. I HAVE tried to represent them as accurately as is possible through the eyes of fictional characters.

I wish to acknowledge the journalists and photojournalists whose books, interviews and articles I have mined, especially those I interviewed for *Bearing Witness: The Lives of War Correspondents and Photojournalists*. I also thank Max Stahl for his email on Christmas Eve in the depths of another English winter and Roberta Mears (aka Bella) for permission to use her email from Italy.

My gratitude and apologies must go to my dear friends who read the first embarrassing drafts of this story and were gracious and inventive enough to find words of encouragement: Jane Morgan, Anne Spencer and Alan Leith. Without the amazing Rosie Scott's initial critical appraisal of the manuscript and her vision of what it might become this book might never have seen the light of day. As always I am grateful for her intelligent and wise counsel.

My deepest gratitude goes to the Literature Board of the Australia Council for a Skills and Arts Development Grant and Ledig House in Ghent, New York, for giving me two glorious months where I could write without distraction while watching the seasons change. Can I please come back?

Handing over a manuscript that you have nurtured for years can sometimes be akin to saying goodbye to a lover too soon. I held onto the manuscript for *What Remains* well after the story had been written, partly because I knew something was missing and had no idea what that might be (thank you, Jane and Catherine), and partly because I was not ready to expose my first tentative efforts at fiction to the world. Mostly, though, I kept the manuscript so I could continue to return to a world and characters I had come to love. I would like to think this behaviour was testimony to the value of the story rather than a reflection of an emotionally impoverished life.

The chapter on Tugela Ferry and the Church of Scotland Hospital is based on my time there. The visit to the AIDS patient's home when the Zulu nurses sang, together with the emotional reaction Kate experienced, is my own. The bitter and wasted life of the little boy in the cot—which cannot possibly rate as anything of significance given the enormity of the AIDS and TB epidemics in Africa—is a memory I will carry to the end of my days, as is my deepest respect and appreciation for the work of Tony Moll and his staff. Your simple dedication gave me faith again.

If you wish to learn more about the Church of Scotland Hospital and their work in combating TB and AIDS within their local and wider communities I encourage you to visit their website: www.kznhealth.gov.za/coshospital.htm. I also encourage you to visit the Philanjalo website, an associated non-profit organisation set up by Dr Tony Moll in Tugela Ferry that works in conjunction with the hospital to improve the quality of life for their AIDS patients and families: www.philanjalo.org.za.

For the opportunity to set my story free, my deepest appreciation goes to all the team at Allen & Unwin, but especially the fabulous Catherine Milne, whose gentle prodding pushed me into emotional territory I had long been avoiding, and whose copious suggestions and sage recommendations improved the story no end. I also thank the talented Ali Lavau for her keen eye and careful line edit, and the insightful and ever patient Elizabeth Cowell, who oversaw the editing process and pulled it all together. Thanks should also go to the wonderful Sandy Cull for designing an evocative and beautiful cover I am proud to have on my book. Most importantly I am indebted to the indomitable and always passionate Jane Palfreyman: a woman of fine integrity. Thank you for seeing the value in my work and the vision of what it could become.

Finally, my thanks must go, as they always must, to Alan and his unwavering belief in me and BSFR!

Please feel free to email Kate at the Bullwinkle email address Pete set up for her: bullwinkle91965@yahoo.com.